THE
BOTOX
DIARIES

THE BOTOX DIARIES

Janice Kaplan
&
Lynn Schnurnberger

 BALLANTINE BOOKS · NEW YORK

0105133 18

A Ballantine Book
Published by The Random House Publishing Group

www.ballantinebooks.com

Library of Congress Cataloging-in-Publication Data can be obtained from the publisher upon request.

ISBN 0-345-46857-0

Text design by Julie Schroeder

Manufactured in the United States of America

First Edition: June 2004

1 2 3 4 5 6 7 8 9 10

In memory of our sweet, wonderful fathers,
Stanley Kaplan and Jerome P. Edelman,

who led us to choose the sweet, wonderful men we married,
Ronald Dennett and Martin Semjen,

to whom we dedicate our hearts and this book

ACKNOWLEDGMENTS

We had so much fun writing this book and are lucky it got laughs from the right people. Our thanks to agent extraordinaire Jane Gelfman and primo editor Maureen O'Neal for supporting us and getting so strongly behind *Botox*. Both are incredibly smart and talented—the best in the business. Kim Hovey at Ballantine has endless energy and enthusiasm and we're grateful that she waved her magic wand on us. Thanks to Johanna Bowman for her hard work and attention to detail.

Writing this book took a tremendous amount of patience and fortitude—on the part of our friends. Thanks to all of them for encouraging and putting up with us. A special note to Susan Fine, Joanne Kaufman, and Emily Listfield, who called almost daily to ask how many pages we'd written. Big hugs to all our great cheerleaders: Margot, Stuart, Robert, Jeanne, Sally, Henry, Allan, Marcia, Linda (both of them), Peter, Susan, Rosanne, Donna, Jimmy, Martha, Anna, Anne, Jean, Nancy, Leslie, Tom, Pamela, Naomi, Maggie, Len and Emily, Ronnie and Lloyd, Marsha and David, Anne and Michael.

We're lucky to have wonderful mothers and mothers-in-law who have always been our greatest champions, not to mention terrific role models. Kisses to Bob and Chris, and Nancy and Frank.

To Ron and Martin—you're both handsome, sexy, funny, smart,

loving, warm, and wonderful. We love you and we'd do anything for you. Especially since you let us read every single page of this book to you over and over. And you laughed every time.

And to our awesome and amazing children, Zachary, Matthew, and Alliana—you're the best. You happen to be the sweetest, smartest, most talented kids around, and we love you. We'd mention how gorgeous you are, too, but that might embarrass you. And we'd never do that.

THE
BOTOX
DIARIES

Chapter ONE

CHAMPAGNE CORKS are popping and it's only five a.m.

"Darling," Lucy trills as I groggily cradle the phone between my ear and my goose down pillow. "I didn't wake you, did I?"

Of course not. Why would I be asleep at this hour when I could be up repotting the azaleas?

"Where are you?" I ask, fumbling for the Brite-Lite clock on the night table to confirm that, yes, it's still two hours until my alarm goes off. "Traveling?"

"L.A., darling," Lucy says. "Working."

I knew that. When she's in New York, Lucy lives around the corner in a big Tudor house, but she regularly packs off to Burbank to produce glamorous TV shows. Being on the opposite coast causes her to sink into saying "darling" too much.

"Everything okay?" I ask, awake enough now for my worry genes to have kicked in.

"Absolutely, yes," Lucy says as I hear what I swear is another champagne cork popping in the background. She bursts into giggles, covers the phone and calls out, "Watch it, darling!"

"What's going on there?" I ask.

"It's not what you think. We're rehearsing for a show and there's a scene with Dom Perignon. We're using real French champagne, even for the sound check."

French champagne. I sit up abruptly realizing that when the phone rang, I had been dreaming about Jacques, my very own Frenchman. We were lying naked, with our arms wrapped around each other at the edge of a warm, sunny beach. He was kissing me passionately as the waves lapped over us. Wait a minute. Didn't I see that same scene in some old movie? I put the phone down and notice the TV across the room is still flickering. I must have fallen asleep watching *From Here to Eternity*. Again.

"Yoo-hoo, " Lucy calls impatiently. "Earth to Jess. You still with me?"

I clear my throat. "Jacques," I say. "We were making love."

"Jacques? Jacques is *there*?" Lucy screams so loudly across the country that she doesn't even need her brand-new cherry red Nokia 120000RICH cell phone.

"No, Jacques isn't here. Of course not. We were on the beach." That's not what I meant to say. "I mean I was dreaming about him on the beach. Nude." I manage to stop myself before I get to the climax. Of the story. Next topic. I realize it's two a.m. on her coast so I say, "But anyway, you're working late."

"I know. All night. Everyone thinks my life is all poolside meetings with Ben Affleck, but all I do out here is work, work, work." Lucy sounds awfully cheerful for a poor working girl. But then again, she's downing champagne while I'm cozying up to a blue plastic tumbler of tepid bathroom water.

"So what's going on?" I ask, wondering why this call couldn't have waited for daybreak—on either coast.

"I'm so sorry to bother you, " Lucy says, taking a deep breath, "but it's about the bake sale."

Ah, right. The fifth-grade bake sale. Now that's certainly worth a call at five a.m. In fact, I bet she's halted shooting on her million-dollar production in order to get this handled.

"I need a favor, darling," Lucy says. "Dan said he'd pick up something for Lily to bring, but that means it will be store-bought. Uck. I'll look like a bad mother. So two questions. What are you making for Jen to take, and would you mind very much making double?"

Double what? I haven't even given it a thought. I've just barely recovered from making nachos to send to school last week for International Lunch Day. The week before it was homemade yogurt for the Dairy-Tasting Project. Did I miss the PTA meeting when they installed Martha Stewart as the new principal? Jen's homework tonight will no doubt include long division, current events, and . . .

"Cupcakes!" I say brightly. "Jen and I are going to make cupcakes."

"I knew it!" Lucy says gleefully. "You make the best cupcakes! And you could make Jen's with pink frosting and Lily's with blue frosting, so they'd each feel special."

I groan. That's just what I need, cooking instructions from three thousand miles away. "Lucy, stick to producing your show and I'll produce the cupcakes, okay?"

"I'm sorry," Lucy says, sounding genuinely contrite. "I don't mean to be so controlling. It's hard being out of town and I just want everything to go right. And I'm only calling at this crazy hour because once we start shooting for real, I won't have a second."

Now I feel bad for jumping at her. So I try to compensate. Or overcompensate, as usual. "Listen, why doesn't Lily come over tonight and the girls can make the cupcakes together. Then they can decorate them any way they want."

And so what that after the girls are asleep I'll probably gorge on gobs of leftover frosting—both pink and blue? I eat when I'm tired, and without a real-life Jacques around to notice, who really cares if a single mom has a little extra frosting on the hips?

"Oh, that's so sweet of you," Lucy says. "Lily will love that. I'll call Dan and let him know."

Dan, the husband of the year.

"Tell Dan that Lily should come for dinner, too. It'll be easier for him."

I have to stop. In another minute, I'll be offering to run over and scrub her bathrooms and sleep with her husband so that her being away doesn't inconvenience anybody too much. Anybody except me.

"Are you sure it's not too much trouble?" Lucy asks.

"Of course not," I say. "I love having girls' night."

"Well, we need one of those girls' nights for just you and me as soon as I get back," Lucy says. Then lowering her voice, she whispers into the cell phone, "You won't believe what's happened on this trip. I can't wait to tell you. You're the only friend I have who'd understand."

Another champagne cork pops in the background, and Lucy dissolves into giggles. This time she covers the phone, but I can still hear her say, "Enough already! I'll be right there."

When we hang up, I pull the comforter up around my shoulders. I should try to fall asleep, but the minute I close my eyes I see Jacques again on that beach. I open them. This will never do. Jacques is my ex. In fact he happened so long ago that he's an ex-ex-ex.

Alas, it's the Triple-X elements of him that I seem to miss the most.

I make myself sit up and flick on the Itty Bitty reading lamp by my bed. As long as I'm awake I might as well get something done since my to-do list is longer than the newly revised tax code. I desperately need to deep-condition my hair, order a new bath mat, reorganize the closets, reupholster the sofa, recaulk the counters and renew Jen's library books. And while I'm at it I should find a faster printer, a faster Internet provider, and a faster exercise program. I'm still spending thirty minutes twice a week on the treadmill, when everyone else is building Better Abs in Five Minutes a Day. With all the time I'd save, I'm sure I could do something about world peace.

But world peace is going to have to wait, because I end up spending the next hour flicking through the Lands' End catalog and poring over pictures of the "Kindest Cut" bathing suits. All modeled by women more-or-less my age, apparently grateful for the extra bra support and the no-ride backside. The one-piece suits are cut high on top, low on bottom and loose all around. How did I get this catalog anyway? Do the fashion police know I'm over forty? I reflexively glance down at my breasts. Still firm, but less than perky. Maybe I just need my morning coffee. I was reading just yesterday that caffeine is a great pick-me-up—for your breasts. No wonder Starbucks stock is on the rise.

I sigh and toss aside the catalog. From the next bedroom, I hear my daughter Jen moving around, humming happily to herself. Why would I worry about long-gone bikini-wearing days when the present is blessed by a loving daughter with a crooked smile who gets up in the morning singing? Sure enough, a minute later she comes bounding into my room.

"Hey, Mom. Wanna hear my new song?" she asks, bursting with more energy than Britney Spears in a Pepsi commercial.

"Sure," I say, sitting back with a smile. My little girl—well, not as little as I think she is—has on a teeny-tiny pink nightgown that makes her look more Baby Doll than baby. Even straight from bed, her skin is dewy and her big brown eyes are clear and bright. I'd need alpha hydroxy, two moisturizers, and Visine just to look half that good.

Jen grins and poses dramatically at the foot of the bed, arms flung out wide and hips bouncing from side to side as she starts to sing. It takes me a minute to register the tune. But then I get it, that Madonna song, "Like a Virgin." *Like* a virgin? She's eleven years old, for heaven's sake. As far as I'm concerned, the only time she should use the "V" word is in an ode to the Virgin Mary. It makes me long for the days when she warbled that unbearable Barney song.

"Love your singing," I venture, trying to be supportive. But I've got to know. "Where the heck did you learn that song?"

"They play it on the oldies station," she says, jumping onto my bed.

Madonna on the oldies station. I shudder to think where that puts the Rolling Stones—or me.

"I'm going to sing it for Ethan," Jen says excitedly.

Ethan, her boyfriend. One of us has to have one. Although hers is twelve.

"You are *not* going to sing that for him," I say just a little too prissily. I look around the room to see if my mother just came in, because that was definitely her voice. I soften my position. "I mean, the whole act might be a little much." *Touched for the very first time?* I don't think so. No use giving the boy pointers.

"Well, I'll sing it but I won't wear a belly shirt, okay?" she asks with a mischievous twinkle. Then suddenly she leans over and looks at me wide-eyed. "Mom, your hair. What happened? It's all gray!"

"What do you mean?" My hand flies up to my head.

"It's all gray," Jen repeats. "Ooh. Eck!"

Horrified, I tug at my roots. Is it possible? I've avoided the L'Oréal aisle at the drugstore for all these years and now it's suddenly an emergency. Who knew this would happen overnight?

"How bad does it look?" I ask anxiously.

"Pretty bad," Jen says. But then she breaks into giggles.

"April Fool's!" she crows triumphantly.

"Got me," I say, laughing and throwing the pillow at her as she ducks, doubled over in laughter. Scary that she knew I'd buy into anything about looking old.

Jen runs back to her room to catch up on more oldies—yup, Britney should be hitting that category any day now—and suddenly it occurs to me what my dream this morning was all about.

It's April first.

My subconscious knew the date, even if I didn't. Sixteen years ago today, over a breakfast of crepes and champagne, Jacques, my passionate French lover, handed me a sapphire-and-diamond ring and asked if I'd marry him. I gasped and said, "This isn't an April Fool's joke, is it?"

To which he said, "What mean, 'April Fool's'?"

Perhaps I should have taken our cultural chasm as a sign that the marriage wasn't going to last any longer than the delicate Chanel sandals he'd bought me. Kisses in cafés, long luxurious lovemaking and out-of-body orgasms—okay, even many of them—don't necessarily a solid marriage make. Although it does take you a while to notice. And I didn't really have anyone to blame but myself when six years later the marriage crashed.

But enough. I haven't even showered yet and already I've dreamed about sex with my ex, been April-fooled into feeling like Barbara Bush, and gotten vicariously giddy on Dom Perignon. But today's a workday and I have a great idea for the charity where I'm gainfully employed—at least part-time. Of course if I don't get moving I'll be presenting the plan in my p.j.'s.

* * *

The day after Lucy jets back from the coast, she calls—during daylight hours, thank goodness—wanting to have lunch.

"There's a new sushi place near my office," she says. "Want to try it tomorrow?"

"Sure," I say agreeably. Lucy's so clued in that she knows what's going to be in Zagat's even before the ballots are counted.

"I'll have my assistant Tracey make a reservation," she says, then adds in a conspiratorial whisper, "By the way, the chef is Iguro Mashi-kuro. I always love his eel."

He has his own eel? Lucy can make anything sound exciting. I wonder what she has to say about his salmon roe.

The next morning at eleven a.m. I'm dressed in black capris and my best TSE cashmere sweater-set when the skies turn black. How can Al Roker have gotten it wrong again? Millions of dollars for the Doppler 4000 and they still can't tell the difference between an April shower and a monsoon.

Maybe I should call Lucy and suggest we postpone. We can always meet tomorrow morning at Dell's instead.

No, braving Hurricane Andrew would be better than breakfast at Dell's, the local landmark that's been serving inedible food since 1952. I never got the appeal. The consistently bad service? The guaranteed watery eggs and watery coffee? For a few precious weeks last fall we did have a Starbucks. Then a group of moms declared it wasn't "quaint enough" for our little town. They organized a rally that was the biggest event in Pine Hills since the Brownies' Walk to School Week. Kids carried placards: BUCK STARBUCKS! FRANCHISED COFFEE IS OBSCENE! And my personal favorite, DEATH TO ESPRESSO! And dammit if Starbucks didn't pack up their lattes and leave. So, I say to myself, reaching for my J. Crew trench, Manhattan or bust.

Thirty-seven minutes later, after I get off the train in Grand Central Station, I head for the taxi stand on Vanderbilt Avenue. The people are lined up, but the taxis aren't, so I start walking through the drizzle. I'm striding up Madison Avenue when I hear the first clap of thunder. I stick out my hand to hail a taxi and three drivers whiz by me without even glancing in my direction. Oh, great. I can't even pay someone to pick me up. Could it be that even the cabbies are trolling for twenty-five-year-olds? At forty-one, have I already become completely invisible? I shiver. This may not be the time for big philosophical issues—the rain is starting to come down in sheets. I'm only on Forty-eighth Street and the restaurant's fourteen blocks away. With any luck my underwear will still be dry when I arrive.

The restaurant has no name out front, and I walk up and down the block where it's supposed to be located three times before I venture up a flight of stairs and push open an unmarked wooden door. A perfectly beautiful Asian woman in a sleeveless black dress, bare legs, and black spike mules is standing behind the lacquered front desk.

"Is this Ichi's?" I ask, trying to close my umbrella and managing to spill a large puddle of water on the gleaming marble floor.

She looks at me blankly. I've pronounced it ITCH-ies, which is obviously wrong.

"ICK-ies?" I suggest.

Still no response.

"EYE-cheese?"

Blank.

"EYE-keys?"

She takes pity. "Welcome to AH-SHAY's," she says.

No way do you get AH-SHAY's out of a place spelled like ICK-ies, but I'm not arguing with a woman who's gone sleeveless on the third wettest day of the year.

"I'm meeting Lucy Baldor. We have a one o'clock reservation."

She looks carefully through her book, as if she can't believe that I actually belong here.

"Ms. Baldor hasn't arrived yet. Would you like to be seated?"

"I'd like a ladies' room first." Maybe I can squeeze some of the water out of my hair and turn it from wet mop to dry mop.

She gestures elegantly. "Just behind you to the left."

"Thanks." I try to step away from the desk, but my dripping um-

brella has turned the floor into the Antarctic ice shelf and I immediately go flying: my umbrella in one direction, my bag in another, and
my butt in the most obvious direction—straight down until it slams
into the cold marble. Ms. Sleeveless Dress pretends like she hasn't
seen a thing.

Nobody offers to help me up, so I slip and slide my way back to
my feet and scurry off to the ladies' room, which is plastered with wall-
to-wall mirrors. What fresh hell. The hair that I'd spent twenty minutes blow-drying into a sleek 'do has been water damaged into a mass
of stringy ringlets, and the blotchy black circle running down my
cheek proves that the waterproof mascara isn't. A hasty comb-through
and a swipe across my cheek with a wad of toilet paper are the best I
can muster. An hour and a half out of the house and I've gone from
having a vague resemblance to Cybill Shepherd to looking like Court-
ney Love, the Kurt Cobain years.

Back out front, I'm led to a table and I heap my wet coat on the
back of my chair. Nobody comes by to take it, to offer menus, or to plunk
down a measly glass of water. It's okay. I can wait. I fumble through my
purse, looking for props and trying to pretend that I have something to
do. Seventeen minutes, two Altoids, and one phone call to check my
messages—there are none—later, I'm strumming my fingers on the
water glass when Lucy comes in. She makes her way across the restaurant with a lean, coltish stride that makes heads turn—literally—at
every table. Her makeup is flawless, her streaked blond hair swings at
the perfect angle around her chin, and her Burberry raincoat and spike
Manolo Blahniks look like they just came out of the box. Does this
woman walk between the raindrops? Even if she came by limousine,
and I bet she has, she had to get from the curb to the door, and as I
glance out the window I see, yep, it's still pouring.

"You look fabulous," I say, getting up to kiss her on both cheeks.

"You too, Jessie," she says, going for the newly chic third kiss. Left,
right, left. I never remember that last one and our noses bump.

A maitre d' materializes from nowhere to help Lucy out of her coat
and whisk it away. He apparently doesn't notice my coat, still heaped

on the seat. With Lucy settled into her chair, two waiters and a busboy scramble over with water, menus, and a chorus of greetings, confirming my taxi-hailing suspicion. Maybe I am becoming invisible.

"I'm so glad to be at this restaurant," Lucy says to me spiritedly when the minions have left. "I'm told the best plan here is to let the chef prepare whatever's freshest. Is that okay with you?"

"Sure." I'm willing to risk my life at Kmart sale days but not on day-old sushi.

Lucy orders for us, chatting with the waiter about the quality of the uni. "That's a sea urchin," she explains, turning to me, to keep me in the loop.

"The uni. Ah, it's superior, today," the waiter confides, with a wink. But of course. For Lucy, he'll probably find a cache of uni-uni. She orders a few more dishes I've never heard of and gives the menus back to the waiter. Then she turns her radiant attention toward me.

"Before we say another word, I just have to thank you for making those cupcakes with Lily," she says. "She hasn't stopped talking about them."

"Oh, it was fun," I tell her honestly.

"But you went to a lot of trouble and I'm really grateful," she gushes.

"I told Dan to come for dinner with the boys the night we made cupcakes," I say, determined to prove I could have done even more, "but he'd already promised them Taco Bell. He's such a great dad."

"Yeah, he is," Lucy says half-heartedly.

"No, really," I say with enthusiasm. "Of all the husbands I know, he's the only one I'd consider. You don't mind that I'm jealous, do you?"

"No, go ahead," she says. "I'm having trouble getting too excited about my life these days so you might as well enjoy it. Sometimes your life can look perfect to everyone else and feel flat when you're living it, you know? You should understand."

What intrigues me about Lucy is that despite her fabulous job, her three wonderful children, and oh, yes, the Mercedes and the six-bedroom house, she has moments when she feels truly and sincerely miserable. She calls it a classic midlife crisis, and for some reason, she's decided that I am the one person who gets it.

"You know what I mean, don't you?" she asks, leaning forward.

Well, maybe I do. I felt that way once myself. After all, I did leave Jacques.

"After all, you did leave Jacques," she says.

What? On top of everything else she's a mind reader?

"Yeah, I did," I say. "Do you want to hear for the four-hundredth time why everyone thought I was crazy but I knew it was the right thing?"

She grins. "No, I think I've got it."

"But what's up with you?" I ask. "When you called from L.A. it sounded like you had news."

"Not really news." Lucy takes a deep breath and looks as if she's about to tell me something important. But instead she shakes her head. "It was nothing. Just a guy I work with who was flirting with me. Kind of fun for a day or two. But hey, I'm married. I stopped thinking about sex a long time ago."

We both laugh and I know she wants to get off this subject. Much as I'd bet there's more to the story, I let her get away with it.

"And what's up with your love life?" she asks, moving on with lightning speed. "Are you still going out with that painter?"

"What painter?"

"The guy you met before I left for L.A."

I make a face. "One date. When I saw his license plate said BLWJOB I decided there was no future. With my bad knees and all it would never work."

Lucy laughs so hard the sake dribbles down her cheek. I feel a secret thrill that my sexless love life can keep her entertained. If you're going to go on 101 bad dates you might as well have a good audience.

"I may have somebody for you," she says, toying coyly with her chopsticks.

"Oh please, not another personal trainer."

"No, of course not. This one's a plastic surgeon. Dr. Peter Paulo."

"Lucy, honestly. Are you trying to fix me up or just fix me? Sometimes I think you should be scheduling appointments for me instead of dates."

"One-stop shopping, babe. Imagine if you and Dr. Paulo fell in love. Maybe he'd give me a discount on the Botox."

"You do Botox?" I shouldn't be surprised but I am.

"Of course. Don't you?"

"Are you kidding? Dove Moisturizing Bar and I call it a day."

I move to the edge of my chair and peer at Lucy's perfect, porcelain complexion. Now that I'm unabashedly staring I can see that there's not one furrow on her brow. None of the crow's-feet under her eyes that have begun creeping up on mine. But is it true that she can never look scared or angry?

"Boo!" I say loudly, out of nowhere, possibly scaring myself more than Lucy.

Lucy jerks back, almost spilling a glass of water. "Jess, have you gone looney?" she squeals.

"Sorry, the Botox. I just wanted to see if your face still moves."

"Of course it does," she says, steadying the glass back in its place. "Except the forehead, I'll admit. But how often do you express yourself with your forehead?"

I think about that one. But it still bothers me that Lucy—who pouts if the lettuce isn't organic—happily injects her face with poison.

"I thought your body was a temple," I say.

"My body is a temple," Lucy laughs. "I just don't want it to crumble like St. John the Divine."

"Oh, Lucy. You're the most fabulous-looking woman I know."

"That's nice of you, but in Hollywood they shoot women over thirty. Out there if you're twenty-three and you haven't had your first mini-lift it's already too late."

"Oh, come on. Get real."

"If I did I'd be the only one," she says wryly, pulling out a mirror to reapply her lip gloss. "Forget about the girls on camera—we don't even want them in the audience. The demos on my shows have to be eighteen to thirty-four because after that the only advertiser who still cares is Viagra."

"Or Depends," I say brightly.

That's a conversation stopper. Before I have a chance to ask any more questions Lucy glances at her watch. "Darling, I hate to do this, but I have to run." She nabs the check and leaves a hundred-dollar bill on the table. "Anyway, are you free Friday?" She doesn't even wait for my answer. "That's when I told Dr. Paulo you'd get together."

Oh, for heaven's sake, this is all Lucy's fault. No one else could get me to the gray granite hallway of a too-chic white box building on East Seventy-second Street at six forty-three on a Friday night. And here I am in brand-new Stuart Weitzman high-heels—I can already feel the blisters coming on—bought for a man I've never met. Wasn't I the dry wit who used to say that "Love may be blind, but dates shouldn't be?" And if I'm going out with Lucy's plastic surgeon, shouldn't he at least pick me up? Oh, that's right. When he'd called to confirm our date for this evening, he'd said that as long as I had to take the train into the city and I'd be out anyway, why didn't I come by his apartment? Certainly wouldn't want to inconvenience him. Maybe I should have called back to see if he needs a pint of half-and-half or a dozen eggs as long as I'm out.

I'm two minutes early, so I pull out my cell phone to give my daughter an early good-night kiss.

"Jen, Jen honey, you there?" I say, trying to hear through a staticky connection.

"Yeah, Mom. What's up? You on your date yet?"

"What makes you think I'm on a date?"

"Lily's here," she giggles. "She told me all about it. What's a plastic surgeon, Mommy? Are you gonna marry him?"

This is not the phone conversation I was hoping for. "No, Jen. We're just having dinner. Nothing special. You're the only one for me. That's why I'm calling."

"Sure, Mom. Whatever. Gotta go. Did you need me for something?"

"No, just wanted to make sure you were all right. Which, I guess, you are. Okay, then. See you later . . ."

Jen clicks off the phone before I can blow her a kiss, leaving me with nothing else to do but tuck in my tummy, straighten my skirt, and ring the bell.

On the other side of the door I hear loud howls and barking. But no one answers. I wait and ring again. No one answers. No one answers. Then the door swings open.

"You're on time," the plastic surgeon says, accusingly. All I can see at the moment is his head, and then he steps back. He's wrapped in a skimpy terry cloth towel and his naked chest is dotted with thick clumps of wet matted gray hair. Obviously, I've interrupted his shower. He looks at me and tilts his head to one side, trying to dislodge some water from his ear. Beads of water are dripping down his leg and he reaches for a corner of the towel to start to dry off. "Don't do that," I think, panicked. He manages to dry his leg without revealing anything that I don't want to see—now or ever, I have a feeling.

"Uh, I'm sorry. I thought we said s-six forty-five?" I say with a stammer. My voice—I *hate* when I do this—rises like a little girl's on the "six forty-five" part.

"We did," he snaps, turning his back to me and leading me into his mirror-walled lair. "But who ever heard of a New Yorker arriving on time? Well, not really your fault," he says, in what I'm sure he thinks is a generous tone. "You're not from New York, I mean New York 'proper,' now, are you? Just give me ten minutes to get dressed."

He disappears into the bedroom, and I try not to think about his peeling off his towel. Maybe I should just leave now. On the other hand, the evening can't get any worse, can it? Yes it can. The dog— an apso-lapso? a lapso-apso? an Alpo? I never can get these designer dogs straight—carries on for his absent owner and starts humping my leg.

I sit down on the white-on-white, never-been-touched-by-children's-hands couch and flip through the copy of *Matisse-Picasso* that's been too casually placed on the glass-and-chrome coffee table. Then I notice a copy of *Hustler* that's been shoved under the sofa.

Why don't I have a secretary who could call me with a pretend emergency to get me out of here? Maybe I could get hold of Jen again and beg her to phone me back with an imagined case of strep. No, Lucy. It's Lucy who should get me out of this fine mess, I'm thinking as the dog, who's now working himself into a frenzy, starts humping more furiously, as if he's super-glued to my leg.

"Um, your dog . . . ," I call out.

"Yeah, I know. He's adorable," he shouts back. "I don't want to make you jealous but he's a real chick-magnet when we're walking in the park."

"Yes, I'm sure . . . but, um, at the moment he seems to have attached himself to my leg and I can't seem to shake him."

"Nonsense. Winston would never do anything like that. Would you, pookie," he says, emerging from the boudoir in a Calvin Klein pullover and leather jeans. He walks halfway across the room toward me, then pauses and turns, posing like a male model at the end of a runway. I don't applaud, so he keeps walking over to the wet bar in the corner of the living room. Wet bar. He must have picked up that decorating tip from *Hustler*. Circa 1978.

"Sorry I kept you waiting," he says in full smarmy-charmy Park-Avenue doctor mode as he uncorks a bottle of Chateau-something-or-other. "I've some cheese and things in the kitchen. Wanna stay in tonight?"

I'm confused. Have we been out so much this week that we have to stay home tonight?

I wouldn't mind going to the Four Seasons. Le Cirque isn't far. And I've always wanted to try Le Bernardin.

"Staying here would be lovely," I hear myself say.

He sashays across the room, hands me the Baccarat goblet and cups his hands around my chin. Then he turns my face thoughtfully from side to side. Am I being kissed already or appraised for Botox injections?

"I know which side of your face is better," he says, pleased to think he's impressing me. "But I'm not going to tell you until later." He actually winks.

Is this his best shot? I hardly know how to reply. And on top of everything, I'm incredibly annoyed to realize that I'm actually wondering which side of my face really is better.

He settles into the sofa and pats a cushion for me to come join him. "You'll never guess who came into my office this afternoon," he says.

"Who?" I ask brightly, sitting down one cushion over.

"No, you'll have to guess." He grins seductively.

Do we really have to play this game? Okay. "Meryl Streep."

"No." He sounds annoyed. I've guessed too high.

"Kathie Lee."

"Getting warmer."

"Go ahead, tell me now."

"Dahlia Hammerschmidt!" he reveals triumphantly.

My face is blank. I can't help myself—I've never heard the name in my life. I try to hide it but he can tell. And he's immediately crestfallen.

Who knew there was going to be a pop quiz this early in the evening? I've blown it already and I didn't even want him.

"I'm sorry," I say sheepishly. "I guess I should have renewed my subscription to *People*."

"It's okay," he says. "I only thought of it because you remind me a little of her."

This could be a compliment. Dahlia Hammerschmidt is probably a once-famous actress, or at the very least, a rich socialite. Then again, she was last seen visiting a plastic surgeon.

I pick up the Baccarat goblet and take a sip.

"So what do you think?" he asks.

What subject are we on now? Ah, I've got it. The wine.

"It's very nice," I say.

He glares at me and then takes a large swig from his own glass. "Come on. That's not a description for a wine. Try again."

If I'd done this badly in college, I never would have graduated cum laude.

"Fruity," I suggest.

"Nope. Oaky. With tinges of acorn. A bit nutty."

A bit nutty. I won't argue with that. I take another sip. "A wonderful kumquat aftertaste," I say.

"Kumquat?"

"Very flavorful."

"It should be, at a hundred bucks a bottle." He's mildly appeased. Maybe I'll just get sloshed on hundred-dollar cabernet and call it a night. I take another sip and Winston, the sex-starved dog, chooses this moment to prove his undying affection for me by catapulting onto my lap in a single bound. As I jerk upright, the red wine sloshes around in the glass, and a few drops land on the snow white sofa.

"Oh, God, I'm so sorry!"

I jump up, dumping Winston unceremoniously from my lap, and rush to the kitchen. A moment later, I'm back with a wet dish towel and I drop down in front of the couch and start scrubbing at the stains.

"Don't worry," the good doctor says graciously. "It's just a couple of drops."

"I want to get them out."

"It's okay." He leans over and grabs my wrist, and when I stop scrubbing, he starts rubbing the underside of my hand with his thumb. We look at each other. "Are you thinking what I'm thinking?" he asks.

I know I'll get this wrong, so I don't try too hard. "What are you thinking?"

"I'm thinking"—his voice has gotten lower and his thumb-action has gotten faster—"I'm thinking that since I'm sitting here and you're on your knees right there, we could have a little fun. Or a large amount of fun, if you know what I mean."

Oh. My. God. And not even a license plate to warn me.

I scramble to stand up as quickly as I can, banging my knee against the glass-and-chrome coffee table and stepping on Winston's tail. I yelp and so does he.

"Listen, I've got to go," I say, grabbing my jacket and purse. "Thanks for the wine. It was very oaky. Sorry about the stains. You can send me a bill, okay? And good luck with Dahlia whatever-her-name-is . . ."

The rest of my sentence is lost to both of us, because I've slammed the door behind me and am back in the hallway, running toward the elevator. Poor Lucy. I hope she trusts someone else to give her Botox injections, because Dr. Paulo may never want to see her again.

Chapter TWO

AT NINE O'CLOCK the next morning, Lucy's husband Dan comes to pick up Lily.

"You look terrific," he says, giving me a peck on the cheek.

"I do?" I'm in jeans and a sweatshirt and since I've just applied Revlon Really Rosie to my toenails and they're not quite dry yet, I'm flapping my feet around like a demented duck.

Dan glances at the toenails. How could he not? "Pedicure?"

"Not a pedicure. I do it myself. Saves twenty dollars and nobody has to sit at my feet."

"Maybe you'll teach my wife how to do that. But maybe not. She loves people sitting at her feet."

Not going there. Girls stick together. "Your daughter was sweet as could be last night," I say, switching topics. "I'm glad she decided to sleep over."

"Nothing Lily likes better," Dan says. "But I figured I'd take her out to breakfast this morning. The boys are at a tennis match and Lucy's sleeping in."

"Too late," I admit. "We already ate breakfast. Waffles, made in our new waffle iron. Drenched in maple syrup."

"I'm suitably impressed." Dan unzips his jacket, revealing a red plaid shirt that offers that suburban-lumberjack look. He's six feet tall, has big gray eyes and the requisite wavy black hair. He looks more muscular than the last time I saw him, which must mean he's part of that pack of middle-aged studs working out at the gym. I don't have to look down to guess that instead of shoes, he's wearing all-weather, all-terrain L.L. Bean boots, even though there's no snow outside and it hasn't rained in a week. That's what guys do around here. They buy four-wheel-drive Jeeps to cruise down paved suburban streets, too.

"How was the big date last night?" he asks.

"The date was great," I say. "Just lovely."

"What'd you do?"

Honestly? Scrubbed a sofa. Had my leg humped by a horny dog. Escaped.

Forget honesty. Why ruin the man's breakfast? Besides, I haven't got the stomach myself for the gory details.

"The usual," I say vaguely. "Some drinks. A lot of talking. Dinner. You know."

"Sure."

He'd ask more, but Lily and Jen burst out of the playroom and Lily rushes to kiss her dad.

"Have a good time?" Dan asks, picking her up and swinging her around.

"Yup," Lily says as Dan puts her down. "Jessie made beaded necklaces with us last night. Look." She holds out the turquoise-and-pink ornament around her neck, which Dan admires appropriately.

"Last night?" Dan asks. "I thought Jessie was out."

"She came home really early because she wanted to make necklaces," Lily reports. "And she hadn't eaten dinner, so we got to eat again. Frozen pizzas."

Dan looks at me with a raised eyebrow. "Busted," he says.

"Busted by an eleven-year-old," I agree with a mock sigh.

But the girls have a different agenda. "Can I stay a little longer?" Lily asks, tugging at Dan's hand. "I don't want to leave yet."

"Okay. Fifteen more minutes," Dan says as the girls run upstairs. He takes off his jacket and tosses it on a chair.

"Want some waffles?" I ask.

"No thanks. I don't want to bother you."

"Don't be silly. You haven't had breakfast yet and I've plenty of batter left."

He grins and a little dimple appears.

"I know, I know, I'm so domestic," I say apologetically. "It's just that—"

"No, I love it." Dan cuts me off before I can start apologizing for waffles. I have to stop this. Last time Dan was over, I apologized because it was raining.

We go into the kitchen—normally I'd be embarrassed that I hadn't cleaned up yet, but Dan doesn't seem to mind—and I briefly whisk the mixture that's still sitting in the bowl.

"What's in there?" Dan asks, standing over my shoulder and peering at the batter. He's tall, and when he leans in to look, my head bumps his chest. I catch a whiff of sandalwood shaving cream.

"The usual stuff. My secret ingredient is vanilla and some cinnamon and sugar."

"Amazing," he says, truly meaning it as he watches me spoon the batter into the waffle iron. "Around our house, defrosting Eggos is a big occasion."

"It helps to have modern, expensive equipment," I say and then realize he won't know I'm joking. "Actually, I bought this relic for five dollars at a flea market last week."

"Incredible. What a woman. I see why Lily loves coming to your house. Good breakfasts. Good company," he says generously. I roll my eyes at the compliment and so he adds, "By the way, nice of you to rush home last night to play with the girls. Leaving your date and all." He grins mischievously at me.

I sigh. "Okay, so the date was a disaster. Trust me, I had a lot more fun stringing beads."

"What happened?"

"You can guess."

"No, I can't. I'm a forty-three-year-old guy with three kids. I can remember when disco fever wasn't retro. What do I know about dating anymore?"

"Bingo," I say. "Nobody who lived through John Travolta in a white suit should still be going on dates. Every time I get fixed up I feel like a complete idiot. Jen and Lily already seem more comfortable around new boys than I do. Of course they don't have to worry about cellulite."

Dan laughs. "Come on, Jess, any man would be lucky to get you." He looks me straight in the eye as he says that with a sweet, sincere smile. I know he's just being the loyal husband of my loyal best friend, but I blush anyway. "And any guy who knew you had that fancy five-dollar waffle iron would propose on the spot," he adds.

"Give me a break. I don't even think I want to get married again. Once was enough."

"Really?" he asks.

I fiddle with a napkin. My great excuse for being the only single woman in the PTA is that I *like* being single. But Dan looks genuinely interested and I hear myself admitting, "I don't know. The grass is always greener, right? I'm the one who left, but now that I'm on my own, all I can remember is the good stuff about marriage. So, yeah, in my heart of hearts I probably want someone to share my life with. Some dreamboat who'll curl up next to me in bed every night. But, hey, I've been there, so I also know that the dreamboat probably snores."

Dan scrapes a last bit of maple syrup from his plate. "Do I sense a little cynicism there? Was the first time around so bad?"

"Not bad. It had its moments.

"So what happened? He snored?"

I laugh. "Let me put it this way. We met on a beach at Club Med. I didn't speak much French, and the only words Jacques knew in English were *Marlboros, bed,* and *You're the most beautiful woman in the world.* You'd be surprised how far that got him."

"Not surprised at all. Sounds like a better come-on than 'What's your sign?' "

"I probably fell for that one once, too," I say. "But when it came to Jacques, I fell for everything. I was young and he was sexy. It was all so passionate. But five or six years down the road . . ." I stop and shrug. Why am I telling Dan all this?

"At least you got that great kid out of it."

"Not even." I stand up and start clearing his plate. "I adopted Jen right after we split. That was one of the big problems. I wanted a baby and Jacques *was* a baby. He didn't want a family, so I left. *C'est la vie.*"

Dan doesn't seem to know what to say.

"Hey," I jump in. "At least my French got better."

"For that you could have gone to Berlitz."

I laugh. "That's what I think every time I go on one of these blind dates."

"I'm so sorry, Jessie. I've known you all these years and I never knew the details."

"It's okay. I don't exactly broadcast it. Lucy's probably the only one who's heard the whole story."

"Lucy. Oh, darn." Dan gets up. "Thanks for breakfast, but I'd better get back. The boys will be home and Lucy has to get to an appointment."

"For what?"

"I don't know." He laughs. "Probably a pedicure."

First thing Tuesday, I'm walking through the kindergarten hallway at Reese Elementary School on my way to Fifth Grade Parents' Morning and I'm already ten minutes late. But I can't resist stopping to look at the collages tacked up on the bulletin board. They're just too darn cute. The sign says OUR IMPRESSIONS OF SPRING, so I'm guessing this one puffy white cotton ball creation is an Easter bunny and not a melted snowman. Either way, it takes me back to when Jen was five and making these same funny, clumsy artworks. Can it be that Jen's only eleven and I'm already nostalgic for lost youth—hers and mine?

I sigh and hurry on to the gym where I grab a cup of coffee and wave to a group of moms who are chatting animatedly.

"Jesse, come on over!" calls the ever-cheerful Melanie, who's standing in the middle of the group.

"I'll be right there," I say.

I head across the room to where the breakfast goodies are—I jogged on the treadmill at six a.m. and now I'm starved—but suddenly Lucy comes rushing at me, her face lit with panic and her eyes popping as if she were being chased by a wild bull.

"Are you okay?" I ask.

She grabs my elbow and starts wheeling me in the opposite direction. "I need to talk to you."

"Well, I need a muffin first."

"Don't go over there!" she says, in a loud whisper.

I look longingly over at the pastry table where a couple of women I know are replenishing the Danish. I try to turn in their direction, but Lucy grabs me with a hold that would bring Vin Diesel to his knees. She steers me to a corner of the gym and finally loosens her grip.

"For heaven's sake, what's the matter?" I ask.

"I can't stand these mornings," Lucy says. "All the women here hate me." She pauses and looks around, then adds with emphasis, "Every—single—mother—in—this—*room!*"

"That would be something of a miracle," I say with a shrug. "You can't get the women in this room to agree on anything. Come get a muffin with me. Cranberry-apple would be nice. Maybe banana."

"*No!*" she says, sounding like a stubborn eleven-year-old rather than the parent of one. "I'm not going back there."

I look over at the Alpha Moms who have her so alarmed and I know what she means. Cliquey girls don't go away—they just get older. I'm always telling Jen that if she doesn't have the Skecher high-tops that everyone else is wearing her social life will *not* be over, as she so dramatically claims. But in their J. Crew uniforms of khakis, crisp cotton shirts, and muted-tone sweaters neatly tied at the shoulders, the moms seem to be sending a different message. Inadvertently, I look down to see if I'm dressed to code. Thank goodness I am.

My gaze turns to Lucy, who definitely didn't get The Memo. She's not dressed like a mom—she's dressed like she thinks a mom should dress. The hot pink sweater, which looks suspiciously like cashmere, shows more cleavage than allowed by Pine Hills law, and her jeans are tight, low-slung, and definitely not Levi's.

"Aren't those the jeans I saw in *InStyle*?" I ask. "The ones that sell for something like five hundred dollars a pair, only in Beverly Hills?"

"They're incredibly comfortable," she says defensively. "Everyone I work with wears them."

Work. So there's the problem. The lightbulb goes off in both our heads at the same time.

"You know what's wrong with the women in this room?" Lucy asks. "They hate all the mothers who have full-time jobs. They scheduled this little event so that none of us could make it. But here I am," she adds, tossing her head defiantly.

"You're paranoid," I tell her, but even as the words are coming out, I realize she's got a point. Nine to ten for coffee and ten to eleven-thirty in the classroom isn't exactly the perfect schedule for anyone with a full-time job.

"You took the whole day off?" I ask, impressed.

"Oh, please," she says. "That's not the point. I'm here and nobody will even talk to me."

"Who'd you try to talk to?" I ask.

"The women at the donut table," she says, "who acted like I had the plague. The women I interrupted standing by the percolator, who were deep in conversation about how you shouldn't have kids if you're not going to stay home with them."

"They didn't mean you," I say.

"No? Who did they mean? Hillary Clinton?"

She's got me there. "Come on, Lucy, what difference does it make? You've got terrific kids. Lily. The twins. Those boys give teenagers a good name."

"Yeah, I have great kids." She grins. I hit a soft spot. "Really great kids. Smart and funny, all three of them. Shouldn't that buy me some PTA points?"

"I think so," I say as I spy the dreaded Cynthia Victor walking briskly toward us. "But here's the person who should know." Cynthia—former president in corporate America, current president of the PTA—is the kind of suburban supermom who never should have left Wall Street. She quit her job to raise her family. Now she coordinates Palm-Pilots with her daughter Isabella and fits in her kickboxing class between tennis lessons and town council meetings. Rumor has it that the year she was in charge of the Girl Scout cookie sale, she assured a "Troop of the Year" victory by ordering two thousand boxes of Thin Mints herself. When the kids had to make a building for social studies class, Jen concocted hers out of dominoes, toothpicks and a whole lot of Elmer's glue. Isabella's model, on the other hand, arrived at school with the label DESIGNED BY I. M. PEI ASSOCIATES clearly visible. Cynthia demurred at the time that "I.M. didn't do it himself. I just called someone in his office for ideas."

Now Cynthia's obviously on another mission.

"Jess," she says, "I'm putting together a little mother-daughter book club. Nothing fancy. Just six or seven of us. We could read some Nancy Drew together."

My face must give me away—what self-respecting preteen would be caught dead reading Nancy Drew?—because she adds, "Or everybody can decide on the books together. I'll just make sure to vet them first."

"That sounds like fun. Jen and I just read the new *Harry Potter* together."

"No *Harry Potter,*" Cynthia says firmly. "I don't like that series."

"Well that's okay, too," I say. Maybe two hundred million people are wrong about Harry. Then trying to draw Lucy into the conversation, I add, "By the way, uh, you know Lucy, right? Lily's mom."

"Oh, yes, of course," Cynthia says. But she looks at Lucy as if she's never seen her before in her whole life and gives her the slow, head-to-toe once-over. Cynthia pauses dramatically when her eyes reach the tops of Lucy's alligator boots. But instead of saying something snide about them, she turns pointedly back to me.

"So how about it?" asks Cynthia. "We'll meet Fridays at seven.

Discussion will be from seven-fifteen to seven forty-five, and we'll have snacks afterwards. Nothing too sugary. Just some fruit and crackers. Maybe cheese. Jen doesn't have a cholesterol problem, does she?" she asks solicitously.

"Not that I know of," I say. Another thing to put on the list. Get her hair cut. Buy Pumas for summer camp. Check Jen's cholesterol.

"Lily's a great reader, too," I say, trying to snag an invite for my best friend and her daughter.

But politeness isn't on Cynthia's to-do list.

"With you and Jen signed up our little group is filled," she says efficiently. "Perfect. See you Friday at seven sharp. My house, of course."

And with that, she's gone.

Lucy looks at me incredulously. "I told you. All these women hate me. Did you see that? It was like I wasn't there."

"Cynthia's just like that. She has her own agenda. I think I'm going to call her and say Jen and I can't do it."

"No, no, don't be silly. I don't care. If anything, I'm out of town so much, it would be Dan who'd have to go with Lily. Might be worth it just to see how Cynthia would handle having testosterone at her mommy-daughter book group."

Lucy's cell phone rings and she looks embarrassed. "It's okay. Answer it," I say.

I hang out for a minute while she says hello, and when she realizes who it is, she turns to me and mouths, "Sorry. I have to take this."

Her business call gives me an excuse to make my way to the pastry table in time to snag a croissant. I chat with a few of the other mothers about birthday parties and dancing lessons. One of them asks me if I can chaperone a class trip and another enlists me to work the book fair. I make my escape before someone can sign me up to sew saris for Diversity Day.

When I wander back to Lucy, she's still on that business call. Or maybe it's not strictly business, I suddenly realize. Lucy has her hand cupped around the phone and her face is flushed. A few strands of hair are sticking to her slightly damp forehead. Every few seconds Lucy, the serious professional, lets out a hoot of laughter. I try not to listen.

Okay, that's a lie. I get as close as I can without grabbing the phone from her.

"I'd love to tell you, but I can't right now. I'm in a school gym," I hear her whisper.

I should probably disappear and give her some privacy, but I can't bear to leave. Something makes her giggle again.

"Then ask me questions," she coos.

I'd give anything to know what the Mystery Caller asks now, because the next thing she says is:

"Pink silk." And then she giggles again.

Another pause. And then, "Just the kind you like."

My face gets red, even though I'm not the one on the phone.

Lucy looks up and sees me, but I might as well not be there. "Yes, you looked great on the show this morning," she gushes into the phone. "I liked the Hermès tie. Is that the one you were telling me about?"

He—because I'm pretty sure by now it's a "he"—must have a self-esteem problem because she quickly says, "Yes, you were wonderful. You always are."

Lucy rolls her eyes at me, pretending she can't wait to hang up, but the guy at the other end won't let go that easily. "You were great, sweetheart, trust me. But I have to get off. Yes, I'll call back in an hour. Promise. Okay. Me too."

Lucy hangs up, stuffs the phone back into her beige Dior hobo bag and says brightly, "So. I'm sorry about that. Now you never told me about Dr. Paulo."

"Not so fast," I say. "Who was that?"

"Just someone I work with."

"The guy who flirted with you in L.A.?" I ask, sensing a plotline.

Before she has a chance to answer, Cynthia—goddamn Cynthia—rings a bell. A real bell. I swear. She's standing in the middle of the gym holding a cowbell. We all look at her, which is what she really seems to want in life, and for a moment it appears that she's going to take a bow. Instead, she chirps, "Ladies, it's time! The children are waiting for us in the classrooms!"

I hope Cynthia hasn't planned the class activities, too. Following the Nancy Drew read-aloud, she'll probably have us playing hopscotch.

After my morning in Jen's classroom, I spend three hours at my computer working on my presentation for the Arts Council for Kids. Great group, bad acronym. Unlike the rest of the staff, I refuse to say "ACK" out loud, unless of course I'm choking on a hot dog. But be that as it may, it's a worthy cause. Since I became their fund-raiser five years ago, I've raised four million dollars for the Council, which sounds like a lot, but in Manhattan terms, it's what certain people drop in an afternoon at Harry Winston. But I have a plan this year to blow it out of the water.

I manage to return a few phone calls although none of my conversations are as intriguing as Lucy's. Maybe I'm in the wrong business. Or not. I like the kids we help, I like the cause, and I especially like that I can work part-time, mostly from home. I get to earn a living without changing out of my sweatpants.

Just before Jen gets home, marking the usual end of my workday, I catch myself staring in the mirror, counting my crow's-feet. Then the phone rings again, but this time it's not business. As soon as I pick it up and say, "Hello," Lucy blurts, "So why did you hate Dr. Paulo?"

I laugh. " 'Hello, how are you' is usually a better way to start a conversation."

"Hello, how are you. Why did you hate him? You never answered me this morning."

"I didn't hate him. He's just not my type. Sorry. Wasn't a great night."

Lucy groans. "I don't know how it could have gone wrong. He's so good with Botox."

Well, that's a quality that never made my list of what-to-look-for-in-a-husband. Kind and caring. Sense of humor. And—who knew?—good with Botox.

"Maybe he sees too many beautiful women all day," I suggest generously. "He's gotten kind of spoiled."

"Okay, I've got to ask this. What kind of underwear were you wearing?"

Am I missing another connection here or . . . Oh, for goodness' sake! Does Lucy think I dropped anything more than my dignity? "Trust me, Lucy. Underwear wasn't the issue. He didn't get to see it, believe me."

"No, no. I'm just thinking that we should go shopping for lingerie. I know a great little place on Madison. Are you free on Monday morning?"

"Shopping, sure," I say. "But why lingerie?"

"Because lingerie always makes you feel better," Lucy says preachily, sounding as if she's quoting from the Bible. The Very New Testament. "I need a lift. You need a lift. My mother used to say you can't hold your head up high in an old bra."

I never heard of a bra holding up your head, but I'm in. "Monday," I agree.

Lucy's Madison Avenue lingerie store looks intimidating even from the outside. A delicate lemony camisole is floating in the window next to a midnight blue lace garter belt. At least I think it's a garter belt. Hard to tell. It's hung so artfully from a thin wire, it might be part of a Calder mobile rather than something to wear. On an awning above a feng-shui red lacquered door, the pseudo-French name of the store is inscribed in intricate curlicues.

"This place is expensive," Lucy admits as we get out of the cab, "but worth it. It's even French."

"La Lovelette," I say, reading the name on the awning. "Not really French, I don't think. Just meant to sound foreign and impress you. Sort of like Häagen-Dazs—made up to sound Danish and sell more ice cream."

"Like Ben and Jerry's," Lucy says distractedly, as she heads toward the store.

"Not at all like Ben and Jerry," I insist, following her. "Ben and Jerry are real guys who live in Vermont, while Häagen-Dazs is . . ."

Lucy stops and looks me straight in the eye. "Jess, I don't really care about ice cream right now, okay? I want to focus on lingerie."

Got it. I pull myself together to enter this temple of temptation.

The store is all polished surfaces—a brilliantly buffed wood floor, gleaming chrome fixtures, and smooth-as-glass marble walls. It's not immediately clear to me that anything's for sale since it feels more like a museum with just a few choice items on display, lit like Picassos. Finally, past the Mies van der Rohe chairs, I notice some high racks where bits of lingerie are hanging on heavily padded hangers, each a foot apart from the next.

"Not very much merchandise," I whisper to Lucy. Whispering seems the way to go in here.

"That's because each piece is spectacular," she says. "All one-of-a-kind."

I walk over to examine a one-piece peach silk garment that's floating in the air, backlit by hidden spotlights, and just as I'm fiddling around, trying to find the price tag, a saleswoman approaches. She's one of those women of indeterminate age who looks like she was born on Madison Avenue. Her blond hair is pulled back in a sleek knot, her makeup is impeccable—that almost impossible to achieve not too matte, not too shiny look that *Vogue*'s declared essential—and her St. John knit suit has to cost a lot more than she makes in a week, even here.

"Beautiful piece, isn't it?" she asks in an excessively cultured voice. "Perfect for any occasion, but if you're getting married, it's what I call a must-have."

"Not getting married yet," I say. "I'm just looking." When she smiles slightly, I add quickly, "Just looking at the—um, lingerie, I mean."

Her smile turns to ice as she notices me hunting for the price tag, and once I hit on it, I almost faint. This little number would have to be a wedding gift from the Sultan of Brunei before I could slip into it. Am I buying underwear here or does it come with a house in the Hamptons?

"Anything that's less 'dear'?" I ask her, rising to the occasion.

"That's hand-rolled silk and the pearls were cultivated from a new breed of oysters in the China seas and individually applied with thousands of gold-thread stitches," she says with just a *trace* of condescension.

Frankly, my Fruit of the Looms seem to be working just fine. And just how comfortable do pearls feel in your crotch, anyway? I guess that's not the point.

"I'm sure it's worth the price," I assure her. "I just can't afford it."

She looks disappointed in me. Very disappointed. I am clearly no longer worth her time and she can barely bring herself to point her chin toward the back of the store in a vague indication that I might find something there.

Heading back, I spy a single rack of lacy bits, hung slightly closer together so I actually have to move the hangers to see them. I go through each one carefully, finally finding a bra that looks as much like my $18 Maidenform as possible, only it costs $185 and has a fancy French label. Now that's an idea. Maybe they'll just sell me a label.

Since this is obviously the lowest-priced bra in the store, I go to the front, prepared to admit defeat. Lucy has her back to me and is holding up something I can't yet see while the saleswoman—who wisely abandoned me for Lucy ages ago—nods approvingly.

"Do you think it's too much for the first time?" Lucy asks.

"I think it's perfect," the saleswoman says. "For the first time or anytime."

I stop. The first time? Hasn't Lucy shopped here before?

And then I get it.

The first time.

Okay, I'm an idiot. We're not in this store to shop for me. Lucy has a *reason* to be here. She's been sending signals for days that something's up, and I've been ignoring them. The popping champagne corks in L.A. The whispered call on the cell phone. The need for a girls' night so she could tell me something private. Now she's going to spend a small fortune on sexy lingerie because a man . . . well, because a man is going to see her in it. And it hits me over the head like a ton of bricks that the man isn't Dan.

Lucy turns around and holds out the skimpy black undergarment for my approval. Her face is glowing.

"Like it?" she asks.

I feel light-headed. Woozy. Like I've swallowed a glass of champagne too fast. I sway very slightly on my heels.

"Are you all right?" asks the saleswoman, who is rapidly getting on my nerves. When I don't answer, she says, "Why don't you sit down while your friend tries this on?"

I obediently follow Lucy into her fitting room, which looks like a small, jewel-box bedroom with muted lighting, flattering antique mirrors, and a soft pale pink love seat. I can't help thinking that it's the perfect spot for *monsieur* to *regarder* his mistress while she models lingerie for him.

I think I'm going to be sick.

"Let's get out of here," I whisper urgently to Lucy.

She holds up the black whatever-it-is. "Don't you like it?" she asks.

"I don't like why you're buying it."

"What do you mean?"

I'm too flustered to be subtle and the words just come tumbling out. "For heaven's sake, Lucy. You're having an affair. Or planning to have an affair. I finally got it. I'm so stupid, I didn't put it together before. And now you're trying to get me to say it's okay by pretending this ridiculous lingerie is worth it."

Lucy plops down on the love seat and drops her head into the six hundred dollars' worth of lace that she's holding in her hands.

"Oh, Jess, it's not like that," she says softly. "There is someone . . . a guy I work with. I'm sorry. You're right, I've been wanting to tell you."

"Who is he?" I ask stoically. I'm usually pretty good at knowing what's expected of me, but this is uncharted territory. Best friend of a woman who's thinking of having an affair. Do I nod my head and listen supportively? Do I express outrage and dredge up Dan and the children? Or do I just admit that I'm completely confused? Somehow, the only words I hear coming out of my mouth are, "Who is he?"

"That doesn't really matter, does it? He's someone you probably know. I mean, not know, know. But you've heard of him. You could guess who it is. He's kind of semi-famous."

Swell. This is like being back in Dr. Paulo's apartment. What's with these people? I'll never guess who Mr. Semi-Famous is, and when I eventually get Lucy to tell me, I still won't know who the heck he is anyway. Oh, forget it. This is all beside the point.

I stand up. "Lucy, what are you thinking? And why in god's name would you do this?"

She turns to me with a look I can only describe as teenage angst. That glassy-eyed gaze of having found the person, the only person in the world who makes you feel tingly, alive, and whole—and who you also know is going to cause you endless, delicious pain. And it's more than a little disconcerting to see this look on the face of my friend. My married friend. Who, in my opinion, should grow up and let her own teens have the angst.

"I don't know. I don't know," Lucy babbles. "It's all just kind of happened. I mean 'it' hasn't happened. Not yet. But we started with a few dinners out in L.A. and there were some good-night kisses. And then one time I couldn't sleep so he came to my hotel room and we shared a cognac and we talked until five in the morning."

Maybe I should suggest pay-per-view. That's what puts me to sleep when I'm in a strange hotel room.

Lucy looks up at me, pleadingly. "I really like him, Jess. He's all I can think about lately. Is that so awful?"

It's too soon for a position paper here. On the one hand I'm appalled. On the other hand, she's my best friend. I want to understand. My practical side kicks in. "When are you going to see him again?" I ask.

"I'm supposed to be in L.A. again next week. And it gets even worse. He's hosting my next show. The pilot I'm doing. We're going to be thrown together all the time. What am I going to do?"

"You seem to have decided. Unless you're buying this lingerie to try to rekindle things at home?" I ask hopefully.

The color drains from Lucy's face and I can tell I've made her feel awful. She stands upright as the padded hanger drops to the floor with a thud. "Come on. Let's get out of here. I want to go home and catch the last half of Lily's soccer game."

For once, Lucy's going back to the suburbs and I have a reason to stay in the city. We say a quick good-bye and I head over to Fifth Avenue, making sure that I'm holding my head up high, despite my cheap lingerie. I walk briskly north to Ninety-second Street and when I get there, I'm slightly sweaty and breathless. Damn. Lucy would never arrive for a business meeting this way. The building is one of those old, elegant Fifth Avenue addresses that requires you to be certified by five old-monied WASPs and the right interior decorator before you're granted the privilege of plunking down a cool three million bucks to nab an apartment.

It requires the skill of three doormen to get me inside—one guy opens the door and asks who I'm visiting, the next one announces me via intercom to my hosts, and yet another leads me to the elevator and discreetly whispers my floor to the white-gloved elevator operator. This is an up-to-date, fully automated elevator. So after the attendant pushes the button marked "14" he doesn't have anything else to do. I figure his job now must be to stand ready to meet my every need. But I'll be damned if I can figure out what to ask for on our twenty-second ride.

The elevator door opens into a gracious foyer, complete with a Chinese rug and a white lacquered Parsons table, which boasts a tastefully huge, but not too huge, bowl of fresh-cut peonies. Thick mahogany doors at either end lead to the only two apartments on the floor. They're unmarked.

"Fourteen-A is to the *left,*" the elevator attendant says, smirking. So this is why he was put on earth. He waits while I ring the bell and is still standing there when a maid in a gray-and-white uniform opens the door.

"Okay?" he asks her, as if his bringing me up to the apartment may be a greater intrusion than she could really bear.

"Yes, fine. Mrs. Beasley-Smith is expecting her," she says.

Thank goodness. I'd hate if she'd forgotten about me in the three minutes since I was last announced.

I follow the maid into a sweeping persimmon-colored living room dominated by a huge trompe l'oeil frieze of naked cherubs circling an English garden. Uh-huh. On the far wall, another sensibility prevails and a silk-screened Warhol soup can screams for attention. Now I'm ready for anything.

"You can wait here while I see if Mrs. Beasley-Smith is ready," the maid says. She seems to like saying that name. Maybe she should go with Mrs. B.S. for short.

But after all the pomposity, I'm not really prepared when a thirty-ish woman in Levi's and a white T-shirt glides in, cradling a baby in one arm and trailed by a golden-haired little girl of about four. Mom is sweetly pretty in a well-scrubbed way, with light brown hair pulled back into a ponytail with a dime-store scrunchie and just a trace of lip gloss.

"Hi," she says, shifting the baby to her other hip so she has a hand to offer. "I'm Amanda. This is Taylor." She bounces the little boy until he grins and then says, "And behind me is Spencer."

"Hi," Spencer says in a teeny, tiny voice.

"Nice to meet you," I say, bending down to her eye-level. "I'm Jessie."

When I stand up again, Amanda thanks me for coming. "I have four friends joining us. I hope that's enough. We're all really excited about getting involved."

"That's great," I tell her. "I'm thrilled to be working with you."

Within a few minutes, the room fills up with moms and various-sized toddlers, and I'm introduced in succession to Pamela Jay Barone, Rebecca Gates, Allison von Williams, and Heather Lehmann. I can't place any of the names, though I have a feeling any money manager would know them. The women are cookie-cutter perfect—pretty and slim, with well-highlighted blond hair (except for Pamela, whose auburn mane is swept off her face by a paisley headband), and they sport huge diamond rings. But they're dressed casually and there's an easy familiarity as they play with each other's children.

Just as I'm beginning to wonder how I'm going to integrate a gaggle of toddlers into my presentation, a girl who I quickly realize is the au pair appears in the doorway. She's about eighteen or nineteen, with luminous skin, curves in all the right places and hair that gleams like it's spun from pure gold. In a room full of almost-blondes, she's the only one who looks like she's never had to pay for it.

"Ilsa and I could take the children now," she says to Amanda in a lilting Swedish accent.

"That would be great, Ulrike," Amanda says. "There are only five kids and Heather's nanny is coming in a few minutes, so you can take them into the playroom."

"Or to our apartment," Pamela offers.

"Either way," Amanda says, then turning to me, she explains, "Pamela lives right across the hall and our au pairs are friends. We're so lucky. Half the time we don't even shut our doors so the kids can play everywhere."

Ilsa comes in—she's pretty, but not as drop-dead gorgeous as the sensuous Ulrike—and the two au pairs round up the children, who happily follow them out.

"I don't know how you can bear to have that girl in your house," Heather says bluntly to Amanda, as the moms settle into various leather wing-backed chairs, damask-upholstered sofas, and cushiony velvet love seats. "I wouldn't want her within a mile of my husband. Why bring the chicken to the fox?"

"Well, Alden's never home, so it's not a problem," Amanda says lightly.

"And Alden would never run off with an au pair," Rebecca says, trying to be supportive. "It would be way beneath him."

"She could definitely end up beneath him," Heather says smugly. "You've got a girl who looks like a Swedish porn star prancing around in the next room, and a husband can't be blamed for getting ideas."

"I think we should start the meeting," Pamela says, in a slightly high-pitched voice. "We're here to talk about charitable work, so let's get to it."

"Absolutely," says Amanda while the rest of us try to banish the image of a sweaty Alden and Ulrike going at it under the gaze of the trompe l'oeil cherubs. "Well then, you've all met Jess, who works with the Arts Council for Kids," she says affably. "Alden and I . . ." she pauses for effect, then repeats, "Alden and I always make a contribution, but this year, I thought—writing a check isn't enough. What really matters is getting involved. And that's why we're here. To form a committee that can do something to help this wonderful charity."

I'm glad to hear why Amanda thinks they're all here. I was worried that I was the post–Pilates class entertainment for a group of rich, bored women who weren't quite rich enough to be on the boards of the New York City Ballet or the Metropolitan Museum of Art. But these women aren't the social-climbing piranhas I'd feared.

I launch into my spiel about what we do and how many inner-city children we reach. How we provide free dance, drama, music and art classes to kids who can't afford them. I tell them about a boy named Rodrigo who came to our music classes every day after school for years to escape an alcoholic mother and who just got a scholarship to Juilliard. They all nod. They're on my side.

"So how can we help?" asks Pamela.

I'm ready. I suggest an auction benefit they could run. An afternoon luncheon-cum-fashion show where we split the proceeds with the designers. If they want to put some sweat into the endeavor, I say, reaching for a joke, five-K runs seem to be in vogue.

"I've got a much better idea," says Rebecca, the one supportive voice in the imagined au pair scandal. I'm prepared for it to be loopy . . . and it is.

"Why don't we put on a show!" she says.

"Just like Mickey Rooney and Judy Garland?" I quip. They look at me blankly. If I want to keep working, I've got to stop referring to things that happened before my clients were born.

Rebecca forges ahead. "What I mean is, why don't we take all the kids in your program and put on an opera—like *Rigoletto* or something—

and that way we can combine music and drama and art. And we could do it at Lincoln Center. Off-season, of course."

Allison, who hasn't said much yet, is suddenly excited. "I love it! And our kids—the older ones of course—could be in it, too!" Quickly realizing she doesn't want to sound self-serving, she adds, "They don't have to have the starring roles. We could get a couple of professionals. . . . If you think we need them."

How do I explain that Placido Domingo isn't taking on any more gigs and that the logistics of their kids, the Arts Council kids and a performance of any kind—let alone an opera at Lincoln Center—is just not going to happen in this lifetime? I hate to be a wet blanket, but I think I better rein in their plans.

"A performance is a great idea," I say cheerily. "But maybe we should do something small and intimate. We have a lovely stage at the Council Center."

"No!" Allison roars. Five heads snap around to her direction. "We have to dream big. Isn't that what your organization is all about? Lincoln Center. *Rigoletto*. All our kids together, rich and poor. If we think it can happen we can *make* it happen."

How many therapy sessions has this woman had? Luckily, having said her piece, Allison retreats to her former docility, and the others quickly agree to ditch *Rigoletto* on the grounds that not all of the kids speak Italian. However, as bad luck would have it, one of their husbands plays tennis with the chairman of the board of City Center, and she's sure there's some small stage she can secure for the event. Great. The ideas keep brimming forth. They know which designer should make the costumes, which caterer will provide snacks after rehearsals, and who should choreograph the routines. I'm in the cross fire of five overexcited women who act like they're the ones who put the exclamation point after *Oklahoma!* After twenty exhausting minutes of inspiration, the ideas start slowing down. In the end, it's decided. A musical show starring all the kids. Tickets will cost one thousand dollars. Ten-thousand-dollar-and-above donors will be invited to a preshow dinner party with real-life underprivileged kids. Whether to hit up Kate Spade or Donna Karan for the goody bag gifts is left undecided.

They look at me expectantly. "It's going to be wonderful, isn't it?" asks Amanda.

"Wonderful," I answer numbly.

As I collect my coat, say my good-byes and stumble into the foyer, I've thought of what I can ask the elevator attendant to do for me. Fetch two Advil.

Chapter THREE

LUCY TOOK OFF for Los Angeles two days ago without even calling me. I'm betting that she's ticked off because I didn't play the expected role of trusty sidekick at the lingerie store. But I happen to like her husband and I don't happen to like what she's doing. Doesn't she realize this has to end badly? I know she's a TV producer, but didn't anybody ever make her read *Madame Bovary* or *Anna Karenina*?

But not talking to her is driving me crazy. We've talked almost every day for the past ten years, since Lucy first spotted me sitting alone in the Pine Hills playground and came over to offer a welcoming smile and a chocolate chip cookie. Lucy appeared so exotic in her white, fur-trimmed Dior parka—which frankly did stand out in a sea of blue peacoat–clad moms—that I suddenly felt like the most popular girl in seventh grade. But it didn't take long to get beyond the faux fur and find her good heart. And boy does she have one. She always seemed to have a sixth sense about what I needed—late-night calls when I was lonely, Friday-night fix-ups that I complained about but secretly enjoyed (well, at least sometimes), and a calm voice when I was sure that Jen had scarlet fever. No, Lucy assured me. Pink cheeks are actually a sign of good health.

So what's going on with her? She's always been the one with the strong moral compass. After all, wasn't it Lucy who absolutely *forbade* me to have what I told her would be "just an innocent drink" with my accountant—who just happened to be married? But I'm still her best friend and she needs to know I'm here for her no matter what. She needs my advice. She needs my support. And since I've sworn off *All My Children*, I need my daily dose of drama.

When I can't get through to Lucy's cell phone, I call her New York office and speak to her trusted assistant Tracey, the latest in a long line of just-graduated-from-Vassar protégées. In a mere six months on the job, Tracey has morphed into a mini-Lucy—she talks as fast as her boss and wears Club Monaco versions of Lucy's designer clothes. She can't afford take-out sushi so she eats tuna fish. She's almost ready to conquer the world, but first, she has to answer the phones.

"I've been having trouble tracking her down this trip, too," Tracey says. "Maybe her cell phone's not working."

No way. Don't TV producers have their Nokias surgically implanted in their ears? If Lucy's not answering, something's up.

"You could leave a message at her hotel," Tracey suggests. "That way she'll get it when she comes back tonight."

If she comes back tonight, I think.

I glance at the clock. Ten-ten in the morning, which means it's only seven-ten in L.A. That's when Lucy has champagne, as I remember. "Maybe I'll call the hotel now," I say. "Do you have the number?"

Tracey gives it to me, adding, "But I tried her room a while ago and she's not in. Must have been an early meeting that I didn't know about."

And what kind of meeting would that be? Television execs don't typically rush to the office before sunrise, as far as I know.

"Doing this pilot is really keeping her busy," Tracey says, as if aware that she needs to explain something.

I bet it's keeping her busy. Didn't Lucy tell me that the host of the new pilot is the guy who . . .

Suddenly, I'm inspired. I take a deep breath.

"Lucy told me about the show. And she can't stop talking about that fabulous host. What's his name again?"

"Hunter Green."

Hunter Green. So now I know. Well, not really.

"Hunter Green?"

"The game show guy," Tracey says. "He hosts *Fame Game.*"

Ah ha. Now we're getting somewhere.

"When's it on?" I ask innocently. "I'll check him out." Boy, will I check him out.

"It's syndicated, so hang on. Let me look." I hear her rustling through some papers, and then she says, "Looks like it's on in New York at ten in the morning."

"That's right now."

"I guess it is. Let me know what you think."

I hastily say good-bye and flick on the TV in my bedroom. Remote in hand, I flip past morning talk shows featuring beauty makeovers, home makeovers, life makeovers, husband makeovers—isn't anybody happy with what they've got?—finally landing on a game show. Wrong one. Another game show. A flashing sign on the set tells me I've found *Fame Game.* And the guy standing center stage must be Hunter Green.

I get as close as I can to the television and stare. Okay, Hunter's cute. Kinda. Not exactly Brad Pitt, but not the pits, either. He's mid-forties, I'd guess, and pudgier than a woman on TV would dare to be, but he's appealing in a bearish, comfy sort of way. His eyes crinkle when he smiles, which seems to be all the time. He's wearing a nice suit and an even nicer tie (maybe the one Lucy approved?) and I can tell from here that he has on a lot of cologne.

At the moment, Hunter has his arm around a slightly overweight contestant with a bad dye job. He's making eyes at her and cooing as if she's the only woman in the world for him, and she's so smitten that a goofy grin is plastered across her face. I quickly figure out that she's lost the round and is being sent packing. But in the thrall of Hunter's heady seduction she wouldn't care if she lost her job, her husband and her year's supply of Lay's potato chips. Hunter announces her consolation prize—a Day of Beauty at Sears (maybe she can have her legs and her car waxed simultaneously)—and she throws her arms around him and plants a big kiss on his cheek. "I love you, Hunter!" she screams.

Hunter hugs her as if she's his long-lost grandmother, then turns to the camera and winks. "We'll be right back with lots more." He winks again. "Don't go away."

Wouldn't think of it.

I wait impatiently through a commercial for an arthritis pill and another for Preparation H—ol' Hunter's not exactly pulling in a young demo, is he, Lucy—and when the show starts again, Hunter has his arm firmly draped around the shoulder of the next contestant. He's cooing. She's smitten. Big surprise.

I keep watching. To be fair (and should I bother?), he's not a bad host. The game itself is thoroughly mindless, and Hunter at least livens it up with some clever banter. Which may be scripted, I remind myself.

By the next commercial break—Tums and a cream for vaginal dryness—I've got the pattern, and sure enough, Hunter comes back on camera flashing bedroom eyes and hugging another hapless contestant. Well, better her than Lucy. My only comfort is that if Hunter's on the air this morning, he's not cuddling with my best friend. But then the credits roll and the screen says, THIS SHOW WAS PRERECORDED. Should have thought of that.

I turn off the TV and start pacing up and down in my bedroom. Oh, Lucy, don't you get it? You may be the most sophisticated woman I know, but you don't stand a chance against Hunter Green. This guy is *professionally* charming. It's his *job* to make women love him. If he clamps one of those beefy arms around your slim shoulders, you're going down.

But what can I do?

The phone rings and I grab it.

"Hey, there, it's me," Lucy says.

"Hi. Where are you?"

"In my hotel room."

"You are not."

"I'm not? I think I am. Room 920. Kind of lovely, actually. I have a marble bathroom with a sunken tub and a Jacuzzi. Much nicer than what I have at home."

"Tracey said you weren't in your room."

"Calm down. I just spoke to Tracey, which is how I know you'd called. I was at the gym early and grabbed some breakfast. Now I'm back."

So she's back. But I know she's lying about the gym. She's prepared a story in case Dan calls, and she's trying it out on me.

"What's going on in L.A.?" I ask.

She knows what I mean. But instead she turns industry on me. "Getting this pilot started is tough," she says. "I've had three meetings already at the network. The guy I work with there says—"

"Lucy," I interrupt, because I can't bear her talking to me as if . . . well, as if I'm Dan. "Lucy. You have to tell me the truth. I want to know what's happened with Hunter."

"Hunter?" Her tone changes abruptly from overburdened exec to squealing teen. "Jess, how do you know his name? I never told you."

I don't say anything and she giggles. "Damn. Has this already made Liz Smith?" She sounds more pleased than panicked at the idea of being an item.

"Doesn't matter, just tell me what's going on," I say. "I need to know everything."

She's quiet for a moment, then says, "You don't really want to know, Jess. You know what I mean? You think you want to know, but in your heart of hearts, you don't."

She's got me there. Of course I don't want to know. Almost as badly as I *do* want to know.

"So you slept with him," I say.

She giggles. She pauses. She relents. "That would be an affirmative."

Now what the heck do I say to that? I'm going to be sophisticated about this. "Was he good at least?"

Another giggle. "Another affirmative."

Isn't that wonderful. I'd hate for Lucy to be throwing her life away for anything less than multiple orgasms.

And suddenly, I think of the one thing Lucy could do that would be even stupider than sleeping with Hunter Green.

"You're not falling in love with him, are you?" I ask.

"No, of course I'm not in love with him," she says, trying to sound scornful, but instead her voice is slightly goopy. So she gives in. "I'm in . . . I'm in infatuation. We have this amazing bond. I just feel so . . . connected to him."

They're connected? Big deal. You can get that with AT&T, too— and with a lot less static. But it also occurs to me that if she isn't careful, Lucy's gonna be slapped with roaming charges.

Time to appeal to her rational side, unless that's been *dis*connected.

"Sex can make you feel connected to someone, even if you hardly know him," I say, the professorial side of me asserting itself. "Prolactin or something. I read about it. The same hormone that's released when you're breast-feeding is released when you're"—screwing? copulating? making love?—"when you're having sex," I say, avoiding any judgment calls. "It makes you feel all lovey and mushy, so you bond to your baby, which is good. But it does the same thing when you're just"—here we go again—"having sex with a guy. Which isn't always good."

Geesch. Where did all that come from? I know Lucy, and she's going to make fun of me now. Tease me for giving her a biology lesson when the subject is chemistry. Or promise me that her chemicals are strictly under control.

But she doesn't. Instead, she just sighs. "I can't explain what's happening, but it's beyond amazing. Hunter's so passionate. And intense. This morning, he held me and looked into my eyes for what seemed like forever. You can't imagine how he looked at me, Jess. Like I'm the only woman in the world. You can't imagine."

But I can imagine. Perfectly. Just so happens I saw that look this morning, too. And while I don't track the Nielsen ratings, I'd have to guess so did a couple of million other women who happened to be watching morning TV. It may be Hunter Green's *only* look.

Lucy's other line rings and I'm spared while she gets it. She comes back swearing that the other call really is business and so we say goodbye, promising to talk later.

I hang up and go back to pacing. I've had all I can take of television stars and lovesick friends and . . . *prolactin?* What the heck was that about? My best friend is screwing around with some beef jerky game show host and I'm giving adult sex-education lectures. But I'm not going to think about that right now. It'll give me worry lines. And that's the last thing I need, even if I am on my way to the dermatologist.

Unlike Lucy, who wouldn't make an appointment with a doctor she couldn't flirt with, I'm about to go to my first visit with Dr. Marsha Linda Kaye. Maybe because she's a woman she takes her patients on time. So at exactly twelve-fifteen I'm lying stark naked on her black leather examining table, my butt sticking to the thin crinkly paper on top, while Dr. Kaye scans my body from head to toe with a magnifying mirror that must make every pimple and pore look as large as Bryce Canyon. I cringe to think of what it must be doing to the cellulite.

"Everything looks okay mole-wise," she says after ten long minutes of scrutiny. "Nothing unusual. At your age you have to expect a few discolorations, but as long as they're not raised there's nothing to worry about."

I point to the one brown spot on my chest that's brought me to this $250 visit. "What about this?"

Dr. Kaye moves the magnifying mirror. She peers. She prods. She takes a thin metal pointer-thingy and pokes the spot a few times. "I don't see a problem," she says reassuringly.

I feel relieved. Momentarily.

"We can do a biopsy if you're concerned," she says, and when I don't immediately protest, she dabs the area with a numbing solution. Before it has a chance to completely work, she's scraping with a tiny razor edge and dabbing the cells onto a prepared slide.

"Ninety-nine percent sure it's nothing," she says, applying a small bandage now to the spot, "but now you won't have to worry about it." She moves the magnifying glass over to my face and adds, "If I were you, I'd be a lot more concerned about the broken blood vessels at your nose. What do you say we give them a *zap* right now?"

From nowhere, she points a Flash Gordon–like laser gun at my nose.

"Ah, nah, that's okay," I say, trying to grab back some dignity by pulling up the paper dressing gown. "Those red spots have been there so long I hardly notice them. I just use a little concealer and—"

"Nonsense, Jessica. This is the twenty-first century. You don't need concealer when we can fix it permanently." She laughs. "Trust me, this is minor. It'll just take a sec."

I'm tempted, but since I've been known to beg for Novocain before a teeth cleaning, and I've already been attacked (however gently) with a razor, I ask, "Will it hurt?"

"Hurts for a second and looks good forever."

Which means it hurts.

"And what exactly do you do?" I ask, stalling for time.

She briefly describes the laser's pulsating electricity, then adds, "This one will be on the house. No charge."

Well, that's interesting. I've heard they give the first vial of crack away free, too.

She reaches for a pair of eye goggles. For herself, not for me, I suddenly realize. Hello, if the laser's pointing at my face, why does she get the protective goggles?

"Are you sure this won't hurt too much?" I ask again.

"Trust me," she says, adjusting her goggles and pointing the gun squarely between my eyes.

Sure, now I can relax. So I close my eyes, grit my teeth and when the jolt comes, I'm okay with the quick, stinging pain that's not much worse than an insect bite. But it's followed by a smell that could be a slab of sirloin on a sizzling grill. Me, medium rare.

"Is my skin burning?" I ask, panicked.

"Take it easy." Dr. Kaye's smiling like a Cheshire cat and holding a gilt-edged mirror in front of me. And darn if she isn't right—my face is slightly flushed, but the blotches that have bracketed my nostrils for twenty years are gone. Just like that. It really is a miracle. Who cares about the Red Sea parting when you can witness the red lines disappearing?

"See, didn't I tell you?" she beams. "Little things like this don't have to bother you. We can fix just about anything."

And now, of course, I'm hooked. Is anything truly possible? My mind races, making a top-to-bottom inventory. Can Dr. Marsha Linda

Kaye do something about those age spots I can no longer pass off as freckles? The blue spider veins that crawl down my leg?

I hesitate, but can't resist. "What would you recommend?" I ask.

She runs her fingers gently across my face. "I'd keep it simple right now. We'll just give you a B&C."

"A B&C?" I have a moment of panic. "Don't you go to a gynecologist for that?"

She laughs, but then she continues on with business. "A B&C—that's Botox and collagen. Start with some Botox right here." She touches an offensive wrinkle I never knew I had. "And collagen on the naso-labial lines. That would make a big difference."

Naso-labial lines? How have I missed those? If I don't attack with collagen and Botox right now, will my face eventually look like an Amish quilt? Even though I'm looking at forty in the rearview mirror, I thought I was holding up pretty well. But Dr. Kaye, with her professional eye, knows better.

"The other procedure you should consider right away is a glycolic peel," she says. "Any of my patients will tell you it takes five years off the face." She glances at her watch. "If you want to wait about ten minutes, I might even be able to do it today."

I sit up abruptly, grabbing at the paper robe and eyeing my own clothes across the room. "No, thanks. No time today. I'll think about it, though." And I probably will, damn it. What happened to the no-maintenance-me who used to leave the house with wet hair and a swish of lip gloss? Just yesterday I was almost reeled in by a spiel about a $155 miracle cream that was developed by a NASA scientist because the saleswoman at Bloomies promised it was "age-defying."

Cream, maybe. But no Botox today. That's too much of a leap. Besides, that first *zap* was on the house, but the rest won't be, and for a B&C—oh gosh, who came up with *that* abbreviation?—I'd have to break into Jen's college fund. Which I won't do because my priorities are still straight. At least I think they are. But I'd better get out of here quickly before Dr. Kaye tells me that she takes American Express.

*   *   *

Back home I log on to my computer to try to get some work done, but fat chance that's going to happen today. Nasty images of Lucy and Hunter performing seminude contortions in an erotic Cirque du Soleil keep running through my head like a broken DVD. And then, so much worse, I see Botox needles chasing the three of us around the room. I ditch the work idea and decide to check my e-mail. I have three new messages, which immediately makes me think I must be popular. Then I start opening them and I realize I'm popular only with retailers. Home Depot is having a spring sale—twenty percent off toilets and fertilizer. Next message: JCPenney is having a spring sale—thirty percent off fancy bras (don't get me started again). And who's having a spring sale in message number three? The subject line says this one is from . . .

Shit!

Shit! Shit! Shit! Shit! Shit!

No bargains here. I know that without even opening it. And I can't open it. I can't.

My blood is racing and I feel like I've swallowed a gallon of coffee. My hands are shaking so hard I'm afraid I'll delete the darn thing the minute I try to open it. So I get up and walk away from my desk. I pace around the kitchen, nibble on a muffin, brew a pot of herbal tea and try to simmer down. I go upstairs, stare into my closet for a solid three minutes, and then I realize the problem. I'm not dressed right for this e-mail. I change out of my ratty sweats into my oh-so-chic black suede pants. Should I reapply the lipstick and mascara I wiped off at Dr. Kaye's office? That's silly. I can probably read this bare-faced. No I can't. I go to the bathroom and pull out a tube of Estée Lauder Sun-Kissed bronzer and a new Bobby Brown deep-wine lip stain.

With a critical eye, I look into the full-length mirror and swivel around. The Butt Master I bought for $24.99 from that three a.m. infomercial was worth every penny. The suede pants look good. I may be middle-aged and divorced but I still have some flair. I hate to sound like a bad self-help tape, but I'm just as desirable and a lot more self-confident than that pretty young thing who was once married to French dreamboat Jacques.

The man who after a decade of silence has sent me this e-mail.

Which—time to face the music—I am now ready to read.

And it's really not that hard to do, is it? I go back downstairs to my desk, stare at the computer, and take a few deep breaths. A double click, and Jacques is back in my life.

Or at least he's back in New York.

Mon Amour,

I'll be in your city next week. Can you meet me Monday nite at 6 for drinks at Les Halles or Tuesday nite at 8 for dinner at Balthazar? Let me know which is better for you.

Avec amour, J.

I reread it six times. Not that there's much to read. I haven't heard from him in ten years but Jacques acts like we just broke baguettes together last week. He must have had some sort of emotional breakthrough, though, because he's actually given me a choice. Something I don't remember his doing in all our years together. Still, the options are limited at best. What if I want to meet him at Les Halles Monday night for *dinner* instead of drinks? What if I'm available Tuesday but hate Balthazar? And tell me, please, is nobody ever going to take me to Le Bernardin?

Another possibility crosses my mind. Clearly one that would never have occurred to Jacques. I don't have to see him at all. I could simply delete the message, erase him from my memory bank, and never have to confront my ex-lover, ex-husband and ex-life again. Jacques, *Monsieur Irresistable,* simply takes it for granted that I'll see him.

And he's right. I will.

I sink back into my ergonomically correct chair, close my eyes and try to picture what Jacques looks like now. Could he possibly be gray? Is he wondering if I am? Has he gained weight? Whoops, I have. How much can I lose before next Monday if I go on my favorite starvation diet? Maybe I should meet him on Tuesday, to give the Slim-Fast an extra day. I think briefly of trying to scare up some black market fen-phen, even if that's the one that kills you.

Ten years. But no matter how hard I try, I can't picture Jacques looking one iota different than the day I met him, standing on that Caribbean beach in one of those skimpy French bathing suits that no American man would ever have the nerve to wear. I barely had the nerve to look. Twenty-four hours later I wasn't just looking, I was having what I thought was the fling of my life with a ruggedly handsome hunk who looked like he'd been cast to seduce somebody's wife in one of those French art-house movies. Instead he seduced me, nobody's wife yet. And how I ended up as Jacques' bride is one of the mysteries that I've replayed eight thousand times in my head.

That first night—the very first night we met—we took a bubble bath together in a luxuriously large tub that overlooked a moonlit ocean. Only a Frenchman would know to reserve a bathroom with a view. And that's how it all started. I was barely twenty-four, still the proper wait-for-three-dates-before-you-kiss-him Jess my mother had raised me to be. But I'd been at my first job long enough to earn this one-week vacation. And why not make it a wild romance with an exotic Frenchman on a balmy Caribbean island? I was so free, so unlike myself. Almost as if the FBI had relocated me with a new name and identity. For seven days, I could be whoever I wanted to be. Or, as it turned out, whoever Jacques wanted me to be.

So there I was that first night, naked in a frothing tub, gazing at the stars, with a hunky man massaging every inch of my body. And then he said, *"Je veux laver les cheveux belles."* "I want to wash your beautiful hair." Could that be what he was saying? My high school French was pretty *mauvais*. For all I knew he was saying he wanted to wash my beautiful *horses*. They both made about the same amount of sense to me—until Jacques actually began sensuously caressing my hair, working us both up into a lather.

Lucy thinks she's infatuated? I'd put my first-week obsession up against hers any day. When my vacation was over, I wanted to die, but instead I went home to Ohio, and that p.r. job at the museum didn't seem so glamorous anymore. Then Jacques started calling. He had an apartment in New York so why didn't I come live with him? He missed me. He wanted me. He needed to feel me in his arms again. Just a short visit, I told my mother, as I bought my plane ticket and packed up the biggest bag I had.

For six months, maybe a year, the passion never cooled. We drank wine, made love, ate dinner, made love, took a bath, made love. For variety, we went to restaurants, drank champagne, and kissed passionately, waiting to get home so we could make love. He stroked my arm so frequently that a friend quipped that like a piece of velvet, my skin would wear out. Getting married was a formality since we were never apart.

Oh, Lucy, you won't believe me if I tell you that the frenzy won't last forever. That the sex might continue to be great but that, eventually, other things will matter, too. One day before Jacques proposed, I made a careful list of the pros and cons of our relationship. The negatives: Language, Religion, Political Differences. He Doesn't Want Children. He Always Expects to Get His Way. Never mind that the French are perversely fond of Jerry Lewis. And on and on for eighteen lines. On the plus side, one lone entry: He Makes Me Feel Alive. That was enough to swing the balance, to change my life, and to carry me over the threshold.

Feeling alive again. Is that the draw of Hunter Green, Lucy? If so, I get it. And what I wouldn't give to feel that way again.

Chapter FOUR

THE WAY LUCY'S FEELING when she gets back from L.A. is lousy. She takes to her bed for two days—a distinctly un-Lucy-like move.

"The whole world is just spinning," she whispers when I come over with a pot of freshly brewed green tea.

"Are we talking physical or the metaphysical here?" I ask.

Lucy looks at me blankly. I decide to rephrase the question. "I mean, are you dizzy? Do you feel sick? Or is Hunter making you crazy?"

"What, are you nuts?" she says, jumping out of her king-sized sleigh bed and smoothing out the six hundred thread count Egyptian cotton blue toile Frette duvet. "Don't talk about Hunter in here." Her eyes dart around the room as if she's looking for microphones, a mini-cam, or James Bond's secretly recording martini glass that Dan might be monitoring.

"Do you think Dan suspects?" I ask, truly concerned.

"Would you shut up!" Lucy hisses. "I'm not kidding! Just shut up in here!" She pointedly turns away from me and goes back to smoothing out the duvet. Her life may be a mess but her room never is.

"Calm down. You're a little overwrought, don't you think? Have some tea."

"I don't want tea."

Well, this is progress. I'm guessing she doesn't want the sugar cookies I brought, either. I sigh. "Come on, Lucy. What can I do for you? If it's a tough time, let me help."

"I don't know what kind of time it is," she says, pausing. "But thanks." She stretches and anchors both hands on her slim hips. "On top of whatever else is going on, my back is killing me. I feel like I'm eighty."

I stifle my impulse to point out that back pain is often related to stress—or sexual gymnastics. Instead, I commiserate. "Tell me about it. I swear I creak when I get up in the morning. I don't care *what* the magazines say, forty is the new eighty."

"I thought fifty was supposed to be the new forty," she says, but at least she smiles.

"What about Botox for the back pain?" I suggest, drawing on my new, all-purpose remedy. "They use it for migraines."

Lucy rolls her eyes. "You're so naïve," she says, patting my hand. "That's just a way to try to get the insurance to pay for it." She pauses, and suddenly her eyes light up. "But do you know what we do need?"

Something better than new lingerie, I pray silently.

"Thai massage!" she says, suddenly bubbling again like the old Lucy. "It's amazing, you'll see. You'll come with me, right?" As usual she doesn't wait for an answer, but snaps her fingers and snaps into action. "I'll make the appointment."

"Face down on the mat, hands behind your head."

Now that's a promising beginning, particularly since I'm standing here with nothing on but a thin cotton robe, held together by a ribbony sash. The burly man barking the order stands inches away, and he flexes his muscular arm so that the snake tattoo on his bulging bicep practically jumps out and bites me.

"Is this a massage or a bank robbery?" I whisper to Lucy.

"Shh, don't make jokes. Pay attention and just go with the flow."

Lucy looks Zen tranquil, which is completely baffling to me since

Mr. Biceps—aka the massage therapist—is forcing us down toward the cushions on the floor. The room is cozy and dimly lit, a lavender lava lamp glows in the corner and the strong odor of vanilla incense makes me gag. Mercifully, Yanni isn't moaning in the background. So far, the Thai massage that Lucy promised would relax every muscle in my body has instead put every muscle on alert.

"You're welcome to take off the robes and anything underneath, ladies," says the guy I met only five minutes ago. And why wouldn't I strip for someone with one day's growth of beard and a mail-order diploma from Massage America? Lucy, however, drops her robe and immediately starts to peel off her thong.

Next thing I know, I'm lying facedown on the mat with Lucy beside me. I shut my eyes tight. I'm going to relax right now if it kills me. Okay, we're starting. But how can I relax? I swear the guy is mounting me. He is. He's sitting on my behind, all two hundred pounds of him, and grabbing my wrists. I try to twist around to see what's going on, but Ravi Master, as he's told us to call him—I'd bet anything that's not what the priest called him at his baptism, but I'm in no position to quibble—shakes my wrists and doesn't let go.

"The tension through your muscles is moving into my arms. Into my arms. Into my arms," Ravi Master chants as he tightens his grip. "So you can relax. You can relax. You can relax. You're at peace with the world. Peace with the world. Peace with the world." Does the man have a stutter or is he just a poor conversationalist?

He's chanting. He's shaking. I'm losing consciousness—not in a good way. My arms have been starved of blood flow for at least four minutes. I think they're dead. They must be dead. They are dead. Now that I'm too numb to reach for a can of Mace, Ravi Master yanks my arms back around his head and clasps my hands to his neck. This makes my back arch so steeply into the much-heralded cobra position that my breasts pop out straight into Lucy's face.

"Feel good?" she asks me. I can't begin to answer because in this stretched-out state, my vocal cords are bulging and all of the air seems to have been socked out of my lungs. Just wait till it's your turn, Lucy, I think.

For a blessed moment, Ravi Master releases my wrists. There is a god. But within nanoseconds he's turned into The Hulk, lifting me up in the air and slamming me over on the mat into the missionary position. Upon which, yes, he mounts me again and pins down my shoulders.

"U-uncle," I stammer. "You win."

But he's not done. Now that he's working on Side Two, he pushes, pulls, contorts and distorts my body into a series of positions that would impress any Pennsylvania Dutch pretzel maker. And much as I resist, it starts to feel good. I don't know if he's loosened my muscles or my spirit, but after about twenty minutes of this I'm all warm and tingly. I'm so at peace that the room is all happy pinks and purples and the meaning of life seems much, much clearer. Uh-oh. What's in that incense anyway? I don't have time to worry the question as I drift into a light sleep and Ravi Master abandons me to minister to Lucy.

Half an hour later, Lucy and I drag our Ravi-relaxed bodies to the sauna where it's a steamy 180 degrees—we're paying $150 apiece to experience the exact conditions that cause thousands of New Yorkers to flee the city each summer. We're sipping small bottles of Evian, sitting on hard benches, staring blankly at glowing coals.

"Amazing, wasn't it?" says Lucy as she wipes away a bead of perspiration and lets her towel slide down from her breasts. Naked again. Makes you wonder why she needs that personal shopper at Barneys.

"Amazing," I agree. "How did you find out about this place?"

"I heard about it in Los Angeles. Ravi Master's bicoastal."

"Never a dull moment when you're in L.A.," I say.

"I find time for a couple of other things when I'm working," Lucy says coyly, and I swear she flutters her eyelashes.

Oh no. Please, no. Not this. "Don't tell me you and Hunter go to Ravi Master out there," I say.

"Hunter?" Lucy squeals. Well this is something new. Lucy never squeals. My sophisticated friend is turning into a puddle, and it's not just from the steam. "That's a laugh. Hunter doesn't have a Zen bone in his body. He's a total guy's guy."

"Meaning?"

Lucy giggles. "You know, he does those guy-guy things, like he eats beef and drinks Jack Daniel's. You should see us in restaurants. He gets the steak with everything on it, I get the salad with dressing on the side. He teases me about what a girl I am. He's just so cute."

She pauses to take a sip of water, but I'm the one who gulps. Hello? Isn't this the woman who considers meat the dietary equivalent of Enron? "Doesn't sound like your usual type," I venture.

"I guess not, but what I love is that he's a take-charge kind of guy. In everything. If you know what I mean." She grins slyly and looks up at me. Waiting to be asked. I don't want to ask. But she's primed. Lucy makes small circles on her chest with a well-manicured finger and she's off and running.

"Want to know how we got together for the first time? We were in the elevator at my hotel and he started nuzzling my neck and whispering how beautiful I was. Then he started kissing me. Hard. He came to my room and there was none of the usual should-we-or-shouldn't-we?—he just pulled off my sweater and carried me onto the bed." She has that faraway look in her eye that you see in women in love and mental patients. And she's not done. Lord knows, she's not done. "He's so forceful. So strong. For once I don't have to make any decisions. He's completely in control. I love that. Sex with him is a whole different thing. It's so different than with . . ."

Okay, I get it. Different than with Dan. At least she has the decency not to finish that sentence. And I don't launch into a speech about how sex with Dan is based on love and commitment and having a life together—while sex with Hunter is about an afternoon at the Four Seasons. Nice real estate, but she's only renting.

Lucy runs her fingers through her hair. "I guess Hunter's so successful because he knows what he wants and he goes after it. And right now he wants me."

I think I saw this in *Gone With the Wind*.

"Here, listen to this," Lucy says as if I've just begged her for another story. "I was driving to his apartment last weekend and he called me on my cell phone to say he was waiting for me and had some instructions. I think his exact line was, 'Your job is to knock on the door. My job is to take care of everything else.' And then he repeated it in this really slow, sexy voice, 'You knock on the door. I do everything else.' I'm getting goose bumps just telling you. Imagine how that made me feel!"

I know how it would make me feel. Like a kindergartner. Still I know what's appealing to her here. Someone else is in charge and taking care of everything. It makes her feel sexy. Post-feminist meets post-Neanderthal and loves it. Dan, Lucy's wonderfully evolved husband with his dimples and denim shirts helps with the dishes and takes the kids to school. But he doesn't throw her on the bed, Ravi-Master style.

"I have my own news," I tell her. Am I desperate to change the subject or do I really need advice? "My ex e-mailed. He's going to be in New York."

"Your ex? You mean Jacques?"

"I don't have any others," I say with a laugh.

Lucy shakes her head. "You've been letting me ramble on all this time when you're the one with the big news!"

How silly of me. Lucy's been holed up in a hotel room with a game show host and a pair of handcuffs—I'm guessing on that one—and my e-mail rates as the big news here.

"So are you getting together with him?" Lucy asks.

"If I can lose five pounds before next Tuesday."

"Stop it, you look great." She looks me over carefully, and I'm grateful that my towel is still in place. "How long since you've seen him?"

"Eleven years and three lifetimes ago. Last I heard he was remarried. No, last I heard he was divorced again."

"Maybe he wants you back."

"Don't be silly. He can get any woman he wants. Besides, he may be rich and sexy but I've been down that road."

"So a little fling for old-time's sake?"

"You're having enough sex for both of us," I say. "Anyway, I know how the story ends."

"That's the great thing about being with Hunter," says Lucy, so self-absorbed right now that after ninety seconds of talking about my life we're back to hers. "Who knows what will happen with us? All of a sudden I feel like there's a world of possibilities. Who knows how my life could change?"

"Yeah, it could change," I say more archly than I mean to. She's just spoiled my one chance to talk about Jacques so I'm not feeling very supportive anymore. "You could ruin everything you have at home. Which hasn't been so bad, you know."

"No, it's been great," Lucy says. She sighs and wipes her eye with the edge of the towel. "I'm not a complete idiot. Despite what you probably think."

I don't answer. Because what *do* I think?

"Look," she says, taking a new tack. "I know what I've got. I love my family. I'm not looking to leave and mess things up. In a bizarre kind of way, Hunter might even help my marriage because he's making me feel good. And when I feel good it's good for the whole family."

Now that's creative. Trickle-down economics as applied to orgasms. I stare at Lucy in disbelief.

"So which is it?" I ask. "You want Hunter because he could change your life? Or because he's your own personal Prozac?"

"Maybe I need Prozac, too," Lucy says with a sigh. "You know what's getting to me? The twins are sixteen. Pretty soon they'll be in college. I feel like a major part of my life is already over."

Is that what's going on here? Classic midlife crisis? Preparing for the empty nest by flying away herself?

"You have a great job," I say, looking for the silver lining. "That won't change."

She shrugs. "My job stopped seeming glamorous a long time ago. Especially when I race to catch the red-eye so I can be home with the kids the next morning at six a.m. And you know what? When the boys are gone and I can stay out in L.A. for all the big late-night parties, I won't give a damn. The best part of my life is the kids. And now that's ending."

I wish the dreaded Cynthia could tear herself from the PTA long enough to hear that you can be a bicoastal, alligator-boot-wearing, Emmy-award-winning producer and still think your kids are the center of your universe. That's what I've always loved about Lucy. She has her priorities.

Her life is under control. She knows what matters. At least she used to. If, on top of it all, Lucy's boys get into Harvard—and they probably will—Cynthia's going to need more than yoga to calm herself down.

"You're only forty-one," I remind Lucy. "Even with the boys in college, you still have your whole life."

"Part of the problem," she says, unconsciously toying with her wedding ring. "Dan and I got married when we were babies. Twenty years ago. Our whole life is built around being a family. So what are we supposed to do for the next twenty years?"

"You still have each other," I say. "And Lily. A lot more years of Lily."

"The one saving grace," she says, agreeing with me. "But when it's just Lily at home, we could move into Manhattan. Or out to L.A. She'd love it."

"You're making plans?" I ask, wondering if the L.A. fantasy includes Dan—or Hunter.

"Not plans, exactly, but I do think about things. How they are, how they could be." She goes back to making those damn circles on her chest, and as I watch her, the world starts spinning. I've had more than enough.

"I'm dying from the heat," I say, as I stagger to stand up. "Let's get out of here before we're permanently pruned."

We head for the dressing room, and as I'm standing under the pulsating shower, I realize that Lucy's affair is really pissing me off. Forget the moral issues. Now all of a sudden she's not interested in me or my dates—or the e-mail from my ex, which once would have been good for at least twenty minutes of mind-numbing analysis. The one advantage of being unattached should be that your married friends wait breathlessly for the latest installment of your single-life soap opera. The drama! The dresses! The sex and no sex! Now Lucy's one-upped me again. Her affair with Hunter is way better than a daytime soap—it's got all the makings of a Jaclyn Smith Movie of the Week.

As I turn off the shower, I realize without any doubt—and without any advice from Lucy, god knows—that I'm going to see Jacques for dinner on Tuesday. Why wouldn't I? I was married to the man once so there's no reason that we can't be friends. Well, maybe not friends. I don't exactly see us going to the multiplex together to catch the latest flick or sipping hot chocolate and chatting about the Paris-London Chunnel. But I'm curious about what's happened in his life. And I guess I wonder if I'll feel that old flutter when his hand accidentally grazes my sleeve or the lump in my throat that used to catch me off guard when he'd sit across a table from me and look soulfully into my eyes.

Besides, I've never had one of Balthazar's famous green apple martinis. And with Jacques paying for them at fifteen dollars a pop, I may even have two.

As usual, I'm early. Balthazar is abuzz with its expected array of tall miniskirted models, squat predatory investment bankers, and—after all these years—average-looking people waiting to get inside. What's the matter with me? Jacques has never been on time in his life. As I step inside, I figure I'll be able to visit the ladies' room, run a quick brush through my hair, and . . .

"Mon petit chouchou!"

Jacques' voice rises above the din at the bar, and before I can turn around, he's embracing me and kissing both cheeks. Then he hugs me tightly, holding me in his strong arms for a moment longer than I would have expected. I'd forgotten how muscular he is and forgotten also petit chouchou, his pet name for me. Only a Frenchman could call you a "little cabbage" and get away with it. He leans back, still holding on to my shoulders and looks tenderly into my eyes.

"Mon amour, you are as absurdly beautiful as ever!"

He looks pretty darn good himself. His curly hair is shorter than before and his deep brown eyes are still piercingly intense. Someone's been spending a lot of time on the Côte d'Azur, because he has a deep even tan the color of cocoa butter, and of course he's wearing a crisp white custom-made Turnbull and Asser shirt, just like in the old days, to show it off. His body is firm without a trace of middle-aged love handles. And is he admiring my equally trim silhouette? As long as I can keep his hands off my waist, he'll never know that I've poured myself into Saks' finest Tummy Tightening Body Shaper. To tell the truth, I'm having a little trouble exhaling, but at least we don't wear girdles anymore. Though damned if I know the difference.

Jacques slides over to the bar to retrieve his wineglass and the maitre d' immediately leads us through the well-dressed throng of waiting patrons to a candlelit table for two.

"Perfect," I say, impressed as always by Jacques' effortless ability to jump the line and set the scene.

"Anything for you," he says as we sit down next to each other on the suede banquette. Too close for comfort, I think. But just then a Château Margaux appears—and Jacques raises his glass.

"Together again," he says. "Where we should be."

We clink glasses and I take a sip.

Together where we should be? Did I just drink to that?

Got to slow down the pace here. I'm not ready for any heavy-duty romancing just yet. "So," I say, asking the world's most boring question, "what are you doing in town?"

"Business and pleasure," he says. "The business is done. You are the pleasure."

The man's not going to be easily sidetracked. Besides, I'm starting to remember how nice it is to have someone flirting with you. Ever since the FedEx man changed his route, nobody's even tried.

"I've missed you," Jacques says. "I think of you every day. Time has passed, but you're always with me."

That old classic movie stuff always did get to me. I feel that flutter, which could be my heart, or else I'm hungry and should go right for the bread basket. Damn you, Jacques, this is how you made me feel the first day we met. Don't do this to me again.

"What's going on in your life?" I ask, trying to keep this conversation on the ground. "I've heard only bits and pieces."

"I'll tell you everything. Business is good. And the rest? I've learned a hard lesson. I was foolish, *mon amour*. I had you. The love of my life. And I lost you. I've had many women," he says, as if he's talking about croissants, "but I never loved anyone the way I loved you."

Jacques never did bother much with small talk. In a funny sort of way it feels like old times. But somewhere between me and the croissant-girls, he must have fed that never-loved-anyone-else line to someone else.

"Didn't you get married again?" I ask.

"I did. But it wasn't like what you and I had. Nothing could be."

Should I let him get away with this? Another gulp of wine and I might, but we've got to fill in some blanks.

"What happened?" I ask, trying to sound nonchalant. "You found someone young and beautiful and you couldn't resist?"

"No, I was *stupide*. After you left I was a . . . how you say? . . . a bachelor boy again. That was okay for a while. But then I had enough. Three years ago we married. Now I am divorced. And back in New York." He smiles. "And your *histoire*?"

I'm ready for this. I've got the Cliffs Notes. I'd planned the speech I would give Jacques about how happy I am and how wonderful my life is. For days I've known I shouldn't dare sit across from this man and say anything else.

"I've been lonely," I hear myself say. Oh my god. Wrong speech. Where did that come from? "I mean, that's not what I mean," I say quickly.

"It's all right. I understand," he says, taking my hand.

He doesn't understand, because neither do I, but here we are in Balthazar holding hands across the table and brushing knees underneath it. We order. We nibble on our overpriced seared scallops. We gaze into each other's eyes—yup, soulfully. We talk about old times, remembering only the moments when we were blissfully happy. He brings up the dreamy cruise around the Aegean where we danced on the ship's deck every night under a full moon. I've always meant to ask Jacques how he managed to make a full moon last a whole week. But now doesn't seem like the right time. Not when we're smiling so sweetly at each other and mumbling about how wonderful life was way back when.

Sitting here, I realize that crash diet be damned, in Jacques' eyes I'll always be a fresh-faced girl of twenty-four. And it feels pretty darn good to be basking in that reflection. Who needs the dermatologist when I have Jacques? No amount of lasering could possibly peel off the years more effectively than seeing yourself through an old lover's eyes.

"So," he says, squeezing my fingertips lightly and taking a last sip of cappuccino, "shall we leave? I'll take you home."

I'm really not ready to leave, but we're going to have to say good-bye sometime.

"I guess I'll get a cab to the train station," I say, wishing desperately that I still lived in the city and could make the evening last a little longer with a romantic walk home through the cobblestoned SoHo streets. "I don't have the apartment anymore."

"Don't worry. I know you've moved," Jacques says. "I planned to drive you home."

Nobody has a car in the city, and even if they did, there are DON'T EVEN THINK ABOUT PARKING HERE signs plastered all over the street in front of Balthazar. (Where else but New York can you get a ticket for even *thinking* about parking?) But as always, Jacques has made his own rules and we step outside into a waiting black Mercedes.

I don't bother giving Jacques directions to Pine Hills because the way the evening's gone, I figure the flight plan's already programmed into the car. The CD player's been programmed, too, starting slowly with U2's "Beautiful Day," moving on to Lenny Kravitz singing "Can't Get You Off My Mind," and heating up to early Barry White, a little clichéd, but it works. I hold my breath, but I know my Jacques is always discreet. Whatever he's planning, Nirvana's "Rape Me" isn't going to be one of the tracks. As he cruises up the West Side Highway, I nestle into the cushiony leather seat and start to drift. Jacques reaches over to stroke my arm. Ah, how lovely. A man who can steer and stroke at the same time.

When we pull into the driveway, he runs around to my side of the car to open the door, walks me onto the porch, and wordlessly follows me inside. I fumble with a light switch and blink a couple of times in the suddenly bright foyer, realizing that back on my own turf, my mood has quickly shifted. That reminiscing romantic who surfaced at Balthazar has been deep-sixed.

"My daughter's at a sleepover tonight, so I'm sorry you won't get to meet her," I say, back to sounding like a suburban mom. "But can I show you around the house?"

"Bien sûr."

We begin to walk around and I feel like an idiot. If I'd wanted to give house tours, I would have joined the Pine Hills Garden Club.

Uneventfully we do the living room, the dining room, and the kitchen, which I brilliantly identify as being the living room, the dining room, and the kitchen. What am I supposed to do? Point out the Sub-Zero? Jacques cooperatively looks around my kitchen as reverently as if he's just stepped into the cathedral at Notre Dame.

"C'est magnifique," he says.

Okay, I think we've milked this floor for all it's worth.

We traipse single file up the stairs to pay homage to Jen's bedroom—also known unofficially as The Shrine to Justin Timberlake—and my IKEA-decorated study. We're really moving now. We pass by my bedroom quickly, with only a nod to its purpose, and somehow land in the guest bathroom.

Jacques peers inside, honing in on the claw-footed soaking tub.

"Old house, old tub," I say cheerfully. "I never replaced it because I think it's kind of quaint."

"Does it work?" he asks.

"Sure."

Jacques strides across the wood-planked floor, kneels next to the tub and turns on the water. He plays with the old faucets until the water is the temperature that he wants. "A stopper?" he asks.

A stopper? Yes, we do need a stopper, but not for the tub. I thought once we'd passed the bedroom we'd made it to the safety zone. How could I have forgotten that Jacques' smoothest moves start with bath oil?

I'm still trying to decide what to do when I spy the cork stopper sitting on top of the wicker hamper and pick it up. I weigh it in my fingers until Jacques comes over, takes it from me, and puts it into the open tub drain.

Jacques, we can't do this, I say, only I guess I don't say it out loud, because his hands are around my shoulders and his lips are brushing lightly against my cheek. When I don't pull away he gently kisses my neck, then nuzzles against my ear, whispering soft nothings in French. I can't make out the words, but I can feel the heat. Tantalizingly, he kisses my eyelids and holds me tighter. My body sways closer to his until our lips find each other and we melt into that timeless space that erases the moment along with the years.

I'm not thinking anymore. He's unbuttoning my blouse and I'm letting him. He runs an appreciative finger across my chest and I can hardly breathe. Maybe some of those six pounds I've gained in the last years have landed on my breasts because when he unhooks my bra and steps back, I see a hint of surprise glinting in his eyes.

"You're more beautiful than ever," he says.

"Older," I say.

"But more beautiful," he repeats.

I resist pointing out that the breasts aren't quite as perky as they once were and the little freckles on my chest are ungenerously referred to as "age spots" by the good dermatologist.

Instead, I let him unzip my black satin skirt and I pull it off in one smooth move, taking the body shaper with it.

"No fair," I say, because he's still fully dressed and I'm now standing in nothing but my black lace bikinis.

But he's not in a rush. Jacques is never in a rush. He kisses my breasts lightly, then just a little harder, and his hips press against mine. I start to undress him and he leads me toward the tub. I dip a tentative toe into the water and let out a small yelp.

"It's freezing!" I say, laughing. Jacques laughs, too, and Sir Walter Raleigh–like, spreads a towel over the wood floor, changing the plans from water to land.

"That floor's still going to be too hard," I say, wishing I'd bought the plush Fieldcrests instead of my Target bargains.

Jacques moves closer to me and cups my face gently in his hands. "Where shall we go, *mon amour?*" he asks.

I think about it for only a moment, looking at his almost-nude body, which is muscular and smooth, and to my great surprise, I hear myself whisper, "Well I have a very, very soft bed."

* * *

Hours later I half wake to realize that Jacques and I have fallen asleep with our bodies wrapped around each other in the cozy entanglement of arms and legs that was our way for all those years. I can feel his warmth and the weight of his thigh pressing against mine. He rouses and gently caresses my shoulders, then cups his hand around my breast. My eyes flutter open and I find Jacques gazing at me with a tender smile. "It's still the same, *mon amour,*" he whispers. "I still love you."

I snuggle closer and bury my head in his chest. "You're wonderful, Jacques. As wonderful as ever." I glance at the bedside clock and it's only four a.m., but I realize that it's almost time for him to go. He's booked on the seven a.m. Air France flight. I'm ready and I'm not.

He gets up reluctantly and as he dresses, I groggily go to the closet and reach past my normal terry cloth robe to find the silk one from Victoria's Secret that's been sitting there unused for umpteen centuries. Jacques stops in his tracks and comes back toward me.

"You're mine," he says, wrapping me in his arms and pressing me against the wall. He kisses me deeply, ready to make love one more time, but Air France waits for no man.

"You . . . it's time to . . . you'll miss your flight . . . ," I stutter between kisses.

"I don't care," he says. "I don't want to let you go."

But he encircles his arm around my waist and we walk slowly down the stairs. At the front door we have a final, lingering kiss. And then he takes both my hands in his.

"It's like we were never apart, *mon petit chouchou,*" he says. "So it's settled. When I come back in three weeks we'll be together forever. This time we won't make the same mistakes."

I want to believe him and I kiss him back wordlessly. Forever sounds pretty darn good.

Chapter FIVE

I FALL BACK into a dreamy sleep almost immediately after Jacques is gone. Nothing wakes me for several blissful hours until Jen comes bounding into my bedroom, lugging her purple Gap backpack, her black overnight bag, her red cushiony sleeping mat and a pink pillow emblazoned PRINCESS. She looks like she's just back from trekking in the Himalayas, not overnighting with Lily.

"How was your evening, Mom?" she asks as I sit up abruptly, trying to pretend that she hasn't just awakened me from a sound sleep. I laugh to myself as I get a good look at my big daughter. The earphones from her American Girl Walkman are dangling around her neck and she's carrying a stack of *CosmoGIRL!* magazines. At age eleven all she knows is she's a Girl. Whether it's one who plays with dolls or reads about boys is a toss-up right now.

"My evening was fine," I say. I try to stifle a yawn. "I guess I'm still a little tired."

"Did you have sex?" Jen asks, casually throwing all of her gear onto my bed.

I gulp. What's that about? Is she guessing here or did she sneak back last night and look in the window? No, more likely telling Jen I was going out with my ex-husband was a mistake. I gotta remember that all those books say single moms shouldn't confide too much in their kids.

So I do the obvious. I lie. "Of course I didn't have sex, sweetheart. You don't have sex if you're not married, remember?" I have to stop letting her watch reruns of *Friends*. Why believe me when all the singles on TV are having so much fun? "Jacques is just an old pal now," I say.

Jen buys it. "That's good," she says animatedly. "Because Lily and I found a better husband for you."

A better husband? I want to tell her that Jacques wasn't so bad when you come right down to it. But that would be back in that category of "Too Much Information." So I clear my throat and say chirpily, "I didn't know I was looking for a husband. But who'd you have in mind?"

She reaches for the stack of magazines and fumbles around until she finds the mother lode—a copy of the real *Cosmopolitan*, that hasn't been "Girl-ed."

"Right here, Mom," she says, waving the magazine at me. " 'The Twenty-Five Most Eligible Bachelors.' I picked one for you. His name is Boulder, like the rock."

"He certainly sounds solid." I laugh. But Jen is distracted, because she's busy flipping through the pages of the magazine.

"All the models in here have big boobs," she says. Jen looks down at her own flat T-shirt and rubs her hand against the fabric, as if willing her breasts to grow.

I could lecture about calling them breasts, not boobs, and promise her that she'll get some soon enough. But she won't believe me right now.

"So tell me about Boulder," I say instead. Rocks and boobs. What a magazine.

"He's thirty-three." She looks at me and frowns slightly. "He's the oldest one, so I hope he's not too old. But he's got big muscles and he's a professional surfer. Isn't that cool? I don't think we should move to California for him, but Lily says we have the Atlantic Ocean right here so it shouldn't matter. I'm writing him a letter."

"I'll help with the spelling," I say gamely. I'd hate for there to be any grammar mistakes when pledging my love to the oldest-known bachelor in America, who still happens to be way too young for me.

"Good, because I'm going to tell him all about us."

Us. Of course. Jen's not just trying to nab a husband for me. It's a package deal. She's looking for a dad.

I reach over and take a look at the picture of this Boulder guy— bare-chested, holding a surfboard and offering up such a dazzling grin that I check to make sure I haven't accidentally flipped to the ad for BriteSmile. Doesn't strike me that I'm looking at my destiny, but I can imagine what Jen sees in him—the perfect guy to carry her on his shoulders for a wave-jumping romp into the ocean.

Jen's looking at me expectantly.

"He looks like he'd make a pretty fun dad," I say tentatively, because the old guilt is seeping back. Most of the time just being the two of us seems perfectly fine. But as much as I love her to pieces, I'm still only one parent. Okay, on my good days, maybe one and a half. Still, I can't help worrying about how much she misses having the standard-issue matched set.

Jen, however, is hankering to make the date and ignores my cue to bare her innermost thoughts on Life with (Single) Mom.

"So I'm writing him a letter to enter the contest," she says, explaining the rules for winning yourself a Boulder. "He's going to read them all—"

Or maybe someone will have to read them to him, I think.

"—and then he'll pick the girl he wants to marry. *Cosmo* will send you on a date first. And oh, Mom? Just so you know. The date might be on TV, too. Is that okay?"

"Sure, hon, if we win, I'm there," I say. At least it's not *The Bachelor*— I don't have to get into a hot tub with the guy. And anyway, what are the odds of any of this happening? Jen scrunches her freckled nose and appraises my chances.

"So, Mom, you know how you've been talking about having your hair streaked? Maybe you should do it now."

"What? Don't think I can land a husband like this?" I say, joking. I give a pretend sigh. "All right, I'll do it. I don't want to let you down."

But for Jen this is serious business. And now she thinks she's hurt my feelings.

She comes rushing over, throws her arms around me, and gives me a big, mushy kiss. "I love you, Mom. You're perfect just the way you are. You could get any husband you wanted."

"Oh, you're a sweetie. I love you, too." I give her a big hug and trace a heart on her back with my finger. Jen giggles.

"Go unpack your stuff and we'll grab breakfast," I say as she dashes off loaded down with her bags. "Wait, you forgot your pillow," I call after her, but she doesn't come back and I have to smile. What self-respecting "Princess" would carry her own?

With Jen gone, I get out of bed and slip into the silk robe. Good thing Jen didn't notice it lying in a heap on the floor—I'm not sure she would have believed I was wearing it to impress Jay Leno. I pick up my own pillow and hug it tightly to my body. It seems impossible that just a few hours ago Jacques was lying here beside me. Maybe I dreamt it. I look around for signs, but there's no telltale forgotten sock. I breathe deeply and get the merest hint of Jacques' cologne. How could last night have been so amazing?

And this morning—when he told me he still loved me. I throw the pillow back on the bed. Oh, god, what did I answer? Something about how wonderful he is. Why couldn't I just say, "I love you, too?" Now that would be simple. The man I'd loved so passionately, so long ago, comes back into my life. After all this time apart, we finally get the fairy-tale ending. Just like a romance novel. And as Jacques and I fell asleep last night, wrapped in each other's arms, I was sure I did love him.

But now?

I pace around my bed fussing with the books on my nightstand and bend down to straighten the fringe on the throw rug. I walk into the bathroom to get a glass of water and stare into the mirror. Do we really have a future? What was it he said at the door as he was saying good-bye? *It's settled.* I feel that familiar clench in my stomach. What-ever else has changed about Jacques, he hasn't lost that old habit of as-suming he can decide things for both of us.

I wander back toward the bed. No, this time, I'm going to have to make my own decision. I put the pillow back against the headboard and get another whiff of his cologne. Maybe I won't change the sheets just yet. And maybe I have to give the man another chance. That is, of course, unless I fall for Boulder.

For the next three days I keep waiting for Lucy to ask me about my date with Jacques, but she never does. And I can't bring it up because Hunter's in town and he's already demanding every moment of her attention. By day four, Lucy's bursting because I have to, absolutely *have to*, meet her *boyfriend*. She's forty-one and married—you'd think she could come up with a better word.

"You're going to love him," she says breathlessly when she calls me with the invitation. "I mean, I'm sure you're going to love him. But I really need to know what you think."

Since Lucy insists that introductions be made over something more exotic than a simple latte or even green apple martinis, she's come up with a plan. Hunter's been invited to a star-studded party for Willie Nelson and we're both going to tag along. We'll even get to go to the concert. Works for me. If I'm chief advisor on my best friend's Hollywood affair, at the very least I should get some perks out of it.

Lucy calls me twice more to ask what I'm wearing, clearly more worried about my making a good impression on Hunter than the other way around. Since I don't own a pair of alligator boots, Lucy agrees that I can wear my fake pleather skirt and she'll lend me her third-favorite pair of Jimmy Choos. Two days later she panics about the pleather and drops off her own real leather skirt—from Ralph Lauren, no less—along with the Choos.

That night, I'm standing on the corner of Thirty-fourth Street feeling like a hooker in my four-inch stilettos when Lucy and Hunter walk by without even noticing me. They have their heads huddled close together, sharing some secret that has them both grinning.

"Lucy?" I call out.

"Oh, Jess!" She rushes over and gives me a quick hug. "I'm sorry. Didn't mean to keep you waiting." She tosses back her hair and then adds, "This is Hunter."

As if I didn't know. He looks just like he did on television, though maybe a little heavier. How's that work? I thought the camera added ten pounds. Maybe that only happens to women—another one of nature's little jokes. Hunter's skin is so smooth that I wonder at first if he's wearing makeup. But no, I recognize the faint smell of Aveda for Men. Which means he's probably just scrubbed, exfoliated, and self-tanned.

"Nice to meet you," I say, extending my hand, but Hunter has another plan and leans in to give me a hug.

"Lucy says wonderful things about you. And now I see why," he says. He squeezes my arm, offers a Clintonesque rub of my elbow, and gives me a heartfelt gaze.

"Hope those blue eyes aren't crying in the rain," he says.

I blink. Huh?

"That's a Willie Nelson song," he says with a playful smile. "Remember? 'Blue Eyes Crying in the Rain.' And you have lovely blue eyes."

"Well, thanks," I say.

"So what's your favorite Willie tune?" he asks.

Oh no. I almost forgot he was a game show host. What is this? Country Music for $200? I can tell already I'm not going to win the Buick.

"I like all of Willie's songs," I say stupidly.

"Come on. One favorite," he cajoles. "So I can make sure Willie sings it tonight."

Already he's doing me a favor. I take a stab. "I used to love 'I'm Walkin' ' when I was a kid."

He grins. "That's Rick Nelson."

"Maybe Willie knows it, too," I say, trying to recover. These country-music guys all sound alike, anyway.

"I bet he does," Hunter says graciously. "Little Ricky Nelson. You must watch a lot of *Ozzie and Harriet* on Nick at Nite."

"I guess I don't get around enough," I say, slightly embarrassed.

Hunter throws back his head and laughs. "Good one," he says. " 'Don't Get Around Much Anymore' is one of my favorites, too." And he gives me a wink, which makes me feel better.

Decent of him. He put me on the spot, but then he saved me. And now that the quiz show's finished, Hunter turns and locks arms with me on one side and Lucy on the other, turning us into a mini Rockettes line. "I must be the luckiest man in New York!" he gushes. "I've got the city's two most gorgeous women."

Lucy smiles adoringly up at him. I don't want to like him, but I kind of do. He's chatty and charming and I can see why he earns the big bucks. As we walk down the street, I notice a few people glancing at him and he notices, too. Is this what Lucy likes? Being on the arm of a television star makes you feel pretty darn important yourself. I'm waiting for Joan Rivers to ask me whose dress I'm wearing. (I'd have to say: "Lucy's.")

But maybe Hunter's gotten a little too used to being in the spotlight. Walking into Madison Square Garden for the concert—we have VIP tickets, Lucy announces—he swaggers down the aisle, looking from side to side, expecting to catch someone's eye. Most people are fumbling with their bags and adjusting the coats on their seats, but a thirtyish woman who's sitting on the aisle glances at him then turns away to pull off her sweatshirt. He stops.

"Yup, it's me. Hunter Green," he says, tapping her on the shoulder. "I saw you staring at me."

"I—I wasn't . . ." she starts to stammer. But Hunter reaches over and snatches her program.

"Here, I'll sign that for you," he says magnanimously, scrawling his name with a flourish.

The woman takes back her program with a startled look on her face that suggests that since she has no idea who this man is, she doesn't know whether to say thank you or call security.

"I like to make my fans happy," Hunter effuses obliviously as we press forward to our seats. "It was just a minute of my time but she'll remember it forever."

Yup, she'll be dining out on the story about the weird guy who grabbed her program at the Willie Nelson concert for days.

In our front-row seats, Hunter sits between Lucy and me and drapes one Canali-clad arm around each of us. Cozy. But two songs in, he's given up impressing me and has both hands firmly anchored on Lucy's thigh. He massages her knee and nuzzles her neck. Should I tell them to knock it off? Come on, Lucy. Just maybe one of the eight thousand people at this concert knows you—or Dan. But Lucy's lost in Hunter World and has forgotten that anyone else is around.

When Willie sings "Blue Eyes Crying in the Rain," Hunter reaches over to squeeze my hand, but a minute later, he's back to pawing Lucy. And it keeps getting worse. Is it getting kind of hot in here? By the time Willie's singing "On the Road Again"—which is where I'd like to be— Hunter and Lucy are going at it like they're auditioning for a remake of *Deep Throat*. I'm expecting someone in the row behind us to tell them to get a room.

When the concert finally ends we make our way outside, apparently heading for Willie's private trailer. A part of me would just as soon go home. Isn't show-and-tell over? I've met Hunter, he's made me laugh, and I've watched him make out—how much better can the evening get? Still, even though my feet are killing me I might as well stay. It's not every day I get to meet Willie Nelson. I just hope I don't end up calling him "Rick."

I'm traipsing three paces behind Hunter and Lucy, like a six-year-old trying to catch up with her distracted parents, except I'm not wearing Mary Janes. Just as my heel catches on a sidewalk crack for the gazillionth time, we're in front of the trailer. Three armed security guards pounce on us. Hunter pulls out his network ID card and says grandly, "I'm a friend of Willie's." One of the guards officiously pulls out a clipboard and runs his finger up and down the list. I guess we're okay because he makes a sweeping gesture and motions us up the steps.

Inside the trailer, it takes a few minutes for my eyes to adjust to the smoky haze. When they do, I can see the guys from Willie's band sitting on a tattered velvet sofa and downing shots of tequila. Each one has a half-dressed girlfriend/groupie/hooker snuggled in his arm. Willie himself is standing in the far corner, and when he spots Hunter, he strides over and gives him a big bear hug. Then Willie turns to Lucy and me, extending one hand and carefully keeping the other one behind his back. "Howdy, ladies," he says.

Hunter laughs and walks around him, grabbing whatever it is Willie doesn't want us to see.

"It's okay, Willie, they're cool," Hunter assures him, taking a deep drag on the cigarette he's snatched from Willie's hand. He holds on to it, takes a second drag and then passes it on to Lucy.

Now I get it. I've never had anything stronger than a double dose of Motrin, but I recognize the smell. So the stories about Willie are true. The man's survived all these years on chocolate chip cookies and marijuana. Sounds good. But look at that skin.

"You don't smoke, do you, Lucy?" I trill nervously. She shoots me a drop-dead look, but sure enough, passes the joint on without taking a puff.

The pot smoke in the room gets thicker and the decibel level gets higher. I struggle to follow what Willie and Hunter are talking about until I'm distracted by a leather-clad musician, who's sitting in the corner with a now completely naked girl. She's straddled on top of him, vigorously rocking back and forth, doing things I've only read about in *Penthouse* letters. (Well, a girl can't learn everything from *Good House-keeping*.)

"Fuck me!" the girl screams above the din. "Take me! Fuck me! Ride me, Daddy!"

This certainly isn't how we do parties in Pine Hills. Where are the canapés and the avocado dip? Still, the entertainment here is pretty darn good, although I'm the only one who seems to be paying attention. I glance around but the boys in the band are all busy with their own babes, and a new toy has appeared on the scene. A bong? Hey, I'm no rube. I saw a Cheech and Chong movie in college. There's so much to take in, but the action in the corner is People's Choice Awards–worthy and I'm riveted. I'd swear that the musician and the screamer are actually doing it back there. And now the young maiden seems to have a new request.

"Fuck me harder! Ride me, Daddy! Ride me!" she screams.

Another girl from across the trailer apparently thinks this sounds like an excellent idea. With a loud whoop, she pulls off her shirt and chimes in, "Do *me*, Daddy. Let's show 'em how it's done!" Suddenly I have the awful feeling that the whole scene is about to dissolve into a giant country-music orgy, with Lucy and the now stoned Hunter ready to jump right in.

I tug at Lucy's sleeve, anxiously. "I have to get home to the babysitter," I tell her through clenched teeth. "Let's get out of here."

She nods—maybe she's feeling as uncomfortable as I am—and we grab Hunter and stumble toward the door. We step past the tight security and I have to laugh. Two dozen of New York's finest are on high alert outside to protect Willie and his boys. If the cops stepped inside, they could make the pot bust of the week.

Blessedly a cab streams by and we all pile in. As we pull up to the Waldorf to drop off Hunter, Lucy looks like she wants to follow him inside, but it's already two a.m. and even she can't think of a good cover for arriving home at dawn. Hunter gives Lucy one last kiss, hands the driver a fifty-dollar bill and tells him, "Take good care of her. She means a lot to me." Blecch. Sorry, Lucy. The only ride you're getting tonight is home with me.

As the cab pulls away, Lucy looks out the rear window and gives a small wave.

"The best, right?" she says, turning back to me with a satisfied sigh.

"The best," I agree. I'm not sure if we're talking about Hunter, the concert, or the orgy, but hey, it was all just swell. Besides, at this hour I'm not up for deconstructing anything.

"Next week we're invited to Cher's party," Lucy says, glowing. "And after that, dinner with Whoopi. It's in L.A. or I'd beg you to come."

"Whoopee," I repeat. And I hope that's enough to sum up the evening.

Chapter SIX

THE AUDITIONS for what I have come to think of as The Benefit Musical of the Century are this afternoon, and my committee of Park Avenue ladies are at the Broadhurst Theater on Forty-fourth Street waiting for the director—the one-hit wonder Vincent Morris—to arrive. Most kids rehearse in a high school gym. But thanks to the connections of one of our ladies, our budding Tommy Tunes will be warbling their off-key renditions of "Tomorrow" on the same stage where *Man of La Mancha* premiered. My hardest job today may be resisting making jokes about "The Impossible Dream."

Just as we're settled into the seventh row of the theater—best seats I've ever had—Vincent flounces in wearing a purple cape and a Sherlock Holmes hat. Kind of the cross-dressing equivalent of *Phantom of the Opera* meets *Hound of the Baskervilles.* I wonder if the wardrobe mistresses on either show noticed anything missing.

"I'm here!" Vincent calls, dashing down the aisle. Heather jumps out of her seat in a flurry of excitement and practically tackles him.

"Darling!" she exudes.

He stops to double kiss her. "You look *mahvelous*, darling," he says, sounding like he's channeling Billy Crystal, or whoever it was Billy Crystal was channeling.

"You're so wonderful to do this for us, Vincent!" she says breathlessly. "Giving your time to our little charity!"

"There's no such thing as a little charity, darling. Only little people." He pauses and tosses his cape back as if this enigmatic tidbit of wisdom should be recorded in *Bartlett's*. Then he repeats the kissy-kissy with Pamela, Amanda, Allison, and Rebecca and finally stops to shake hands with me. How could he tell I was just the hired help?

"So you're the genius behind this production," he says, pumping my hand and staring at my breasts. No, it's not my breasts he cares about. He's trying to decide whether the cashmere is from Kashmir or Daffy's.

"So tell me," he says, spreading his arms theatrically. "Do you know why I'm here? Why I agreed to direct your fabulous production?"

No, but I can guess. Your last play flopped. You're out of work. Heather's husband is the richest man you've ever met and you're trying to get backing for your next real show—one that stars actors over four feet tall.

"You're graciously giving us your time because the Arts Council for Kids is a terrific organization and we're all here to help the children," I say, spouting the party line.

"Well that, of course," he says dramatically. "But mostly I'm here because I love, love, love, love, *love* children."

Oh dear. This may be bad news.

"And I *love The Sound of Music*," he says, practically clapping his hands.

Pamela steps in front of Heather and grabs Vincent's arm.

"Heather didn't tell you we're doing *The Sound of Music*, did she?" Pamela asks anxiously. "The committee voted against it. That show is just too controversial. Too many Nazis. And then there are all those nuns. We don't want to offend anyone."

Right. And then there are all of those people who hate lederhosen and are allergic to edelweiss. Lucky for Julie Andrews that she didn't have to deal with my committee.

If Vincent is disappointed that he won't get to make the hills come alive, he recovers quickly. "Right-oh," he says cheerfully, moving along. "What's the new pick?"

"*Chorus Line!*" Pamela says brightly.

"No!" Allison retorts loudly. "We said no because that's the show with a gay director." She glances over at Vincent and then looks mortified. "Not that there's anything wrong with that."

"For goodness' sake, Allison. Don't you remember? I told you at the last meeting that the director in the play isn't gay. It was the real director of the show who was gay. And he's dead now."

Vincent shakes his head. "I *hate Chorus Line*. Even though Michael Bennett was a dear, dear friend of mine. A brilliant man. A *mahvelous* man."

We all bow our heads in a moment of silence.

But before a creative consensus can be reached, a busload of the ACK kids from Harlem come streaming in, flinging Phat Farm sweatshirts and JLo backpacks on eighty-five-dollar orchestra seats.

"*West Side Story!*" Vincent declares, snapping his fingers, obviously having found inspiration in two rowdy eleven-year-olds who are spontaneously staging their own rumble in the aisles.

"*My Fair Lady!*" says Pamela with a decisiveness that not even Judge Judy would mess with. So we all nod. Sure. *My Fair Lady* it is. And I can't wait to see what the kids do with a Cockney accent.

The rest of the gang—the Park Avenue kids in their neatly starched uniforms from Brearley, Dalton and wherever else they go—stroll in accompanied by babysitters, nannies and iPods. They sneak glances at the earlier arrivals, who are bunched together on one side of the aisle, and take their own seats directly across from them.

With a flourish of his cape and a high-pitched "He-l-l-ooooooooo," Vincent takes the stage. Amazingly, the kids stop fidgeting, the chatter ceases, and all eyes are focused on the purple-clad figure in front of them.

"I'm your director," he roars out to them in a voice he must have used last when he auditioned for the part of God. "We're going to work, work, work, but we're going to have fun, fun, fun."

He tells about the fabulous play we're all going to be doing together and gives his "heartfelt and deepest thanks" to the wonderful women who have made the show possible. Then he moves on to the auditions.

The kids sit up straighter. "You'll come up and sing," he says. "I may stop you, but that doesn't mean you haven't done a fine job."

My Park Avenue mothers have figured out the order for auditions. By school. The girls from Spence—because it's the former home of Gwyneth Paltrow?—are up first.

A tall, fine-boned blonde takes the stage, and she's so pretty that it looks like the auditions might be over before they've started. But then she opens her mouth and Vincent bites his lip, resisting, for the moment, the urge to banish her from the stage—forever.

Three more girls follow her up and it's painfully obvious that Spence is not currently harboring the next American Idol. But at least the ice has been broken and the first wave of my Council kids are up next.

A wispy twelve-year-old black girl with cornrowed hair and skinny legs climbs hesitantly up the steps to the stage. She looks around wide-eyed, takes a deep breath and says in a tiny voice, "I'll be singing 'Tomorrow.' "

Oh god, I think. Don't do that, Tamika. But it's too late. Let the warbling begin. Tamika takes center stage.

> *The sun will come out, tomorrow.*
> *Bet your bottom dollar that tomorrow,*
> *There'll be sun . . .*

Did Bette Midler sneak on stage while I wasn't looking? Is Barbra Streisand hiding behind the curtain? Tamika must be lip-synching because no one that small could sing that big. She's blowing the roof off the place and she's not even on the second chorus. Vincent lets her sing the whole song and he'd probably like her to sing the entire score. I glance at my Park Avenue mothers, who look stricken. So much for acting classes and hundred-dollar-an-hour singing coaches. Tamika's a natural.

The auditions lumber on for the next two hours and the kids stay surprisingly well behaved. By the end, Vincent even has both groups talking to each other. Amanda passes around petits fours and boxes of Godiva chocolate and doesn't even seem to be offended when one of the kids asks if she has any Krispy Kremes. Day one has been a success and the kids look genuinely pleased to hear that parts will be announced next week and they'll be back on Wednesday to start rehearsals.

"This is going to be even better than I thought!" Vincent says enthusiastically to our little committee after the kids have left. "Isn't that Tamika amazing? Don't you think she'll be an incredible Eliza! Thank goodness we have our star!"

He pauses, waits a beat, and when nobody answers, goes for a wrap. "I'll cast the rest of the parts and e-mail the list over to each of you," he says.

Sensing that everybody's about to leave, Amanda works up her nerve and clears her throat. "Um, I'm not sure how to say this but don't we need to pay some attention to the people who, well, will be paying for this event?"

"Yes," pipes in Heather. "And I thought that Nicole Walters—you know her father Jerry is the CEO of Morgan Stanley—was just divine."

"I like the girl who's father is the CEO of Citibank," says Allison, who's apparently confused our auditions with a leveraged buyout.

Vincent hesitates, probably trying to decide whether casting the girl with the most talent is worth alienating the man who might fund his next project. He looks at me, figuring I might referee this round.

"Before we get to Eliza," I say diplomatically, "I think we can all agree that Pierce is our Henry Higgins." Vincent looks at me, needing a little more help on this one.

"Nobody could possibly accuse us of favoritism on that," I say. "He was just so much better than any of the other boys. Is that okay with you, Pamela?"

Pamela looks down at her Ferragamos in an effort to be appropriately humble.

"I wouldn't want anyone to think that my Pierce got the part because I'm on the committee. But," she says blushing, "his father and I are so proud." She turns to Vincent, solemnly. "If you believe in him as much as we do, I promise you, he'll never let you down."

I have to remember that speech. I'm sure I can score some points with it during Jen's next parent-teacher conference.

Vincent's sold on Pierce Barone, loaded with talent—and let's face it, just plain loaded—and nods eagerly. "But of course Pierce's role was never in doubt. I should have made that clear from the beginning."

Now that a place for one of their own has been secured, there's a palpable sense of relief.

"Well, that Tamika girl was pretty talented," Amanda ventures.

"She was," Heather agrees. "But don't you think Nicole and Pierce would look just darling together on stage? And their parents are already such good friends!"

I keep waiting for somebody to point out that Nicole's thin soprano voice won't make it past the orchestra pit. But the Park Avenue moms are too busy cooing and envisioning where this perfect casting of Nicole and Pierce could all lead—the dating, the debutante ball, the inevitable nuptials at the Plaza. Or maybe the Plaza Athénée.

"No!" Allison cries out. Didn't this happen at our last meeting? The girl doesn't say much, but when she does, it's a tidal wave. "The whole idea was that all our kids would be together, rich and poor, remember? So it has to be Tamika and Pierce. One from each side. That's what this is about."

A general hush settles over the group. Nobody dares argue and Vincent seizes the moment. "Well, well. Good, good. If that's what you all want then I'm with you. Tamika and Pierce it is." Still, he's not quite sure whether he's back in the director's chair or still playing diplomat. "Anybody have any other favorites?"

"I'm sure you can figure out the rest of it, Vincent," Heather says dismissively. Now that the leads have been cast, she's done. Handling details is for the hired help. "But I do have some big news about the benefit party," she enthuses to the rest of the ladies. "I called Kate and she's with us."

Where are we off to now? Kate who? Hepburn? Hudson? Couric?

"Kate's going to donate her newest line of pink leather wallets for our goody bags," Heather says triumphantly. "But only for donors over $1,000. I got her to throw in some notepads for contributors over $500. You know those wallets are *precious*. Everyone wants them. It's fabulously generous of her."

I get it. Kate as in Spade. I like her wallets myself. In fact, I bought a knockoff from a street vendor on the corner of Fifty-second and Sixth for five bucks just a week ago. I start to suggest that I could get some of those for the under-five-hundred-dollar donors, but I stop myself just in time. The ladies here probably don't know that you can get anything from a street vendor besides a pretzel and I don't want to burst their bubble.

We wrap up, do our kiss-kiss good-byes, and dash outside where a lineup of chauffered Town Cars are purring at the curb. Amanda quickly slips into one while Pamela and Pierce duck into another, and they wave to each other through the tinted glass windows. No carpooling for these girls, even if they do live across the hall from each other.

Having no Town Car, driver, or even taxi waiting, I cross the street until the Park Avenue posse have pulled away, so they won't see that yes, my feet are actually going to touch the ground and I'm going to walk to the train station. I glance at my watch, trying to decide if there's a prayer I can make the 6:11 train home. There's always hope. I head crosstown on Forty-fifth Street at a pace that would impress Marion Jones, veer into a back entrance to Grand Central Station and come into the home stretch, sprinting breathlessly to Track 11, landing a seat in the front car with ninety seconds to spare. Damn! I could have stopped for a package of Twizzlers. A minute later, the crush of got-it-timed-to-the-last-second commuters jump on—all of them with Twizzlers, I bet—and start scrambling for seats.

"Mind if I sit here?" asks a man who's apparently spotted the seat next to me and doesn't mind asking me to push aside what I'd hoped was an intimidating pile of stuff.

"Sure," I mutter sullenly. But then I look up and see that it's Dan standing there, smiling at me.

"Hey, I didn't realize it was you," I say, suddenly cheerful. I slide over to give him the aisle seat, dragging my pocketbook, tote bag, newspaper and umbrella with me. I used to worry that my sinking mutual funds would turn me into a bag lady—now I realize my accessories might have already done me in.

Dan unbuttons his Burberry coat—does Lucy buy them in bulk?—and tosses it on the overhead rack. Even in a suit and tie he looks casually handsome—he's tall and toned and confident, just like Lucy. Geez. The guy's gorgeous and he's the real deal—not like some people I've seen on Lucy's arm lately. What's the matter with my idiot friend? Doesn't she realize what she's got? If Ralph Lauren saw Dan and Lucy together he'd snap them up for a three-page ad campaign— the Perfect American Couple. But it's more than just looks. Dan's supportive, he loves her, he's in it for the long haul. Why don't the two of them stick to the storyboard and just head off into the sunset together?

Dan sits down next to me and tucks his one slim briefcase at his feet. How is it that men never have anything to carry? If they're supposed to be the hunters and gatherers, the very least they could do is bring home a bag of groceries once in a while.

"So," Dan says, settling in. "Great to see you. Everything good?"

"Terrific," I say, balancing my pocketbook on my lap and leaning over to shove everything else under my seat. Whoops. My head ends up just a little too close to Dan's knee. I sit up abruptly.

"How was the Willie Nelson concert last night?" Dan asks, ignoring my umbrella, which has now rolled onto his foot.

"Really, really fun," I say. "It was so great of Lucy to take me."

"Yeah. Absolutely," Dan says, just a little too heartily. "So was it only the two of you?"

What does that mean? And what the heck am I supposed to say? Lucy never told me the cover story she'd cooked up for Dan, and I never thought to ask. If he wanted to come to the concert last night, did she give him a reason why he couldn't? Or why she was taking me instead? I'm guessing she didn't explain he'd be a fourth wheel, what with me and her lover already signed on.

Dan is looking at me, waiting for an answer.

"It was a lot more than two of us there," I say brightly, trying to buy time. "Madison Square Garden was packed. What would that be, ten thousand? Fourteen thousand? I didn't get the count."

Dan chuckles. Okay, that worked. But I'm not out of the woods yet.

"You guys got home pretty late last night," he says, pressing on. "Should I be worried about my wife going out on the town with the only single woman in Pine Hills?"

"Uh, yeah, right," I say. "You know me. Totally wild. Two Diet Cokes and I call it a night."

"So what'd you do until two a.m.?" he asks, prodding.

Got stoned on secondhand pot. Watched Hunter and Lucy make out. Saw naked girls screwing band members. "Nothing special," I say.

"C'mon. Gimme a hint."

"I think I'll let Lucy tell you about it," I say feebly.

"Big secret, huh?" He laughs, but I'm worried that he's worried.

"I've got it!" He snaps his fingers. "Lucy's having an affair with Willie Nelson and you don't want to tell me!"

I can only imagine the wan smile that's pasted on my face about now. If only you knew, Dan. Or maybe you do.

"Speaking of affairs," I say, going for a bad segue, "I saw Jacques the other night. Remember I told you about him? My ex."

"Sure. Jacques. The French guy who was a whiny baby."

"I never said that."

"Well, something like that," Dan says.

"No, I said he didn't want to *have* a baby."

"Because he *was* a baby."

I sit back in frustration. "Well, maybe I did say that but it's not what I meant," I say petulantly.

Dan raises an eyebrow. He gets it immediately, even though I wasn't trying to tell him.

"Sounds like you two got along pretty well. That old French charm still works, huh?"

I feel my face flushing. I'm pretty sure I didn't just fall for the French charm but maybe I should get another opinion. I haven't talked much to anybody about this. Dan might as well be the one I open up to. He's here. He's a pal. All that testosterone has to be good for something. And the male viewpoint might be helpful.

"Tell me I'm crazy, but I like him," I say simply. "I can remember all the reasons I left him, but the minute I saw him it felt so comfortable." I shrug. "I don't know. Just so right."

"You mean you two are going to get back together?" he asks.

Now that's the good thing about talking to guys. They're blunt. Get right to the point. Okay, so I will, too.

"He still loves me," I say, as if that explains it all. And maybe it does. But Dan looks at me dubiously.

"After all these years? And you're back in love, too?"

Well, well, we are moving along quickly, aren't we. Dan's clearly never spent three hours a week with a shrink on the Upper West Side, ruminating on the subtleties of a failed romance. This is more like analyzing the stock market. Who are the players? Does it look good or bad? Are we buying or not?

But Dan must be good at the market, because he's asked the million-dollar question. Am I in love? I've been thinking about it all week, and I still don't have the answer. Yes. No. Sometimes. I wanna be. Maybe I am. Who could ever tell for sure? The sex. The sex was great. But what if I'm just prolactating? No, we really connected. There's something there. But has he changed? I don't know. What about Jen? Would we have another kid? Is he ready to be a father now?

I take a breath. Enough. I can't keep doing this. I wish I were a man.

"You never *really* know if you're in love," I say, weaseling out yet again.

"Of course you know," he says adamantly, surprising me with his surety. "You either are or you aren't."

I'd like to ask him if he's still in love, but I wouldn't dare. He probably is, and it's too painful to think that Lucy might not be anymore. At least with him.

"Give me a couple of weeks to figure it out," I say. "Jacques is coming back and another date or two's gotta help." I gaze out the window and start fantasizing about another date—or more specifically, another night with Jacques loving me and folding his body into mine. But the train's almost at Pine Hills, so I start collecting my scattered belongings, then surprise myself by asking Dan, "Want to meet Jacques when he's in town?"

"Sure," Dan says agreeably. "I might pick up a few good lines from the guy. The four of us could have dinner."

The four of us. Funny, I wasn't thinking about it that way. I've got to remember that Dan and Lucy are still a couple.

The train stops and we step off onto the platform. "Walking home?" Dan asks.

"Of course," I say, shifting my tote bag from one arm to the other. "Who'd pick me up? And you?"

"Yup," Dan says. "Who'd pick *me* up?" He chuckles at the very idea of Lucy joining the fleet of devoted wives waiting patiently in their minivans to collect their hardworking husbands.

"Let's go," Dan says. We weave our way through the parking lot and when we turn onto the street, Dan drapes his arm seductively around my shoulder, drawing me close. *"Mademoiselle, you are so very beautiful,"* he says in a faux French accent. *"So very, very beautiful."*

"Don't mock me," I say, laughing. But I notice that he doesn't remove his arm as we start to trudge up the hill.

At home, I open the door and can't decide if I've stumbled into a Gotti family funeral or the perfume aisle at Macy's. An overpowering scent of rose and gardenia—and would that be a top note of primrose?—hits me immediately. When I step inside, I see luscious bouquets of flowers spilling out of dozens of cut glass vases—green vases, pink vases, crystal clear vases. The front hall table isn't nearly big enough to hold them all, so the flowers are everywhere—some on the floor, others on the staircase, and even one short, squat vase balanced precariously on the needlepoint chair.

"Mommy!!" Jen comes bounding toward me, shrieking in delight. "Look at this!"

I am looking, since I'm too stunned to do anything else.

"I counted every one of them! Sixty-four roses! Twenty-two lilies! Thirty of those pink thingies! Twelve of those purple and yellow ones! Aren't they the best? And sixteen of these." She thrusts a gardenia at me. Can't miss that fragrance.

"Who are they from?" she asks, still shrieking. "Maggie wouldn't let me read the card!"

Maggie, the high school senior who comes over twice a week after school to look after Jen and help with homework, wanders into the foyer with a small smile on her face.

"Hey, looks like you have an admirer," she says.

Maggie must have plenty of them, being a cute seventeen-year-old with wavy red hair and a warm, inviting manner. Suddenly I flash on the Swedish au pairs at Amanda's Park Avenue spread—and the interesting question Heather raised about bringing the chicken to the fox. Would I keep Maggie once Jacques moved in? I'd want to, of course, Jen adores her. But Jacques is not a fox. And he's not moving in. And if I think he's still a fox, he's *definitely* not moving in. Besides, who knows what's going on in his head? Maybe he expects us all to move back to France. Well, that's certainly not going to happen. He has to know that right off. Though Jen would like Paris, for a year or two anyway. She'd get a head start on her foreign language requirement, not to mention picking up some great clothes.

I shake my head. How am I ever going to stop this endless tape from running at the drop of a Jacques?

Jen and Maggie are both grinning at me.

"Open the card, Mommy, open it!" says Jen, bouncing up and down. She points to an elaborately beveled vase, bursting with at least two dozen blooming peonies, and motions to a ribbon-bedecked card dangling from the side.

Dazed, I walk slowly over to the vase.

"Oh, Mommy, you know I told you I counted? It came to 144 flowers. That's twelve dozen. Twelve *dozen!*" She's jumping up and down and I'm unexpectedly pleased, but not just because of the flowers.

"Pretty good math," I say. "Did you do it all in your head?"

"She did," Maggie says proudly. "I figured I wasn't dragging her away from the flowers until you got home, so we played math games with them."

Okay, Maggie's definitely not out of here no matter who moves in. Anybody who gets my daughter to play math games has a lifetime option on babysitting.

Jen can't wait any longer, and she pulls the card from the vase. "Here it is, Mommy! Read it out loud! It has to be from Boulder. He must have gotten the letter and really likes you. We'll be on TV, Mom!"

Boulder's an interesting possibility, but even from here, I can see the ORDERED FROM address on the outside of the envelope and—big surprise—it's Jacques' home in Paris. No, I'm not going to read the card aloud, at least not until I've read it to myself first.

I take the card and the vase that's perched on the needlepoint chair. "This one will look pretty in my room, don't you think?" I say to Jen. "Pick one for your bedroom."

Jen makes a beeline for a pink vase holding a dozen pink roses. My decorating her baby room in nonsexist yellow and green obviously had no effect. "Like this one?" she asks.

"They're perfect. You picked the best one. Let's bring them upstairs and then we'll have dinner and I'll tell you what the card says."

Maggie says good-bye and Jen, with her nose poked in the fragrant roses she's selected, heads to her own room, leaving me alone in mine. I quickly place the vase on my dresser and rip open the card.

Mon amour . . . There aren't enough flowers in New York to tell you how much I love you. Our love will live forever even though these flowers will die . . .

Dead flowers? Maybe that lost something in the translation.

. . . I can't wait until we're together again. In two weeks, my darling. Just two weeks more. Toujours, Jacques.

He needed 144 flowers to tell me he'd be back in two weeks? I thought we settled that at the door. I guess all this is better than a bunch of limp tulips from the Korean grocer or those balloon-festooned mums from FTD. On the other hand, this must have cost a thousand bucks. *A thousand bucks?* He could have sent the industrial-strength Oreck vacuum.

I check my watch. Seven o'clock, so it's one a.m. in France. Knowing Jacques, it's not too late to call. And even if it is, he won't mind my waking him up. I dial the familiar number and listen as it rings four, five, six times. Where could the man be at this hour? The answering machine clicks on and I hastily hang up as if I've been caught doing something I shouldn't. Or maybe it's Jacques who's doing something he shouldn't. Well, why shouldn't he? We haven't made any promises. Still, twelve dozen flowers say he loves me. I was about to tell him the same. But even twelve million flowers don't mean that he's suddenly monogamous. And it's just as well that I'm not making a life decision based on my house having been transformed into the botanical gardens.

Chapter SEVEN

ONLY IN PINE HILLS does the fifth grade travel to Appalachia for spring break. What a getaway. Nine hundred dollars and Jen will be spending a week living in a tent building houses with Habitat for Humanity. Against all logic, twenty-two girls but only three boys signed up for this little adventure—which must be because eleven-year-old girls are so handy with a nail gun. For that price, some of the parents are hoping that the kids will be hammering side by side with Jimmy Carter. I'm just hoping there's a nurse and a first-aid kit.

At the bus stop, I kiss Jen good-bye and remind her to be careful around the power tools.

"You promised me you wouldn't use the chain saw," I say one last time.

"Sure, Mom," she says dismissively.

"No, I mean it," I say.

"Yup," she grins, giving me another quick kiss and getting on the bus.

I smile to myself at her polished technique. No way I can argue when she's agreeing with me—whether she means it or not.

As the yellow bus pulls away, I wave madly and swallow hard against the lump in my throat. I always hate when my baby leaves. But this time I have something to ease the separation anxiety. I reach into my pocketbook and pull out the packet that Lucy dropped off last week. First class plane tickets to Puerto Vallarta. Our own little escape, she called it. She's jetting down from L.A., and we'll meet up tomorrow. As for the tickets—she wouldn't hear of my arguing. Or paying. And with all her frequent-flier miles, it would be foolish if I *didn't* go first class.

I haven't traveled alone in ages, and I'd almost forgotten what it's like to fly solo. Usually I'm on a plane with Jen, my trusty travel companion, and we pull back the armrests on our seats—invariably Row 36, next to the bathroom—and snuggle together to see who can make the three-ounce juice can and miniature pretzel-snack last longer. This time after I've boarded, I take the iced goblet of Perrier that the flight attendant offers—I'm in the first row window seat, no less—and fumble with the personal-video screen attached to my oversized seat, trying to pretend that it's not my first time out of coach.

"Need help with that?" asks the male flight attendant.

"No," I say, but then I look up and realize that the cute ones obviously get assigned up front. "Well, sure," I amend. "It seems stuck."

He reaches across my body to get to the controls and when his arm grazes against my shirt, he winks and says, "Sorry." Is this how Erica Jong got over her fear of flying?

As soon as we take off, the woman next to me in 1B stretches back in the leather seat, which is suddenly as big as a bed, and falls asleep immediately, apparently not as excited as I am by the warm cashew nuts that start off my three-course, gourmet meal. She wakes up just as I'm polishing off the last teaspoonful of the crème brûlée, and politely asks the flight attendant for the special Zone-Diet dinner that she'd preordered.

I glance over at her and realize she looks vaguely familiar. I can't quite place her—and then I think I do.

"Did we go to high school together?" I ask.

She smiles. "That's what people always think. I look familiar, right? No, you probably know me from TV."

"Oh, of course," I say. This is why I shouldn't be allowed to fly first class. Is she the wife on a sitcom? No, not blond enough for that. One of the girls from *Saturday Night Live*? No, too thin to be funny. Maybe she picks the Power Balls for the lottery on the Metro Channel.

After an awkward pause she decides I've probably placed her by now. "I so love Puerto Vallarta," she says, continuing the mile-high chitchat. "Where are you staying?"

"Le Retreat," I say, feeling first class again.

"Really? It's supposed to be glorious. And so romantic. Meeting your guy there?"

"My girlfriend."

"What a drag. I hear it's the place for sexy couples massages. And sexy . . ." She pauses awkwardly, and looks at me. "Oh, okay. I get it. I'm down with that. Rosie's a personal friend."

I have no idea what she's talking about, but the conversation is apparently over because she slips the sleep mask back down over her eyes and nestles into the farthest side of the seat. Her Zone-Diet meal sits untouched on the white-tableclothed tray in front of her for the rest of the trip. I don't blame her. I wouldn't wake up either for three grains of rice and a palm-sized portion of tofu.

At the airport, a limo from Le Retreat whisks me away, zipping along the highway before turning off onto a dirt road that has been hacked out of the jungle. For forty-five minutes, the car meanders along, finally pulling into a clearing near a turquoise reflecting pool where I'm greeted by swaying palm trees and a thicket of richly scented fuchsia-and-white tropical flowers. When I step out, I notice iridescent-beaked toucans perched in the trees, and since, blissfully, there are no chirpy counselors handing out mai tais like there were on my one and only visit to Club Med, I think I'm going to like it here.

The concierge meets me smartly at the front entrance—I'm guessing the driver called ahead—and apologizes endlessly for my room not being ready. "But your friend's already here, Ms. Taylor," he says grandly, taking my bag and escorting me inside. "I'll call her suite."

We're not sharing a room? I should have realized this isn't the economy tour. Lucy said she'd take care of everything, but I didn't expect all this. I'll need to bake more than a couple of dozen cupcakes to repay her this time. Maybe a bundt cake.

I plop into a plush rattan chair in the lobby and a handsome waiter glides over immediately, offering champagne, on the house. I'm sipping peacefully, gazing dreamily at the ocean and not even minding all the happy couples walking hand in hand on the beach. Then the happiest couple of all breezes in, heading in my direction. I'm looking at them contentedly without registering who they are.

Until everything comes into focus.

Lucy's not alone.

She's wearing a bikini top and a clingy flowered sarong. Her red manicured toenails peek out from strappy pink sandals and there's a freshly cut hibiscus tucked behind her ear. Her best accessory, however, is the glow on her face that came either from the ninety-five-dollar oxygen facial in the spa or from fabulous sex with Hunter—at even greater cost. And since Hunter is standing right next to her, I'm betting she didn't have a facial.

I stand up uncertainly and Hunter leans in and gives me a kiss. "How was the flight?" he asks buoyantly.

I'm still too stunned to speak, but Hunter never needed another person to have a conversation.

"Great place, isn't it?" he asks expansively, spreading his arms to take it all in. "They love me here. Wait until you see the suite they gave us. And your room should be just fine. I've already told them to send you a fruit basket. On me."

"Nice," I sputter. "Really great." I pause, distracted for a moment by the swirling pink pattern on his Hawaiian shirt. Could those be flamingos? But I have to stay on course. "I didn't realize *you'd* be here," I say, my voice a little edgier than I'd intended. "I thought it was just me and Lucy."

He chuckles. "You and Lucy at *Condé Nast Traveler*'s Most Romantic Resort in the World?" Hunter chuckles again. "I don't think so. You're cute, but she's mine." He puts his arm around Lucy and squeezes her.

Lucy cuddles into the nook of his arm, but then she catches the expression on my face and straightens up. She, too, leans in for the air kiss. "You look terrific, Jess," she says. "I hope you're not too surprised that Hunter's here, but it's going to be great. Wait till you see the spa. I've already got you booked for a full body aromatherapy massage. I'm told it's heavenly. But if you'd rather do the rose petal facial, I can change it, no problem."

I decide to ignore the spa menu. "Why didn't you tell me Hunter would be here?" I ask, not worried that the man under discussion is standing right in front of me.

"I was just trying to spare you another one of those awkward scenes on the train with Dan. If you didn't know, you wouldn't have to be part of the cover-up."

"But I *am* the cover-up," I say.

She pauses. It's hard to argue when I've hit it on the nose. But Lucy didn't get to be a powerful Hollywood producer without a full load of charm and an arsenal of comebacks. "You know me, I always think I deserve everything," she says earnestly. "My best friend and my favorite guy together in the most beautiful place in the world." She smiles at Hunter who, ever the pro, picks up his cue.

"In fact, I insisted that you join us," he says magnanimously. "Come to think of it, having you here was all my idea."

We all know he's gone a little too far with that one. But at least it's on the table. My getaway vacation is really about Lucy and Hunter trying to get away with something. And from the look on Hunter's face, he's already scored. He has that shit-eating grin men get when they draw a straight flush. And his hand is a doozy—he's got the girl, had the sex, took a nap, ordered room service, chugged tequila and now expects to shmooze-over the situation with the best friend.

I have a few options. I can throw a tantrum right here in the middle of the lobby, jump in the limo and head straight back to my house. Make that my empty house. And spend the weekend doing what? Finally repotting those azaleas? Next option: I can do a Dr. Phil and lecture Lucy on moral turpitude: *Who the hell do you think you are, woman? Lying to your best friend and betraying your husband! That's two for two on how to screw up your life!*

There's one other possibility: I can keep my flip-flops planted firmly where they are and try to enjoy that rose petal facial. My storming out isn't going to save Lucy's marriage or make life any better for Dan. But I'm not going to wimp out, either. When I finally get Lucy alone, I'm going to point out that her little midlife fling has crossed over into *Dangerous Liaisons* territory. If this is how she's saving her marriage, I'm glad she's not in charge of Homeland Security.

But for the moment, if I'm going to stay, I might as well be gracious about it.

I look outside at the long stretch of pink sand glowing under the bleached light of the midday sun.

"It's glorious here," I say. "Maybe I'll just take a walk on the beach by myself until my room's ready."

"Wouldn't hear of it," says Hunter, ever convivial. "Come on, you must be hungry. Let's have a snack."

I glance at Lucy to see if three's more company than she'd planned on this afternoon. But she's all welcoming smiles.

"Let's eat down by the beach," she says enthusiastically. "It's already our favorite place."

"And great food," says Hunter. "They have killer filet mignon enchiladas."

"Told you," she says, playfully rolling her eyes at me. "I adore everything about this guy except the way he eats. But he'll come around." She giggles girlishly and slips her arm through Hunter's. "Before the end of the weekend I'll have him munching the wheatless tacos."

Okay. I'll keep my mouth shut if she feeds him a taste of her taco. But if she tries to cut his meat, I swear, I'm leaving the table.

Hunter and Lucy stroll down the flower-bedecked path on the beach, while I veer onto the talcum-powder-smooth sand, relishing the warmth beneath my toes and relaxing as the sun beats down on my shoulders. Maybe I'll get an early start on a summer tan.

"Watch out for the sun," Lucy calls out solicitously. "It's dangerous here. Do you need some SPF-40? I have SPF-80, too."

"That's okay. I don't smoke and I don't drink much. Figure I'm entitled to one vice. I'll make mine sunshine."

I reach into my straw bag and pull out my own tube of Bain de Soleil SPF-8. The highest I'm willing to go right now.

Lucy leaves Hunter and hurries to my side.

"Darling, really," she warns in a low voice. "This is too irresponsible of you."

"I know. Risk of skin cancer. I've read the articles."

"That too," Lucy says. "But I'm talking age spots and wrinkles."

"I hear you. But I look better with a little color in my face. And I don't care if in my old age I end up as wizened as Georgia O'Keeffe. Doesn't seem to have hurt her. Maybe she looked like a tiny old raisin, but at ninety, she snagged a twenty-year-old lover."

Lucy looks impressed. And I can tell she's tempted to switch to my SPF-8. Instead, she points out the couple a few paces ahead of us—a stunning twenty-something blonde on the arm of a much older man whose face is the color of a worn baseball glove and just as leathery.

"Looks like around here, May-December romances work only in favor of the men," she says.

She's right. Due north, I see another young blonde in a stunning string bikini doting over an old bald guy sporting an ill-advised Speedo. I'm sensing a trend. A lot of rich old sugar daddies escorting lithesome young girls tells me this place doesn't cater to people celebrating their wedding anniversaries. I never thought I'd have anything good to say about Lucy's affair, but at least Hunter picked someone his own age.

"And here we are," Hunter says, coming over to both of us. "Not such a long walk. I sure am ready to eat."

Here we are? I'm looking around at beach, ocean, palm trees and a big, blue open sky, but I don't see a restaurant. Or a café. Or even a lone pool boy with menus. Could it be that Hunter's been out in the sun too long and he's hallucinating? But then Hunter stoops behind a tree and seems to disappear, which, frankly, at his size and with those pink flamingos on his shirt, is pretty hard to do.

"Come on into our cabana," Lucy says, and then I notice that what I thought was just overgrowth is a thatch-roofed hut, tucked between two trees.

We duck inside, but this is no modest beach shanty. Instead of the usual plastic lounge chairs, the lush interior boasts a huge silk-covered chaise, piles of overstuffed pillows, and a teakwood table set elegantly for two. Hunter is already on the resort-issued mini-PC ordering the filet mignon, the wheatless tacos, and oh yes, an extra place setting.

"Now I really feel like I'm intruding," I say, looking helplessly at Lucy. "Couldn't we just go to the restaurant?"

"Not really," she explains. "Everything's served in your own cabana. Le Retreat is *very* discreet."

"Very discreet," says Hunter, caressing Lucy's shoulders and swiveling her around for a kiss. A very long kiss. A very, very long kiss. Am I supposed to look or look away? Where's Emily Post's granddaughter when you really need her? After several minutes of staring at the patterns on my chipped pedicure, I hear a gentle rapping from outside.

"May I disturb you?" a deep, velvety voice asks.

Thank goodness, food is here. I rush to the doorway to welcome room service but the buff, good-looking guy standing there isn't holding a tray. Instead he has a small blue bag slung over his shoulder and a huge, colorful beachball tucked under his arm. He has slicked-back hair and his muscular legs gleam with a perfect tan. Doesn't look like the sun has done *him* any harm. His biceps are bulging under a white polo shirt emblazoned with a pink logo: LE RETREAT THERAPY.

"Therapy? Nah, I'm feeling just fine, thank you," I tell him. "But I would like a lobster salad for lunch. Hold the mayo."

"Manuel, come in!" Hunter calls out from behind me.

"No, we canceled!" Lucy shouts, stepping away from Hunter's embrace. "Didn't you get the message? Our friend is here now. We'll have to do this later."

Manuel looks at me, then at the two of them. "Nonsense," he says. "We can all work together. I'll make it part of the experience."

What experience? I was expecting to experience lunch. Maybe go wild and have a margarita. But now Manuel seems to be on the menu.

"I don't think this is a good idea," Lucy says warily. "Jess missed the first lesson. She'll never catch up."

"She looks like a quick learner to me," Manuel says. "And the more the merrier, to coin a phrase. Come on, let's get started. We'll begin with some simple pelvic thrusts." He demonstrates, bending his knees. Oh no. Don't tell me this is leading up to group sex. I haven't even showered. Instead of thrusting, I stand rigidly in place. Make that I stand perfectly erect. No, forget that, too. I can't get my language—or my body language—right on this one.

"Loosen up," Manuel says, squeezing my hand. "You don't have to be embarrassed here. It's just the four of us."

Which is what I'm worried about.

Hunter, apparently already loosened, flexes his knees and thrusts his groin forward, calling out, "One . . . two . . . three!" He pulls back upright and—oh, please save my soul—takes a deep breath and does the little exercise a second time, this time chanting, "Four . . . five . . . six!" How high do we have to get here? Can we please stop at six? Don't want the man to strain himself.

Lucy also seems to be thrusting and counting—mercifully to herself—and I've apparently been forgotten.

I pull my hand back from Manuel. "What's going on here?" I bristle.

"Preliminary exercises," he says. "Just pretend you're volleying a Ping-Pong ball back and forth between each other's groins. I'll do it with you."

I was never any good at sports. Which is beside the point. "Preliminary exercises for what? And what kind of therapy is this anyway?"

"I'm the Tantric Sex Therapist," Manuel says grandiosely. "I have a degree if you'd like to see it."

Hunter and Lucy are still volleying, only they've inched forward so the imaginary ball doesn't have so far to go.

"I'm sure you know Le Retreat is famous for our sex workshops," Manuel says helpfully. "We have Jungian, Freudian and for our older clients, what we like to call 'Viagrian' therapy."

I would have thought Hunter was too engrossed in his ball game to be listening, but this catches his attention. "I certainly don't need the Viagra," he pipes up, missing his volley.

"No, of course not, honey, you're already a sex machine," Lucy coos, also quitting the game. Then she turns to me. "Isn't it amazing that I got Hunter to do tantric sex? Sounded too touchy-feely for him at first. But it's really about making our orgasms together last and last and last and last."

"Tantric sex orgasms can go on for hours," Manuel says dreamily.

Who has that much time? I have trouble finding twenty minutes to wax my legs.

I glance in the direction of the door and Manuel picks up that he has at least one unhappy camper. "Let's move right along," he says, snapping out of his reverie. "We can practice with the beach ball or go right to the group orgasm."

Now there's a choice I'm eager to make. But I don't have to. "The group orgasm," Hunter says gleefully.

That's it. I'm outta here. "I'm going to take that walk on the beach," I say. "I think the tide's in." Or out. Who cares.

But Manuel braces his strong arm around my shoulders, anchoring me in place. "No, we need you. It takes four to have a really good group orgasm. And I'm starting to feel a very special vibe in this room."

He reaches for his beach bag, which apparently isn't holding towels, and pulls out four black silk scarves. He deftly steps behind me, and so quickly that I don't have time to protest, ties one of the scarves tightly around my eyes. A moment later Lucy and Hunter are both equally secured—I'm just guessing since I can't see—and Manuel is preparing us to achieve true sexual ecstasy. Without even taking off our clothes.

"Deep breaths, everybody. And now unleash that orgasmic energy."

Almost immediately, Lucy, doing the best Meg-Ryan-at-the-deli imitation I've ever heard, comes first, moaning and groaning and yelping. Hunter, never to be one-upped, joins in, the grunts of his sexual passion even louder and more out of control.

If this is all it takes to have an orgasm, why did I spend $24.95 on that vibrator?

I feel Manuel's hand on my back. "Release. Release. Join in the pleasure. Feel the ecstasy, young lady."

Young lady? I want to tell him that I never have an orgasm with someone who doesn't know my name. Except for that one time in 1982.

Suddenly there's a marked change in the intensity of Hunter's Group Orgasm.

"EEYYOOOW!" he screams.

"That's good! That's great!" Manuel screams back.

"NO IT'S NOT!" Hunter hollers.

"It is! Trust me! Go, Hunter, go! Ladies, stop and listen to Hunter. That's how to have an orgasm."

"IT'S NOT AN ORGASM!" Hunter screams, so loudly that we all simultaneously rip off our scarves and look at him, holding one leg and hopping up and down on the other. "IT'S A CRAMP, GODDAMN IT!"

Lucy immediately drops to her knees and begins massaging what I hope is Hunter's leg.

Manuel, flustered, rushes to their side. "Do you need a doctor?" he asks. "There's always one on the premises. We average four heart attacks a week. But not from the sex therapy," he hastens to add.

"No, that's okay, I can handle this. It happens all the time," says Lucy, still massaging but sounding—could it be?—slightly annoyed.

Hunter's wailing, Lucy's rubbing, Manuel's hovering and I'm exiting. Nobody notices as I scoop up my flip-flops and make a hasty getaway, dashing back up the path to the main building. The concierge is waiting for me when I slip in the back way, and he's holding the keys to my now-ready room. How did he know I was coming this time? A GPS tracking system for each individual guest? I couldn't even afford one for my Subaru.

"Delighted you're back," the concierge says solicitously. "May I escort you upstairs? Your bag is there and the valet has unpacked." Who asked him to do that? Now everyone will know that my Lacoste lookalike T-shirts came from T. J. Maxx.

My room lacks the silk chaise and teakwood table of the beach palace, but it does boast the largest bed in the smallest space I've ever seen. The king-sized—no, this must be czar-sized—four-poster is luxuriously draped with layers of sheer fabric that look like mosquito netting. I'm hoping they're there for the romantic effect and not to keep out czar-sized bugs. Since I missed our snack, I follow the sweet scent of fresh papaya over to the fruit basket that Hunter, as promised, has sent. I munch my way through one papaya, two mangoes, three kiwis, one guava, a handful of blackberries and an excessively large bunch of grapes. Lying by myself on the bed and sucking the luscious guava juice is about as sensuous as my three-day stay here is going to get. And frankly, it's a lot more satisfying than that group orgasm.

But maybe solitude is against the rules at Le Retreat because there's a knock at the door. I decide to ignore it. Can't I just sit here by myself with my fruit? And then a second knock.

When I open the door, Lucy glides in. "Hunter's fine and Manuel's taken him to the Jacuzzi," she says, giving me a peck on the cheek. "So I get a whole uninterrupted hour just with you." She takes in my room with one glance, then strides across to open the terrace door and let in the sea breeze.

"Nice view, but sorry the room's not bigger," she says apologetically. "Hunter took care of it. Should I have you moved?"

"No, I like it," I say, not needing any more favors. "Want a piece of fruit? I have one kiwi left."

She shakes her head. "Thanks, but I already grabbed a lobster salad."

Would that be the lobster salad I was dreaming about when Manuel came?

"Come on, we have another appointment back down on the beach," Lucy says, stepping off the terrace. "Put on your swimsuit and sarong." She heads over to the blond-wood dresser to assess my wardrobe. I should know by now that Lucy doesn't trust me to pick out my own clothes when Hunter's around.

"You won't find one there," I say firmly. "I don't wear them."

Lucy, misinterpreting, turns in surprise and eyes me appraisingly. "You can wear a bathing suit. Your body's fine," she says, in what I assume is meant to be a comforting tone. "Your breasts are still good. And your thighs aren't that bad. A little cellulite, but we all have it at our age. If you get in the water really fast, nobody notices, anyway."

Well, that's a reason to live.

"I've got a bathing suit. It's the sarong that never occurred to me," I say, peering into a drawer studded with chamomile-scented sachets. More bug protection, or are they there for romantic reasons, too? The stacks of valet-folded clothes are so neat that I handle my fifteen-dollar cotton tees as if they were hand-painted Stella McCartney blouses and gently nudge them aside to pull out my sarong-alternative.

"How about denim cutoffs?" I ask brightly.

She looks at me like I'm talking in Urdu. Clearly denim cutoffs aren't part of her wardrobe. Or her vocabulary. And since I'm not going to translate, she moves right along.

"Not to worry. I have an emergency sarong right here," she says, reaching into her Tod's tote. "Always carry an extra. I hate when they get sandy."

Me too. I strip down to pull on my alluringly named Miracle Suit, guaranteed to make me look ten pounds thinner. And where exactly do those ten pounds go? Shoved down to my thighs? Or does some poor unsuspecting woman who didn't buy the Miracle Suit end up with them?

I fumble with my new sarong—cutoffs were easier—and look at Lucy's, which is elegantly secured at the side in a neat butterfly knot that highlights her sit-up-perfected abs. I try to emulate her impeccable style, but my wrap ends up crumpled and bungled and clumsily held together with a four-square knot that wouldn't win a Cub Scout any badges.

Back on the beach, Lucy leads me toward two straight-backed wooden chairs sitting high above a low-stepped platform that reminds me of a shoe shine stand.

"Reflexology treatment," Lucy says, climbing up gracefully into our very high seats. "Sort of like a foot massage, only it's supposed to be healing. Marianna and Mariella will be here in a sec. I hear they're amazing. They can get rid of all the toxins from your body."

And they send those toxins where exactly? The same place as those ten pounds? Someday I just know I'm going to run into that fat, toxic woman who got my giveaways, and she's going to be mighty pissed.

"Reflexology can cure all sorts of disorders," Lucy goes on, sounding like an infomercial. "Pick your problem. Any problem. You can ask the therapist to concentrate on the instep, which is good for kidney and liver function, or the toe area to cure allergies."

I blink hard into the sunshine. "I don't have allergies," I tell her. "At least not since I used to break into hives every time I saw Davy Jones. Not the Monkee. The boy who sat next to me in fourth grade." I pause. Haven't thought about him in a long time. Wonder if he's still single. "The therapist can do anything she wants," I say with a sigh. "Except try to cure my spleen. Don't have one anymore."

"Really? What happened?" asks Lucy, impressed.

"Motorcycle accident, second year I was married to Jacques. Remember I told you about it? I'd finally learned how to ride the Harley myself, but I wasn't so good above eighty."

"For a sweet suburban mom, you've had a pretty adventurous life," Lucy says.

"*Had* is the operative word. Not anymore."

Lucy hears the admonition in my tone.

"Come on, Jess, adventure is what it's all about, isn't it? We can't quit taking some risks just because we're all grown up. There's a whole world out there. Live free or die."

"Isn't that the motto of New Hampshire?"

"I don't know. I think I did see it on a bumper sticker somewhere. But it's right, isn't it? If you're not going to do anything new or different for the second half of your life, why live it? I don't want a straight path for the next forty years. I want some bumps in the road."

"Well, you're making them," I say. "Bumps. Potholes. Construction detours. Jackknifed tractor-trailer trucks. Anything else you'd like to put in your way? Vehicular homicide? Does that make life more interesting?

Lucy straightens up. "Well, excuse me, darling. Feeling a little testy?"

We sit silently in the chairs and within moments, the reflexologists arrive. They're long-haired, long-limbed and clad in string bikinis that would make a Brazilian blush. "Anything special we can do to help you relax?" asks the girl who introduces herself as Marielle.

Yup. Gain ten pounds. Flash me some cellulite. Put on some clothes.

"No, just the usual. Whatever that is. My feet are in your hands," I joke.

"First they'll go in the soak," she laughs back.

Marielle places my feet in a frothy chamomile bath, rubs briskly with a terry towel until my toes turn rosy, and then with light, staccato movements, begins searching for pressure points.

"Don't be surprised if you feel some tingling in your chest when I'm massaging the back of your foot," Mariella says, settling into a cushion at the foot of the stand. "It's the energy flow. Pressure on the heel stimulates the breasts."

So that's why women spend so much on shoes.

Lucy extends her foot as the other therapist kneels down on the sand in front of her. Maybe I should tell Marianna to steer clear of Lucy's heels—her breasts don't need any more stimulation.

"Listen, are you upset with me because Hunter's here?" Lucy asks, squirming in her chair. Wonder which toe did that.

"No, I get it. Hunter. Le Retreat. Something new. Making your life more interesting, right?" I pause. "Maybe that's what I'm doing with Jacques, too."

"You see, we're in the same boat," she says exuberantly. "I have Hunter, you have Jacques. Great sex for everyone."

"I'm kind of hoping Jacques is more than a few nights of great sex," I admit.

"You never know," says Lucy, who'd been thrilled when I first told her about my night with Jacques. She'd even consulted an editor friend at *Modern Bride* about whether you wear white to a re-wedding ceremony and called me with the answer: Ecru.

"By the way, I'm sorry if all that with Manuel was a little over-the-top," says Lucy, "but it might be something fun for you to try with Jacques. Keep him on his toes, so to speak. If Hunter went for it, anyone will. Oh, and about Hunter. Can I tell you what he did with me last night?"

"You could, but no, don't," I say just a little too harshly. I'm finished talking about toes, spleens, breasts, tantric sex and whatever the heck else they dreamed up last night. I promised myself I'd tell Lucy what I think about all this, and I'm going to. I take a deep breath.

"Look, I'm not mad," I say, "but I've got to tell you the truth. I'm sure you had fun last night, whatever you did. But I look at you with Hunter and the whole thing's just wrong. He's not the guy you're meant to be with. He isn't your soul mate."

"I don't know about the soul mate thing," she says, shrugging, "but we have so much fun. I love his life. It's so different from mine. We go to fancy Hollywood parties. I never thought I'd like that sort of thing, but with him it's fun. He knows everybody. Did I tell you that two nights ago he took me to dinner at Sting's house?"

Sting's house? I wouldn't have minded eating there myself. Two nights ago I was at the mommy-daughter book club. Whatever Sting served had to have been better than the low-cholesterol Jarlsberg and low-sodium saltines that Cynthia offered up. But Sting's seaweed-wrapped hors d'oeuvres are beside the point.

"Lucy, you say this is a little fling, but don't you see what's happening? It's totally out of hand. You're going out in public with the guy. You're lying to Dan. You're risking your marriage. You're being totally self-centered. Plus you're gaining weight."

Lucy whips around so fast that I think she's going to fly off the chair. "Oh damn, am I really?"

"Which part of that worries you?"

"The weight." She takes her thumb and forefinger and starts pinching her inner thigh. "Maybe I'm just bloated."

"No, you're fine," I say impatiently. "I was just trying to get your attention. Did you hear anything else I said?"

"Of course," she says, still inch-a-pinching her thighs and moving on to her totally toned midsection.

"You're not fat. Just stupid."

Well, that was a bucket of cold water. Her face reddens—not from the sun—and her mouth quite literally drops open. I always thought that was just a figure of speech. Then she swoops around, eyes flashing.

"I'm *stupid*? *I'm* stupid? Really? I'm one of the goddamn smartest people I know. I'm a television producer, remember? Important people talk to me. I interviewed Carl Sagan three weeks before he died. Stephen Hawking gave me a full sit-down interview."

"He always sits down. He's in a wheelchair."

Lucy glares at me with an expression that would wither Sting's rain forest. But I'm not stopping.

"You know, if you had a single ounce of intelligence you'd be kissing Dan's feet every morning. Rather than whatever parts of Hunter you're doing I-don't-care-what with."

"This has nothing to do with Dan," Lucy says imperiously.

"Nothing to do with Dan? If you think that then you really *are* stupid."

I'm so furious that all I want to do is jump off the chair and storm away, but Marielle has me by the ankles. Who knows what will happen to my energy flow if I jerk my foot around—could end up needing my appendix removed. So I sit back with my arms folded across my chest, fuming. And the best I can tell, Lucy's steaming, too.

Hours pass. The tide comes in. The sun sets. The leaves change. Stephen Hawking walks. Carl Sagan zooms back on a shooting star.

Or maybe it just feels that way.

Lucy ends the standoff. "If anything's stupid, it's this argument," she says finally, sounding apologetic. "You're my best friend, Jess. I'm sorry I lost my temper. I know you mean well. It's just you can't really understand."

"What can't I understand?" I ask, not quite ready to uncross my arms.

"What my life's like."

"Not really different than anybody else's," I say. But then I pause. "Well, you do have more men than the rest of us."

We both smile and hell unfreezes. Lucy leans over and rubs my arm. "Jess, stop worrying about me. I know what I'm doing. I love Dan, I really do. That will never change. I've got things under control."

That's what they all think. I decide to make one last stab.

"Want to hear how it feels from the other side?" I ask, as we slip our totally massaged and relaxed toes back into our sandals and head up the beach. "I've never told anybody about this. But you know all those reasons I've always given you for why I left Jacques? You know, we didn't have enough in common. He didn't want a child. All that? Well, it's all true. But there was one more. He didn't think I'd get hurt, either."

Lucy stops dead in her tracks. "He was having an affair?"

"Yup. It's not something I've ever been able to talk about. Even to you. I was too embarrassed. I thought somehow it was my fault. But Jacques didn't even think it was a big deal. He said it had nothing to do with me. Wouldn't change our relationship. He loved me."

"I bet he did," Lucy says fervently. "Who wouldn't love you?"

"Funny, you don't feel so loved when you find out something like that," I say, flooded with memories. All the bad memories I've been trying to keep at bay since Jacques has come back into my life.

"I'm sorry you got hurt. But Dan won't find out," Lucy promises.

We walk a few steps in silence and Lucy links her arm in mine. Maybe some of what I've said is starting to sink in.

"You never forgave Jacques?" Lucy finally asks.

"Hard to say," I admit. "At the moment, the whole question's up in the air."

Chapter EIGHT

WHEN I GET BACK from Puerto Vallarta, the message light on my answering machine is flashing like a Las Vegas slot machine. I try to count the neon pulses but give up at seventeen and press PLAY. First comes a round of irate calls from Park Avenue stage mothers, shocked—shocked—that their children's talents at singing, acting, and sucking up haven't been properly rewarded with a key role in *My Fair Lady*. I'm trying to figure out how they knew to call me when one mother reveals that my number was on the bottom of the casting announcement, put there by our ever-clever director Vincent. Who apparently takes calls only from Nathan Lane.

Then comes a series of increasingly agitated message from Jacques. He's had a change of plan. Instead of New York, his business meeting will be in Dubai.

So sorry to disappoint you, ma chérie, he says sorrowfully. *You were looking forward to seeing me, non? Another time. Soon. Je promis. Téléphone-moi.*

In the next message—an hour later? the next day?—he isn't *très content.* Why didn't I call him *immédiatement?*

I know you're out of town, he says, his voice now slightly agitated. *But you must call.*

Apparently he doesn't know I'm the only person in the universe who shells out $150 a month to Verizon and still hasn't mastered the art of beeping in. *Time* magazine may put me on the cover.

Are you mad at moi? he asks in the next, an edge of panic creeping into his tone. *Je t'aime. Je t'aime. Do not be mad at moi.*

Two more calls to tell me I shouldn't be upset. He's had a change of plan, not heart. He'll make it up to me. He loves me.

I kick off my shoes and sit down. This is taking longer than I'd bargained for.

Here's what we will do, he says, panic gone and confidence restored. *You will come with me to Dubai on Thursday. I am sending the ticket. You will have it tomorrow.*

There's a plan. Fly out Thursday to Dubai. Which is where, exactly? I seem to remember it's in Africa. Or possibly Arabia. Is there still an Arabia? Maybe I'm thinking of Abu Dhabu. Abba Dabba? Yabba dabba doo. No, that's what Fred Flintstone said.

I take a deep breath. Never mind where Jacques wants to send me, my mind seems to wander all on its own.

Next beep. Next message.

My Chauncey doesn't go to Dalton so he can be cast as a fishmonger! screams a furious mother's voice. *Chauncey will not be in the play! He's joining the lacrosse team instead! Get someone from Stuyvesant to be your fishmonger.*

I guess that's not Jacques.

But maybe this last one will be.

Thursday, ma chérie. My car will meet you at the airport. Jacques' voice is smooth as crème fraîche. *We will make love every night. During days I have meetings, but for you there is shopping. A tour of the city. A hike in the mountains. And I will arrange a desert camel ride, je promis.*

The desert. At least that helps me pin down the continent. And here I am lusting after a man who's promising me camel rides. But enough. I click off the machine and notice the International FedEx package sticking out from my pile of unopened mail. Jacques' secretary always was efficient. How is it that all of a sudden, I'm everyone's favorite travel companion? My biggest trip last year was to the opening of Sam's Club. Now between Jacques and Lucy, it's raining airline tickets.

Still, meeting Jacques in Dubai, Dubuque, Des Moines, or wherever the heck he has me going is out of the question. Because unless some family in Appalachia has decided to take her in, Jen will be home this afternoon. I can't wait to get her back. Come on, Jacques. Please tell me you remember I have a daughter, and that I can't pick up and fly six thousand miles to have sex with you. Though god knows I'd like it.

I take my suitcase to go unpack and, as if on cue, the phone rings. I wish I had caller ID. I'm not talking to Chauncey's mother about the indignity of her precious progeny playing a fishmonger. And I'm not prepared for Jacques just now. But what if it's Appalachia calling and the nurse is on the line? I warned Jen about those power tools. There's been an accident, a horrible, bloody accident. My poor baby's been hurt.

I drop my suitcase and grab for the phone, almost knocking it off the desk. "Hello, is everything okay?" I ask anxiously.

"*Oui, oui, mon amour.* Now that I have you I am happy again," Jacques says, his honeyed voice calming me even from so far away. "So you got the ticket? I will see you in two days?"

"I wish," I say, surprised at how glad I am to hear from him. "But it's impossible."

"Nothing's impossible. Not where we're concerned."

"I can't meet you this time. My daughter. You forgot about Jen."

"Ah, Jen. Your little wren. But that's easy—another ticket! Think how much she will love the camel ride!"

I laugh and cradle the phone closer to my ear. Yes, I'd love to see Jacques on Thursday. Would do anything to see him. Except leave my daughter. "Unfortunately, school vacation's just ending and it's going to be a big week in history class," I joke, thinking ahead to next week's schedule. "They're just getting to Lewis and Clark."

"Lewis? Jerry Lewis?" Jacques asks, perking up to Jen's academics.

Oh please, not that French thing with Jerry Lewis again. Best just to ignore it. "I'm sorry, Jacques," I say. "I wish you could still come here. I miss you."

"Moi aussi," Jacques says, crestfallen. "I've been dreaming about our being together. But *c'est d'accord*, I understand. Your little girl. She's the only reason I would take no for an answer. But I must hold you in my arms again soon."

"I want that too."

"A thousand kisses."

For the first three days after she gets back home from Appalachia, Jen drives me crazy and I can't figure out what's going on. Maybe I should have gone to Dubai. She insists on dragging me to the mall and trying as hard as she can to max out my Discover card. Limited Too isn't good enough for dresses and we have to go to Betsey Johnson. Never mind that the styles are too sophisticated for her and too teenagey for me—she loves them. She wants fancy sandals with heels and I should get the same pair. Her wish list includes dangling earrings for me, a sparkling bracelet for her, glossy pink lipstick for both of us, long-lasting lash-enhancing mascara (which I won't even discuss) and seventy-five-dollar José Eber haircuts. Thinking I'm being a sport, I give in on the dresses and splurge on the bracelet. But when I won't pony up for the rest, my usually even-tempered sweetie stomps away in a huff.

"You don't understand. You don't understand anything," she pouts, turning her back to me on the escalator.

This time she's right. I don't.

Sunday morning, for some reason, Jen wakes me up unnaturally early. She's a vision in the new Betsey Johnson, the glittery bracelet, and the six bejeweled barrettes that Lily gave her last birthday.

"You gotta get up, Mom," she says urgently. "Put on your new dress. And I picked out a pair of shoes for you. They're not as good as the sandals you wouldn't buy, but they'll be okay."

I blink, trying to figure out what's going on. Why is she all dressed up? Is it Easter again so soon?

"I'll be okay for what?" I ask.

"I'll tell you later. C'mon. You've got to make pancakes. You've gotta hurry."

Jen and I always have pancakes on Sunday morning, but today she's so jumpy she can barely sit still long enough to eat one, never mind her usual stack of four with fresh banana topping.

When the doorbell rings, she shoots up like a rocket. "Get it! Get it!" she shrieks, so excited you'd think Clay Aiken was coming for a playdate. "You should have worn the new dress, but I guess your jeans are okay."

"Why? Who's here?" I ask, trying to figure out what she knows that I don't.

"Just get the door, now!"

I fold my arms. "Tell me what's going on, young lady."

By now, Jen is apoplectic. "Just open it! Open it!" she shrieks.

So I do.

Standing there is a model-gorgeous guy with spiky sun-bleached hair, a grin plastered on his face, and a bunch of pink roses in his arms.

"Congratulations!" he says, giving me a big sloppy kiss on the cheek. He's about two heads taller than I am, athletic-looking, and wearing a cutoff Abercrombie & Fitch T-shirt that declares he's "Surfer Dude."

"I'm Boulder!" he exclaims, as if I should be as excited by the news as he is. "You won! I'm your date!"

He lunges in for a hug, and, forgetting about the armload of flowers, crushes the roses between us. Would that be a thorn that's now lodged in my cleavage? I always did prefer orchids.

"Look! Give us a big smile!" Boulder says.

He spins me around and I see eager photographers, stocky men with videocameras, and young, stylish women with notebooks and stopwatches all swarming up my front lawn. In the driveway, the high school marching band, dressed in full beribboned regalia, strikes up the only song they really know. "Stars and Stripes Forever."

Suddenly a microphone, a clipboard, and a makeup brush are simultaneously thrust in my face.

"What the hell . . . I mean the heck . . . is going on?" I ask, pulling away from the microphone. One of the cameramen steps in so tight that I don't know if he's going for a close-up of my crow's-feet or a shot of the thorn in my cleavage. I stick my hand out to push him away and then decide that's the wrong move. Only time you see a hand blocking the camera is when some corporate bad guy is trying to keep his face off *60 Minutes.*

"What is this?" I demand again. "What's going on?"

"I picked you!" Boulder says, the sunlight bouncing off his unnaturally white teeth. "Seven thousand letters. Or maybe it was seven-hundred thousand." He looks over at one of the young women with notebooks. "Mindy, how many people should I say wrote in for a date with me?"

"Whatever you want," she calls out.

"Millions of letters!" Boulder says enthusiastically. "And you're my perfect match! *Cosmo*'s Most Eligible Bachelor has found his girl!"

It's all coming back to me now. The date Jen found in the magazine. The letter she wrote in my name and must have sent off even though I never corrected the spelling. But maybe Boulder didn't notice.

"Jen!" I call, looking out into the sea of lights and lenses. "Jen, where are you? Come here, now!"

She pops up in front of me, giggling and hopping from foot to foot in her white patent flats. Okay, maybe she is getting a little old for them. I should have bought her those high-heeled sandals.

"Mom, I kept the secret! I did, didn't I? You didn't know anything, right? I promised not to tell and I didn't."

"Really natural reaction," Boulder says to me, admiringly. "You seemed just like a suburban mom."

I'm glad a decade in Pine Hills has accomplished something, although not everyone would take that as a compliment. Just then, Mindy steps forward, waving her clipboard marked SEGMENT PRODUCER.

"Perfect, Jess, you did great," she says cheerily. "I'm so glad we don't have to reshoot the surprise arrival. Got it on the first take. You really acted surprised."

"I *was* surprised," I say, offering an explanation that obviously hasn't occurred to anyone yet. "But what's going on here? You can't just show up on my doorstep this way."

"We got all the permissions we need." Mindy grins. "From your daughter."

"She's only eleven."

"Right!" Mindy beams.

How did Jen know about all this and not tell me? Maybe I've gone overboard teaching her to keep promises. Better add a codicil: Sunday school lessons do not apply when dealing with reality-TV producers.

"Now you and Boulder can go inside and talk a little while we re-set. But don't give away any secrets," Mindy warns. "We want to capture all that getting-to-know-you stuff on tape."

"Sure. Perfect way to start a relationship. Get intimate on tape."

"And by the way," Mindy continues, "I'd like the next shot in the kitchen, if that's okay with you."

"No, it's not okay with me," I say, bristling. "There's pancake batter all over everything. Let me go clean up a little first."

"The set dresser and two prop guys are here to get the kitchen ready," says Mindy, as if every household includes a cleanup crew of three teamsters. "We even brought oatmeal in case you don't have any. Quaker Oats paid for product placement."

And I thought all I was getting was Boulder.

Inside, away from the sunshine and bright lights—a double whammy that must be ultra flattering with me in no makeup—I try to regain my composure.

"Would you like something to drink?" I ask Boulder, falling into my best hostess-with-the-mostest mode.

"No thanks, I'm in AA," he says happily.

"How about orange juice?" I ask, since that's what I meant in the first place.

"I don't drink that, either," he beams. "Though maybe if it's low-acid. Do you have any soy milk?"

"No. Do you drink water?"

"Sure. If it's Perrier or Pellegrino. Or even Poland Spring," he says good-naturedly.

"How about Pine Hills?"

"Never heard of it, but I'll take a flyer," he says adventurously.

I hand him a glass of tap water and try to think what we have in common. Nothing. "Are you really a surfer?" I ask, remembering the magazine article.

"Sure thing. I'm out there hanging ten in Malibu every day. But what I really want to do is be in movies," he says, as if he's the first person to come up with that idea. "By the way, just so you know, I'm only in AA for the contacts. Seven a.m. meeting in Santa Monica at Shutters on the Beach gets all the studio execs. That's where everyone gets discovered."

"I'll remember that," I say, though why I'd use up precious brain cells over that, I'm not sure.

"And stay away from the four p.m. meetings in Venice Beach," he adds helpfully. "That one gets all the winos."

I look around the kitchen which the prop guys have already cleaned up. They do a nice job on sinks. Maybe we could shoot in Jen's bathroom next.

Boulder squeezes by the camera tripod that has been installed next to the table, and then he traps me in another bear hug.

"Can you believe this?" he asks, thoroughly thrilled with himself. "We made it! You and me! Not just in the magazine—we're on the TV show!"

"Yeah, I'm pretty surprised myself," I say, honing my skills in understatement. "I mean, I know why they picked you, but what made you pick me?"

"I was amazingly smart on this one," Boulder says, so pleased with himself that the grin spreads—I didn't think it possible—even wider. "I figured all the other *Cosmo* bachelors were gonna go for the sexy girls. But only ten of us would get picked to be on the TV show. And I thought, Go for an old one! A mom! Somebody nobody else would pick! Somebody you'd never expect! They'll love it!"

"I guess it worked," I say, stunned. Who knew that being old enough to have my memory and my collagen break down would land me a date? But hold on. I'm not looking for a date. And this is worse than one of Lucy's fix-ups. Why would I go through with this?

"You know, this whole thing was my daughter's idea," I say, inching away from him. "Maybe you should get someone else. Someone sexy. Your own age."

"No, hey, I really wanted you," Boulder says earnestly. "I like moms. And you remind me of my own mom. She's pretty cool."

"Maybe she and I can have lunch sometime," I say frostily. "But let's face it. You and I are never going to work out."

"No, don't take it wrong," he says, adjusting the Surfer Dude T-shirt around his six-pack abs. Which in his case are a twelve-pack. "You're pretty good-looking. You've really kept yourself up for someone your age." He pats me on the backside with about as much passion as a ten-year-old petting his Saint Bernard.

My patience is wearing thin. "Thanks, but you know, I think everyone should just get out of here." I wave my arms broadly, as if that's all it takes to shoo him away.

"No way. You gotta do it. This is our big chance."

"My chance for what?" I snap. "I'm a happily single mom. I love my life. I love my daughter. I just turned down a trip to Dubai. I mean it. I want everyone out of here."

"Hey, please?" he asks imploringly. "I really need to do this. Don't say no."

By now, Boulder's lower lip is trembling and his brow is starting to furrow. Suddenly he's a little kid, and all my maternal instincts kick in.

"You gotta help me out here," he adds dolefully. "I don't make any money surfing and my agent says I might get a commercial out of this." His baby blue eyes glisten and he blinks hard.

Ten feet away, I see Jen looking equally scared, shocked that I'm getting mad instead of married. She was trying to make me happy. She had a plan about Boulder, and gosh-darn if she didn't get him here.

I can't disappoint Jen. I just can't. And besides, I'm desperate for Boulder not to start crying right here in my kitchen.

"All right, all right," I say, capitulating. "I'll do it. Just tell the crew not to scuff my floor."

"Thanks." Boulder grins. "I won't forget this." And just like that, all's right with the world again. He must have been an easy child.

"So isn't this whole thing too fabulous, Jessica?" Mindy gushes as she rushes over. "In your wildest dreams, could you have imagined that today would turn out like this? I love making people's dreams come true."

Boulder looks over at me nervously, but I'm as good as my word and I don't utter one nasty thing about this not being my dream date.

"Anyway, we're about to start up again," Mindy says, fixing the collar on my shirt. "Scene Two. Breakfast. The set's ready."

The set? I usually refer to it as my kitchen.

"Your letter says you're a great cook," Mindy says, now fussing with my hair. She leads me over to the breakfast table and fusses with the gold heart locket I'm wearing.

"It wasn't my letter," I say, repeating my mantra for the day. "Jen wrote it. In fact, she should be part of this." I look around the room to see what's happened to my contest-entering daughter and spot her standing excitedly in the doorway.

"Come over and have some breakfast with us," I call out. Jen starts to run toward me but Mindy grabs her.

"Not yet, honey!" Mindy says. "We have Boulder bike riding with you later. We don't need to see you twice."

I stand up. "Set" or not, this is still my house, and I get to make some of the rules. "I need Jen with me," I say firmly. "I'm not going to do it without her."

"Whatever you want," says Mindy. "But I have a better idea." Turning to Jen she asks, "Would you like to be my assistant?"

"Awesome!" Jen answers.

Overruled, I sit back down and notice how *Elle Decor* my kitchen table now looks. I turn over one of the cups. Where have I been hiding these Wedgwood dishes? Not to mention the Irish linen place mats with the matching napkins and the Kosta Boda crystal glasses.

"Boulder, before we roll, the writer has some notes," Mindy says, motioning to a skinny guy standing next to her. "He's really good. He just came off a gig on *Survivor*."

"*Survivor* has writers?" I ask, surprised. "Isn't that a reality show?"

"Of course," says Mindy. "But you can't count on real people. They just never sound authentic without a script."

The writer, predictably decked out in thick glasses, black Keds, and disheveled shirt, steps forward. "Hey, Boulder, remember your claim to fame is that you're the bachelor who loves kids," he says, fumbling with his yellow pad. "Tell her how cute the kid is." He looks over at Jen. "What's your name again, beautiful?"

"Jen," she says helpfully. Great. The television crew's been in my house for less than an hour and already my eleven-year-old answers to "beautiful."

"Right. And remember to keep complimenting your date. Tell her you like her hair and her big brown eyes. Or maybe they're blue. Green? I can't see from here. Can somebody find out what color the date's eyes are?"

"I'll check," Mindy says, making a note to herself. Guess they'd never think of asking me. I might get it wrong.

"Anyway, just talk about her eyes," says the writer, continuing on. "Girls eat up that compliment stuff."

So this is what they mean by revenge of the nerds. The geeky writer gets to tell the stud muffin how to seduce me.

"And don't forget that one of the reasons you picked Jess is because she's such a good cook," Mr. How-to-Get-a-Girl continues. "That's important to you in a woman. So for breakfast she made you a carved-pineapple fruit salad, a whites-only omelet, and oatmeal pancakes. Quaker Oats pancakes. Be sure to mention how healthy and delicious they taste."

The prop man comes to the table to deliver my homemade breakfast and two cups of double cappuccino.

"Okay, roll tape," Mindy calls. "We're ready to go. Hit it, Boulder."

On cue, Boulder reaches across the cutlery to place his hand on mine. "Great breakfast you made for me," he says. "And I want you to know first thing it doesn't bother me at all that you're eight years older than me."

Wait a minute. I agree to do him a favor and he thanks me by telling America I'm robbing the cradle. Why don't we just paint a sign on my forehead, OVER FORTY. Or maybe Mother Nature already has.

"Older women have their advantages," I say, trying to win some points back. "We have experience, you know. We've learned how to do a thing or two."

"Whoo, whoo!" Boulder whoops. "I'd like to see some of that experience later." He winks at me, or maybe the camera. "I have some things I'd like to show you, too, if you know what I mean."

I grimace. Weren't we supposed to be talking about my great cooking skills? I look over at the egg-white omelet in front of Boulder. Looks kind of bland. Maybe I'll offer salt and pepper. That sounds safe.

"I didn't know if you like things spicy," I say.

"Like everything spicy," he says, going for yet another frat-boy double entendre.

Where's that geek writer when you need him? Probably off polishing his Keds.

Hoping to move things along, I pass Boulder the tall, oversized, prop-man-supplied pepper mill. Could they have found a bigger one?

"Pretty thick, isn't it," Boulder says lasciviously. "Takes two hands, huh?"

That knocks me over. No, actually, I do the knocking over. In a split second, the pepper mill goes crashing into the crystal, sending the fresh-squeezed orange juice flying all over the nonabsorbent Irish linen and the no-longer-picture-perfect omelet.

"CUT!" Mindy cries.

I sit back, watching the rivulets of orange juice splashing off the table and onto Boulder's crisp khaki pants. For once in my life, I don't apologize. And having learned my lesson at Dr. Paulo's, I'm not getting down on my knees to clean up, either.

The prop guys rush forward to take care of the mess, and instantly new goblets, napkins, place mats, and orange juice appear.

"Let's do that one more time," Mindy says. "We're ready to roll again."

"But my pants are soaked," Boulder complains.

"We're not shooting below the waist," Mindy says efficiently. "Just take them off."

Boulder does what he's told, unabashedly stripping off the drenched khakis. Spilled o.j. probably isn't the kind of accident his mother had in mind when she told him always to wear clean underwear. Still, at least this answers the age-old question. His are boxers, not briefs.

But now a real crisis emerges.

"We're out of egg whites," an assistant reports tremulously, hurrying up to Mindy. "Can't make him another egg-white omelet."

"Then make him a goddamn *yolk* omelet," Mindy snaps.

Boulder, who's been willing to woo an older woman, to get all his good lines from a geek, and to sit at my breakfast table in his underwear, now takes a stand.

"I won't eat a yolk omelet," he declares. "I haven't had a yolk in a year and a half!"

That does it. I should be upset, but instead, I burst out laughing. Loud, giddy, peals of laughter that keep building. Boulder looks stricken, which only makes me laugh harder.

"It's not you," I sputter, between gasps. "It's not the yolks, it's not even the boxers. Or maybe it is the boxers," I say, cracking myself up all over again. "I would have guessed briefs."

Across the set, I hear ripples of laughter as Jen and various members of the crew break into guffaws. In a moment, the whole room is rocking with laughter. My Surfer Dude date looks embarrassed, but then his good nature wins out, and he's doubled over, too.

"I'm sorry," he tells me, "I rarely take off my pants this early in a date. You're a good sport."

And goddammit, I am.

But now the writer chimes in. Again. "Hey, Mindy," he says, knowing that his paycheck depends on his bright ideas, "as long as Boulder's pants are off, do we want him to sleep with Jess?"

Is this another product placement opportunity? Did they bring condoms along with the Quaker Oats?

Mindy consults her notebook. "Good idea, but three of the other bachelors ended up in bed with their dates," she tells the writer. "This one's slated as the heartwarming segment. No sex. Just gooey family stuff."

That's a load off my mind. I can only do so many new things in one day.

We finish up in the house and head off to the park for what is apparently the gooey family stuff. The writer, out of ideas, leans against a tree. But Jen doesn't need any help with heartwarming. And neither, bless him, does Boulder. They ride bikes and shoot hoops. They get Fudgsicles at the Good Humor truck. And they even have a water-gun fight that makes her screech in delight.

Clearly, Jen picked the right guy, if not for me, then for her. Instead of marrying Boulder maybe I should just adopt him.

Six hours, five locations, and four outbursts from Mindy later, we wrap.

"When's this show going to be on?" Jen asks, as the crew spiffs up my house one last time before leaving.

"We air late August," Mindy says. "An hour special."

"A whole hour?" I ask, impressed.

"Well, it's really forty-four minutes, after commercials," Mindy amends. "Then we leave ten minutes for host wraps. Three minutes with the *Cosmo* editors. Maybe four. A two-and-a-half-minute tape on all the letters that came in. Interviews with each of the top-ten bachelors. And finally the date segments. Yours should be . . ." She hesitates. "Well, your stuff was good. We might even get two minutes out of it."

Two minutes? So much for my fifteen minutes of fame.

But Boulder's happy. And he's the last to leave.

"You're a cool kid," he tells Jen, who's already crumpled onto the sofa, exhausted from the day's activities.

"I had fun," she says happily. "Thanks for the bike ride."

Boulder, her new buddy, gives her a kiss on the top of her head, then comes over and hugs me.

"I really enjoyed myself. Maybe we can do this again," he says, giving me the final Boulder grin of the day. "And I meant what I said before. You're really swell for someone your age."

"Thanks," I say, and I can't help smiling.

As he's walking down the front path, I call out after him, "Say hi to your mom for me, okay?"

Chapter NINE

FOR THE NEXT WEEK, Jen is a hero at school and her friends are convinced I'm the new *Cosmo* girl. One of her buddies sends me a glittery construction-paper heart that says "Boulder Loves Jess." The bridal shop in town calls to offer a discount on my dress—if I can get them a credit on the show. They don't believe me when I say I'm not getting married. And if I were going for product placement, I'd call Vera Wang.

"Get the dress," Lucy urges. "You never know. Better Boulder than Jacques."

"I thought you liked Jacques."

"Not since you told me about his affair," she says vehemently. "I *hate* him now."

"All he did then was what you're doing now," I say simply.

"It's different. He hurt you. I'll never hurt Dan."

And maybe she's learned a lesson, because when I see Lucy and Dan a few days later at the school Science and Technology Fair, they're huddled close and holding hands. When Dan whispers something to her, Lucy giggles and glides her manicured fingers over his chest. They look like the coziest couple around. I try to decide if I should interrupt them. Yes, I've already seen Lucy having tantric sex, but this scene seems a lot more intimate. And less fake.

I mill around the elementary school fair, looking at the baking-soda-and-vinegar exploding volcanoes, the plastic-and-duct-tape exploding rockets and the Malthus-inspired exploding-population graphs. Didn't I build that same volcano a million years ago? Science marches on but science fair projects haven't changed since Archimedes jumped out of the bathtub yelling "Eureka!"

I go over to check out Jen's entry. Mounting her graphs on a floral-patterned poster board was a nice touch. Though the rest of it is pretty lame.

"Good-looking project," Dan says, coming up behind me.

"Looks good, but it's phony data," I admit.

Dan laughs, thinking it's a joke, but I'm not kidding. Jen's project was supposed to be simple. Three identical plants. One plant watered regularly for ten days. One overwatered. One not watered at all. What would happen? We checked every morning, but who knew Home Depot stocks houseplants that could survive even Cruella de Vil? Ten days without water and Philodendron #3 was dry as dust but not even drooping. Poor Jen. I had no choice.

"See that plant that has no leaves?" I ask Dan. "Had 'em until last night. I pulled them all off."

Dan eyes me suspiciously. "Really?" he asks.

I shrug. "Science fair was today. I had to do something."

"I see," Dan says, mulling over my confession. "Good thing you don't run the Human Genome Project."

"Yeah, with my data I'd have us all related to Yoda."

Dan looks me over carefully. "No family resemblance yet," he says amiably.

"Just wait nine hundred years," I warn. Reflexively, I stroke my face, wondering if wrinkles could ever possibly look as cute on me as they do on Yoda. Good thing he didn't use Botox. Spielberg would never have cast him.

We stroll over to join Lucy. She's standing by Lily's project, which has a big FIRST PLACE blue ribbon proudly pinned in the corner.

"THE EFFECTS OF HABITAT DESTRUCTION ON ENDANGERED SPECIES," I say, reading the headline on the poster. "Wow. Sounds complicated."

"But important," Lily says with the passion of a new Greenpeace recruit. "Everything on the earth changes so fast now that lots of species can't keep up."

Yup. Know just how they feel.

I ponder Lily's poster, which shows how many "breeding females" are left on Earth for six endangered species. Figures. The boys' projects explode. The girls' projects breed.

But Lily's not fooling around here. She's taking the fate of the Komodo dragon and the Goliath frog pretty seriously. Someone has to. And look at that. Only one hundred thousand female leatherback sea turtles left. Exactly how many do we need? Fifty thousand sounds like plenty to me. Just a thought—which I won't share with Lily.

"Hey, Jess," says a young man behind me. "What's a big TV star like you doing at the science fair?"

I turn around as Dean and Dave, Lily's tall, handsome twin brothers, come over, all confidence and jocular good cheer.

"Figured I should be prepared in case the Discovery Channel calls." I laugh.

They banter with me for a few minutes—are high school boys supposed to be this polite?—and then drape their arms around their little sister. They tower over her, and she looks up at them adoringly.

"My sister, the big winner," one of the boys says good-naturedly. I don't know which one. I can never tell them apart. It was easier when Lucy put Dean in a red snowsuit and Dave in blue.

"Not as big as your tennis blue ribbon, but not bad," Lily says happily.

"You might have won a better prize if you'd let me help," the other one jokes, punching Lily playfully on the arm. "I'm the one who got an A plus in physics."

Lily punches him back, giggling. "Yeah, right, Dave. If you'd helped, I'd have proven the Earth is flat."

Dave laughs and hands her a small shiny box that he pulls out of his pocket. "From me and Dean," he says. "It's a really cool, glittery frog pin. For our sister who's going to save the world."

"We looked for a frog on a *lily* pad, but couldn't find one," Dean teases. "Get it? Anyway, we're really proud of you. I mean it. Really proud."

What's the matter with these kids? Never heard of sibling rivalry? Didn't they read the handbook?

Lucy and Dan are beaming and they wrap their arms around each other, exchanging a warm don't-we-have-the-best-kids-in-the-world gaze. I guess that's the look you get to share when you've been married a long time and you've made it through all the tough days and the ordinary days, the sleepless nights and the family fights—and then someone gives you a blue ribbon. Whatever else Lucy and Dan have done wrong, they've done one thing—the big thing—just right.

"You're a great mom, Mrs. Baldor," Dan says, squeezing her tightly.

"And you're a great dad," Lucy says affectionately. "We did a darn good job with these kids."

It's a *Walton's Family Christmas* photo-op if ever there was one. And I might feel jealous—if it weren't so nice to see Lucy and Dan this happy together.

While Lily's glued to the spot in front of her first-place project, trying to convince all comers not to forget the Komodo dragon, I spot Jen across the room with a group of friends. I stroll around the rest of the fair, hoping to come up with some ideas we can use next time. Although given our plant debacle, maybe I should just hire Dave and Dean to oversee Jen's next science project and be done with it.

Above the science fair din, I hear the piercing voice of Cynthia, the dreaded PTA president.

"I can't believe Lily Baldor won," Cynthia wails loudly to one of her acolytes. "She couldn't have deserved first place. Her mother wasn't even home last week."

That's an interesting twist. Lucy had to be home for Lily to win? Was it against the rules for the kids to do the projects by themselves?

"I've heard Lily's mother doesn't just work. She *travels*," says Cynthia's sidekick, supermom-in-training Martha, rolling her eyes back in disgust.

Now there's a woman who probably needs to get out of the house more. And didn't her mother ever tell her that if she rolls her eyes like that, they might get stuck that way forever?

"I thought your Isabella's project was fabulous," says Martha, groveling to get on Cynthia's better side. As if she has one. "I would have given Isabella first place."

"I would have, too," Cynthia agrees loudly. "We had Bill Nye the Science Guy to dinner and he said her planet mobile was as creative as any he'd ever seen."

Planet mobile. Now it's all coming back. *That* was my fifth-grade project, not the volcano. Of course, Pluto was still a planet back in my day. Which means Isabella had one less Styrofoam ball to worry about.

"Maybe we should think about letting Lily into our mother-daughter book club," Martha proposes. "I'm still not sure about the mother, but Lily might add some cachet. She did get first place."

"Fine, as long as we all understand that she didn't *deserve* it," Cynthia says huffily.

Catching my eye—and probably realizing that I've heard every word—Cynthia tosses me a plastic smile and waves me closer. "Jess, you're friends with Lucy, aren't you? You can give her the good news. She's in the book club."

Cowabunga. Lucy will be thrilled. But to paraphrase Groucho Marx, why would she want to join any club that would have Cynthia as a member?

"Sure, I'll run to give her the good news," I say, grabbing the excuse to get away. "In fact, I'll go find her right now."

"I saw her getting her husband some coffee a minute ago," Cynthia says promptly. "Wearing a new diamond necklace, I think. Very pretty, but a bit much for a school event, if you want my opinion."

No, I don't want her opinion. And besides, for anyone who needs to know, it's not diamond, it's Swarovski crystal. Given how much Cynthia supposedly dislikes Lucy, she sure pays a lot of attention to her. But then again, who doesn't?

I'm about to say good-bye and look for that coffee urn when Martha grabs my arm. "Oh, Jess, before you go. I meant to call you anyway. Can you drive my Marian to dance class on Saturday morning? Cynthia's called an emergency PTA meeting."

PTA emergency? A vote on whether to serve lemonade or fruit punch at the school picnic? Could take hours. "Glad to drive her. I always take Jen," I say generously.

"Dance class? Saturday?" Cynthia asks, in a tone that suggests she's Mother Superior. "Don't tell me you two still go to Miss Adelaide."

Martha looks slightly cowed, but sticks to her guns. "Of course we go to Miss Adelaide," she says. "Everyone tells me Miss Adelaide is the best."

"Not anymore," Cynthia gloats. "Now it's Miss Danielle in Glendale. Forty-minute drive—each way—but worth it. She's *definitely* the best."

Martha looks stunned. "I didn't know about her," she murmurs. "I'll switch Marian immediately. If Miss Danielle's the best, we're there."

Ah, yes. The Best. Here we go again. Do any of us settle for anything that's not The Best? Cynthia once poured out all her Absolut vodka in the middle of a party because someone told her Grey Goose was better. I regularly schlep to the Upper West Side of Manhattan to prove I can buy New York's best bagels. It goes without saying that nobody would dare have her daughter's overbite corrected by the "second best" orthodontist. And ever since a cabal of mothers declared Sal the best barber in Pine Hills, no one will go to anyone else. Now all the boys in town have identical haircuts that make them look like cloned miscreants in *The Matrix*.

So dare I ask, why does Martha's Marian, the chubby little girl in the beginner ballet class, need the best dance teacher? The best nutritionist, now that I could support.

Martha sighs heavily and turns to me. "You'll switch, too, Jess, right?"

No, I won't. I like Miss Adelaide, all 102 tyrannical pounds of her. And life's too short to keep chasing the new best.

"Ballet's not very important right now," I say dismissively, making the decision on the spot that Jen can join the chorus of our benefit *My Fair Lady*. She's been begging and Vincent won't mind. "Didn't I tell you? Jen's making her musical debut on Broadway in a few weeks."

Cynthia looks stricken. Trumped twice. First Lily's blue ribbon and now Jen's shot at a Tony Award.

"Does your daughter sing?" Marian asks reverently, desperately trying to figure out why my daughter—and not hers—is slated for Broadway.

Cynthia's way ahead of her. "I'll definitely get a singing coach for Isabella," she says, pulling out her PalmPilot and efficiently adding another hoop for Isabella to jump through. "You must have a good one. We'll go to him."

"Won't happen, sorry. Jen's working with a very famous director who simply isn't taking on new students," I say condescendingly. "I'm sure you'll find a coach for Isabella, someone capable. Too bad though. Our Vincent is . . . *the best.*"

Someone should give me my own blue ribbon. Because for once, the supermoms are speechless.

I'm getting a stomachache. Joshua Gordon, new vice-chairman on the Board of Directors of the Arts Council for Kids, has left me three icy messages. I can tell I've done something wrong, but for the life of me, I can't figure out what it is. My little part-time job doesn't usually require massive doses of Pepto-Bismol. But every time I hear Mr. Gordon's steely voice, I want to reach for that bright pink bottle.

"Am I'm finally speaking to the *real* Ms. Taylor and not her machine?" he asks officiously, after his weary-sounding assistant puts him through at nine o'clock on Wednesday night. So the man works late. I'm impressed. Wonder how his assistant feels. "I don't have a lot of time but there's an issue we need to talk about. I'm sure we can settle it quickly, in person. Does tomorrow around five work for you?"

Five o'clock? Must be his lunch break. "Sure," I say, trying to be accommodating. "I'll come into the city. Do you mind someplace near Grand Central?"

"Grand Central's fine. How about the Oyster Bar? This won't take more than ten minutes."

Yes, it will, I think when we hang up. He'll run over from his office. But I'll spend the morning blow-drying my hair, changing outfits, fishing around my drawers for my good jewelry, poking a nail through the first pair of pantyhose I put on—for ten bucks can't DKNY make them last longer than ten minutes?—and changing outfits again. If I have any time, I should probably run out and buy a new pair of shoes. Lucy insists my Nine Wests are embarrassing to wear in front of board members.

At three-ten, I'm standing in the middle of Grand Central trying to figure out what deep trauma from my childhood requires that I arrive early for everything. Must I leave enough time for traffic, train breakdowns and tornadoes every time I travel? And I've really outdone myself today. Getting here an hour and fifty minutes early may be a new record, even for me. I'm not sure why this Joshua Gordon character is causing me such anxiety. Usually I at least have to meet a man before he can make me nuts.

I waste half an hour in the bookstore at Grand Central, reading the first twenty pages of a bestseller I'm too cheap to buy. Sure it's funny, but I'll wait until it's in paperback. I browse through a pen shop, a cigar-and-chocolate emporium, and an expensive stationery store. Who decided that this is what every commuter needs? The Origins store at least is my style. I browse the shelves, picking up the Fret-Not body soufflé and the Gloom-Away cleanser. Why down a Xanax when you can just wash your face? Then there's one that has Lucy's name written all over it—the Never A Dull Moment spray. The label says the crushed papaya in it gobbles up lackluster skin cells. My luck, the papaya will eat the wrong cells. And another one not to miss—the Perfect World Gift Collection. Although I think that's setting expectations for bubble bath just a tad high. Still, I go wild, buying grapefruit body scrub for Jen, tangerine-scented candles for two friends who have birthdays coming up, the complete line of Plum Passion lotions for my mom, and an oversized loofah back-scrubber with an extra-long handle just for me. Because nobody else is around to scrub my back lately.

"If you have time, I could do your makeup and give you some of our product samples," says the ever-helpful salesgirl.

"Not short on time," I admit, looking at my watch and seeing it's not even four yet.

"Really?" She seems startled. Am I the only person in Grand Central not rushing somewhere? "I could do a quick-foam facial, which takes about ten minutes. Then your makeup should take another fifteen. Still okay?"

"Well, I wasn't planning on it, but why not?" I say, climbing onto the makeup stool. Maybe this will help me relax. And better to wait here than in the cigar shop.

"By the way," says my salesgirl/aesthetician/makeup artist, "my name is Eve."

That's too good. I wonder if everybody at Origins is named Eve.

In seconds, Eve's slathering a thick, ginger-scented goop all over my face.

"Should tingle, but feel good," she says pleasantly. She places two thin slices of cucumbers on my eyes and a spritz of citrus balm across my lips. I'm starting to turn into the fruit plate special.

"Just sit here for a few moments and let all the botanicals make you younger-looking," she instructs. As if I could leave looking like this. But I'm afraid if I sit here too long I'll start to ferment.

I settle back into my chair, enjoying the sensations of my pores tightening and my lips softening. But just how is this fruit-on-the-face thing going to make me younger-looking, anyway? Fruit doesn't seem to age all that well if you ask me. Never seen a wrinkle-free raisin or a smooth prune. And then there's that old puckered apple at the bottom of my refrigerator. Oh well, at least the fruit facial is cheaper than Lucy's Botox.

"Feeling pretty?" Eve asks, as she comes back over to me. "We'll take off the mask in another minute. And I've wrapped your purchases. They're at the register."

"Do you have my credit card?" I ask, remembering that I didn't take it back.

"Did I leave Jessica Taylor's card over there?" Eve calls out loudly to a colleague across the room.

"Yup, right here," another salesperson sings back. "Jessica Taylor. Got it."

Eve removes the cucumber slices from my eyes just in time for me to see an impeccably dressed, silver-haired man put down the over-sized gift basket he was considering and look at me quizzically.

"Jessica Taylor? The Jessica Taylor I have an appointment with at five?" he asks, taking a few steps toward me.

"Um, no," I say, mortified, turning the swivel chair around and fu-riously wiping the glop off my face with the nearest wad of cotton. "Not me. No appointment."

He pauses and stares conspicuously at my blue Arts Council for Kids tote bag sitting on the counter. My god the man is handsome. Chiseled features. Perfect profile. I bet his picture looks great in the an-nual reports. And me? A gucky mess with ginger mask coagulating around my ears. I try to brush my hair back and end up with a fistful of foam.

"You're not the fund-raiser Jessica Taylor? You sure about that?" he asks dubiously.

"No, I don't raise funds. I raise . . . um . . . poodles," I say, thor-oughly humiliating myself. "I'm the poodle-raiser Jessica Taylor."

He's not buying it. What's the matter, don't I look like a dog per-son? "Listen, Jessica," he says, glancing pointedly at his watch, "we can talk right here and save some time."

This can't be Joshua Gordon. It just can't. Not now, not like this. I've been planning all day how professional I'll look when he sees me. I've got on my best business suit and I brought a briefcase instead of a pocketbook. The only reason I agreed to the makeup here in the first place was I thought Eve could give me that understated-but-polished-working-woman-of-the-world look that Lucy knows how to do all by herself.

"Don't know what you're talking about," I say, tucking my chin down as far as it'll go. Go away, please just go away. "Nope," I shake my head vigorously.

"I'm sorry," he says, backing off. "I'm supposed to meet someone with your same name. My mistake. I guess no top-flight fund-raiser would be so frivolous as to get a facial in the middle of the workday, now would she?"

He leaves and I watch him dissolve into the crowd at Grand Central. What was I thinking, having my makeup done here? How many people come through this terminal a day? Let's take a wild guess. Ten thousand? A hundred thousand? A million? But of all people, why Joshua Gordon? Why him? The real surprise is that I didn't see more people I know. Or that more people didn't see me. Maybe they did. There'll probably be a picture of me getting a facial on the front page of the *Pine Hills Weekly*.

But for now I'm stuck sitting here licking my wounds. Not to mention licking citrus balm off my lips. So much for my dignity. I want to disappear, but somehow, I have to make myself go to that meeting. And it won't help my case to show up without makeup, even if I am freshly foamed. I try to sit patiently while Eve applies her magic creams and chatters on about the latest light-reflecting foundation, the silicone-smoothing eye cream and the retinol moisturizer that's supposed to take ten years off my face. Between that and the fruit, I'm going to end up looking younger than Jen.

The fifteen minutes of makeup turns into thirty, because Eve tells me that putting on enough makeup to get the natural look takes longer. I don't want to look natural. I want to look like someone Joshua Gordon has never seen in his whole life. Maybe he won't recognize me, anyway. It was just a quick glance.

While Eve's busy applying three different blushers to accentuate the apples of my cheeks, I swipe my lips with my own color-tinted ChapStick and jump off the chair. Enough. I have to get out of here.

"You look gorgeous," Eve says. "Hope you're going somewhere special."

"Business meeting," I say, bustling toward the door. And then I stop. "But damn, I can't go to a business meeting carrying Origins shopping bags. Can I leave them here until afterward?"

"Sure, but they're excellent bags," Eve explains innocently. "Recyclable. All natural. Nothing to be embarrassed about."

Well, that would be the only thing not to be embarrassed about today.

Despite everything, I arrive at the Oyster Bar at five o'clock on the dot, but Joshua Gordon is already seated, drumming his fingers on a table.

I take a deep breath. I can do this. I've raised a child on my own. I've dated on TV. I've climbed Kilimanjaro. Not really, but I read about someone who did. All it takes is a little faith in myself. I walk over to the table.

"Hello," I say, blooming with confidence as I extend my hand. "I'm Jessica Taylor. You must be Gordon Joshua."

"Joshua Gordon," he corrects me.

"Right. Sorry. You have two first names. It could go either way."

"No it couldn't. It's Joshua Gordon."

"I bet people do that all the time."

"No, this is the first time, actually."

"Of course. Joshua Gordon. Got it. Check." I wait, knowing it's his turn to say something. But anxiety gets the best of me.

"I had another friend with two first names," I say, babbling into the silence. "Steve Roberts. Only his real name was Steve Robert Gravano. Dropped the Gravano when he was buying a co-op on Fifth Avenue because he thought it sounded too Italian."

"I'm not Italian."

"No, of course you're not," I say. "I mean, you could be. I could be, too. But I'm not, either. Not that it matters. For either of us. You know, some of my best friends are. Italian, I mean. And some are not. Italian. And I'm friends with, um, all my friends."

I want to die. Lord, please kill me right now. This minute. Do that lightning-bolt thing you do so well. But no such luck.

"I'm glad for you. I'm relieved to hear you have friends." I'd like to think there's a little glimmer of a smile when he says that, but I'm probably deluding myself.

"Anyway, it's good to meet you," I say. "After all our phone calls."

"You're right, I feel like we've already met," Joshua says. He looks meaningfully at my Arts Council for Kids tote bag to let me know he knows. I know he knows. And he knows I know he knows. But civility reigns and the subject is ignored. Though with both of us so in the know, so intelligent, you'd think this conversation could move up a notch.

But instead, it turns monosyllabic.

"Fishmonger," he says, finally getting down to business.

"Pardon?"

"Fishmonger," he repeats, as if that explains everything. "Did you really cast the son of Lowell Cabot III as a fishmonger?"

Now I'm the one who's silent. Nice technique, it turns out, because he keeps talking.

"His son is Chauncey. Goes to Dalton. Tried out for your play. The mother tried to reach you."

I get it. That call I ignored in the midst of all Jacques' messages. Though I took her advice. Cast a boy from Stuyvesant as the fishmonger.

"Not happy with his part and his mom pulled him out," I say, to prove I'm keeping up.

Joshua Gordon nods. "His father's one of my partners. Good man. But he and his wife are furious and threatening not to send a donation to the Arts Council this year. So your little production has made our biggest benefactors angry—which isn't the point of having a benefit."

"I know the point of having a benefit," I say tartly.

"You need to raise money, not alienate donors," Joshua says patronizingly.

"I'm sorry if your partner's not happy—but a lot of other people are," I say steadfastly, surprised at how strongly I'm reacting. "The benefit committee's actually humming along, which is more than I can say for a lot of benefit committees. They're raising lots of money and getting new people involved." Then going on just one point too long, I add, "They've gotten Kate Spade to donate wallets."

He ignores the wallets. In fact he ignores my whole speech. "The bottom line here is the bottom line," he says. "You need to apologize to the Cabots."

"For what?" I ask archly. "For letting them know that their money can't buy everything?"

He pauses and I wonder if he's deciding whether he can fire me right on the spot. On the other hand, they hardly pay me enough to fire me.

"Look, tell them whatever you want," he says, issuing an executive command. "Just take care of it."

"Don't worry. I always take care of everything," I say.

"Good."

"This is going to be the best benefit the Arts Council has ever seen," I add enthusiastically. Too enthusiastically. "You'll see. Everyone's going to love it." When did I turn into the cheerleader from Delta Delta Delta? And to think they rejected me all those years ago.

"Glad to hear that go-get-'em spirit," Joshua says. Does he mean it or is he making fun of me?

"I'll figure out the Cabots," I tell him. I don't know how, but I will.

"Thanks. Listen, as long as we're here, can I get you something to eat? A cup of clam chowder?"

I'm starved, but I don't dare risk having soup dribble down my chin. Maybe a salad. Something small and green with fresh grilled tuna? No, I'm not eating with the arrogant Joshua Gordon.

"I really should be going," I say, gathering my things together. "We said ten minutes and I don't want to keep you."

"Maybe another time," he offers distractedly. But he's already pulled out his cell phone and has moved on to his next task.

"By the way," I ask boldly, before he finishes dialing. "What were you doing in Origins?"

He looks up, surprised by my admission, then sits back in his chair and takes me in from head to toe. "I got to Grand Central early. Figured I'd pick up a gift for my assistant. Have her working late a lot."

"Thoughtful," I say.

"But I didn't get anything. Couldn't make up my mind. Good thing my clients don't see me trying to shop. They'd never trust me with million-dollar mergers."

"Here," I say, reaching into my pocket. "You might want to get your assistant these. Origins' Peace of Mind gumballs. Don't really know if they work as advertised. But it's worth a shot."

He pops one in his mouth. "Not bad. Peace of Mind, huh? I feel better about the benefit already."

"I should have thought of this when I first came in," I say, laughing, handing the whole box over to him.

He clicks the cover open and shut a few times, then picks up his cell phone to get back to work. "I'd never been in Origins before," Joshua says, giving me one final meaningful glance. "But from what I can see, they do nice work."

Chapter TEN

LUCY IS PERCHED at the gleaming counter in her Poggenpohl-perfect kitchen, leafing through *The Barefoot Contessa Cookbook,* while I'm hunched at her travertine-granite cooking island, gazing in disbelief at the *New York Post.*

"Lucy, we need to talk about this," I tell her.

"Sure, eventually. But right now we need to get back to making the sauce," she says.

"We?" I ask dubiously.

"Okay, you," she agrees, with a half laugh. "Anyway, I have plenty of recipes, if you want a different one."

"I don't, but why exactly do you collect cookbooks?" I ask, looking at the stack in front of her. "You never cook. You're like a nudist subscribing to *Women's Wear Daily.*"

"My great vice. Recipe pornography. I read and drool. Like listen to this," she says, opening another book from her pile. "Lusciously Rich Sugar-Glazed Fruit Trifle. Slather raspberries with brown sugar and molasses, cook it all in butter and serve it hot with vanilla ice cream. Mmm. Don't even need to eat it to feel satisfied."

"And you'd only eat it if you were on the All-Sugar Diet. *Sugar-Boosters.* That's the book I'm waiting for someone to publish."

"It'd make a fortune," she agrees, smacking her lips seductively.

"I'm into real estate porn myself," I admit. "Read listings for country houses I can't afford. Lust over ads for six-bedroom mansions with three fireplaces and five wooded acres. And probably kitchens like this one," I add, pulling a glinting, high-carbon tool from her maple block.

"Use it anytime you want," Lucy offers as I cross to the inlaid cutting board to prepare the herbs for the dinner party she's throwing tonight for Dan.

"What's that green stuff you're chopping?" she asks.

"I'm mincing. And it's cilantro."

"And the other stuff?"

"Basil. And this one's parsley," I say pointing with the knife. "Come on, you've seen parsley before."

"Why does everything come in green? It's confusing," Lucy says, playing with the lemon grater I left in front of her, foolishly thinking she might actually grate. "Even those other things you've got there. The ones that look like Christmas decorations. Green."

"They're serrano chiles, imported from Mexico and twice as hot as jalapeños," I say, sounding like I'm auditioning for Nigella Lawson's job on Style Network.

"How hot are jalapeños?" Lucy asks.

I put down the chopping knife. "Lucy, you couldn't possibly care. The sauce will be delicious, I promise. Dan will be thrilled. His guests will be awed. Now are we going to talk about parsley—or that picture of you and Hunter in the *Post*?"

"Parsley," Lucy says. "Much more interesting. Lots of pictures in the *Post*. But nobody's ever chopped herbs in my kitchen before. Or used that Wüsthof Culinar Chef's Knife, if you can believe it."

"Why wouldn't I believe it? I've seen kitchens at Expo Showroom that get more use than this one. If the Viking range people knew you tried to fry chicken in the microwave, they'd probably come over and haul this baby right out of here," I say, patting the barely-been-used ten-thousand-dollar commercial-quality stove.

"Want it?" Lucy asks, as if I could cart off the 30,000 BTU range along with the pile of slighty worn cashmere sweaters she's donating to the Aruba Relief Fund. Nice of her to want to help. But only Lucy would send cashmere-aid to Caribbean hurricane victims.

"What I want is for you to talk to me about the New York Post. I warned you something like this would happen," I say stubbornly, shaking my head.

"It's not a big deal," she insists. "So there's a picture in the paper of Hunter and me together at Cher's party. We work together, remember?"

"You're so in denial. Hunter has his arm around you. He's grinning. He's eyeing you like you're the icing on a cupcake. What's Dan gonna think?"

"Dan? Come off it. If it's not above the fold in the Wall Street Journal he never sees it."

"Used to be you wouldn't let me whisper Hunter's name in the house. Now a lusty picture in the Post doesn't even faze you?"

"Stop worrying about this. We've got more important things to do. I've been waiting all day to see you butterfly a fish," she says, changing the subject. "Sounds vaguely against the laws of nature to me."

"As so much is," I say, delicately filleting the red snapper with the haute cuisine flair I learned back in the days when I was married to Jacques. Never made this Snapper Vera Cruz before but it's looking good. Maybe I'll whip it up for Jacques when he gets back to New York. Won't tell Lucy that I'm using her dinner party as a test run.

Lucy comes over and puts her arm around me. "You're such a great friend, Jess," she says. "You worry about me even when it's not necessary. And I'll tell you again—this is the best birthday present anybody ever gave me. A dinner party cooked in my very own kitchen. A personal chef. I feel like Oprah."

"Don't get too used to it," I joke. "This is one night only. And by the way, I thought the party would be for you. Sweet of you to make it for Dan's clients."

"I thought this would mean a lot to him," Lucy says tenderly. "I've never cooked a gourmet meal for him before."

"You still haven't."

"Technicality," Lucy says, laughing. "And you don't mind being regifted, do you? You're in good company. I usually only do that with Gallo wine and Godiva chocolate."

I finish filleting the fish and begin blackening the chiles in one of the dozen copper pots Lucy has hanging overhead. I guess it's easy to keep them shiny when they're never used, but they must be a royal pain to dust.

"So what's Dan giving you for your birthday?" I ask, staring into the pan and trying to decide if the chiles are looking properly blistered.

"We'll see. He wants to take me shopping Sunday," she says indifferently, "but there's nothing I really need." Then perking up she adds, "The big question is what I'll get from Hunter."

"Heartache?" I suggest.

"Very funny," Lucy says. "I'm expecting something pretty fabulous, though. He brought a nine-hundred-dollar bottle of wine to Cher's party to celebrate her comeback tour."

"That woman has a comeback every two months. Hunter'll go broke," I say, searching through the sleek, modular pantry for sea salt. The one ingredient I forgot to bring. But never mind sea salt, I can't even find a box of Morton's. Maybe Lucy's worried about hypertension.

"Did it taste any different than an eight-hundred-dollar bottle of wine?" I ask facetiously, trying to figure out if some extra onion will make up for the missing salt.

"Wasn't for drinking. It was for showing off. You should have seen the way he carried it in, cradled in his arm like it was Michael Jackson's love child. He was so damn proud of himself."

"Do I hear a tinge of disapproval?" I ask hopefully.

Lucy takes a second to mull. "Hunter wants everyone to like him. I know that. He's all about the grand gesture, which can make him seem kind of shallow. On the other hand," she says, "shallow has its advantages. Being with him makes birthdays more interesting."

"Dan would buy you anything you want for your birthday," I remind her. "You don't need Hunter."

"Gifts from your lover are different than gifts from your husband," Lucy explains patiently. "When your husband gets romantic, it comes out of joint checking. Like Dan bought me that diamond bracelet from Cartier last year, and all I could think was that we should have been putting that money into a 401k. But Hunter can blow a fortune on me and I don't feel guilty. It's sheer indulgence."

"Having an affair is nothing *but* indulgence," I say righteously, on behalf of Pat Robertson. And my mother.

"Well, maybe it is," Lucy says defensively. "But that's what's so incredible about having a lover. With Hunter I feel totally pampered. We take bubble baths together. We have sex in the afternoon. When was the last time Dan squirted whipped cream all over my body and licked it off?"

"You mean Hunter did that?" I ask, interested. Maybe there's something to this affair thing after all.

"Not yet, but we've talked about it. We'll have to use soy cream, though. Hunter's lactose intolerant."

"Oh, for heaven's sake, Lucy," I say, slamming the knife back into its slot. "The problem is you stopped trying with Dan. You take him for granted. You don't realize what a great guy you've got."

"Of course I do. Dan's the best. I want to be with him forever. I just want to have sex with someone else for a change. Is there anything so wrong with that? I'm forty-two now, which is a woman's sexual peak more or less. Aren't you having the best orgasms of your life?"

"I probably would be if I had someone to have them with," I say ruefully. "My vibrator's not up to par lately."

"Check the batteries," Lucy advises. "Duracells never let you down."

"Thanks for the tip. And here's one for you. You want great sex? Next time you go to Le Retreat, take Dan. Or go to the Mandarin Oriental for a weekend and have rousing orgasms for two days without worrying about the kids. Bring Reddi-wip, if you want. As far as I can tell, the best thing about an affair is you have sex in fancy hotel rooms and you don't have to make the bed afterwards."

"I do love room service," Lucy says. "Especially those rolling trays with a single red rose."

She's missed the point. I take some cellophane out of the drawer to wrap up the extra herbs—not that I think Lucy'll be sprinkling them on tomorrow night's dinner—and then wave the box at her.

"Saran Wrap," I say as if I've just discovered a new twist in DNA. "That's the solution. I remember reading about it years ago. You meet your husband at the door dressed in nothing but plastic wrap and a smile. Then he throws you to the ground and makes mad, passionate love with you. *Voilà.* The marriage is saved. Works every time."

"I read about it too but I never got it," Lucy says. "Doesn't sound practical. For one thing, how flattering is Saran Wrap? I'd probably look like a side of USDA choice beef."

"Prime beef," I suggest, going a grade better.

"Well, fine, but then there are all those sticky layers of plastic. Dan'd give up. It took him long enough to learn how to unhook my bra."

"You're impossible," I say, heading into the living room with a bowl of lime-and-thyme-scented salsa for the crudités. On the way, I pause at the dinner table, which Lucy has creatively arranged with her collection of antique china and silver. To Lucy, eating well has more to do with the plates than with what's on them. Each setting is different, with unusual pieces she found at quaint New England consignment shops and get-there-before-dawn flea markets. If I tried to pull this off, I'd have a jumble of mismatched crockery. But Lucy turns the mélange into a work of art. Judy Chicago's Dinner Party has nothing on Lucy's.

"You set a nice table, but you're still impossible," I say. "Do you have a spoon for the salsa?"

"Try this one. London fiddle pattern circa 1845. Bought it from a British importer in Vermont, but I'm sure it's authentic."

"So's the salsa," I say, putting down the bowl. "New Jersey tomatoes. Bought at ShopRite."

Lucy goes upstairs to change and I set to work on the first course, individual chèvre-and-pine-nut tartlets drizzled with raspberry vinaigrette. In the time it takes to make these, I could probably solve the national debt crisis. I'm just putting the tart crusts in the oven to bake when I hear the back door open.

"What's all this?" Dan calls out as he walks in. "Smells great in here. Are you really *cooking* tonight, honey?"

I take my head out of the oven—the tarts will be fine—and turn around, face flushed from the heat. Dan stops, startled, and puts down the case of wine he's carrying. "Oh, Jess. Wow. I'm sorry. From the back, I thought you were my wife."

"No, darling, I'm your wife," says Lucy, as she drifts into the kitchen, dressed now in a gauzy white blouse, flowing black palazzo pants, and spike-heeled Jimmy Choos. Guess she's not planning on getting up to serve.

Dan gives Lucy a peck on the cheek, then comes over and gives me a kiss, too. "Well, it does smell amazing in here. I got that part right," he says.

"Everything should be great," I say, talking about the food. "All under control."

Dan nods, then hands Lucy the *Post* he has tucked under his arm. "So what'd you think of your picture in the paper?" he asks casually.

"Lousy picture of me," she says without missing a beat. "My nose looks funny from that angle."

I gulp and start putting away the peppers, but Lucy seems unfazed.

"Everyone else seemed to like it," Dan says. "At least four people in my office gave it to me, so I have extra copies, if you need them."

I try desperately to decide if there's an edge of anxiety to Dan's voice, but instead he starts unpacking the wine bottles.

"Heitz Cellar. Great vintage," he says, holding out one of the bottles. "A nice cabernet sauvignon."

Or nice enough. Probably not nine hundred dollar a bottle.

Lucy frowns. "Jess is making a fish for dinner," she says disapprovingly. "Shouldn't we have white?"

"Oh," Dan says, slightly abashed. "I thought you'd like the Heitz. But the other half of the case is Sonoma chardonnay. Is that better for you?"

"Either is perfect," I say. "The sauce for the fish is spicy and a little heavy. Why not serve both?"

Spirits restored, Dan heads off with the wine, and as soon as he's out of the room, I hiss to Lucy, "You said he'd never see the *Post*. He saw it. Now do you feel bad?"

"Of course not. It was no big deal," she hisses back. "Just like I told you."

"You're lucky, but you can't stay lucky forever," I tell her.

The guests arrive and I meet everybody, but by the time we sit down to the table, which Lucy has bedecked with a dozen glowing candles, I can't remember a single name. And all I've had is one glass of Diet Coke. What is it about me with names lately? I was trying this time, too. When Dan introduced me to the man who's now sitting to my left, I did that memory-by-association thing. He's bald, so I visualized a bald eagle. Eagle. America. Uncle Sam. Was his name Sam? Probably not. Maybe I just went from bald eagle to birds. Robin? Nah, too English. Woody? In that case, I would have visualized his . . . oh, never mind.

After the proper oohing and aahing about Lucy's gorgeous table and my amazing tartlets, the mousy woman across from me downs her second glass of wine and asks for a third. I'm pretty sure she's married to bald eagle—she's small and timid so I visualized an eagle eating a mouse. Maybe she's Mickey. That'll do.

"I saw your picture in the paper," she says to Lucy, in a rush of chardonnay-boosted confidence. "Your life must be *so* glamorous. A party at Cher's and you're there with Hunter Green. I watch him on TV every morning. I just love him. Seems like the nicest man in the world. So charming. Is it just the most fabulous thing in the world to work with him?"

"He's a bit of an egomaniac," Lucy says grandly, rolling the warm chèvre around on her tongue. "But so's everyone I work with. And can you believe these tabloids? Can't even stand next to someone at a party anymore."

"You mean you didn't arrive together?" asks the woman I now think of as Mickey.

"Bread sticks, anyone?" I ask loudly, figuring I can derail the conversation. What could be more neutral than bread sticks?

"Please, no, get those off the table, immediately!" calls out a moon-faced woman in a blue dress. "Don't you know carbs kill?"

So much for a neutral topic. I'm glad I didn't mention seven-layer cake. The woman would have gone straight into cardiac arrest.

Mickey ignores the carb controversy and keeps her attention glued to Lucy. "I once tried to get on Hunter's show," she says. "I took the Internet quiz but I never heard back. Any chance you could put in a good word for me with Hunter when you see him again? Are you two really close?"

"Wine? Who needs more wine?" I jump up, grabbing for the bottles. "Dan has red and white," I say as if these are the two most original colors to hit wine stores in fifty years.

But Mickey—what made me think she was mousy? The woman's starting to sound like Janet Reno—stays riveted to Lucy and persists in her line of questioning. "Isn't Hunter the host of your new pilot? You must be together day and night."

"Oh, you know Lucy, always busy, busy, busy," I say, interrupting yet again. "Where do you get your information?" I ask Mickey, hoping to divert her attention. "You seem to know a lot about TV."

"I'm on the fan websites all the time," Mickey says, as if that's the first step toward her Daytime Emmy. "I know everything about Hunter Green. His favorite color, which isn't green. Where he gets his ties. His shoe size." She stops for a moment, trying to decide if she should share her information, then decides to take the plunge. "The only bad news is he has very small feet," she confides. "And you know what that means."

"Very small socks?" I ask hopefully.

"But the good news is he just got back from a fabulous weekend with his secret girlfriend at a really romantic hideaway. I forget what it's called. Oh that's right," she says triumphantly. "Le Retreat."

Lucy manages not to spit out her wine, but she looks up just a little too anxiously at Dan. And their eyes lock for a beat too long.

"Isn't that interesting," Dan says calmly. "Lucy was there last weekend, too."

For once the unflappable Lucy seems shaken. Her usual quick

comebacks aren't coming, and she carefully smooths the napkin in her lap with the palms of her hands. Nervous gesture or wiping off the sweat? Come on, Lucy, say something. "Jess was there with me," she ventures lamely.

"Yes I was," I say boldly, speaking on behalf of my very, very guilty client. "And it didn't seem at all romantic to me."

"Me either," Lucy quickly agrees. "How do these places get their reputation, anyway?"

I get up to clear the first course plates. And, I hope, the air. "Snapper Vera Cruz coming up next," I say. "Mickey? Would you mind helping me clear?" I look over at Hunter's number-one fan but she doesn't respond. Nikki. That was it. Nikki. I guess I'll clear the plates myself.

When I finally get home from the dinner party, I find Boulder fast asleep on my mid-century modern sofa. Paid a small fortune for it, and the couch looks just like the one my mother bought from Sears when I was growing up. Hated it then—what made me think I'd like it now? And I don't know why Boulder's sleeping on it.

"I had to use my judgment, and I thought it would be okay to let Boulder in," says Jen's babysitter, Maggie, walking into the room. "Everybody in town knows about you two."

"That's fine," I say, wondering what brought Boulder to my doorstep when there's not a camera crew in sight. "Sorry I'm so late." Party was over by midnight but I wasn't in a rush to leave. Figured I'd stick around in case Dan had anything more to say about Lucy's weekend, the picture in the *Post*, or *l'affaire* Le Retreat. But Dan seemed tired, and after he dried a few dishes, he went to bed. With or without Lucy I can't say, although I'm sure she'll tell me tomorrow.

I empty out my wallet to pay Maggie. When did babysitters in Pine Hills start earning ten bucks an hour? I know she's saving up her money to go to college—but should I tell her that any job she gets after graduation won't pay nearly so well? Once Maggie's gone, I turn my attention to Boulder, who's curled up like a sleepy puppy. He looks so comfortable that I'm certainly not going to wake him. I toss a light

afghan over his bare feet, start to tuck it around his toes, then stop myself. Wait a minute, I certainly *am* going to wake him. What the heck is
the boy doing on my couch at two a.m.?

But how to rouse him? A gentle shake to the shoulder? A kiss on
the cheek? A glass of cold water dumped on his head? I settle on the
shoulder shake. Which does nothing. Nice to be young and male and
a sound sleeper.

"Boulder?" I say loudly. "Boulder? *Boulder?*"

He finally sits up, wide-awake immediately. Nice to be young and
male and wake up on a dime.

"Hey, Jess, how ya' doin'? Did you hear our show's going to be on
next week?"

"No, really? I thought it was scheduled for August."

"Everyone at the network loved it and they put it on the fast track
for sweeps," he says, stretching. "I figured we could all watch together.
It'd be cool."

"Cool," I agree, wondering whether he's planning on sitting on the
couch until next week. "Is that what you came here to tell me? It's
kinda late." I rub my eyes and yawn for emphasis.

"You sure had some night partying," he says with a grin. Here we
go again with the grin. "You can tell me about it if you want."

"Nothing to tell," I admit. Still, good manners require I offer him
something to eat. He's a growing boy and he's probably hungry. But
I'm not going back into the kitchen at this hour for anything. Well,
maybe some grapes.

"So what's going on? Why'd you come over?"

"Actually, I want to talk to you seriously," he says.

Then not grapes. I have some leftover beef stroganoff. That sounds
serious.

But now the grin is gone and his expression has turned solemn.
His range is increasing. He must be studying hard in acting classes.

Boulder clears his throat and summons his lines. "Listen, Jess, I
know that after the show's on everyone's going to think we're a couple. And I like you a lot. I really do. Love Jen, too. We really all could
be very happy together."

No, we couldn't. But I don't want to interrupt his big scene.

"Unfortunately, that being together can't happen right now, and I wanted to tell you the truth myself." He pauses for effect, stroking his perfectly one-day stubbled chin. "I'm already involved with someone."

This doesn't sound too upsetting. I've been kissed off before. And by people that I've actually kissed. "That's okay," I say, probably a little too quickly.

"Really? You're not upset?"

"No. I understand. We met on a TV show. These things can't last," I say philosophically. Should I add how great it was getting to know him? And that I've learned from the experience? No, I think I'll leave well enough alone.

"My agent got me to do the whole thing," Boulder says, still apologizing. " I said I didn't want to mislead anyone, but he said a break's a break."

"It's a tough business. You do what you can," I say, trying to make him feel better.

"So can we just be friends?" Boulder asks. "I'd hate to lose you completely. Especially now that I'm sticking around New York for a while to go on some auditions."

Oddly enough, I realize that I'd be glad to have sweet, spike-haired Boulder as my friend. He's fun to be around, and I wouldn't mind walking into the PTA Parents Spring Swing on his arm. For once I'd have a good time dancing—and Cynthia would have a seizure trying to figure out what was going on with me and Surfer Dude. Win-win.

"Glad to be buddies," I say. And now that we're confidantes, I get to ask, "So, who are you seeing? Are you happy?"

"Happy most of the time," he says, getting comfy again on the couch. "We have so much in common. We met surfing. We're both trying to break into acting."

Surfing and acting. Relationships have been built on less. Although not much. "Sounds good," I say supportively.

"It is," he says thoughtfully. "I'm just not sure if he's the forever person."

He? Did I hear that right? Okay, I was born in Ohio, but I've lived in New York for a long time. I shop on Christopher Street. I watch *Will &* *Grace*. I'm not shocked. But "he" sounds a lot like "she" and I don't want to jump to conclusions.

"So, tell me about your . . . forever person. What's . . . their name?" I ask, searching for the right pronoun.

"Cliff," says Boulder happily. "He's gorgeous. He looks just like me. And we're both Aries."

"And me a Sagittarius. Guess you and I just weren't in the stars, Boulder."

"Maybe that was it," he says, nodding. Because obviously it was astrology and not our slight difference in sexual orientation that kept us apart.

"So why isn't Cliff your forever person?" I ask.

"Maybe he is," Boulder says. "We're so right together. The only big problem with the relationship is my mom."

That I can understand. "Is she having trouble accepting Cliff?" I ask sympathetically. "At least she won't have to deal with a daughter-in-law."

"Oh, she really loves Cliff," Boulder says eagerly. "She loves every-thing about him. She just can't get over the fact that he's not Catholic. She's pretty strict about my not dating boys outside the religion."

A nice post-modern twist. Mom's good that he's gay. But she's a traditionalist. Still yearns for a church wedding. No matter what the Pope says.

"Your mom's pretty devout?" I ask.

"You bet. She's the last person I know who still eats fish on Friday. She doesn't care that Vatican II declared the Mass can be in English— she reads it in Latin. Well, she doesn't really read Latin. All she knows is *veni, vidi, vici*. Doesn't get her very far."

"Only Latin phrase I know is *carpe diem*. Seize the day," I say. "Which is exactly what you need to do here."

"I'll do it," Boulder says eagerly. Then pausing, he asks, "But do what?"

"Take action. Go for what you want. Have you talked to Cliff about converting? Might solve the problem for your mom."

"I never thought to ask," Boulder says.

"You have to," I say resolutely. "If this is a serious relationship, everything gets put on the table. You make sacrifices for each other. Every relationship has obstacles, but if you want to be together, you work them out."

Boulder looks at me wide-eyed. "You're right, I'm going to talk to Cliff. Thanks, Jess. You're smart. How do you know so much?"

Now there's the question of the evening. I seem to be good at everyone's relationships but my own.

"Mostly I read a lot," I say. "Everything I know is from Chekhov."

Boulder stares at me blankly. I better explain it in a way he'll understand. "Chekhov. Think of him as the guy who wrote the original *Sex and the City*. Russian version."

Boulder grins affectionately. "See, you really are smart. And I was so smart to pick you as my date. We're going to be BFF."

Now I'm the one who doesn't get it. It's late and he's speaking in initials. "Help me out on this one," I say.

"BFF," Boulder says, coming over and locking pinkies with me. "Best Friends Forever."

Boulder spends the night on the couch, and in the morning, he brews a pot of coffee for me, leaves a note signed with a happy face, and is gone before Jen or I wake up. I have to get out of the house quickly, too. I'm meeting my Park Avenue benefit friends Amanda Beasley-Smith and Pamela Barone for a fashion show at Chanel. And what in heaven's name can I wear? I've read about the quandary celebrities face before these events—put on a Versace for the Versace show and a Prada for Prada or is that too much pandering? Lacking couturier choices, I settle on a little black dress. It isn't Chanel, but I think of it as my *homage* to the great Madame Coco, who, when her lover died, vowed to put the whole nation in mourning. And darned if every fashionable woman in New York isn't still wearing black.

Three blocks from the store, I realize that I've forgotten my invitation, and my name probably won't be at the door. Even the security guard will know at a glance that the dress isn't the real deal. But I don't have to worry because Amanda and Pamela are standing outside, politely waiting for me. Those girls were well brought up. Swiss finishing schools are good for more than snagging a rich husband.

"Thanks for inviting me here," I say as we head up the grand staircase to the private showroom.

"We thought it would be fun," says Pamela. "Private viewings are always so much better than those big fashion-week productions."

"Always such a terrible crowd at those," agrees Amanda. "You can never buy anything. And the private viewing is all about buying."

I'd love to buy, but I forgot to bring my trust fund. Best I can do is spring for the Chanel Pink Mink nail polish. Yummy color, but at $16, is it really worth it? Any better than my $2.50 Wet 'n' Wild? I know this outing is Amanda's way of thanking me for all the work on the benefit and making me feel like one of the girls. But it's making me feel like one of the poor girls.

As we step into the private viewing room, a salesgirl who's barely older than Jen hands us each an elegantly embossed pad of paper—definitely better stock than my wedding invitations—and a gold pen.

"Feel free to mark down the numbers of as many outfits as you want," she says, standing in a perfect pose to show off the classic pink Chanel suit she's wearing. I wonder if the rules here are like McDonald's and she had to pony up for her own uniform. If so, that pink number should be fully paid for by the time she's ninety. Maybe I should tell her about the economic advantages of babysitting in Pine Hills. And she can do that in jeans.

The show begins, heralded by hip-hop music pulsating so loudly that I wonder if they're trying to drive out everybody over thirty. The fifty or so young socialites in the audience give a smattering of applause as the models prance out in the latest variations of the classic Chanel suit—this season, micro-mini short, Pilates-body-tight, and finished—or not finished—with frayed edges. Maybe hems cost extra. The traditional ladylike links that used to be strung delicately at the waist have been replaced by clunky metal biker chains ripped off from the Hell's Angels. I used to think you had to be old enough to wear Chanel. Now you have to be young enough.

Amanda and Pamela, obviously in their element, are delightedly nudging each other and scrawling down notes faster than Joyce Carol Oates churning out a new novel. I'm very busy, too, trying to identify the lovely thin blond woman in the front row, wearing jeans and a wispy, sheer blouse with sprays of flowers on it. Her perfectly high-lighted hair is gathered back loosely in a rubber band. It couldn't be Gwyneth Paltrow. Maybe it is Gwynnie. Gee, her pale features look washed out when she's not done up in movie makeup, and that painted porcelain pendant hanging from her neck definitely didn't come from Harry Winston. Look at that—five minutes at Chanel and I'm already a snob.

Each model—none of them weighing more than a lettuce leaf— struts past, thrusting her angular hipbones from side to side, showing off the last of the daytime ensembles. Then the hip-hop music changes to Ella Fitzgerald, the lights go from bright white to amber and a model sways toward us, wrapped in a pale-nude column of fluttery chiffon. There's a murmur of pleasure, and a stirring of excitement as pad pages flip and numbers are furiously recorded. Entranced, I make a note about the diaphanous, mint green strapless gown. Wouldn't that look spectacular hanging in my closet? Maybe not, because I have noth-ing to hang next to it. I bet half these women have whole rooms dedi-cated exclusively to their designer evening wear. As they say on Park Avenue, you can't have too many ball gowns.

The music stops, the lights go back up, and there's a pause in the action while the models regroup—maybe it's time for their vitamins— and the first wave of orders are placed.

"I have to get that floaty chiffon," Pamela says eagerly. "Gorgeous, wasn't it? And so romantic. It reminds me of the tulle skirt I wore last year to the Metropolitan Opera Ball."

"Didn't save it?" I ask.

She looks at me askance. "I could never wear anything from last season," she admits.

I could. And I accept hand-me-downs. Because even if I won the lottery, would I ever plunk down four thousand dollars of my own for a designer dress? Seems so frivolous. But just looking at clothes this beautiful makes me feel good, so I can imagine how I'd feel wearing them. Completely spectacular. Completely invincible. Ready to take on the world. For now, though, I guess I'll have to conquer the world in khakis. Easier for getting in and out of the subway.

Amanda and Pamela trade notes, making sure that they're not going to end up at some gala in identical dresses. There's a little brouhaha over the absolutely divine number nineteen. Neither of them can remember exactly what it was, but they're both sure that they have to have it.

"Rock, paper, scissors?" I suggest helpfully.

"No, that's okay," Pamela says with a little smile. "Amanda can have this one. But the next one we both want goes to me." I wonder if the pact applies only to Chanel—or if Pamela will invoke it to claim the best nanny, the choicest Aspen ski rental, or the ground-floor co-op they've each been dying to buy for their housekeeper.

They hand their forms to the girl in pink, who seems surprised that I don't offer up mine, too. "You didn't find anything you liked?" she asks with concern. "Is there something I should tell Mr. Lagerfeld? He always loves feedback."

"Not that he does anything about it," sniffs Pamela, who's obviously expressed her opinions before.

"It's true," says Amanda politely. "Calvin takes our comments much more seriously."

"So does Ralph.

"And Oscar."

"Mr. Lagerfeld has been very busy lately," the young salesgirl offers in his defense. "You know he just lost ninety-two pounds."

Amanda and Pamela nod, as if this non sequitur actually means something. Maybe it does. Hard to take feedback on an empty stomach.

The salesgirl wiggles away on her stiletto kitten mules and Amanda and Pamela wriggle around on the hardback gold chairs. As with everything I've seen here, the chairs are a triumph of form over function.

"By the way," Pamela says to me with her best Cheshire cat smile. "Amanda and I have something for you after the show. A little gift to thank you for the benefit. You deserve it. Everyone on the board's been talking about what a great job you're doing."

"Everyone?" I ask. "That's really nice. But I'm betting there's one exception."

"Why would you think that?" asks Amanda quizzically.

I bite my lip. Should I admit it? "I had a little run-in. With Josh Gordon," I say, trying to figure out how much to tell them. "The man hated me sight unseen and once he did see me"—with my face slathered in fruit goop; okay, some things you don't share even with the girls—"and once he did see me, it only got worse."

"I haven't heard a thing about it," says Pamela with a shrug.

"Probably not your fault anyway. Josh's having a hard time lately," says Amanda, looking over to Pamela to see if she's heard the gossip. But Pamela looks blank and realizing that she's the one with the scoop, Amanda tantalizingly adds, "Alden told me all about what happened with Josh's wife. Everyone kept it quiet for a long time. It's so, so sad."

"My gosh, what is it?" asks Pamela, concerned. "An accident? Is she sick?"

"Worse," says Amanda, serenely crossing her hands in her lap. "She left him and ran off with her tennis pro."

That happens in real life? Wives still run off with the tennis pro? Now that we're into a new millennium, I would have thought it would be her Bikram yoga instructor.

"Oh my god," says Pamela. "She ran off with Dawson? The guy with the ponytail and the silver stud earring? He's the best pro at the club. I always liked him."

"Everyone does. Or did. He's adorable," says Amanda.

"But he's going to suffer," says Pamela archly. "I don't care if he has a great backhand. Nobody will go to him anymore."

"You're right. Such a scandal," Amanda says, pursing her lips.

"No, no, not that," says Pamela huffily. "If Dawson's hooked up with Mia, he's just not going to be available off the court. So what good is he? Won't be able to go out to lunch. Or to those black-tie things our husbands think are so boring. He had such a gift. I took Dawson with me to the Polo Dance two summers ago and I have to say, he was divine." She looks off dewy-eyed, leaving us to wonder just where else Dawson might have been divine.

But Amanda's not worried about Dawson's career or Pamela's need for a new pro. She has more details that must be shared.

"Anyway, Josh was devastated. As you can image. He had no idea. He didn't even know she was taking tennis lessons."

"Mia's a fool," Pamela says. "You have your little affair, fine. But you don't walk away from a good husband for a tennis pro. I'm sure she'll come back."

"Josh won't let her. Filed for divorce. Alden says he gave her a huge settlement and it's over."

Pamela pauses, too well bred to ask how much.

"Who got Ireland?" she asks instead.

"The country?" I ask, thinking that these people are so rich they even divide Europe between them.

"No, the daughter," says Pamela.

"Joint custody. Josh is such a dear," Amanda says loyally. "He has such a good heart and he takes care of everybody. Including Mia. What could she have been thinking?"

"Just another woman facing forty and panicking. Promise me we'll stay with our husbands," she says to Amanda. "If we need some rejuvenation, we'll just go off and have face-lifts together."

"Let's start with our eyes and go from there," says Amanda conservatively. Then turning back to me, she explains, "So with all that, you've got to understand that Josh isn't quite himself. He's been on edge all year. I'm sure it was nothing personal against you."

Abruptly, the music starts up again and more gossip about Josh Gordon is tabled as the models swirl out to tempt us a few more times.

"So did you pick your favorite?" Amanda asks me when it's all over.

"Loved everything," I say with a laugh. "Not that it matters."

"But it does," says Amanda gleefully. "That's our surprise. We've arranged with the Chanel publicist for you to borrow a gown to wear to the benefit."

Pamela and Amanda are both grinning in delight and waiting for my reaction.

"Are you serious? You didn't have to do that. But I'm really glad you did," I say, truly pleased at the prospect of my Cinderella night.

"I think the apricot strapless would look perfect on you, but if you really want," Pamela says beneficently, looking to Amanda for approval, "we could let you have the floaty chiffon."

"No, that's yours," I say. "Any Chanel gown would be more than I ever dreamed of." And it would. But now I'm wondering if they can get me a deal on the shoes.

Chapter ELEVEN

WHEN I SEE DAN Wednesday morning at the Pine Hills train station, I tap him on the shoulder, reaching across the tight cluster of commuters who are packed at the exact spot where the first-car doors will open for the 7:57 express.

"Hey, handsome, come here often?" I ask.

Two disgruntled men look up from their newspapers, annoyed that someone would be joking within their earshot this early in the morning.

"Hi, Jess," Dan says listlessly. His shoulders are slumped and he looks puffy and bleary-eyed.

"You okay?" I ask.

Instead of answering, he distractedly rubs the car keys in his pocket, his mind obviously far away.

"Dan, you okay?" I ask again, concerned.

"Not really," he admits.

"What's the matter? Anything I can do? Do you want to talk?"

He pauses. "Yeah, I kind of do." The train pulls into the station, and I start to push forward, figuring I can grab a two-seater. But as the other commuters surge around us, Dan puts his hand on my arm. "Can we get out of here? Do you have time for a cup of coffee?"

"Miss this train?" I ask, in disbelief. He must have some big problem to talk about. "I mean, sure. Of course." There's always the 8:17. Or if it's a major problem, the 8:41. And getting more coffee—I've had only two cups this morning—can't hurt. Great diuretic. With Jacques coming here in a few days, I need to get rid of this bloat any way I can.

At the Starbucks across from the train station, I ask for a venti toffee nut latte—not ordering sprinkles saves me fifty calories—and Dan gets a small Earl Grey tea.

"I'm leaving Lucy," Dan says as soon as we sit down.

"*What?*"

He doesn't repeat it. I put down the latte and wipe the froth from my mouth with a scratchy napkin. Should have gotten the sprinkles. I could use a surge of chocolate-fueled serotonin right now.

"No. No, you're not. No way," I say. "You'd never leave. You love her."

"Lucy's having an affair. Which you probably already know. I might be the only person on earth who didn't."

I don't say anything for a long time. Then I realize that whether or not I know isn't the point here. "People have affairs all the time," I say finally. "It doesn't have to end a marriage. Sometimes it's just stupid. A fling that doesn't really mean anything."

"I know that," Dan says. But at the moment, he doesn't seem to know anything at all. He stares at his tea, as if confounded by how he's supposed to drink through the straw hole in the lid.

"It's crazy to leave," I say, leaning over the table to take the bubble cover off the cup for him. "There's got to be a better solution."

"I don't think so. At least not now."

"Lucy hasn't said a word to me about your going," I say, wondering how my best friend forgot to share this little tidbit.

"Just happened. We were up all night. I found out and finally confronted her. I've sensed something was wrong for a while, and I guess I haven't wanted to know. But if this is how she's behaving and she doesn't love me, then screw it, we're over."

"Of course Lucy loves you," I say firmly. "I mean, I saw you two at the science fair the other night. You looked so happy together. With the kids and everything. I was thinking that after all these years, you're still in love."

"*Were* in love. Past tense," Dan says. "Sure, we're pretty good with the family thing. But Lucy says she wants adventure. Excitement. Something new every day. And she doesn't get that with me."

"She said that?" I blurt out, surprised that even Lucy would have been that callous.

"Not right away. First she apologized and kept saying how much she loves me. But I wasn't buying it. If you're in love with your husband, you don't screw around. Then she was trying to explain. As if it could be explained. She's bored. We've been married a long time. The kids are leaving soon. Well, great, she's practically a cliché. But that doesn't mean I have to play the long-suffering husband."

"Maybe it's just a phase. Not a very pleasant phase, I admit, but a phase. You just have to ride it out. You and Lucy will get through it."

"I'm not sure I want to get through it," Dan says defiantly. "This didn't just happen overnight. We've been on a downward slide for months. She's been distant. I go to work, she goes to work. When we talk, it's only to figure out logistics for the kids. The last time we had fun was probably Coney Island, 1997."

"You went to Coney Island?" I ask, distracted for a moment by the image of Lucy eating a Nathan's hot dog—with or without the sauerkraut—and riding the Cyclone.

"Yeah, once."

"Was it safe? I've never been to Brooklyn."

"Never?" Dan asks, momentarily distracted himself. "Wait, didn't we all once go to a Lou Reed concert at BAM?"

"That was Brooklyn?"

"Brooklyn Academy of Music," Dan says, finally smiling. "Remember you crossed a bridge? Brooklyn Bridge?"

"At least I didn't buy it," I offer. "And see, that was a fun night. And just a couple of years ago."

Dan nods solemnly, falling back into his dour mood. "Okay, we've had our good moments. Glad we have the videos. But I don't see any more terrific times ahead for me and Lucy. If she wants her own life, I'll have my own life, too. Have my own adventures. See how she likes that."

"She won't," I say. "You're just hurt right now. Don't make any hasty decisions. Give it some time."

"Sure," Dan grumbles. "I won't call the realtor until this afternoon."

I hear the cell phone in my tote ringing. It's probably the other side checking in and I bet Lucy's even more upset than Dan. I've done all I can here for the moment and my services are needed elsewhere. Boulder, Dan, Lucy. If I take on one more client, New York State's going to require me to get a counseling license.

Dan glances at his Rolex, a birthday gift from Lucy. I wonder if he's going to throw it out now and replace it with a symbol of his new adventurous life. Probably the TAG Heuer chronograph that will tell him the time in six zones, the altitude when he's mountain climbing and the depth of the deep blue sea when he's scuba diving. And he's going to need it. He's about to be in for some extreme highs and lows.

"Should we catch the next train?" I ask Dan, finishing off my latte and eager to call back Lucy.

"Nope. You go ahead," Dan says, putting the lid back on his tea. "I've had it. I'm taking the day off."

"The whole day off? That's not like you. What are you going to do?"

"Anything I want. Just like Lucy. I can do anything I please. Just as soon as I figure out what that is."

When I call Lucy from the train and tell her I've just been in Starbucks with Dan, she's relieved that she doesn't have to break the news to me.

"I'm so upset. I've been popping blueberries and Ativan all morning," she says.

"Ativan? On top of everything else are your allergies acting up again?"

"No, that's Claritin for allergies. Although I probably should take one of those too. My nose has been stuffy."

"Crying?" I ask.

"Oh, right, that's probably why. Anything I can take for that?"

"I don't know. What does the Ativan do?"

"It's a benzodiazepine," she says helpfully, as if that explains everything.

"Yeah . . ." I coax.

"I don't know exactly. My assistant Tracey gave me one with a Diet Coke. She says she takes them all the time when I yell at her. Calms you down. Takes the edge off."

"And the blueberries?" I know we'll get to Dan eventually.

"Atkins."

"I thought that was the diet where you eat bacon cheeseburgers without the bread."

"Too many people were switching to Weight Watchers. Atkins had to add blueberries to compete."

"When they add ice cream sign me up."

Lucy sighs. "You're right. Screw Atkins. You want to meet for ice cream as soon as you get in the city?"

"That'll be 9:42."

"Perfect," says Lucy, obviously off her diet and slightly out of her mind.

Sure enough, when I get to Serendipity 3, Lucy is sitting with a huge ice cream sundae in front of her.

"It's called the 'Kitchen Sink,' " she says. "Can I order one for you?" She dips her spoon into the bowl, swirling up a mouthful from the six scoops of ice cream, hot fudge sauce, caramel, bananas, whipped cream, nuts, and maraschino cherries. Four of them. At least they don't have red dye no. 3 anymore.

"I don't think I need a whole sink," I say diplomatically. "Maybe just a taste of yours."

Lucy looks down trying to decide if she can spare a spoonful. "No, I'll order you your own," she says. "I think I'm going to need all of this. Seems to be working better than the Ativan."

Or maybe everything's just starting to kick in. Including the reality of what she's done.

"Did Dan seem really upset when you talked to him?" she asks.

"He was threatening to leave, but I'm sure he won't." She goes for another scoop then drops the spoon back down. "That stupid Le Retreat. It's all their fault. They're supposed to be so discreet. And instead, they're a bunch of idiots. Hello, the room was registered in both our names. Hunter Green is not 'Mr. Baldor.' "

"Huh?" I say, feeling like my edges are getting fuzzy. "What happened?"

She licks some hot fudge off the tip of the spoon, then sighs. "Hunter forgot his watch in the room and for some moronic reason they sent it back to Pine Hills, addressed to 'Mr. Baldor.' So Dan opens it thinking it's for him and there's Hunter's Rolex. The one I gave him for his birthday that I'd inscribed on the back: TO HUNTER, HUGS AND KISSES, L."

"Lucy, are you out of your mind? You bought both Dan and Hunter Rolexes?"

"I expensed Hunter's to the TV pilot," she says dismissively. "He'll wear it on camera."

"Have you no decency? You don't buy two men the same watch," I say, as if I have experience with these things.

"I know," Lucy says mournfully. "I'd do anything for another chance. I'd definitely get Hunter the Baume & Mercier."

"You're in trouble," I tell her bluntly.

"Dan's mad?"

"Yeah, Dan's mad. And that threat to leave sounded pretty real to me."

"Hunter says he'll marry me," Lucy announces. "It was the first thing he said this morning when I told him what'd happened. Actually, it was the second thing. He was really happy they found the Rolex."

"And marrying Hunter's going to be your solution?" I ask, dumbfounded.

"No, I don't think I want to marry him. But you never know. If Dan's going to be so impossible, everything's up for grabs. It's amazing, isn't it? I thought my husband loved me, and now this." She plays with a spoonful of ice cream and then decides to eat it. And another one. And another one after that.

"Lucy, may I point out that you're the one having an affair? Did it ever occur to you that maybe Dan thinks you don't love him?"

"Don't be ridiculous. We've been married forever. He knows I love him. I tell him every day. Well, maybe not every day. But he knows."

This is starting to give me a headache. Maybe that counseling license isn't such a good idea.

"You have to understand this is serious, Luce. Stop pretending it's some little spat over not putting the cap back on the toothpaste. Dan's talking about calling the realtor and you're sitting here self-medicating."

"Self-medicating? I just took one Ativan. Don't be so dramatic."

"Not the pills. The ice cream. You've eaten enough to send the defensive line of the Pittsburgh Steelers into sugar shock. And you don't seem to give a hoot. Two days ago you would have run three miles if you'd slipped up and had an orange Popsicle."

"Okay, I'll run this afternoon," Lucy says lackadaisically, completely missing my point. "Anyway, I don't want to talk about this anymore. Cheer me up. Give me some good news. What's up with Jacques?"

I sigh. "I don't know if this will brighten your day or not. But he's taking me to a fancy inn in Vermont when he comes Friday night."

"Jacques in Vermont?" Lucy says, indeed perking up. "Does he know they have cows there?"

"He thought it would be romantic." I laugh. "Somewhere far away where all we have to think about is each other."

"Did he have his inoculations?"

"He's totally up to date. Malaria. Dengue fever. Leptospirosis. Mad cow disease. Just in case."

"So when do I get to meet him?" Lucy asks. "Weren't the four of us supposed to have dinner? I remember Dan saying that."

The ice cream's working—really has numbed her brain. How can we have a foursome when it's not clear that Lucy has a twosome? "You'll meet him," I offer vaguely. "By the way, with everything going on, can you cope with having Jen this weekend? That still okay?"

"Why wouldn't it be?" asks the Princess of Denial. Make that the Queen. Lucy's always the best at what she does.

"Listen," Lucy sighs, "you should get going. You've babysat me long enough now. You must have stuff to do." She looks ruefully at the rest of the supersized dish in front of her. "And I have at least another four thousand calories to plow through."

"Well, enjoy yourself," I say. "And don't give up. I hear that if you polish off one Kitchen Sink you can get another one. On the house."

Last time I went to Vermont, I spent six hours trapped in a car, stopped twice to use grimy restrooms, got a ticket at a speed trap and spilled a Roy Rogers chocolate shake all over my white shorts when I slammed on the breaks to avoid two Canadian geese crossing the road. Should have sued—but whom? Canada? Mother Goose? Roy Rogers? Dale Evans? Anyway, the shorts looked kind of hip with that brown-and-white tie-dye look.

But on this trip I'm snuggled next to Jacques six thousand feet in the air, looking out the helicopter window at the rolling hills, meandering streams, and yes, cows. I'm loving Vermont, or maybe I'm loving that Jacques and I are kissing and caressing for the entire one-hour ride. When we land, I manage to get out from under the whirring blades with my head intact, if not my hairdo. As we dash away, Jacques has his arm protectively around my shoulders and I feel like I'm a 1940s movie heroine being whisked off by Cary Grant.

The Bradford Inn could be right out of a movie, too. Though not from the 1940s. Looks more like it was decorated by Betsy Ross—and updated by Terence Conran. There's a huge antique brass bed, but instead of a handmade lace throw, it's covered by a distinctly modern geometric-patterned comforter. An authentic hand-woven rag rug rests gracefully next to the bed, but sits on top of plush wall-to-wall carpeting. An oversized rosewood Early American hutch houses a flat-screened TV, a DVD player and a Bose sound system, all of which are controlled by remotes on either side of the bed. Another modern dilemma. Who drives the remote if you each have one?

But Jacques doesn't need a remote to take control. We've barely closed the door when he pins me against the wall.

"At last," he says, kissing me hard and urgently pressing his body into mine.

I drop the cashmere cardigan I've been holding and wrap my arms around Jacques' waist, leaning in to kiss him languidly. But Jacques' usual slow tempo seems to be on fast forward. With little prelude, he pulls my T-shirt over my head and grabs hungrily at my breasts.

"I want to make love to you right here," he says, tugging at his belt and pushing me forcefully against the wall.

Well, okay. Sounds interesting. But I could use a little more build-up. Maybe he's counting that hour of kissing on the helicopter as fore-play. But that was airplay. Aren't there rules about starting over once you change altitude? I better stop thinking and just get into this.

Jacques is standing in front of me, completely naked now. Obviously ready to go. I'm a couple of steps behind.

"Are you all right, my darling?" he asks.

"No" seems like too complicated an answer. We can make love if that's what he wants. So what if I don't have an orgasm. It's going to be a long weekend. My turn will come. And I remember reading some-where that sex standing up is good exercise for your quadriceps.

Jacques doesn't seem to notice that I'm not totally on his wave-length, and within minutes, he explodes with pleasure inside me. I don't exactly fake it, but I make a few murmurings of satisfaction, truly enjoying his excitement.

"That was wonderful, yes, darling?" he asks, now gently stroking my cheek.

"Yes," I whisper back, eyeing the bed and thinking how nice it would be just to lie down under that comforter and luxuriate in his strong arms.

But we seem to be totally out of synch today because Jacques has other ideas.

"So," he says, pulling away and heading toward the bathroom. "I have a plan. Canoeing?"

Canoeing? Could we make that canoodling? I look longingly again at the bed, which is clearly going to stay unrumpled for a while longer. Maybe we're both getting older. Took me too long to get in the mood and now he wants a respite before round two. In the old days, making love with me was the only activity he seemed interested in. Now it's just one item on the list.

Jacques quickly pulls on a pair of shorts—Nautica, of course, we're going boating—and I head to the enormous double-sinked bathroom for a quick shower.

"Don't take too long," he calls out as I'm soaping up.

"Why are we rushing?" I ask.

"Don't want the river to go dry," he calls back, joking.

We get down to the boathouse with plenty of time and water to spare, and Jacques pulls a two-person canoe to the edge of the beach.

"Hop in," he tells me, slipping two paddles into the bottom of the boat and extending a helping hand.

I climb awkwardly into the boat and perch precariously on the front seat.

"Get on your knees," Jacques commands.

Figures. I just showered and now he's ready for another go.

But he goes around to the stern, explaining that I need to kneel to keep the boat balanced. He manfully pushes the canoe away from the shore, running until he's knee-deep in water, then jumps into the boat.

"Do you know how to stroke?" he asks, handing me one paddle and taking his own. He gives me a sixty-second lesson in paddling procedures and reminds me that since he's in the stern, he sets the pace and I'm supposed to follow along. The theme of the day.

"Stroke, feather, stroke, feather!" he barks. I manage to keep up, and the boat moves briskly, cutting cleanly through the water. This is more fun than I thought. But in a few minutes, my unaerobicized arms begin to ache and my paddle strokes get weaker. Doesn't seem to matter. The boat's still going straight and fast.

"You can relax, *mon amour,*" Jacques calls out from behind. "I can handle this alone. Let me take care of you."

I can live with that. I lean back, enjoying the warmth of the day, the sun sparkling on the water, and the glorious backdrop of green mountains. We glide blissfully through the quick current, the water making a peaceful, thwacking sound as it laps against the sides of the aluminum canoe. Looking out at the passing panorama on the shoreline of thick maple trees, distant farmlands, and tiny twittering birds, I realize how nice it is to have a strong man behind me, guiding the way.

I close my eyes and settle into the moment. How easy life can be when you're part of a couple. When there's someone else's strength to rely on. My mind is drifting when there's suddenly a loud splash in the water, and the boat jerks precipitously to the side.

"What . . ." I spin around and see Jacques swimming powerfully alongside the boat.

"The water is delicious," he calls out. "I couldn't resist. Just a short swim. I'll be right back."

So much for someone to rely on.

Figuring I can keep pace with Jacques, I dip my paddle into the placid water. But instead of going straight ahead, the boat veers around in a circle to the left. Did I learn nothing at Camp Nepakawanee? Nope, I didn't. Unless you count braiding lanyards. I try putting the paddle on the other side and now the boat makes a circle to the right.

Goddamn Jacques. Why did he leave me alone here?

Okay, I can handle this. I flex my arm, get the boat straightened out, and to my enormous surprise, start moving forward. I'm feeling confident and humming bits of a boating medley—"Michael Row Your Boat Ashore," "Bridge Over Troubled Waters," and "Down by the River I Shot My Baby." Given that last one, maybe I'm madder at Jacques than I realize. The current picks up, making my paddling all the easier. I notice some rocks just ahead and steer clear of them. Gosh, I'm good. A small swirling rapid coming up doesn't look too dangerous, but just to be safe, I pull the boat in the opposite direction.

The canoe slams hard into a slab of jutting rock and I hear the heart-stopping crash of metal as the boat flies into the air and flips on its keel.

Suddenly it's pitch-dark and I'm flailing around at the bottom of the river, flapping my arms furiously, like a trapped otter. Water is filling my nose and my lungs feel like they're exploding. Can I be drowning this fast? My foot seems caught between two rocks and I can't pry it loose. Definitely drowning, except my life isn't passing before my eyes. I can't panic. Oh yes I can. Isn't this how Meryl Streep died in *River Wild*? No, she couldn't have died. That was her only commercial movie.

I reach down and with strength I never knew I had, push at the rock and wrench my foot free. I'm so disoriented that I'm not sure which way is up, but I kick as hard as I can and power myself to what I think is the surface. Only there's no sky or sun—it's still dark. I stretch my arm over my head and hear the echo of my hand banging on the aluminum boat. Okay, thank god, I'm safe. I'm in an air pocket. I take a deep breath and dive down to swim out from under the boat when all of a sudden I feel a pair of strong arms around my waist, holding me back. It must be Jacques, trying to rescue me, but this isn't the way to do it. I try to shake free, but the harder I pull away, the tighter he holds on.

Now I do see my life passing before me. How the heck do you scream "Let me go!" underwater? We struggle—he pulling, me pushing, but both of us finally bobbing to the surface, sputtering and coughing.

"I have you!" Jacques calls, bracing his arm around me in the Red Cross–approved cross-chest carry position and dragging along my waterlogged body. "The shore isn't far. Hang on. Just *deux minutes.*"

The shore? What about the boat? I catch a glimpse of it, still upside down, being whisked by the current far away from us downstream.

And then as we get to the sandy embankment on the side of the river, I utter my first words since tragedy struck.

"My Stephane Kelian sandals!" I scream at Jacques. "I bought them just for this trip! Why didn't you rescue those?"

"I rescued *you*," he says petulantly. "I saved your life. Am I not your hero boy?"

I look down at my sandalless foot, which is scraped and bleeding.

Is it fair to blame that on Jacques? You betcha. Who left whom alone in the boat?

"What do we do now, hero boy?" I ask, looking around at the river to the left and the thick forest to the right.

"Too far to swim back. We walk. *Marchons*," he says, heading toward the trees.

I follow him and we pass single file through the thick underbrush. I'm soaked through and chilled to the bone. I should probably take off this wet T-shirt, but I'm not ready to have Jacques see me in a bathing suit. Even though he sees me naked when we're making love. Maybe if I'd lost more weight he'd at least offer to carry me.

We trundle on for what seems like miles—but isn't—until up ahead, I spy a ray of light and a clearing. I happily head toward the sunny field—and civilization.

"A farmhouse!" I say excitedly. I start a hobbled run, but I'm stopped short by a barbed-wire fence that is holding back a herd of— can it be?—Vermont's fabled cows. Spotted brown and white, just like my Roy Rogers–splattered shorts.

"Don't get too close, these fences are always electrified," Jacques warns knowingly from behind. When did hero boy turn into Farmer Jack? He walks parallel, a few feet down the fence. "Look," he says encouragingly. "This part's slightly raised. We can crawl under right here. Flat on our bellies."

I don't have a flat belly. And then there's the issue of my ample butt. But Jacques is already on the ground, and in an instant, he slithers snakelike right under the fence. I don't hear any sizzling sounds, so I prepare to follow him. I tuck in my tush and pull in my tummy, just like they taught me at Lotte Berk. The instructor always said that good posture is a lifesaver, although I don't think this is what she had in mind.

Once past the electrified fence, I stand up proudly, only to confront the next obstacle. A herd of curious cows coming toward us.

"Take off your shorts!" I scream to Jacques. "Quickly!"

"Not here, darling," he says, taking my hand. "Let's wait till we get back to the inn."

"No, the shorts! They're red!" I say frantically, tugging at his waistband. "Take them off now. The cows will charge!"

"*Non, non, mon petit chouchou,*" he says tousling my wet curls and kissing my nose. "Cows are the women. They're docile. It's the bulls that charge."

Docile? I'll show him docile. Although I'm more than a little relieved to hear that Elsie's not a killer.

But then a new thought crosses my mind.

"How do you know there aren't any bulls around?"

"Never in the same field. They only get together to mate. Otherwise the males are too aggressive."

Tell me about it.

We nudge aside the inquiring herd and pick our way through the cow patties. Well, this is pleasant. Now I'm bloody and muddy and I probably smell like dung—which is obviously an aphrodisiac, because Jacques chooses this precise minute to throw his arms around me and pull me close to him in a deep kiss.

"You know, *ma petite,* you're right. We should make love right here."

"In the pasture? Haven't we already paid for the room?" I shake my head. "Anyway, don't you think the day's had enough drama?"

"Drama? What drama?" he asks, raising an eyebrow.

Surely he jests. "I almost drowned," I tell him sternly. "The electric fence could have killed us. And who knows about these stampeding cows."

Jacques bursts out laughing. "Oh, this was nothing more than a—how you say? Boy Scout hike."

And my Boy Scout is always prepared. So why not. The sun is shining, the cows are mooing, and he's deciding that I was right about those red shorts after all. They're coming off.

That night, after one of our famous bubble baths, I'm finally nestled under the Pratesi comforter with my head cradled on Jacques' shoulder. All is forgiven. Two orgasms, a bottle of Veuve Clicquot and a candlelit dinner will do that for you. We're drifting off to sleep when a loud beeping sound makes me drowsily lift my head.

"The fire alarm?" I ask, not sure whether to be worried or annoyed. And I thought today's adventures were over.

"No, just my mobile," Jacques says, getting out of bed. He glances at the caller ID, walks to the far corner of the room, and then, in a muffled voice, whispers into his cell phone, *"Bonjour, ma chérie."*

Well maybe there is another adventure in store. Just not the kind I was planning. I roll over and pretend to go back to sleep.

"Oui, Vermont est très belle. J'ai vu les vaches aujourd'hui."

He saw cows today. That doesn't sound too romantic.

"J'ai nage, aussi."

You're damn right he went swimming. But who would care? Sister? Secretary? Girlfriend? Make that a girlfriend other than me.

He continues talking for a few more minutes, but the conversation never gets more exciting. Until the end.

"Je reviens tout de suite." I'll be back soon. And then after a long pause, he adds, *"Moi aussi."*

Me too? Me too what? Not a good sign.

He gets back into bed, curls up around me and strokes my hair.

"I'm sorry, *ma petite.* Just some unfinished business I had to take care of. Sorry it disturbed you."

How disturbed should I be? I don't know, but I want to.

"Who was that?" I ask quietly. "Do you mind if I ask?"

"Of course I don't mind," he says, gently kissing my neck. "You can always ask me anything. I will always tell you. I want that you are happy. We should have no secrets. *Bien?"*

Bien, I think, as mollified, I fall asleep in his arms. And it's not until I wake up much later that I realize he never answered the question.

Chapter TWELVE

"ARE YOU ALONE?"

It's Lucy, calling Monday at midnight. Like Wal-Mart, she's up and running twenty-four hours a day. And this time she's not even in L.A.

"Yup. I'm alone. Why?" I flip off Jon Stewart. Now that I hang with Boulder, I'm way too hip for Jay Leno.

"I'm looking for Dan," she says anxiously "Do you know where he is?"

"Not here," I say, in case that's what she's suggesting.

"I know he's not *there*." She sounds so patronizing that I briefly wonder why Dan *couldn't* be here. What's the matter, I'm not pretty enough?

"Dan never came home last night," Lucy says. "I'm beside myself. He hasn't called. I'm worried that he was in a car accident."

"But he never drives," I point out. "He always takes the train."

"Then a train accident," Lucy says. "Maybe he touched the third rail. What else could have happened to him?"

I have lots of answers, none of which she's likely to appreciate. "Could be he's taking some time to think," I suggest.

"That's what his study is for," she says, sounding slightly irritated.

"A place for him to relax. I just redecorated last year. In earth tones, very masculine. And he has his own Herman Miller chair. An original."

"I always liked that chair."

"I know. You have one, too."

"No I don't. Mine's a copy. But I saved two thousand dollars and you couldn't tell the difference anyway."

"Yes, I could have. If I'd looked. The armrests are always different," says Lucy, torn between being defensive, distracted and worried. "But anyway, do you think Dan's all right? He's not in his office. He's not answering his cell. It's goddamn midnight. Doesn't he care that I'm worried about him?"

Lucy's feelings might not be high on his list right now. If I know the ever-practical Dan, the soaring costs of rentals in Manhattan and the fact that he doesn't have a clean pair of socks to wear tomorrow are probably all he can deal with tonight. Best I can tell, he OD'd on emotion a few days ago. Now he's probably just going for a plan of action. Any action.

"I'm sure he's fine," I say. But I do wonder where he is. The Carlyle? The Pussycat Club? Camped out in Central Park with a bottle of gin? Not Dan. My guess is he's tossing fitfully on the couch in his office.

"Somebody should tell him that this isn't the way to win me back," Lucy grumbles. "But if you're alone, that means Jacques's not there. How come?"

"Had to fly to Washington for some meetings. He's coming back this weekend. And we're not doing anything that has to do with canoes or cows."

"Want to surprise him when he gets back?" Lucy asks. "We could do something to make you really beautiful."

Not pretty enough for either Dan or Jacques, I guess. Amazing they let me out of the house. "Didn't know I look that bad," I say.

"That's not what I meant at all," she says appeasingly. "It's just that now that we're over forty—I hate saying that number out loud—we have to be realistic. Give Mother Nature a helping hand."

"She did pretty well on the trees, the flowers, and Mount Rushmore," I say. "Did she do so badly on me?"

"Darling, Mother Nature didn't make Mount Rushmore. That's the one with the presidents. See, even the mountains needed some cosmetic work. A little chiseling, a little nipping, a little shot now and then."

I sigh. We've been around this block before. "No way I'm getting Botox injections," I remind her. "And no way I'm seeing your favorite plastic surgeon again. Once in Dr. Peter Paulo's apartment was enough, thank you. I don't need to go to his office."

"Oh, forget about Peter. I don't go to him anymore," Lucy says, shrugging off Dr. Paulo as being as yesterday as Jenny Jones or Susan Powter. Wonder whatever happened to her. Disappeared faster than the pounds she was supposed to help you lose.

"So who's the new miracle worker?" I ask. "Annie Sullivan?"

"Better," Lucy laughs. "Dr. Herb Parnell. He has a new book that's going to be huge. *The Needle of Youth*. There's a bagels-and-Botox book signing party for him tomorrow."

"That's an interesting menu," I say. "Actually, I prefer my bagels with cream cheese."

"But this is so much fun," Lucy says. "You eat a little, you have a happy hour, and you all have your Botox done together."

"Of course it's a happy hour. You can't move your face to frown," I say. "Anyway, how much does this little Botox-and-lox event cost?"

"No lox—it's in Connecticut," Lucy says. "And since it's a book party, the shots are free. Besides, it's at Dahlia Hammerschmidt's. You'll love seeing her country estate."

"Dahlia Hammerschmidt? I thought she was Dr. Paulo's patient."

Lucy pauses, suitably impressed. "Jess, you never know anything about anyone. How in heaven's name did you know that?"

For once, I'm feeling unbearably smug. Liz Smith has nothing on me. At least I don't think she does.

"Not revealing my sources," I say.

"Oh, I've got it," Lucy says, making a quick deduction. "I bet

Peter was name-dropping during your date. Seduction by celebrity-association. That's so New Jersey of him. Just one of the reasons we've all moved on. Well, that and the rumor about Farrah Fawcett's droopy eyelid. Not that I ever believed it."

I sigh. "So what's so good about this latest Merlin? Other than that he's newer than the old one?"

"He's got the latest of everything," Lucy says conspiratorially. "All the drugs that haven't been FDA approved yet."

"That's confidence-inspiring. I thought FDA approval was a good thing."

"Please, they move way too slowly for us. At our age we can't wait for those ten-year studies. What's the worst? You blow a few dollars and it doesn't work?"

"Or you blow a few dollars and end up dead. But with a perfectly unlined complexion."

"At least you look good for your funeral," Lucy says flippantly. "Be ready. I'll pick you up at three."

Lucy pulls up to my house in a flashy silver Porsche 911 Carrera convertible. The top is down and she's wearing dark oversized sunglasses with a scarf tied around her hair.

"I didn't know I was going to Connecticut with Grace Kelly," I say, climbing in and landing on the low-slung seat with a thud. "What's this all about?"

"Traded in the Mercedes. Way too matronly. Fabulous acceleration on this baby," Lucy says, zooming away from the curb.

"But a silver Porsche?"

"Trite, isn't it," Lucy says, smirking as she revs past a gawking teenage boy in a Honda Accord. "Turn forty-two and buy a sports car to try to prove I'm still young. Just like the guys. Midlife crises are equal opportunity these days."

"My understanding was you have an affair *or* you buy the midlife crisis car. How come you get both?"

"Just lucky," she says, lovingly stroking the stick shift.

"Guess when I have my midlife crisis I'll have to get a tattoo or dye my hair purple. I never learned to drive a manual."

"Neither did I," Lucy admits. "On this car, you can leave it in automatic. Then the stick's just there for show."

"Wonder if Mario Andretti used it that way." I want to stretch my cramped legs, but there's no room. Lucy turns onto the highway and whips into the left lane. My hair is flying wildly around my head and I try to tie it back with my fingers. Lucy purses her lips, jams her foot on the gas and hits eighty.

"A little reckless today?" I ask, clutching the sides of my seat.

"Sorry," she says, dropping back down to seventy-five. "Check the glove compartment. I have just what you need."

"A steel-plated crash helmet, I hope." But I should know better. I reach in and find an extra head scarf. Won't save my life, but at least it's Gucci.

By the time we hit Route 7 in Connecticut, I'm enjoying the wind in my face and the envious glances of every man we pass who's trapped in a family sedan. I'm starting to feel like the coolest girl in high school—if only my aching, scrunched-up knees weren't reminding me that I won't be trying out for the cheerleading squad anytime soon. With Metallica blaring from the CD player, we pull into Dahlia Hammerschmidt's circular driveway and the young valet eyes us—or maybe the car—approvingly. Lucy springs out and tosses him the keys.

"Hope you can drive stick," she challenges as she waltzes away.

We walk past perfectly manicured hedges that must keep a topiary-team of Japanese gardeners working 24/7. I can't even keep my bushes from drooping over into the neighbor's yard, and Dahlia's evergreens are a menagerie of bears and elephants. Once inside the massive ornamented front door, a butler hands us a small bound pamphlet with a grand, curlicued title page that reads "The Hammerschmidts at Versailles." I look helplessly at Lucy.

"Dahlia's ballroom is an exact replica of the Hall of Mirrors," Lucy whispers. "She figures if it was good enough for Marie Antoinette, it's good enough for her."

We walk down an endless parquet hallway hung with dozens of ancestral portraits. The Hammerschmidts have either a fine family tree or a good art dealer. Once we reach the football-field-sized ballroom, I stop short, awed. Probably the desired effect. The room is done entirely in white and gold and mirrors—the same decorating scheme of every apartment I've ever seen in Miami. But this faux-French rendering boasts a dozen enormous hanging cut-crystal chandeliers, two-dozen statues of gold nymphets hoisting up shimmering candelabras, and enough three-story-high arched French doors and windows to have kept the Pella company busy for two years. Dahlia even copied the red velvet ropes currently used at Versailles to block eager tourists from touching the gilded treasures. Apparently nobody told her Louis XVI wasn't the one who put them there.

Lucy spots an editor of *Allure* across the room and goes off to compare notes on their slow-weight training class. Talk about the latest. Instead of hours in the gym pumping iron, the new in-the-know technique requires hefting something the weight of a small Brinks truck just once or twice. Verrrryy slowwwly. Makes no sense, but apparently it works. Just twenty minutes a week and they both look like goddesses. Muscle-spasmed goddesses, but goddesses. I decide to get something to eat, but all I can find here at Versailles-on-the-Housatonic are a few bacon-wrapped figs and one tiny tray of cucumber sandwiches with the crusts cut off. Dahlia must be very, very rich, if she can afford not to feed her guests and expect them to come back.

But obviously they do. Looking around, I realize the room is packed with celebrities—or people who think they are. Fox News anchors, '70s sitcom stars, and the local weather woman from WPIX. Wouldn't they prefer to get their Botox shots in private? No, maybe not. Letting people know you've had plastic surgery is the fastest way to land a *People* cover these days. Right behind starting a twelve-step program for sex addiction. Or hiring a surrogate to give birth to your babies, preferably triplets.

Lucy comes wafting back, trailed by an attractive, bespectacled doctor in a polo shirt and cashmere jacket. The man of the hour. And dressed right. If you're performing appendectomies, hospital scrubs and white lab coats offer reassurance. But for elective beauty procedures, good looks and a custom wardrobe are the ticket.

"Jess, darling, meet the fabulous Dr. Herb Parnell. Every girl's new best friend."

"Nice to meet you," he says, scrutinizing me as he extends his hand, and I notice his long tapered fingers. Concert pianist might have been a more fulfilling career option. Or maybe not. "Lucy tells me you're a virgin."

"Plastic surgically speaking, of course," Lucy adds hastily.

Ever the professional, Dr. Parnell appraises my face. "Even if it's your first time, you'll be easy," he says cupping my chin. "A little Botox on the forehead. Some Cymetra under the cheekbone. A couple of shots of Restylane around the lips. And CosmoDerm to fill in the laugh lines around your eyes. You're lucky, not too much damage yet. Two, three dozen injections tops and we're done."

Done with what? With any chance to remember that forty isn't twenty and doesn't have to be? The good things about getting older— wisdom, experience, all that—are fine, but I guess nobody wants them to show up on her face. Still, how can you age gracefully if you're at the doctor's office all the time?

"Why would I need an injection under my cheekbones?" I ask Dr. Parnell, curious despite myself. "And what did you say would go there? The one that sounded like a new STD?"

"Cymetra. My new favorite," he answers, warming to the subject. "All pure. Made from ground-up human skin. A little hard to get since it's made from cadavers. We're fighting for FDA approval. But my real dream is to have it part of the donor form on the back of your license."

What an idea. Who wouldn't jump at the chance to make the ultimate sacrifice and save someone from a lifetime of wrinkles?

"He's recommended Artefill for me," Lucy bubbles enthusiastically. "For my laugh lines. Lasts longer than regular collagen. It's got acrylic beads in it."

"The beads stimulate your skin to make its own collagen," Dr. Parnell explains. "There is a little downside, though. Sometimes the beads show through. Especially if you have thin skin."

"That won't be a problem for me," Lucy says cavalierly. "Can't last in my business with thin skin."

We've obviously monopolized the book-writing doctor long enough, because just then, Dahlia Hammerschmidt sashays over. A diminutive woman in size only, with pouffed-up hair, pushed-up breasts and diamond jewelry that weighs more than she does, she drapes a proprietary arm around Dr. Parnell's waist.

"Howya doin, *Hoib*?" Dahlia asks in a perfect New Yawk accent, which reveals that she isn't old money, she just married it. "Everything still hunky-dory?"

"I'm great," he says, beaming. He stands up a little straighter—not taller, but straighter—blossoming under her doting attention.

"You all know this boy's the best, don't ya?" she asks, squeezing his arm and pressing herself a little closer to him.

"You're too nice to me," he says, pretending to be modest, but obviously basking in her adulation. I always wonder how some women do that—make a man feel ten feet tall even if he's barely five-foot-eight. If I went all honey-tongued and pressed myself against a guy, I don't think I'd get the same results. I've never been good at obsequious. Can spell it, though. Which gets me almost nowhere.

"Another drink, sweetie?" asks Dahlia, still hanging—make that dripping—on "Hoib."

Another drink? Isn't he going to be wielding needles soon? I'd like to think the AMA is at least as strict as the pilots' union. No alcohol consumption for six hours before going on the job.

Dahlia signals a waiter who takes away one empty glass and hands the enthralled Herb a refill. Thank goodness. Seltzer.

"Bottoms up," Dahlia says, taking wine for herself and clicking glasses with her guest of honor. "As soon as you're done, I have seven guests ready for their Botox. Don't worry. They've already bought your book. All you have to do is sign and shoot."

Herb takes a final gulp of seltzer, and lacking a scrub sink, wipes his palms along the side of his pants. Then moving to the center of the ballroom, he sits down at a white and gilded Louis XVI desk and lines up half a dozen ballpoint pens and an equal number of hypodermics.

A nurse—or at least someone in a white uniform—makes her way through the gaggle of waiting women. "Ladies, who wants Emla? Emla anyone?" she asks perkily.

"Numbing cream," Lucy translates for me.

Most of the women accept her offer. Using a long cotton-tipped stick, the nurse swabs their foreheads with a greasy ointment, then slaps a piece of white gauze over it.

"Starting to look like a war zone," I say to Lucy. "What'll happen when they're done?"

"Just some light bruising," Lucy shrugs. "Usually, anyway. Though there was that one time when I got collagen and the needle marks looked like a row of bullet holes."

"Great. Maybe after this Botox party we can stage a little reenactment of the War of 1812."

Could be I really am the only virgin in the room, though, because nobody else seems to be paying much attention to the shooting gallery in the middle of the party. I, on the other hand, am riveted as the good—we hope—doctor yanks on a plastic surgical glove and picks up an oversized needle. His first patient eagerly comes forward.

"So the most beautiful woman steps up first," he says with an easy charm. A flattering line beats a Harvard Medical degree anytime. Especially if you want all the rich women in New York flocking to your door. "Scrunch that pretty forehead for me and we'll see if there's anything at all we need to fix."

She scrunches and he nods. "We can take care of this little problem quickly," he says, and rapidly begins shooting into the offending wrinkle. Three, four, five, six quick injections. I stop counting.

"Done," he says, smiling and bidding the nurse to get an ice pack. "You'll be perfect. But we want to make sure the Botox doesn't move around. You know the rules. Don't bend over or lie down for the next four hours."

"Another reason I could never have Botox," I say to Lucy as the first patient moves away, ice pack pressed to her forehead. "How could I ever go four hours without touching my toes or having sex?"

"You can have sex standing up," Lucy counters.

"I know," I say grimly. "Did that in Vermont."

"Good, then there's no reason not to have Botox," Lucy concludes, gently nudging me forward. "You can go ahead of me."

"That's okay." I snag the last of the bacon wraps from a passing waiter. "For now, I'll stick with food fat to fill in the wrinkles. Although usually what it does is fill out my hips."

"We can make that work to your advantage," Lucy advises with a laugh. "Herb can liposuction the fat from your thighs and inject it into your face. It's like winning the daily double."

An X-ray-thin octogenarian standing behind us waves her cane excitedly. "I've done it three times," she chirps. "You don't have to worry if you don't have enough fat of your own, because Herb will arrange for a lipo donor."

Lipo donor. Now there's a job I'm well equipped for. I pat my wholesome thighs. Who knew these chubby babies could open up a whole new career for me?

One woman after another comes up to Dr. Parnell for the scrunch and shoot. When it's finally Lucy's turn, she gives her copy of *The Needle of Youth* to Dr. Parnell who scrawls, "In Beauty We Trust," and hands it back to her.

"So what's up for you today?" Dr. Parnell asks, quickly getting down to business. "I don't see a lot of problems but give me a scrunch."

Lucy tries mightily but she can't. I know because I can see her nostrils flaring and her eyes half-closed. But her forehead is scrunch-proof.

"I just had Botox five weeks ago," she says apologetically. "But I was thinking I could use a booster."

"Don't think so. Nothing's moving," says Dr. Parnell. "Maybe some place other than the forehead?"

"Be careful not to overdose her or she'll die," I pipe in, as if I know what I'm talking about.

Dr. Parnell laughs tolerantly. "Nobody's ever died from Botox," he says.

Right. Botox is just botulism. I spent my whole life avoiding dented cans and now it's the choice *du jour*.

"One thing *has* been bothering me," Lucy says, glancing down at the deeply cut V-neck on her wrap dress.

Surely she can't be expecting Dr. Parnell to do on-the-spot breast implants. And why would she need them? Another new toy? Aren't the Porsche and the boyfriend enough?

"The top of my breasts are starting to get crinkly," Lucy whispers so softly you'd think she was a mole for the CIA. "There's some creasing."

Dr. Parnell traces an imaginary fault line on her chest. "I think it's just cleavage. But if it's bothering you, consider it gone," he says.

"How can you—" Lucy starts to ask. But Dr. Parnell's done talking. Before the question's even out of her mouth, he's stabbing a needle into her chest.

Lucy squeals and looks up, too startled to say anything.

Dr. Parnell points the glistening, used needle into the air and smiles proudly. "Botox. Love it. As far as I'm concerned, it's a miracle drug. Right up there with penicillin. Cures headaches. Backaches. Wrinkles. And why not cleavage crease. Can always find a new way to use it."

"New way?" Lucy asks, slightly tremulous from the unexpected shot. And the news that she's a guinea pig in the war against aging.

"The line is disappearing before my eyes," the doctor says approvingly. The line he never saw.

Lucy, slightly hunched over and rubbing the tender shot spot, walks away, looking vaguely shell-shocked as the octogenarian steps up for her turn. I step back, having seen enough, when suddenly Dahlia's at my side. I look her up and down, remembering that on my ill-fated blind date with Dr. Peter Paulo he'd said that Dahlia reminded him of me. He must have been really desperate for a line. Because except for the ten fingers and ten toes, I don't see it.

"You goin' next?" Dahlia asks me, eager as a Lucille Roberts telemarketer to initiate me into the club.

"Not doing it," I repeat for the thousandth time. "Not today."

Though I have to wonder why I'm holding out. The Botox babes look pretty good—in fact, darn good. Not at all like the androids I'd expected. And nobody's acting like it's a big deal. With Botox becoming as common as an American Express card, why leave home without it? Being natural might have once been a point of honor, now it's a point of embarrassment. To these women, aging without Botox is like wearing Birkenstocks—philosophically correct and comfortable, too. But you don't want anybody to see you doing it.

"I'd think twice about saying no to Botox," says Dahlia, who has two more cents to add. "No wedding ring, I notice. Gotta do what you can to compete." She winks and gestures grandly around her palace. "Think I got all this on my natural charms? Becoming Mr. Hammerschmidt's third wife wasn't exactly a cakewalk, ya know."

I pause reverently to think what might have been involved. The three B's? Back rubs, Botox and blow jobs? Given the size of this place, Dahlia probably made her way further through the alphabet than that. What starts with Z?

Lucy comes over, looking pale and clutching her chest.

"I think . . ." Lucy says, gasping for air. "I think I'm having a heart attack. The Botox. It must have paralyzed my heart muscles. I can't breathe."

"I'm sure that can't be," I say soothingly. Though who knows. What if she bent over or had sex while I wasn't looking?

"Not here, not here! You'll ruin Hoib's book party!" says the pint-sized Dahlia, rushing over and grabbing Lucy. With the strength of a Navy SEAL commando, she hauls her out of the room and dumps her unceremoniously in a royal bathroom which is twice the size of my living room.

"Lie down here," Dahlia directs, gesturing to an overstuffed love seat. Lucy, misunderstanding, settles onto the bidet.

"Maybe you should call an ambulance, just in case," I say, hustling in after them.

"Absolutely not," Dahlia says staunchly. "I've planned this event for months. There's a reporter here from the New York Post. No way I'm letting it be known as the heart-attack party."

She turns on her red suede Christian Louboutin heel and swivels out, slamming the door behind her. I have a feeling it's locked.

Lucy gets up and, clutching her chest, begins pacing around the bathroom. "Oh god, what an embarrassing way to die."

She lurches over to the medicine chest and throws it open.

"What are you looking for?"

"Aspirin. I heard it prevents heart attacks. Though maybe it's too late." She starts rifling through the vials and reading off labels. "Xanax, Zoloft, Lipitor, Ambien, Ativan, Percocet. Just what every well-stocked house needs. Everything but a goddamn aspirin." She pauses, studying two more bottles. "Viagra and birth control pills. How's that for a match made in heaven."

If Lucy's making jokes about Dahlia's sex life, she's probably not destined to die on the bidet.

Instead of swallowing a pill, Lucy turns on the gold faucet and runs some cold water on her wrists. She takes a few deep breaths, delicately rubs her temples, and sits down on the love seat as the color returns to her face.

"Feeling better?" I ask her.

"Feeling kind of stupid," she admits. "I think I just panicked. Maybe you're right. Pretty idiotic to put your life on the line for vanity. We're all getting way too obsessed with trying to look perfect."

Great. I'm starting to see the value of some renovation work and she's going natural.

Lucy rubs her chest. "He really did jab that needle in kind of deep," she says apologetically. "Scared me. For a minute there I had a flash that my obit would read TV PRODUCER AFRAID OF FORTY DIES OF BOTOX IN THE BOOBS."

"I can top that," I say, shaking my head. "Last weekend, mine was almost CLUMSY CANOER LOSES LIFE AND SHOES."

"At least neither of us ended up HEADLESS WOMAN IN TOPLESS BAR," Lucy says, invoking our favorite tabloid headline.

We both chuckle and I go over and put my arm around her shoulder. "Listen, of course you panicked. You're having a tough week," I say sympathetically.

"It's been more than a week," she says dispiritedly.

"Let's just get out of here," I say. "Grab an Atavin if you want. Or better idea. I saw a Baskin-Robbins down the street."

After Dahlia's party, I don't have much time to think about worry lines, because I'm too busy worrying about the lines the kids are learning for our *My Fair Lady* benefit. With not much time to go, the kids are in the rehearsal hall every day, practicing songs and painting sets. And today they're brandishing gigantic brushes like swords as gobs of red, yellow and blue poster paints are flying everywhere.

"Hey, guys, get some of that paint on the mural," I call out over the cheerful din. Not that I'm complaining. The Park Avenue and Arts Council kids have merged so seamlessly that nobody but their mothers could tell them apart.

"Yeah, let's get going," urges the new stage manager. "The Coventry Garden mural is looking great. But we still have to do Professor Higgins' apartment."

Amazingly, the kids troop over and follow him to the next stretched canvas panel. My idea to make Chauncey the stage manager was inspired, but even I didn't know it would turn out this well. The kid can't sing but he sure can organize. He's got the cast sewing costumes, building sets and getting to the rehearsals on time. Knows how to get people working. And the Krispy Kremes he always brings along don't hurt.

"Ms. Taylor, what color should the flowers be on the Professor's wallpaper?" Tamika, our star, asks me politely.

Now there's an executive decision I can handle. "Lilac," I say, basing my choice on absolutely nothing. But five kids immediately dip their paint brushes into the light purple paint. Heady with power, I spin around to pick the color for the wood paneling on the bottom half of the set and land smack against Pierce's outstretched brush. I yelp, realizing I'm now covered with orange paint from cheek to chin.

"Gosh, I'm so sorry," he says. "I'll get some paper towels."

"You look silly," Tamika says to me, starting to giggle.

"Not the first time," I say, smearing my hand across my face, probably making matters worse. And definitely making my hands orange, too.

Vincent, our flamboyant director, sweeps over in a dither to collect the children who are supposed to be rehearsing Scene Three. But he's stopped short by my orange face.

"Goodness, Jessica," he says disapprovingly, "don't tell me you still use Coppertone."

He grandly tosses his head back and twirls his ever-present Phantom of the Opera cape. As the kids cluster around, he glances at the newly begun mural. "Who chose lilac for the flowers on the wallpaper?" he bellows, wrinkling his nose in distaste. "That's just wrong, wrong, wrong, wrong, wrong! Hasn't anyone here ever been to London?"

"I have," pipe up at least nine Park Avenue voices.

"Then you know that the wallpaper flowers *must* be yellow," he says imperiously.

Nobody asks why, and with the Scene Three children in his wake, Vincent swirls dramatically to the other side of the hall.

"Okay, guys, yellow," Chauncey instructs the kids who are left behind. "Let's paint over that lilac."

So much for my authority. I move over to watch Vincent's rehearsal, tapping my foot as the stage fills with the cheerfully in-tune sounds of the children belting out "I'm Getting Married in the Morning." This number's going to be a showstopper. But at age twelve do the girls really need to know how hard it is to get a guy to church on time?

Behind me, I hear a brusque man's voice rising over the last bars of the song. "Does anybody know where Lowell Chauncey Cabot IV is?" he asks officiously.

I look over my shoulder as none other than Joshua Gordon steps carefully across the concrete floor, trying to keep his perfectly polished shoes clear of the minefield of splattered paint.

"He's over there," I say, thrusting my chin in the direction of the mural.

"Oh, Jess. I didn't realize it was you," he says. Then catching a closer look at me, his face breaks into a wry smile. "Nice look. Orange is a good color on you."

Goddamn, goddamn, goddamn. Not again. Where's Pierce with those paper towels?

I wonder how man-handler Dahlia would fawn her way out of this situation. I take a deep breath and decide to go for lighthearted. "The Origins facial was so much fun, I thought I'd try this," I say saucily. "Could open up a whole new marketing line for Benjamin Moore."

"I'll mention it to them," he says, parrying back. "They're a client. So's Quaker Oats, by the way." He looks at me pointedly.

I'm blank. Does he want me to show up next time in oatmeal?

"I'm thinking of telling the CEO they're doing way too much TV product placement," he says. "Not worth the money they're spending. Probably nobody but me noticed the oatmeal box in your kitchen."

My kitchen? The oatmeal box? That would mean . . . Oh no, it can't mean that. I clear my throat.

"You saw me on the *Cosmo* bachelor reality show?" I ask.

"Yup."

His expression doesn't give anything away, but I can guess what he's thinking.

"Not my finest moment," I say too apologetically.

"I can understand your wanting a hot date. But the surfer's way too young for you. Go for someone your own age."

"What's wrong with young and laid-back?" I ask the man who's obviously neither. I guess I'll never make a guy feel taller than five-eight. Even one like Josh who's already six-two. Took less than nine words to turn me into the anti-Dahlia.

"I don't know what all you women find so appealing about these under-earning, pretty-boy jocks," he says indignantly. "Wouldn't hurt you to look for a grown-up man who earns a living."

Wow. My TV date really touched a nerve. But Josh looks way too upset to be thinking just about Boulder. Then I remember about Josh's ex-wife and the tennis pro. No wonder he's overreacting.

"Just so happens Boulder's gay," I say, thinking that might be a comfort.

"You certainly do make interesting dating choices," he says tersely.

We stare at each other for a few awkward moments. I could try to explain about Boulder. Or maybe tell Josh it's not his fault that his wife is insane. But Joshua Gordon isn't standing around waiting for a group hug.

"Listen, I'm just here as a Board member," he says, reverting to business-only mode. "I came to see Chauncey so I can report back to his father."

"I did a good job with the Chauncey problem," I say, patting myself on the back since Josh is obviously not going to. "Turns out he's a great kid. Once I talked to him I figured out pretty quickly he'd make a mean stage manager."

"Smart solution," Josh concedes grudgingly. "Glad you took care of that."

"Happy to be of service. That's my job. I'm good at it."

"Don't get too cocky," Josh says, scraping his custom-made English leather shoe against the concrete in an effort to wipe off some imaginary blob of paint. "Your judgment in men still leaves something to be desired."

Chapter THIRTEEN

HUNTER IS PACING AROUND the lobby of the Regal Hotel like a wildcat in the new Tiger Mountain habitat at the Bronx Zoo. Nice environment, but he doesn't want to be here. And he's pissed at his handlers—in this case, Lucy.

"Sweetheart . . ." he says through clenched teeth to Lucy. "Sweetheart. Swee*theart*."

"It's okay. It's really going to be okay," she says, as he paces out tighter and tighter circles in front of her. She reaches over to pat his arm but he pulls away.

"Sweetheart, you're a fabulous producer and I trust you," he says, a little too loudly for the genteel surroundings. "You're the best in the business. I'm proud to host your pilot. But what the fuck were you thinking dragging me here to do a fucking second-rate interview?"

"Darling, please don't swear. It's not good for your image," Lucy says.

"Fuck my image," Hunter says, voice rising. "You think the fucking Olsen twins are good for my fucking image?" He's screaming above lobby limits and two out-of-towners standing at the concierge desk look up from their *Around New York* guide to check out the fracas. The show going on in the lobby is hotter than *Hairspray*—and the tickets are a lot cheaper.

"Lower your voice," Lucy says, her own jaw tightening.

"Not until you tell me why you booked this interview. The Olsen twins. The *fucking* Olsen twins."

"Excuse me, but despite what the tabloids say, I don't think both of the Olsen girls are fucking yet. Maybe one of them," I say, entering the fray to keep the facts straight. Lucy hired me for the day as a researcher, and if she's shelling out a per diem, I'm damn well going to earn it. "I'll stay on top of it. Could change any day."

Both Lucy and Hunter look at me like I'm crazy. But today I'm just the lowly research girl, so Hunter doesn't bother explaining that he meant fucking as an adjective, not a verb. Not that he'd be likely to articulate it quite that way.

"Lucy. Sweet. Heart," Hunter says, speaking in measured tones. And making it clear that "sweetheart" is his Hollywood-speak for "moron." "You promised me a big-name interview. I was thinking Brad Pitt. Renée Zellweger. Julianne Moore. She didn't win the Oscar, but I'd be okay with her. But not a couple of Mouseketeers."

"The Olsens weren't Mouseketeers," I say, setting the record right once again. "That was Britney and Christina. And it was ages ago." At least I learned something poring through two hundred back issues of *YM*. "The Olsens got their big break on *Full House*. On ABC, which is owned by Disney. But I don't think that's what you meant."

"I don't care if they fucked Walt Disney himself and every one of the seven dwarves!" Hunter roars, finally exploding. "I'm too important to interview mall rats!" His voice ricochets around the room and Lucy looks alarmed. An ever-growing group of fans at the concierge desk have tossed aside their theater guides. Our little lobby drama is standing-room-only. If Hunter keeps this up, the lights on Broadway may not go on at all tonight.

"Calm down," Lucy says tersely. "These girls have a billion-dollar business. Every preteen in America collects Mary-Kate and Ashley videos. Not to mention CDs, clothes, sheets, and perfume. They have a line at Wal-Mart. Their own magazine. They're practically a bigger conglomerate than AOL Time Warner."

"What isn't?" Hunter asks. "AOL's out of the name, and have you checked out that stock price lately? It's sunk lower than Blackbeard's pirate ship. Practically tanked my portfolio."

"How much did you lose?" Lucy asks, sounding a trifle concerned for Hunter's future. And her birthday present.

"Doesn't matter. I'll always be a rich man," he says cockily. "The network pays me a pretty penny."

She nods, ready to get Hunter back on track. "And you get those big bucks because you're so talented. All wit and charm. You could interview Al Gore and it would be exciting." She pauses, overcome by her own hyperbole. "Well, maybe not Al, but definitely Tipper. Anyway, those Olsen girls will be putty in your hands. We all are." She moves closer, straightens the knot on Hunter's tie and playfully kisses his ear.

"Okay, I'll do the interview," Hunter says, momentarily mollified. "But only if somebody gets me a cappuccino. Double. Soy. With two Equals. No whipped cream."

"Right," I say, "you're lactose intolerant."

"Jess, I'm flattered," says Hunter, looking inordinately pleased with himself. "I didn't realize you knew so much about me."

More than you can imagine.

Lucy looks over at me. "Would you mind handling the cappuccino?" she asks. "I didn't budget a go-fer for today's shoot."

Ah, yes. Still another career choice for me. Go-fer. And they say there are no opportunities for women my age.

"Don't think getting coffee was in the job description," I say, thinking I'm making a post-feminist joke.

Lucy shoots me a withering glance. "In TV, it's a team effort. We all do what it takes to make a good show. Get coffee. Comb the talent's hair. Stroke their ego—"

"Or stroke whatever else," says Hunter, suddenly beaming. "Cardinal rule is to keep the talent happy. And lucky me, I'm the talent." He puts his arm around Lucy and rubs her shoulder affectionately. "You give me what I need off the air and I give you what you need on the air. The best fucking show in television."

"The best," Lucy says, kissing his cheek. "But could we stop with the 'fuckings' now?"

"Sure. Till later," he says with a wink.

Hunter swaggers toward the hotel's cavernous restaurant, where the cameras and lights are already set for the interview, and settles into a banquette. The audio engineer clips a wireless mike on Hunter's lapel and hands him the remote to snap onto his belt.

"Actually, we're not starting the shot right here," Lucy says diplomatically. "Darling, I didn't mention this to you, but the network's having a little problem with the rough cuts of the pilot they've seen so far. They want a few changes."

"What's the matter, they don't like me? They want a new host?" Hunter asks jocularly, confident that the network's about as likely to replace him as the Pope is to announce his engagement.

"No, no, nothing like that. Not yet," Lucy says. "We're not nearly at that point."

"At that point?" Hunter asks in disbelief. "What do you mean 'at that point'?" His ego is so fragile that with three words he's flip-flopped completely. Now he's expecting that the invitations to the Pope's wedding are already in the mail. And he's not even on the list.

"Don't worry, darling. I think we can solve it with more behind-the-scenes. The network thinks that's where you're stronger. So we're going to start this shot in the kitchen. With you working with the chef to make the Olsen girls' lunch."

Now Hunter's ego is flat-lining faster than WorldCom.

"You mean I've got this great opportunity to have a sit-down with the Olsen twins and you're shuttling me off to the kitchen?" he asks in despair.

What's happened to the teen twins not being worth his time? I guess compared to flipping burgers for them, an actual interview with Mary-Kate and Ashley is looking better every moment.

"It's pretty nice in the kitchen," I say, handing Hunter the just-brewed double soy Equal cappuccino no whip that I've fetched. "The chef's terrific. Did you know they invented the rum-and-Coke right here at this hotel?" And who's to say not? Love this research gig. I wonder if encyclopedic knowledge of the Olsen twins and unprovable claims about mixed drinks will get me into Mensa.

Lucy, working hard to keep the talent happy, takes Hunter by the hand and leads him into the kitchen. "So here's the lineup," she says. "We'll shoot the girls with their menus and then cut to you in the kitchen. You'll give America all the behind-the-scenes on what really happens in a famous restaurant kitchen. Then—and this is the best part, darling—you'll come out with the tray."

Hunter is now too deflated to ask how his carrying a tray could possibly be the best part. Good for pumping up his pecs? So Lucy helps him out.

"I can just picture the shot, can't you? The girls think the waiter's coming and then it's *you*. Hunter Green. They'll be so thrilled to actually meet you. I can hear them squealing now."

"That could work," Hunter says, hearing those very same squeals of delight.

I, however, can hear only the steady buzz of the air conditioner. I guess you have to work in TV full-time to share an audio hallucination.

The Olsen twins arrive in a whirl of tight tees, long hair, and dozens of long-looped necklaces. They plunk down their pocketbooks and sit shoulder to shoulder, just as adorable as advertised. But gosh, they're young. Maybe if you add their ages together with Hunter's and divide by three you hit the key demo. There's an equation Einstein never thought of. Mensa, here I come.

Even hidden away in the kitchen, Hunter knows how to make a scene shine. Once the cameras are rolling, he ties on an apron and schmoozes with the chef. You'd think that learning how to make the perfect Salade Niçoise is all he ever wanted to do in life.

"This is fabulous," Hunter swoons to the chef, theatrically tossing olives into the bowl. "I never imagined the drama that goes on back here. So much hustle and bustle. So much tension. It all seems so calm when you're sitting out there in the dining room. But now we're seeing everything that really goes on."

Well, not everything. The cameras carefully avoid the sous-chef who drops a piece of raw chicken on the floor and casually picks it up and throws it on the grill, as if it's an everyday occurrence. Which I guess it is. Then there's the recycled coleslaw. What's left over on one person's plate just gets sent out with a new order. And as a pièce de résistance, we have the assistant who's garnishing the dishes. Alas, he seems to be having a sneezing fit. So along with the beautiful edible flowers, he adds his own finishing touch. A spray of germs. Not on the menu.

With lunch ready, Hunter trades in his apron for a crisp maroon waiter's jacket. Size XLG. This isn't menswear at Barneys—nobody's sized down the uniform to spare his feelings. Ready for his big entrance, Hunter hoists the tray in the air, pushes through the swinging doors and heads out to the Olsen twins.

"Lunch is ready," he carols.

The girls are deeply engrossed in conversation—they obviously don't get enough time together—and never look up. So Hunter, the consummate performer, takes the oversized salad bowls and places them carefully in front of each twin, appropriately serving from the left. Or maybe he's just the consummate waiter. What actor isn't.

Finally, the ever-polite Olsens look up and flash him their million-dollar smiles. "Thanks so much," they say in unison, as they dig into their salads. But there are no squeals of delight or even minor hints of recognition. Hunter hovers awkwardly, not sure what to do next.

And then he decides.

"Can you just scoot over a little bit?" he asks an astonished Ashley, trying to nudge his way onto the banquette.

I'm worried that the girls are going to scream for security. Or Hunter, feeling insecure, is going to start screaming at Lucy. But instead, he puts his hand lightly on Mary-Kate's and offers a friendly grin.

"You have no idea who I am, do you," he laughs. "And no reason you should. But I know that you're the amazing Olsen twins. Honored to meet you, I'm Hunter Green."

Look at that—the Olsens have turned from "fucking" to "amazing." And Hunter's saving the day.

"Oh!" squeals Ashley. "We know who you are."

"Of course we do!" squeals Mary-Kate.

Love those squeals. At last. And with charm to spare, Hunter wins over the Olsens and starts chatting so comfortably with them that they almost forget they're on camera. My research has paid off. He knows which twin is older and joshes that pretty soon that won't seem like an advantage.

"A few birthdays from now you'll be insisting you're two minutes *younger*," he teases.

He banters about boyfriends but doesn't ask anything embarrassing. He mentions that they're on the list of the richest teens in the world—and artfully leaves room for Mary-Kate to point out that they earned their money while the others inherited it. He tells a story about Eminem, then confesses that the first time he heard the singer's name, he thought it was a candy. When, after thirty minutes, the cameraman stops to change tapes and Lucy calls a wrap, the girls don't want to leave.

"We're having so much fun!" Ashley gushes to Hunter, her new best bud.

"Maybe you could be in our next movie," offers Mary-Kate.

"Right, I could play the irascible grandpa," Hunter laughs, making a joke at his own expense.

"No, you're a cool guy," Mary-Kate says cheerfully. "You could play the father."

Hunter would probably have preferred the on-screen role of boyfriend, but he accepts the compliment.

Hunter and the Olsens exchange kisses and e-mail addresses. And then he has one more request.

"I know of two sweet little girls who'd love an autographed picture," Hunter says. "Can you sign one to 'Lily' and the other to 'Jen'?"

"Sure," they say, signing the pictures and loading him down with a stack of DVDs and CD-ROMs before heading out to their limousine.

"That was so incredibly sweet of you," Lucy says when the girls are gone, the cameras are packed and the tumult has died down. "Wonderful interview. And after all that, you think about the kids. You do everything right."

"That's why you adore me," he says, pulling her close.

"Maybe," Lucy says.

I'm back in school. And the wire-haired, bulbous-nosed teacher standing at the blackboard has an announcement for the thirty-five parents fidgeting uncomfortably in the dim, overheated classroom.

"We should encourage our children to masturbate," says Ms. Deitch, the phys-ed teacher, in a whiny, high-pitched voice. If anyone knows, she does. She's obviously never had sex any other way.

She and her accomplice, an overweight, greasy-haired science teacher with a thin pencil mustache and big sweat rings under the armpits of his short-sleeved Dacron shirt, nod knowingly.

I always thought it was a good idea that our kids would be offered sex ed next year in the sixth grade. But now that I'm seeing the instructors, who are giving us a preview of what they'll be teaching, I'm having doubts. These aren't the people I want Jen to conjure up every time she thinks about sex. Although maybe they are. It could help promote teenage abstinence.

Sitting in the wooden classroom chair next to me, Dan leans over and scribbles a note on my pad.

"Cn u believe this?"

"Shh, pay attention," I whisper.

"I already know it all," he whispers back.

"Excuse me, could we have one conversation here?" Ms. Deitch asks sternly, peering out over her bifocals at Dan, clearly now branded as the class troublemaker. "Young man, did you have a question about masturbation or may I continue?"

"Sorry, please go ahead," Dan says. Then he adds to me under his breath, "I think I've got the topic in hand."

"Would you stop it," I say, punching him on the arm. "I don't want to get in trouble, too."

"As soon as everyone's comfortable with masturbation, I'll move right along," says Ms. Deitch.

If this overview of the sex-ed syllabus is turning Dan into an adolescent, I can only imagine what it's going to be like when the class is taught to the kids next year. Are they ready for this? The stats say it's not unusual for kids to be having sex by seventeen. I didn't even have my ears pierced by then.

Ms. Deitch drones ahead, managing to make masturbation, menstruation and copulation all sound equally boring. She has learning tools for the children, including a detailed drawing of the female reproductive system and a three-dimensional polyethylene model of a penis. Looks better in real life. Well, usually.

"We're just about at the *climax* of the evening," says the science teacher, Mr. Johnson, making a bad joke and laughing nervously. Oy. If this is how Jen learns about sex, I'll never have grandchildren. "Before we get to our *climax*," he repeats, not knowing when to leave bad enough alone, "let's take some questions."

Everyone is silent.

"Come on," he cajoles. "There must be something."

Finally one woman in the back nervously raises her hand. "I think all this information is so important for our children," she says in a timorous voice. "We didn't have this when I was in school. So there's one thing I'm wondering about." She pauses, working up her courage. "What can you do if your husband always comes before you do?"

"You can get a new husband," says Mr. Johnson efficiently. "Next question?"

Maybe I underestimated Mr. Johnson. He does have a natural flair for comedy. Dan is smirking and I refuse to catch his eye, knowing that if I do, I'll burst out laughing.

"Come on, one more question," Mr. Johnson prompts.

"Here's one," says the dreaded PTA president Cynthia importantly. How did I not notice her here before? "What does it mean when the children say they're 'hooking up'?"

"Glad you brought it up," says Ms. Deitch evenly. "You might want to write this down because it's a little complicated."

Dutifully thirty-five parents poise their pens to pad.

"Hooking up," she says, as if she's narrating a BBC documentary. "We'll go through it step-by-step. In seventh grade it's kissing. Eighth grade, French kissing. Ninth grade, fondling. Tenth grade, oral sex. Eleventh grade, intercourse. Did everybody get that? Did I go too fast?"

No, but it sounds like the kids are. I make a note to call Boulder's mother, the good Catholic, to find out where the closest convent schools are.

"So what happens in twelfth grade?" asks Cynthia.

"You don't want to know," calls out another mother. Who obviously has older children.

That topic taken care of, our instructors are ready to forge ahead.

"Now my favorite part of the evening," says Mr. Johnson eagerly. "Pick a partner. We're ready for a practice session."

Now I can't even look in Dan's direction. But I don't have to. Because he's started laughing so loudly that he's attracting attention.

"You again, young man?" scolds Ms. Deitch, trying to rein in the class member most likely to be sent to the principal's office. "Do you need a moment to collect yourself in the hall or may we continue? I have something to distribute."

If this is how she's going to handle things next year, she'll be teaching the entire class in the hallway. But Dan, trying to redeem himself and prove that he's ever the good boy, springs to his feet.

"Let me help you give those out," he volunteers, taking charge of the box and starting up and down the rows.

I can't see what Dan's passing out until he gets to my desk.

"Oh great, thanks," I say, looking at the offering, grateful for the snack break. "I'm hungry. A banana. Exactly what I needed."

I start unpeeling the banana when Cynthia leaps up and snatches it out of my hand.

"What do you think you're doing?" she screams at me. "You can't eat that banana. They're visual aids. Paid for by the PTA."

Okay, now I get it. I'm glad to know my PTA dues aren't being wasted.

After Dan finishes distributing the bananas, Cynthia—wanting to reclaim her position as the Student Most Likely to Succeed—hijacks the supply box. Her chore—handing out condoms. Trojans. All shapes and sizes.

"I have one mantra that I insist all the children memorize," says Ms. Deitch emphatically. Repeat after me. "No penis . . ."

We all look at her in shock.

"Please repeat after me," she barks. "This is absolutely the most important thing you'll ever learn. Ready? *No penis . . .*"

By now, too battered down to argue, we dutifully repeat, *"No penis . . ."*

". . . is too big . . ."

". . . is too big . . ." we chime in, warming to the subject.

". . . for a condom."

". . . for a condom!" we boom in unison, thoroughly caught up in the group spirit.

That felt good. I'm finally bonding with these people. With all the uncertainty in the world, it's important to have something you can count on. The air is crackling with so much energy we could be at a revival meeting. Before we burst into "The Hallelujah Chorus," Mr. Johnson breaks open his condom package

"Face your partners, banana between you," he instructs. "Any of you married people who are still monogamous might not have done this in a while."

Following Mr. Johnson's lead, I tear into the condom package with gusto—managing to rip the contents.

"Whoops," I say. "I guess I'm out of practice."

Dan looks over. "Not your fault. Looks like you got the lambskin. Not very durable. You can share mine. It's a lot stronger. And glow-in-the-dark."

I get that we want the kids comfortable with condoms. But glow-in-the-dark? Just how young are we aiming here? Did Cynthia provide Blue's Clues condoms, too?

Ms. Deitch, not quite as forgiving as Dan, comes over to my desk.

"What *happened*?" she asks as if I'd just dropped Michelangelo's *David*. "Please stand up and show the class what you've done."

I shuffle to my feet. "I had the lambskin," I offer, meekly looking for an explanation while next to me, Dan snickers. But Ms. Deitch isn't letting me off the hook so easily.

"Go ahead, show the class," she orders, hovering over me with arms crossed until I limply wave the torn condom in midair.

"This is how babies get born," she says accusingly, as if I'm personally responsible for the population explosion. "Parents, I want you to go home tonight and practice, practice, practice!"

Practice having sex or opening condoms? Little chance I'll do either. Chastised, I sit back down and the instruction continues: How to unroll a condom onto a banana. Are we going to get graded? I hope so, because Dan and I ace this one. What a team. But the woman behind us is encountering some difficulty.

"This isn't working," she complains loudly. "My banana's too soft."

"I only got the very firmest bananas," Cynthia shoots back defensively. "I checked every one myself."

Hate to be standing behind her when she's buying grapes.

As we finish protecting our bananas and wrapping up the session, Mr. Johnson has one final announcement. "Just to let you know that starting in ninth grade, condoms are provided in the nurse's office to the children," he says. "No questions asked."

Very reassuring. I have to sign in triplicate before they'll let Jen go on a class trip to the Museum of Natural History. But she can have sex, no permission slip needed. Then again, I could sign in quadruplicate forbidding Jen to have sex until she's thirty-five and it wouldn't make any difference. Ultimately it's going to be her decision. The best I can do is teach her my values, light a candle and pray.

Before anybody can get out, Cynthia makes a beeline for the door. "Turn in your bananas," she orders. "No one leaves with a banana."

Most of the parents dutifully return their visual aids to the box.

"Condoms, too?" asks one man.

"No! You can keep those if you want," Cynthia says. "Just make sure they're off the bananas. Last bake sale of the year is next week and I'm making the banana bread."

Well, I won't be buying. There's nothing about bananas that's very appealing right now.

Dan and I head out to the parking lot. After our adolescent antics inside, outside alone we're as awkward as teenagers and both turn quiet.

"When's Lucy get back from L.A.?" I finally ask.

"Day after tomorrow. Then I'm going back to the corporate apartment. It's made it easier that my firm keeps a place on Seventy-eighth and Madison. You should come by."

"How's it going?"

"I don't know," Dan says, his good spirits draining faster than a swimming pool in September. "Some days are better than others. Lucy and I aren't talking much. I guess I'm still too angry. Right now I'm just focused on the kids."

"You're a great dad," I say, meaning it.

"I don't know about great, but the kids still come to me for everything. I've been giving Dave girlfriend advice. How's that for irony?"

"No irony. The boys are both so gorgeous, girls must be falling at their feet. And they look just like you. No question here who the father was." Well, that was a clever comment, given Dan's current situation. Another reason I'm not in the diplomatic corps.

But my careless remark seems to have gone right by Dan, who continues on with his story.

"Anyway, Dave's got this girl named Emily he's been best friends with all year. And now he's trying to figure out if he can ask her out, make her a girlfriend, rather than a friend. I told him absolutely. Best way to start a relationship is to pick someone you already like a lot. Don't you think?"

"You bet," I say emphatically. "Sometimes I think the biggest mistake I made with Jacques the first time around was falling in love with love. It was all about romance and not enough about real friendship. Now I'm older and wiser. I won't make that mistake again." At least I hope not. Most of me understands that there's more to marriage than cow pastures and moonlit nights.

"Dave took my advice. He and Emily are going to the Red Hot Chili Peppers concert this Friday night at Madison Square Garden. I'll let you know how it turns out," Dan says, opening my car door for me.

I slide into the driver's seat and turn on the ignition, but Dan's still resting on the door.

"Can I give you a lift somewhere?" I ask.

"No, my car's right over there. Thanks," he says. But he lingers another minute before leaning in to give me a light kiss on the cheek—and then he finally closes the door.

"Keep me posted on the Chili Peppers romance," I call out after him, through the open car window.

"Yup, I'm hoping I'm right about this one," he says, giving me a thumbs-up sign as he walks away.

When I get home, there's an emergency message from Lucy in L.A. She's the only person I know who actually uses the "Urgent" option on the voice mail system. Is she that desperate to find out what happened in sex ed tonight?

"I got the most unbelievable earrings for my birthday," she gushes, the moment I call her back. "From David Orgell on Rodeo Drive."

Who's this David Orgell? Another man in her life? Oh no, that must be a store. And from the address, a very fancy store. Must be that Hunter came through.

"They're three-tiered gold filigree chandeliers with pearl and ruby drops. Very Nicole Kidman. Terribly expensive but absolutely exquisite. I've been coveting them in the window for weeks. And now they're mine. So gorgeous. I'm looking at myself in the mirror right now. Stunning."

"That's great," I say, genuinely pleased that she's happy. "Good for Hunter. I can see what you like about him. Jen was thrilled with the autographed photo he got for her."

"Yeah, Mr. Thoughtful," Lucy says, not quite as warmly as I might have expected.

"He's starting to grow on me," I admit grudgingly.

"What, like a fungus?" she snips.

"Lucy, for once I'm being nice about Hunter."

"Well, I'm not."

What, she was expecting the matching necklace? I sigh. "Help me out here, Luce. You got the guy. You got the present. What's wrong? Are you upset because he spent too much money?"

"Ha. Did you hear any mention here of Hunter spending money? Apparently he spends oodles of money—on everybody but me. I bought the earrings myself. Hunter gave me a heart-shaped Christofle paperweight for my birthday, inscribed TRUE LOVE."

"Not earrings, but that sounds nice, too," I say. "At least it was romantic."

"Might have been, if it wasn't the second one I got this week. Came in a beautiful red-velvet box. Publicist at NBC sent them out. Promos for a new sitcom. At least Hunter remembered to take out the press release before he passed it on. Rewrapped it, too."

"Maybe he didn't know you'd already gotten one," I offer.

"He does now," Lucy says venomously. "I left it outside his door. And just so he didn't miss the point, I rewrapped it—in the press release. Then I marched over to David Orgell and bought the earrings."

"My, my, you've been a busy girl," I say. And all I've been doing is learning how to put a condom on a banana. "I've never bought jewelry for myself that wasn't costume."

"Don't think it was easy," Lucy says. "The salesman was properly unctuous, but he kept asking if he should hold them so I could come back with my husband. Or boyfriend. Or even both, he joked. That he could picture. What he couldn't imagine was my buying them myself. But goddamn it, I can. And why shouldn't I? I don't need Hunter or Dan. I've had it with the both of them."

"Oh, Lucy. Calm down," I say.

"No, really. I've been making my lists for both of them. Columns. Pluses and minuses. Okay, mostly minuses. Did I ever tell you about Hunter's penis?" she asks viciously.

How much am I going to have to hear about penises tonight? "No," I say cautiously. "But Nikki, at your dinner party, did say something about Hunter having really small feet."

"Turns out that little axiom is true," she says ruefully.

"And Dan?" I ask, not really wanting to know, but not being able to stop myself.

"That was one of his big pluses," she admits. "But he hums."

"When?"

"Never mind," she says mysteriously.

I'll be deciphering that one for months. "But I bet he doesn't snore," I say.

"That's true. And I have to confess, Dan got mostly pluses," she says, momentarily softening. "I've always said I loved him. He's the guy I can count on. The one I want in my lifeboat. But he left me, so screw him. Hunter's big attraction was that he made me feel on top of the world. Really special. Then came this sorry regifted Christofle. So screw him, too."

"You've regifted things yourself," I remind her. "It doesn't make you a bad person. A person without a lot of time to shop, maybe."

"I've never regifted anyone I was having an affair with," Lucy says indignantly, making a moral distinction that I'd never really considered before.

"I give up," I say, sighing. "But I still better not ever get a box of Godiva from you."

"Promise," she says, with a grudging laugh. Then clearly done with Lucy's Top Ten Problems of the Day she moves on. "Hey, this is the weekend Jacques is coming in, right? Did you do what I told you?"

"The Brazilian bikini wax thing? I can't possibly. It's just not me. I have a feeling I'm more the Polish bikini wax type. Instead of removing hair, they paste on some extra."

"You're hopeless," Lucy says, laughing, but I can practically hear her shaking her head at the sorry state of my glamour goals. "Can I at least talk you into an eyebrow shaping? It takes six months to get an appointment with Miss Barrett but I have one tomorrow and I'm not going to be home in time. Take it. Please."

"Six months' wait, huh? Maybe I could sell it for you on eBay."

"No, you won't. It's my present for you. Not even regifted. But tell Ms. Barrett you want threading. It's the latest. No more tweezers. They just tug away with knots of string."

"So it doesn't hurt?" I ask hopefully.

"Of course it hurts. What doesn't?"

"Are we still talking about eyebrows?" I ask, hearing the plaintive note in her voice.

"Everything hurts," Lucy repeats. And then she quickly hangs up the phone.

Chapter FOURTEEN

I'VE BEEN PREPARING for this date all week, and I have nothing to wear. The pink flowered sundress is completely wrong. I stare at myself in the hallway mirror on the upstairs landing. What was I thinking? I head back to my bedroom closet for the third time in fifteen minutes. This may end up being a record-setting day, even for me. But I don't really have another decent outfit to change into. Maybe that first yellow skirt didn't make my hips looks so big, after all. I put it back on. Yes it did. How about blue jeans? This is an afternoon date. I could just go casual.

The doorbell rings and I freeze. No, I can't possibly answer the door in these Levi's. I have to remember to buy the Gap Modern Retros. Lucy says they look great on everyone.

"Jen sweetie, will you get that?" I call out, trying to keep the anxiety out of my voice. You'd think that a simple date—especially with somebody I've already married and divorced—wouldn't be so hard. "It's Jacques. Tell him I'll be down in a couple of minutes."

That buys me a hundred and twenty seconds to knit myself a new outfit. Or see how quickly the Gap delivers. Oh, what the heck. I'll go back to the sundress. At least it shows off my Wonderbra-ed cleavage. Which Jacques won't notice anyway because I'm sure his total attention will be focused on my fabulous eyebrows.

I gently trace my fingers across them. How could getting rid of a few stray hairs make me so happy? The now perfectly curved arches seem to have changed my whole face. Bigger eyes. Fresher look. Or maybe I just have to believe that some good came out of twenty minutes of being yanked and tugged and tortured. For the record, though, I'm not ready to go Brazilian. What's the point? By the time a guy has a chance to take that in, he's either interested or he's not.

From downstairs, I hear Jacques trying to make conversation with Jen. They say hello and talk briefly about the weather. After an awkward pause, he turns down Jen's offer of cookies and chocolate milk—I've taught her well about being a hostess—and then flails around for another topic. Given the fractured dialogue I realize he's probably never bothered to talk much with anyone under the age of consent.

"Such a nice house," he finally says to Jen, in his most charming manner. "What made you decide to move here?"

"My mother," says Jen. I hold my breath, but mercifully she doesn't add, "Duh."

"How are the taxes?" he asks, thinking he's hit on a topic that crosses international boundaries. "In France they're *très terrible*."

"I like your accent," Jen says, non-sequitur-ing onto something that for her is more interesting. "I know a song in French. Everyone at school is singing it. Wanna hear?"

I expect Jen to break out into *Frère Jacques*, but apparently that's not what they're singing around the old schoolyard these days.

"*Voulez-vous coucher avec moi ce soir,*" my little baby trills in an innocent, sing-song voice. "*Voulez-vous coucher avec moi?*"

Blue jeans be damned, I'm going down there.

I rush down the steps and give Jacques a quick kiss hello. "I'm sure she doesn't have any idea what that means. You know kids," I say, putting my arm protectively around Jen's shoulder.

"*Non, non. C'est très charmante,*" Jacques says.

"What'd I do wrong, Mom?" Jen asks. "I like that song. It's pretty. What's it mean in English?"

"Nothing, sweetie. I'll tell you later." In about two years, maybe.

No, sooner than that. Can't leave it to Ms. Deitch to translate "Would you like to sleep with me tonight?"

"Tell her what it means now," Jacques says, with a twinkle in his eye. "I'll wait. Do you have a comfortable chair?"

"Not a single one," I say, grabbing his arm. "We should get going. Banana Republic closes in eight hours."

Jen looks me up and down and I can see my outfit hasn't made the grade. Maybe I should have taken the extra minute to put on the sundress.

"You're not going out like that, Mom, are you?" Jen asks, her voice dripping with disapproval. What happened to the bright-eyed ten-year-old who thought everything I did was perfect? She turned into an eleven-year-old who's afraid I'm going to embarrass her in front of her friends. I used to tell her what to wear. Now she's telling me.

"Jeans, Mom, jeans. Is that what you wear on all your dates?"

"All her dates?" Jacques asks, turning for the first time with real interest to Jen. "Tell me about your mother's dates. *Les rendez-vous.* So many, I'm sure. After all, *elle est très belle.*" He strokes his hand appreciatively across my cheek. Has he noticed the eyebrows?

"Yes, tell us both about them," I say, baffled. I can't remember having any dates, never mind any where I wore jeans.

"Mom!" Jen says, exasperated, her voice rising in that contemptuous teenage wail that I expect to hear for the next nine years. "Boulder! How could you forget! We love Boulder!"

Jacques looks at me quizzically. "Who is this Boulder we love?" he asks. "I am sure I do not love him."

"You would," Jen promises. "He's so much fun."

"Actually, you would," I say, going upstairs to change into my sundress. "I'll tell you about it in the car."

Five minutes later—with all this practice I've become a quick changer—we've dropped Jen at Lily's and are speeding toward the city. Jacques' first destination really is Banana Republic, and for some reason it has to be the one in Rockefeller Center.

"The biggest. The most American. The best," he says authoritatively, as we step inside the long, cavernous store. The best? Did he catch that disease passing through Customs at JFK? Or has Jacques met Cynthia?

Jacques enters the men's department, jaw set, as determined as Napoleon at Waterloo. Except Napoleon lost that battle and Jacques never does. He's ready to put in whatever effort it takes to find effortless-looking clothes. He thoroughly inspects each rack, selecting eight nearly indistinguishable pairs of chinos. All size 32 x 32. Love that slim French waist, but I never thought of him as a perfect square.

"Eight pairs. Good idea. You won't have to do laundry for a whole week," I say, as if my French prince knows there's a Tide other than the one at the Côte d'Azur. I start toward the cash register, but Jacques is going in the other direction.

"I have to try these on, *mon amour*. They must fit just so."

Jacques goes in and out of the dressing room eight times, trying on each pair and modeling them for me as he stares intently into the three-way mirror. At least he's not lazy. He comments on the place-ment of the pockets, the width of the cuffs, and the length of the leg. Which happens to be the same thirty-two inches long in each case, but I don't point that out. Then there's the color, alternately described by Jacques as "a little too khaki" or "not khaki enough." He says "khaki" so many times that it starts to sound like a French epithet. Which I'm thinking of using.

"I'm leaning toward pairs two, four, and six," Jacques says, preen-ing in front of the mirror in the last pair. "I'll just try those on again. Unless you liked three. *Le troisième* is still in the running if you say so, *mon amour*."

"No, definitely not three," I tell him. Figure I'll just vote for the even numbers. A girl has to have some rational system for making de-cisions. "In fact, you don't need to try them again, those pairs look perfect on you."

"*Merci, mon chouchou*, but let's just be sure."

And oh, are we sure. He tries on pairs two, four, six followed by four, two, six, then six, two, four. And the big decision? I've lost track by now. But we leave with a huge shopping bag. Which also includes six polo shirts, all in various shades of light blue, selected to be worn with the khakis. Why the shirts don't need to be tried on eludes me. But I certainly don't bring it up.

"Such fun shopping with you," Jacques says grandly when we're finally out the door. "I think we did well, *non*? And now we go buy you a little trinket."

"A little trinket? How about one of these?" I suggest as we pass a street vendor hawking beaded necklaces and "gold" bracelets. The sign on his table makes an irresistible offer: 2 FOR 5 DOLARZ. YOUR CHOICE. And just who else's choice would it be?

"No, something I think you'll like even more," Jacques says, laughing.

He takes my hand as we stroll up Fifth Avenue and I feel my spirits soar. It's one of the three or four days in the year when the city is perfect. The sun is shining but there's no humidity. A gentle, light breeze stirs the air. The flowers in Rockefeller Center are blooming and so are the colorful umbrellas at the outdoor cafés. People are smiling and no one seems to be rushing. Jacques buys two salted pretzels from another vendor who even tells us to "Have a nice day."

The six-block walk takes a little longer than usual because we stop every hundred feet to kiss and peer into store windows.

"Here we are," Jacques says as he ushers me through the revolving door on the corner of Fifty-seventh Street. Tiffany. Haven't been here since I returned the three identical silver candy dishes Jacques' relatives sent us all those years ago for our wedding.

"You know what this store is famous for, *non*?" he says looking around delightedly.

"The blue boxes," I say.

"Yes, that too, my darling," he says, chuckling. "But *non*. I mean diamonds. The most beautiful diamonds in all the world." He clasps my hand close to his and we walk by the sparkling cases of glittery jewels. "I love you. Today we buy you a diamond."

I stop short and pretend to study the baubles in one of the cases. A diamond? I feel a lump in my throat. A few dates, a few nights together, a few hundred flowers and he's won me back? That's all it takes? I promised myself that this time I wouldn't be swept off my feet.

And appearances to the contrary, I'm not going to be. All week, I've been tamping down doubts about who could have called Jacques that night in Vermont. And where he is when I don't hear from him for days at a time. But he still makes my heart beat faster than anybody else ever did. Or maybe ever will.

I must hesitate way too long because Jacques throws his arms around me and kisses me fervently.

"Why look so worried, *ma chérie*? Diamonds are to make you smile. You prefer the sapphires?"

"No, no, diamonds are fine. But maybe just not now."

"Of course now. We're here. Together. Come." He turns to one of the perfectly chignoned saleswomen standing behind the nearest counter. "Diamond earrings. The most beautiful ones you have. For a woman I love."

So we're not going for the ring yet. That's a relief. But what's the matter, he's not ready? We're here. Together. How long should this courtship have to take? It is the second one, after all.

"Diamond earrings. That's way too extravagant, Jacques," I say, pulling myself together.

"For you, the moon," he says. "You brought me back to life."

Well, whatever I did, the saleswoman now brings me exactly what Jacques requested. The most beautiful diamond earrings she has.

"Not quite that big," Jacques says with a wave of his hand. "Something more discreet."

"Yes sir," says the saleswoman, snapping shut the velvet tray and mentally scaling back her commission. "Just how much love would you say you'd like the diamonds to express?"

"Maybe that much," he says, spacing his thumb and forefinger about an eighth-of-an-inch apart.

"About a half carat each," she says, with a twinge of disappointment.

"Make it a carat each," he says expansively.

The saleswoman comes back with four choices and I begin to scrutinize each one. Gosh, they're beautiful. Look at them shimmer. Jacques has his arm tightly around me and the pleasure of our being here together shines as brightly as the diamonds. I don't often feel bad for Lucy, but right now I can imagine how she felt purchasing those chandelier earrings all by herself. Then again, wonder if they're nicer than mine.

I tenderly cup the first pair in my hand, moving it every which way to catch the different light. I hold one up to my ear. Makes my whole face brighter. Better than the eyebrow shaping.

"All right if I try it on?" I ask the saleswoman.

"Of course. Try them all on. See which you prefer. I have others if you wish to see more."

"*Non,* not necessary. We'll take those. I like them the best," Jacques says, pointing decisively to one pair. "You agree, *mon amour?*"

"They're gorgeous," I say. On the other hand, so are the other three pair. And who knows which will best complement my skin tone until I've tried them all on? Oh no, that's pearls. Still, I'm sure there's some difference between them. But I'll never get to find out. Maybe that's the advantage of buying jewelry for yourself. You can spend at least as much time deciding what you want as your boyfriend did at the Banana Republic.

The saleswoman wraps our purchase carefully, and we're still out of the store with earrings and robin's egg blue box in record time. Jacques has our next stop already planned—the obvious place to go after an extravagant purchase. His hotel. Conveniently located a block away.

"I want to see you wearing nothing but your diamond earrings," Jacques says provocatively, kissing me in the elevator.

As aphrodisiacs go, I've gotta say that an afternoon at Tiffany beats oysters every time. I'm totally in the mood. We barely make it off the elevator and into his suite before our clothes are off.

"The earrings," he reminds me. "Put them on."

I tear off the ribbon, but I'm careful with the box. Might want to use it again sometime.

"Come over here. Stand in front of me, my darling. Let me look at you," Jacques says, lying naked on the bed, propped against the pile of pillows for better viewing.

Instead, I slide next to him on the soft sheets and thrust one glittering ear in his direction. "Gorgeous, so gorgeous. How can I ever thank you?" I ask seductively.

"Stand up. I want to see you all."

"There's only one of me," I laugh.

"And that's the one I want to see," he coaxes. "You are beautiful. *Tu es très belle.* Let me enjoy."

Reluctantly I swing my legs over the side of the bed and look down at my rounded tummy. How long can I hold my breath? And why is it so hard to believe that my lover finds my naked body beautiful? That looking at me in full he really would be appreciative, and not be making a mental list of my spider veins, my dimpled thighs, or the extra womanliness on my hips.

Trying to be brave, I stand up and toss back my hair. Probably a bad move. My neck has never been my best feature. But when I catch Jacques' eye, I see a look of pure pleasure and I almost will myself to bask in his admiration.

He rises slowly from the bed and walks toward me.

"*Très, très belle,*" he repeats, taking me in his arms. He kisses me ardently and I'm intoxicated by the passion of the moment.

"Come to me," he says, and with one fell swoop, he scoops me up, one arm around my shoulder, the other anchored under my awkwardly flailing knees. Well, that's a mood breaker. Maybe this sort of thing works in the movies, but all I can think about is how much I weigh. He probably didn't realize I'd be this heavy, and now he's too gallant to drop me.

"Put me down. You'll get a hernia," I tell him. How romantic. Why don't I add that at his age, he should bend his knees to protect his lower back.

"*Non, non,* you're as light as a butterfly," he says. But he does rush over and dump me on the bed pretty quickly.

"It's the diamonds," I joke. "You got me such big ones. I'm heavier with the earrings on."

"Shhh," he says, muffling my silly banter with dozens of kisses. "Ssshhhhh," he repeats again, stretching out the sound, then lightly

kissing my breasts and slowly caressing the length of my body. Somehow, my insecurities vanish—as do any thoughts of anything. For the
next two hours, all I do is feel.

For dinner, I want champagne and caviar in bed, but Jacques insists
he's made a reservation at a must-visit restaurant.

"It's my favorite," he says. "Everyone loves the Four Seasons."

The Four Seasons? That's up there on my list with Le Cirque and
Le Bernardin. Who cares that my sundress isn't swank-restaurant ready.
With my new diamond earrings, I can go anywhere.

"I'd love to go over to the Four Seasons," I say enthusiastically.

"*Non,* just downstairs, *mon amour.* Maybe you didn't notice that
this is the Four Seasons hotel. The restaurant has some silly name—
Fifty-seven Fifty-seven—but I call it the Four Seasons."

Oh good. And we can pretend we're sitting in the Grill Room. Or
is the Pool Room chicer for dinner? I can never remember.

"Should I just wear my diamonds?" I ask, still feeling flirtatious.
"Or do I need to put on something else?"

"Something else," he says. "I have something very important to
talk to you about. You'll want to be dressed."

I feel that lump again in my throat. He's bought me the diamonds.
We've made passionate love all afternoon. Now he has something very
important to say. Or is it that he has a question to pop? No matter how
good I'm feeling right now, I'm still not ready. I don't have to answer him
tonight. I tell myself that again. I don't have to tell him anything tonight.

The restaurant may not be the original Four Seasons, but it seems
pretty nice to me. The maitre d' is attentive and the service is elegant but
restrained. The waiter, thank goodness, doesn't feel compelled to tell us
his name or what his favorite dish on the menu is. The wine steward offers
three suggestions and Jacques predictably goes for the French Bordeaux.

"To us," he toasts, once the wine has been poured into the oversized goblets. "Together again. It's been so good."

"We click," I say, touching my glass to his and going for a metaphor. Which he probably doesn't get. Every so often, I wish Jacques knew the language well enough to share my humor.

He puts down the glass. "I'm not always serious, *mon amour,* but I must be tonight. I have it in my heart to tell you how much you mean to me."

"And you mean a lot to me, too," I tell him, reaching for his hand.

"*Bien.* That is good," he says, lacing his fingers through mine. "But let me tell you. When I first came back to you, such a sad time. I had just divorced. She and I, it was never so good. She was like so many girls who meant nothing. I thought there would never again for me be love. And then I thought of you. Of us."

I stroke his thumb with mine and he squeezes my hand then takes a long sip of wine. If I'm supposed to say something here, I don't know what it is. So I wait. And Jacques continues.

"After all the years, I called and you let me back into your life. And I thought 'This woman knows love. Knows that love is forever.' I was no more sad. From you, I learned that I could love and be loved again. And for that," he says, reaching across the table and taking my other hand in his, "I will thank you forever."

If this is a proposal, it's taking a long time. And there's something in Jacques' tone that tells me he's about to go in a different direction.

"The week you couldn't come to Dubai, I met a woman at the hotel," he says, trying hard not to meet my eye. "Catrine. She is in my same business and was at the conference. A very smart woman, just like you."

I pull back one of my hands to take a gulp of wine. Right now, I wouldn't mind a nice light Californian. Wine or guy. Reflexively, I finger one of my earrings.

"And you slept with her?" I ask cautiously, thinking we're back on familiar ground. Ground I don't want to be standing on.

"Yes, of course," he says a little too quickly. "But it's much more. And it is because of you, my darling. You taught me that when you ask for love, sometimes it is there. So my heart was open again. And Catrine walked into it."

Now I pull my other hand away. I suddenly have a vivid image of

Catrine—all blond, perfectly coiffed, 105 pounds of her—walking into his heart. I hope it was bloody.

"Jacques," I say, steeling my nerves and trying to keep my dignity intact, "why didn't you tell me about this earlier? Why did you keep coming back here?"

"Because we have such a wonderful time together, I didn't want to spoil it," he says blithely. "And I don't want it ever to change. Catrine, yes, she will move to Paris to be with me. But I come to New York still often."

Now there's a different proposal than I was expecting. Good sex three or four times a year with a man who's fallen in love because of— but not with—me.

"It's not in me to do that, Jacques," I say, struggling with all the different emotions I'm feeling. Here's a man who clearly cares for me—I know I'm not fooling myself about that—who's breaking my heart. Not quite tearing it out, but pretty darn close. I might not have chosen to make a life again with Jacques, but damn it, I wanted the decision to be mine.

"Whatever you decide, I will always be here for you," Jacques says, playing with the bread basket since my hand is unavailable. "I'm so proud of you, *mon chouchou*. You have made a life. Your life with Jen. And now me, I am ready to start over, too."

"Well, I wish you well," I say, because what else am I supposed to say? I look down, and for several moments, we're both quiet. Jacques picks up his menu, obviously relieved that he's said his piece and I don't seem too angry.

I pick up my menu, too, but there's no way I'm making it through dinner. Even an appetizer sounds wholly unappetizing. I play distractedly with my wineglass. I'm not the kind of woman who does this. I'm pleasant. Affable. Always want everybody to feel good. Worry about their feelings more than mine. So it's totally out of character—but feels surprisingly good—when I rise gracefully from my seat and dump the full glass of red wine over Jacques' head. His *stupide* head.

"I'm sure someone as smart as Catrine is good with stains," I say, making what I hope is a memorable exit from the restaurant. I'm glad we're not at the original Four Seasons. I still hope to go there one day.

Chapter FIFTEEN

"BUT YOU KEPT the earrings, right?" Lucy asks, leaning forward on the sofa and brushing back a strand of hair from my face.

"I already told you I did," I say, blowing my nose for the zillionth time. Wish somebody would find a constructive use for snot. There seems to be no limit on how much your body can produce.

"I want to see them," Lucy says, obviously worried about my morals. That they were too high. And that I sent back the earrings—or threw them away.

"I've put them in the safe-deposit box. For Jen. My legacy to her for having an idiot for a mother."

"I told you weeks ago I hated Jacques," Lucy says fiercely. "Anybody who screwed around on you once is going to . . ." She pauses, the subject hitting a little too close to home. Her own home. "Anyway, you're as far from an idiot as anyone could be," she says loyally.

"Right. A lot of women sleep with a man an hour before getting ditched. Happens all the time. Regular feature at the Four Seasons. The hotel's probably considering a whole new promotional package—'the Hump-and-Dump Weekend.' You have sex and then you break up."

"Actually, they're thinking of calling it the 'Come-and-Go,' Lucy says cheerfully, getting into the game.

"Yup. The restaurant could have a special section with extra-large glasses and wine-resistant seats."

"I love that you threw the wine at him," Lucy says, her eyes glistening. "It's so Katharine Hepburn."

For some reason, that makes me start crying again. I reach over to the mountainous pile of used tissues next to me, but Lucy efficiently sweeps them away into a garbage bag and hands me a new box of Kleenex.

"I have something to make you feel better," she says. "I made you chicken soup."

Now that stops my crying. "You *made* me chicken soup?" I try again. "*You* made *me* chicken soup?" This must be worse than I thought. Lucy would never go into the kitchen for a simple broken heart. I must have cancer. Inoperable cancer. If Jacques hadn't dumped me, I never would have known.

"Why are you so surprised?" Lucy asks, genuinely abashed, as she pulls a plastic Tupperware container out of a Prada shopping bag. "Try it."

I open the blue lid and look at the watery broth that has a few unidentifiable objects floating on top.

"Mmm," I say. "I never saw pink chicken soup before."

"Of course not. I added food coloring to make it prettier. That chickeny yellow can be so dreary."

I stir the soup slowly with the silver spoon Lucy has thoughtfully provided and cautiously bring a taste up to my lips.

"For heaven's sake, you don't have to eat it," Lucy says, stopping me.

"Might as well. Can't make me feel worse," I say, sipping. Then I take another spoonful. "Not bad. A little salty, maybe, but not bad." I continue slurping my way through the half-gallon container.

"If you're eating this, you're in worse shape than I thought," Lucy says. But she looks pleased. "Maybe I'll bring some to Dan as a peace offering."

"Peace offering. That's good. You should do something. But if it's soup, you might want to add some chicken. And maybe a noodle or two." I stare into the bowl. "How'd you make this anyway? Stones from the backyard?"

"Homemade chicken soup's really not very hard," Lucy says, my new Galloping Gourmet. "I just mixed Knorr's bouillon cubes with some red food coloring."

"Get that recipe out of *Budget Living*?" I ask.

"No, I made it up. I see why you like to cook. It's very creative."

"What's floating in it?" I ask. "The little silver bits?"

Lucy looks into the container, then sticks her index finger in to pull out a sample. She holds it up to the light.

"Maybe some wrapping from the bouillon cubes," she says. "They were sticky."

"Festive," I say, undeterred. I take a few more desultory sips, and when the doorbell rings a minute later, I look up wearily. Could be more people with food, though I don't think word of my grieving state has spread around the neighborhood this quickly.

"I know it's not Jacques," I say, not moving to get up.

"And I know it's not Dan," says Lucy, also not budging.

"You get it, I can't cope."

"No, you get it, it's your house. And while you're up, would you turn off that depressing song? I don't care if it's the Beatles—I'm not listening to that loop of 'Yesterday' one more time."

The bell rings again, and this time I shuffle to the door and hear Boulder's buoyant voice. "Open up! Open up! It's us! The Queers with Cheer!"

"The *what*?" I ask, swinging open the door to a grinning Boulder, who's holding the largest cake I've ever seen. Standing right next to him, wearing the same grin and the same lime green shirt, is his doppelganger with dark hair. If this were a soap opera, I'd figure Boulder was playing both parts. But the evil twin, who doesn't look very evil, comes in first.

"Hi, I'm Cliff," he says, sailing past me with a huge cooler. "Sorry you got so screwed over by the French guy. But we're here to make you forget all about it."

Boulder steps behind me to fasten on a necklace of pulsating blue-and-orange neon lights. "Party time!"

I go over to the sofa and plop back down. "Thanks for trying, but I'm useless," I say resignedly. "Anyway, meet my friend Lucy. She's more fun."

"Are you the one whose husband left her?" Boulder asks. "God, you must be in a lousy mood, too."

Lucy glares at me. I squirm and mouth "Sorry."

"Guess I've been having too many late-night conversations with Boulder," I tell her. "But we won't sell the story to the *National Enquirer*. I promise."

"Scout's honor," Boulder agrees. "But come on. We came here to bring you some fun."

"I can see we have our work cut out for us," says Cliff, pulling a dozen CDs out of his backpack. "But if I can get rich, jaded thirteen-year-olds dancing at bar mitzvahs, you girls'll be a cinch."

"Cliff spent his first six months in L.A. as a d.j.'s assistant," Boulder says proudly. "He taught the Electric Slide at Adam Sandler's cousin's friend's bar mitzvah."

Even I know that qualifies as fame in Los Angeles. So I'm suitably impressed. Still weepy, but impressed.

"First, drinks to loosen everybody up," says Cliff, opening his cooler. "Daiquiris, margaritas and piña coladas. Which'll it be?"

"Piña colada," says Boulder, lining up for a cup.

"No way," I tell him. "What are you going to say at your next AA meeting?"

"They're all nonalcoholic, silly," he says gaily. "Who needs rum? The best part of the piña colada's the coconut, anyway. This is the party where nobody feels bad in the morning."

I look over at the gigantic cream cake, now filling most of my dining room table. "I'll feel pretty bad after I eat that," I say. "And the way I'm going, I'll devour the whole thing."

"Can't. It's cardboard and shaving cream. Just like I got for my twelfth birthday at fat kids' sleep-away camp," Boulder says sadly, reliving the painful memory.

Cliff comes over and puts his arm around him. "That was a long time ago, sweetie. Look at those abs. You're gorgeous now."

Boulder, still feeling like a chubby twelve-year-old, doesn't perk up, so Cliff says, "I'm not the only one who thinks you're gorgeous, right? How about Barry Rivers? Tell the girls about Barry."

What's Barry Rivers have to do with Cliff and Boulder? I hope it's not another romantic triangle. Give me squares. Circles. Octagons. Anything that doesn't involve Pythagoras.

But Boulder smiles now and so does Cliff.

"TEEEEELLLLL HERRR!" Cliff calls out, turning the two syllables into an entire song. "No, better yet. SHHOOOOW HERRR!" Not a bad tune. If he thinks up a few more lines, he might make *Billboard*'s Top 100.

Boulder obliges and takes center stage in my living room. He bends his knees slightly, plants his feet about a foot apart, extends his arms like an airplane, and begins wiggling his hips.

"Party game! Party game!" says Cliff. "Everybody plays! Guess Boulder's good news."

Boulder's knees are bent a little deeper and his hips are swinging in bigger and bigger circles. But I refuse to guess the obvious.

"Hula hoops?" I offer instead. "Something to do with hula hoops?"

"Genius!" says Cliff. "You're in the right place already! Hula hoops! Hawaii! His good news happens in Hawaii!"

I don't want to break his heart and tell him that hula hoops weren't invented in Waikiki.

"Hawaii," says Lucy, moving to the edge of the sofa, totally in the spirit of the game, and bursting with tropical word associations. "Luaus. Pig roasts. Leis. Are you getting laid in Hawaii?"

"Only if Cliff visits," says Boulder righteously.

Not having hit the jackpot, Lucy keeps going. "Let's see. Waterfalls? Volleyball? How about surfing? You're going to Hawaii to surf?"

"Bingo!" says Cliff, the perpetual d.j.'s assistant, reaching into a goody bag and tossing Lucy a gold-wrapped Hershey's kiss. "You win part one. Now WHHHYYYY is Boulder going to Hawaii to surf?"

"Because I got a Dr Pepper commercial!" Boulder screams, unable to contain his excitement any longer. "Not even Diet Dr Pepper. The real thing!"

"Ohmygod that's so great!" Lucy and I say, practically in unison, rushing over and hugging him so energetically that we almost knock him over.

"It's all because of you," Boulder says, hugging me back. "Barry Rivers saw me on our TV date and called. He's only the biggest casting agent in the whole world and he had me come in right away."

"Boulder had four callbacks," says Cliff. "First he had to take off his shirt and Barry just loved his body. Second time, Barry asked him to smile. You know he aced that. Third time, he had to chug a can of Dr Pepper. No dribbling. And finally . . ." Cliff pauses for effect. Or maybe to get his vocal cords ready. "He got to RRREEEAAADDDD."

"You have a speaking part?" asks Lucy, grasping the profound meaning of shilling soda. "You'll get great residuals. Money every time they run the commercial. Better than a credit line at Citibank."

"Do your part for them, sweetie," says Cliff, the proud partner.

"I don't know if I'm ready," demurs Boulder.

"He's only been practicing since yesterday," Cliff explains. "He's still getting the character."

We nod solemnly. "We're all friends here," I remind him. "Go for it."

Boulder resumes his surfing position. He bursts into the famous Boulder grin, then looks straight at us, camera ready.

"WHOOOOOSSSSHHHH," he says, stretching out the syllable in what is clearly a Cliff-influenced performance. I'm waiting for the rest of the line, but it never comes. I look over at Lucy to see if a future fortune can be built on one word.

"Yup," she confirms. "That's a speaking part."

"Isn't he perfect? He's going to be so famous," says Cliff.

"He's fabulous," says Lucy. "That's my professional opinion."

"Everybody on the dance floor!" says Cliff, bouncing on his Pumas. "We're celebrating!"

He puts music on the CD player that I've never heard before. "The

Electric Slide!" he announces with enough enthusiasm to end the California energy crisis. "Come on everybody! I'll teach you!"

Bolstered by Boulder's announcement and Cliff's coaxing, we fall in line. Why not? If it's good enough for Adam Sandler's cousin's friend, it's good enough for me.

Those L.A. kids must have had some bar mitzvahs, because for the next hour, my living room rocks. I'm lousy at the Electric Slide but turn out to have a gift for the Macarena. We go through a Motown set and then on to the Rolling Stones. Sixties music is like Beethoven—lives on forever. Can't tell me our kids will be dancing to 50 Cent forty years from now.

We scream out the lyrics "I can't get no . . . SATISFACTION!" at the top of our lungs and act like a bunch of raving groupies at Lollapalooza. We're rowdy and raucous, and after a riotous rendition of "I Will Survive," we all collapse in exhaustion on the couch.

But Cliff's not done. "One more song," says our favorite d.j., who's wrapped up enough parties to know how to do it right.

From the CD player comes James Taylor's soothing croon, and we circle our arms around each other, swaying side to side. At the chorus, we all join in.

"*Winter, spring, summer or fa-all . . . All you've gotta do is call,*" we warble emotionally. "*And I'll be there . . . You've got a friend.*"

We're maudlin now, as if we've gotten tipsy on our alcohol-free piña coladas.

I lean my head against Boulder's shoulder. "To Dr Pepper," I say emotionally. "And to your future. May it be all you want."

"To all of us. Making the future we want come true. Because we know we can," Boulder says. Now it really does sound like we're at a bar mitzvah. He's good at sincerity. Maybe his next gig could be for Hallmark.

I'm teary-eyed again—but this time I'm happy. Because JT's got a point. It's nice to have friends.

* * *

I may be working with Josh Gordon these days, but it's pretty clear I'm not going to be adding him to my buddy list any time soon. The next morning I'm at his office, having been summoned for an eight a.m. conference. At least I talked him out of meeting at seven.

I take the elevator to the thirty-second floor where his assistant Peggy leads me into an enormous corner office with breathtaking views in three directions. So this is what they mean by on top of the world.

"He's just finishing up a conference," says Peggy, an efficient sixty-ish woman who, making small talk, has already told me that she's been with her boss for twenty-two years. Considerably longer than his wife lasted. "Just make yourself comfortable until he gets back. Can I get you some coffee?"

"I'll be fine," I say. But the moment she walks out, I'm not. I want to look settled—but not too settled—when Josh Gordon walks in. Give the appearance that I don't mind that I've been kept waiting, but that I do have many other pressing things on my agenda for the day.

I go over to a bookcase and peruse the silver-framed family photos gracing the second shelf. The cute blonde who morphs in the pictures from baby in a pram to little girl riding a pony must be Ireland. Cute kid. In every photo, she's either alone or with Josh. No apparent scissor cuts where the ex-wife has been expunged, but she's nowhere in sight.

Five minutes pass. I've got the pictures down pat and I've memorized all the titles on the bookshelf. Milton Friedman's *Economics* I understand, but why is he reading *Atlas Shrugged*? Time to sit down. I lower myself carefully onto the couch. It's way too soft and I sink down deep into the cushions. Better move since this position always makes my legs look too fat. Maybe the hardback chair in front of his desk. I give it a try. But this is worse. If I'm sitting up this straight while I'm talking to Josh, he'll feel like he's taking a meeting with Queen Elizabeth. One's too soft, one's too hard. What am I, Goldilocks?

I stand up and notice that the zipper on my skirt has managed to make its way to the front. I try to swivel it back around but the hook snags on the top of my panty hose and won't move. I'm tugging furiously at it when Josh makes his entrance. At least there's nothing on my face this time. He glances at me. He's busy—clearly fitting me in between deals—and my disarray barely registers.

"Have a seat," Josh says, gesturing to a comfortable chair near his desk. Why didn't I try that one before? It's just right.

"I've been going over the finances for the benefit," he begins, not bothering with small talk. Guess I didn't have to spend an hour last night boning up on CNN's headline stories.

"Contributions look good," Josh continues, rifling through a sheaf of papers on his desk. "Ad sales for the program are strong. But I'm confused about some of these costs."

"Everything's been donated," I assure him confidently, or as confident as I can be with my arm twisted into a contorted angle as I try to cover up my errant zipper. "Except a few minor costs for the production. Vincent said he'd send those off to you."

"I got them," says Josh, coming around with his papers and leaning on the side of the desk. "Some interesting ones. For example, did you approve the four thousand dollars in pink gels?"

"Of course not," I say stalwartly. "No expensive gels or powders or pancake makeup. I told Vincent to buy Maybelline at Duane Reade. Under no circumstances was he to splurge on real greasepaint."

"The bill wasn't for makeup," says Josh, handing me the invoice, which is labeled THEATER LIGHTING SUPPLY, INC.

Oh, those gels. Boy, I'm in total control today. Josh must be impressed. But even looking at the bill, I'm still baffled.

"All that money for extra-soft lighting? Pink gels?" I ask. "Doesn't make sense. These are twelve-year-old kids. Even Joan Rivers doesn't need that much help."

Josh gives me one of his little smiles. From him, that's like seeing the sun in Seattle. Doesn't happen often. But when it does, it's warmer than you'd think.

"How about this one?" Josh asks, pulling out another bill. "A thousand dollars to Millicent M. Who's she?"

"Definitely not Vincent's girlfriend," I say quickly.

I take the receipt and realize it's for artificial flowers. Probably for the Covent Garden scene. Would have been cheaper to grow our own.

I sigh and reach over to take the whole pile of receipts. "Sorry, Josh," I say. "Vincent's used to overblown Broadway budgets. You know, where they pay for union musicians who don't play. For stagehands who don't move anything. And for dressers who stand around during the nude scene in *The Full Monty*. Broadway has more padding than Tim Allen in *The Santa Clause*. But I'll try to rein Vincent in."

Josh nods, apparently softened by my rant. "I appreciate that. I've heard Vincent's a little temperamental. I'll talk to him if you want. I deal with financial problems every day."

"I can do it," I say tentatively. "I'm no Alan Greenspan, but I'm not bad at managing money." He can't argue. He's never seen my checkbook.

But Josh, amazingly, picks up on my hesitancy. "Look, not a problem for me," he says generously, with another small smile. "You've been doing a great job on the benefit. I can help you out. Let your director be mad at me instead of you."

What's going on here? That's so nice of him. I better check the weather in Seattle. Global warming seems to be affecting everything.

Peggy peeks her head in the door before I get a chance to thank Josh and take him up on his offer.

"Sorry to bother you, but Mia's on the phone," Peggy says. "I told her you were in a meeting, but she asked that I interrupt."

"I'll call her back," he replies tersely.

"I offered. She says it's an emergency."

Josh glances over at me.

"Should I step out?" I ask.

"No. I'll just be a moment. Sorry. My ex-wife."

More irritated than worried, Josh snatches up the phone.

He issues a brusque "Hello" into the receiver then paces behind his desk as Mia talks. And talks. And talks. He seems to be losing patience.

"I don't call this an emergency," he says, finally hearing enough. "You could have waited. You interrupted an important meeting."

So now I'm important. Hey, that's not bad.

Josh listens to Mia for a couple more minutes.

"Of course I paid your therapy bills," he says, exasperated. "I told you I'd take care of them for as long as you need."

Which could be a long time, from the sounds of this conversation. Poor man. First the benefit's bills and now Mia's.

"Mia, if your psychiatrist doesn't want to see you anymore, it's not because he hasn't been paid," Josh says tartly. "It must be something else."

And I can guess what it is. I don't know Mia, but I do know shrinks. Could be she's whining too much. Or not keeping her therapist properly entertained. It's not enough just to go into your therapist's office and cry anymore. In New York, you're competing against some of the unhappiest people in the world. Bored with your husband? No longer satisfied with Frederic Fekkai? Anguished by recovered memories of inadequate SAT scores? Oh, please. They've heard it all before. You've got to dig deeper and constantly come up with new material. Keeping your shrink happy is tougher than holding on to a stand-up gig at The Comedy Club.

"Mia, I have to get back to work," Josh says in a tempered voice that he's obviously honed after too many calls like this. "You know I'm here for you if you really need me. But we're divorced now. You can't keep calling me for things like this."

He hangs up the phone and distractedly thumbs through some messages on his BlackBerry. Looking up, he seems surprised to realize that I'm still there.

"Anything you need?" he asks randomly.

Sure. I can think of a few things. I'll take a husband, a house in Montauk, a better prescription drug plan, and a DVD of the first season of *The Sopranos*. And I'll settle for any two of the four.

"No, I guess we're okay," I say.

"Fine, then we're done," he says. "Keep going with the benefit. And talk to Vincent about his expenses. Let's get this under control."

I hesitate. Not the time to remind him that he said he'd deal with Vincent for me. Mia's ruining things for everyone.

"Call me if you run into a problem," he says dismissing me. "I take all sorts of trivial calls from women."

Guess we're not his favorite species right now.

*   *   *

"Maybe Josh Gordon would be nicer to you if you got a face-lift," Lucy suggests to me an hour later, as we're sitting in the waiting room of Dr. Gloria Roget, the latest addition to Lucy's beauty maintenance crew.

Lucy peers into the large daisy-shaped mirror that dominates an entire wall of the outer office and immediately makes "The Face"—the one every woman over forty regularly tries out, though usually in the privacy of her own home. She draws up the skin across her cheekbones with her forefingers and pulls it tight, then uses her palms to stretch out her jowls. Or what she worries are jowls.

"What do you think?" Lucy asks, turning to me with her pulled-back face. "Wouldn't I look better?"

"You look good now."

"I'm thinking future perfect," she says. "Try it."

I copy the same maneuver and study The Face—mine—in the mirror. This firmer, smoother me is an improvement, but I'm not ready to go under the knife. Maybe I'll just get some duct tape on the way home. Wouldn't matter as far as Josh Gordon is concerned, anyway. My face could be as taut as an Army recruit's cot and it still wouldn't change his grumpy opinion of women.

"This isn't what we're here for, anyway," I remind Lucy, releasing my hands and letting my face fall—literally—back into place.

"I know. That's for another time. Today's about boobs," Lucy says, still looking into the mirror. She moves her hands from her face and cups them under her breasts, pushing them forward. "Breasts like this would change my life," she tells me. "You wouldn't understand. You're lucky. You'll never need implants."

"You don't, either. You're just unhappy with everything right now."

"Maybe. But that doesn't mean I'm not unhappy about my boobs, too. Who isn't? You spend your whole preadolescence waiting for them, and then they're never right. Too big, too small, too round, too flat. You hate it if men look at them, and you hate it even more if they don't."

"I know. We all knock our knockers. Look at this," I say, putting my hands under my own slightly heftier breasts and hoisting them up a few inches. "This was me in 1989. And this," I say, pulling my hands away and letting my breasts fall back into the underwire of my Maidenform, "is me today."

"Oh, Jess, you look fine," Lucy says.

"That's only because of my new 18-hour bra. Figure I've got six more hours left on this baby. Don't ask me what I do after that."

"At least you're not worried about springing a leak," Lucy says, playing with the padding on her own bra. "This water-filled stuff is supposed to look more natural than foam. But it makes me nervous."

"If you're smaller, you never sag," I parry, jiggling from side to side, now thoroughly mesmerized by watching my own breasts in the mirror.

"It's amazing we ever became friends at all," says Lucy. "You're the kind of girl I hated in high school. Great tits, and always pretending they were such a *burden*."

"Let's call it a draw," I say, refusing to explain how embarrassing it was all those years ago being the first one in my class to sprout. All my friends were still in training bras. Although I could never figure out what they were training—or training for. I spent the whole year slouch-shouldered so boys wouldn't stare at my chest. Something else not likely to arouse Lucy's sympathy. But I'm still not sure why she's making such a big deal about this.

"Lucy, you're gorgeous. You're perfectly proportioned. What's wrong with a 34-B anyway?"

"In Hollywood, everything," says Lucy. "I must be the only woman in town who has her original set. California's the land of plenty. People talk about grapefruit and cantaloupe and they don't mean fruit. And Hunter's a watermelon guy. I catch him ogling big-chested women all the time."

"So this is about Hunter?" I ask, fairly incredulous that she's made a decision about the man in her future. And that it requires surgical enhancement. Not his. Apparently she's over the small birthday present. Not to mention the small penis.

"Not really," Lucy says. "I'm not doing this for Hunter."

"For Dan?"

"He likes my breasts."

"Then who?"

"Jess, I'd never do this for a man. What kind of woman do you think I am?"

"The kind we all are. Insecure. Tell me the truth. Do you think Jacques' new girlfriend has better breasts than me? Is that why he picked her?"

"Who knows why any of us are doing anything lately," Lucy says with a sigh.

I sit back. "I'm not going to let you do anything stupid," I say.

"Right," Lucy says, as a nurse finally ushers us into the doctor's office. "Ask all the questions I forget to."

Lucy gives the nurse all her vital stats, including health history and insurance policy. Implants aren't covered on her plan, but a case could be made, I suppose, for including them under her mental health rider. Then a procession of stunning assistants bustle in and out of the consultation room. Either God or Dr. Roget is responsible for their firm breasts, and since none of the young ladies seems older than twenty-five, I'm betting on God. But Lucy would call me naïve.

Finally, the good doctor herself comes in. She's tall and sinuous with pixie-short blond hair and—I'm not being naïve about this one—collagen-plumped lips. The diploma on the wall says Harvard Medical School, but I wouldn't be surprised to see "Playboy Pin-up" also listed on her résumé.

Dr. Roget seems ready to give a peppy presentation, but first she needs to know which speech to give. She stares at Lucy's chest, then searches through the notes the nurse has handed her.

"So, your breasts," she says finally. "Are you here to make them larger or smaller?"

If the contractor has to ask whether to paint the inside or the outside of the house, I figure you don't need any work done at all. But Lucy's taking no such cues.

"Larger," Lucy says.

"Good choice," counters Dr. Roget.

And with that, New York's premier boob specialist launches into her lecture, covering all the bases—size and shape, silicone versus saline, nerve damage and nipple numbness. I'm sure this particular form of torture is illegal under the Geneva Convention, but Lucy doesn't blanch. It's all in the name of beauty. No Pain, No Gain. Might as well tattoo that on Lucy's butt. Which is what I'm afraid we'll be correcting next.

"So," says Dr. Roget, encouraged by Lucy's continuous nods of agreement, "one important question. What level of pertness are you going for?"

"How many levels of pertness are there?" asks Lucy, scribbling down notes and hanging on the doctor's every word.

"Many," says the doctor, leading us over to her computer screen and hitting a few keys. A 3-D image of Lucy's torso, scanned in from a photo one of the nurses took earlier, pops up. With a few keystrokes, the doctor enlarges Lucy's breasts, changing her from pretty producer to bodacious babe. Two strokes later, and Lucy looks like Betty Boop. Much more of this and those torpedoes are going to explode.

"Isn't this equipment incredible?" asks the doctor proudly. I'm not sure if she's talking about the computer or Lucy's potential bazooms. "Anyway, your choice on size. What will it be?" Dr. Roget's so casual, she could be asking Lucy to pick out a new mascara.

Lucy takes a moment. "Second one," she says conservatively. The first middle-of-the-road choice I've ever seen her make.

"Done," says Dr. Roget, pulling a photo album off the shelf. "Now take a look at some of our before-and-after shots. I think you'll be amazed at the changes. We get some impressive results."

Lucy and I flip through the pages, oohing and aahing as if it were J. Lo's wedding album. Whichever one. Frankly, none of the women in the pictures look that transformed—except in the "before" photos, the lighting is less flattering. And in the post-surgery shots, the underwear is a lot nicer. But Lucy sees magic, not good lighting.

"It *is* amazing," Lucy says, transfixed. "Exactly what I imagined."

She's ready to sign on the dotted line, and Dr. Roget, ready to close the deal, flicks to the calendar on her Microsoft Outlook.

"You're in luck. Somebody just canceled her surgery," says Dr.

Roget, clicking through her schedule. "How's nine a.m. four months from yesterday work out for you?"

"Lucy's busy," I jump in. "Not a good day for her. She already has a hair appointment. And an eyebrow shaping."

Lucy glares at me. But I take my responsibilities seriously. Time for me to speak up. In quick succession, I rat-a-tat my questions. Post-operative pain? Can be lots of it. Scarring? Might happen. Asymmetry? Ditto. Or not ditto. Your breasts may not end up the same size. Dr. Roget seems to be getting annoyed with being treated like a hostile witness on *Law & Order,* but I don't mind because when I glance over at Lucy, she seems to be coming slightly to her senses.

"And what about hardness?" I ask Dr. Roget. "I've heard implants can make your breasts feel unnatural."

"Not really a worry. Happens sometimes. But don't even think about it," she says, lightly tossing off my concern.

"I don't know how you could do something like this to your body without knowing what it will feel like," I say, shaking my head. "I wouldn't even buy a peach without squeezing it first."

"Well then come on. Squeeze them," Dr. Roget challenges, pulling down her stretchy V-neck shirt and lacy La Perla bra in one swift motion. Her breasts pop forward. Wow. Walking advertisement for her own work. But wait a minute here. Can't be her own work. If Lucy were smart, she'd ask for the name of Dr. Roget's plastic surgeon.

But okay, if she wants me to squeeze, I'm there. I'm not shy. And this is all in the name of medical research. I reach across the desk and grab a handful of breast. First lightly and then not so lightly.

"Lucy, come try it!" I say.

But Lucy, now pale, is glued to her chair.

"Because the point I'd like to make," I say, turning into the senior physician at attending rounds, "is that even breasts that look this good can have some subcutaneous scarring." I'm good. Very good. All those nights scrolling through WebMD.com have paid off. "At first squeeze, the breast may feel normal. But even a baby would know the difference. Especially a baby."

"I'm not having any more babies," Lucy says, finally able to speak.

"A devoted husband—one who's loved you for twenty years, for example—would be able to tell. And wouldn't like it. And even a self-absorbed lover would notice and object."

"Unless his big thrill came from showing you off in a low-cut Versace at Spago in Beverly Hills," Lucy says. I'm not sure if that's a pro or con.

"I don't know what you're possibly feeling," says Dr. Roget, now squeezing her own breasts vigorously, as if she's searching for a misplaced earring in there. "They feel fabulous to me. I don't know what all the commotion's about."

"That's because you've been doing this so long you don't even know what natural feels like anymore. Here, feel mine."

"No thank you. I only touch people who've made an appointment," says Dr. Roget, snapping her shirt back up. "If you have any more questions," she says to Lucy as she stamps out of the room, "feel free to come back. Without your friend."

Chapter SIXTEEN

"I'M HAVING a mother-in-law problem," Lucy complains, as we sit down at a cracked red plastic booth at Dell's dingy diner. My feet stick to the gummy green-and-black linoleum floor and I flip the selection chart on the tableside jukebox, last updated with Nancy Sinatra's "These Boots Were Made for Walkin'." Which still passes as popular music in Pine Hills.

I stare into my watery cup of coffee and dump in two packs of Equal, thinking it might mask the bitter taste. Before I get to Lucy's mother-in-law, there's a more pressing issue.

"Why are we at Dell's again?" I ask.

"Because I was hungry," says Lucy. Who, best I can tell, does nothing but eat these days.

She calls the waitress over and orders blueberry pie à la mode. "Don't give me one of those skimpy pieces," she says, getting up to point out the slice she wants under the plastic-domed pie plate on the counter. "And I need a few packages of Splenda, too." She walks back to the booth and slides in.

"I don't get it," I say, sipping carefully at my coffee. Didn't need to bother. Dell's always serves it lukewarm. "Why do you need Splenda when the blueberry pie is already five thousand calories?"

"Why make it worse?" asks Lucy blithely. She contemplates the piece of pie that the waitress has now plunked down in front of her. Dell's pastries are made strictly from canned fruit and cornstarch, which doesn't make them land lightly on the table—or the stomach.

Lucy digs in with gusto and swallows hard. Not easy to get Dell's pie down. The place has been here since 1952 and I'd guess the pie has, too. "By the way, you should stop using that Equal," she rebukes me between bites. "Splenda is all natural. Pure sucralose."

I have to remember to ask her where those all-natural sucralose fields are. Kennebunkport?

"What happened to your perennial diet?" I ask. "And don't tell me Atkins has stretched the blueberries into blueberry pie. You've been eating everything in sight and you're still as skinny as the Pine Hills Yellow Pages."

"The Aggravation Diet," Lucy says. "Eat anything you want. The pounds melt off."

"Only you, Lucy," I say, putting down my coffee. "Even when you're miserable, you're golden. Most people eat when they're stressed and next thing they know, they end up at Lane Bryant. You get depressed and you're still buying size fours at the Armani sample sale."

"Size two. But the truth is, I don't care anymore. I've given up. On everything." Lucy sighs theatrically and puts down her fork. "At least that's how I'm feeling today. I seem to bounce back and forth. One minute I'm all excited about what surprises lie ahead in a Life Without Dan. The next, I can hardly get my head off the pillow, wondering how I've blown everything that's ever meant anything to me."

"You haven't blown it yet," I tell her. "Messed it up a little, I'll admit."

"No, blown it," says Lucy. "I told you. My mother-in-law."

That's right. Lucy's mother-in-law. Not only is Lucy blessed with the Aggravation Weight-Loss gene—which is what the scientists at NIH should really be working on cloning—but she has the only mother-in-law this side of Mars who actually thinks her precious baby boy married somebody worthy of him. She and Lucy genuinely like each other. Zelda, who's short and round and wears her salt-and-pepper hair pulled back in a scrunchie, started one of the first women's consciousness-raising groups in the '60s. Now she's raising politically astute undergrads as a tenured professor at Smith. Her book—*Women in Basket-Carrying Cultures, 1952–1974*—is a standard text in the field. She and Lucy go on twice-yearly outings to the Metropolitan Museum of Art—to see the paintings, not the gift shop. She's proud of Lucy's job and actually applauds her daughter-in-law's ordering Christmas dinner from Dean & DeLuca. Not exactly my experience. The one time Jacques' mother caught me using frozen peas instead of shelling fresh ones myself, she acted as if I were Lucrezia Borgia, poisoning the family.

"Lucy, what problem could you possibly be having with Zelda?" I ask. "She's practically perfect."

"I know, I adore her," says Lucy, suddenly near tears. She pours a Splenda into her glass of ice water, stirs it with her finger and then gulps it down. I watch, mesmerized. Maybe that's what keeps her so thin. What the heck, I'll try it, too. I suddenly feel like a little girl at a Barbie tea party, drinking sugar water. Not even sugar water. Sugar-substitute water. This is pathetic.

I push aside the glass. "Is Zelda taking Dan's side in this?" I ask sympathetically. "Not so surprising. She loves you, but she *is* his mother."

"No, she's amazing. She's trying to be neutral. She told me that she understands what I've been going through. Not what I did, but what I've been going through. She was even the one who suggested I buy a Porsche for my midlife crisis. Or take up basket-weaving. She offered to teach me. Chapter Seven in her book."

"Try it," I shrug. "You've tried everything else. At least basket-weaving's constructive."

"Too late," Lucy says, sounding anguished. "Zelda's having a sixty-fifth birthday party this weekend. Dan's going with the kids. He asked me not to come."

"I don't get it," I say. "Sounds like Zelda would still be happy to have you."

"She would. That's what really hurts. Dan told me he doesn't want me there. He said it's a family party."

"But you're . . ." I stop, suddenly understanding what Dan meant.

"I'm not part of the family anymore," Lucy says bluntly, tears starting to stream down her face. "How could I not be part of the family? It's *my* family."

I dig through my bag for a Kleenex to give her, but Lucy's already dabbing her eyes with a neatly pressed handkerchief. Monogrammed with an "HG." Unless that hankie came as a bonus with a magazine subscription to *House & Garden,* I'm losing patience. Lucy's crying about her family and wiping away her tears with her lover's handkerchief. Ironic. Metaphoric. Anthropomorphic. No, that's something else. But so is Lucy's behavior.

"Lucy, if you want Dan back, you've got to stop crying on Hunter's shoulder," I say.

"I'm not," she protests.

"You're crying into his hankie, anyway," I say, reaching over and fingering the corner of the sodden white square. "Why would you even carry that around?"

Lucy shoves the offending handkerchief back into her pocket. "Didn't even know I had it," she moans.

"You need to make a choice. That's what it means to grow up."

"Grow up? If I have to get much older than this I'll kill myself."

"Nothing quite that drastic required. But tell me the truth. Is Hunter still in the picture, or just his hankie?"

"I don't know," she says uncertainly.

"Don't you think Dan deserves to know that he's your one and only? Don't you owe him that?" I ask.

"Hunter's never been a keeper," Lucy says. "He was just a toy, just for fun. But what if I give him up and Dan doesn't come back?"

"Won't happen," I say, though I'm not sure I completely believe it. Who knows what men will do. Even Dan.

Lucy pauses and looks seriously at me. "Dan's going off this weekend without me. Maybe he'll decide he likes his life better that way.

Why does he need me around? I've been acting kind of bitchy the last few months."

"I've noticed," I say.

"Don't be nasty," Lucy says, starting to cry again. "Not now when I'm so scared about everything."

"I'm sorry," I say, stroking her hand and trying to be comforting. "What are you scared about?"

Lucy sniffles. "Used to be I could look down the road and predict that every day would be just like the next. I thought I hated that. Now I'm terrified that I can't see down the road at all. I don't even know what'll happen tomorrow."

"What would you like to have happen?"

"I want to be happy," Lucy says, patting away a stray tear with the back of her hand. "I want to feel like I did when I was twenty and anything seemed possible. The whole world was in front of me. One wrong decision didn't matter because I'd get to make a million more. Every door was open. Now the only sound I hear is doors slamming shut."

"Okay, some doors close," I concede. "You'll never be a ballerina. You're not going to grab the Olympic gold for high-diving. And you'll never be a model, unless it's for age-defying makeup. But isn't the upside of getting older supposed to be that you have some perspective? You know what's important in your life. Kids. Husband. Friends. Great job. Family. And for you, a week every year at Canyon Ranch."

"I'm so over Canyon Ranch," Lucy says. "Next year I'm going to try kayaking down the coast of Costa Rica. Wanna come?"

"No thanks. I fall out of rowboats," I remind her.

"That was a canoe."

"Same difference."

"Then you're right—don't come with me."

"All right, I won't. But do you get my point? Maybe you should stop complaining and start appreciating."

"I know. I've had everything anyone could want. I see that now."

"About time," I say.

Lucy turns pale and clutches her stomach. Could be I was too harsh.

"Are you okay?" I ask. "Didn't mean to hurt your feelings."

Lucy shakes her head and doubles over. "You didn't," she says rushing toward the exit. "Just another door closing. Can't eat Dell's pie the way I used to."

When Jen gets into my car after school, her face is contorted into the kind of pout I haven't seen since I served deviled eggs with little olive eyes instead of pizza at her sixth birthday party.

"What's wrong?" I ask as she throws her knapsack into the back-seat and slams the door.

"Nothing."

"Have a bad day?"

"Nope."

"Somebody do something mean to you?" I try again.

"No."

"Well, at least I feel we're communicating," I tell her, pulling away from the curb and trying to ease into the row of shiny SUVs ferrying children from school to soccer games, tennis clinics, art workshops and orthodontist appointments. "I hear about mothers and daughters who can't talk about their problems. Thank goodness that's not us."

She gives me a condescending look and turns her head to stare out the half-open window.

"Ethan's an asshole," she mumbles, barely loud enough for me to hear.

So here's that famous parental conundrum. I want my daughter to talk to me, and when she finally does, I don't like her choice of words. But complain, and I may never hear another word out of her again.

"Why is Ethan an asshole?" I ask. Not a word I'd normally use. But kind of rolls off the tongue. Might have a few people I could say it to.

"All boys are assholes," she says definitively. "Men too."

Now we're getting somewhere. She hates half the human race.

Maybe I can narrow it down to a chosen few. "Did you and Ethan have a fight?" I ask gingerly.

"We broke up," she admits.

I don't want to make too little of this, but I don't want to make too much of it either. "Isn't that what has to happen? You're only eleven."

"Yup," Jen agrees. "It wasn't that much fun being his girlfriend since I'm not allowed to go out on dates. I kind of liked breaking up, though. All the girls came around me at recess. I cried and they gave me presents to make me feel better." She pulls the bounty out of her jean pocket. Two fluorescent ponytail holders, one handmade string bracelet, a rock, a squished Nutri-Grain bar and two partially dead dandelions.

"Not bad," I tell her. Nice kids—the kind who'll grow up to make chicken soup and throw dance parties for the dumped.

"I'm never going out with a boy again," Jen says, unwrapping the crumbly Nutri-Grain bar and taking a bite.

"Never's a long time," I say gently. "Sure, it hurts right now. But it goes away and you try again."

"Yeah, Drew gave me the rock. He said if I'm not going out with Ethan anymore, I can go out with him."

Oh, to be eleven again. I suddenly know what Lucy meant about all those open doors when you're young. Always a new man lined up just waiting to replace the last. Still, I wouldn't want to face final exams again. Or first love, for that matter.

"Mom, do you hate men, too?" Jen asks.

"Of course not. Some are nice and some aren't. Just like all people."

"But what about Jacques? Lily says you hate him. That's what her mom says, but I thought you liked him again."

I have to be careful about this one. Hate him? Well, yeah, that's a pretty good description. So is pissed, angry, hurt, insulted, outraged, offended. Fill in the blank. But that's not what Jen needs to hear.

"Sometimes people disappoint you," I admit. "You expect one thing and you get something else. But that's okay. The reason you date somebody is to find out what he's like."

"Ethan's really popular. When I was with him I felt popular, too. Now no one will like me."

"Whoa. Wrong. You know what, Jen? You're smart and funny and pretty and you're a good person. Never forget that. That's who you are. It doesn't matter who you're with."

"Yes it does," says Jen, twisting her hair around her finger. "Like if I go out with Drew, everyone will think I'm a dork."

"Or else everyone will think he's really cool. As long as you believe in yourself other people will, too. Sometimes it takes a long time to understand that. I even know some grown-up women who get confused about who they are."

"Do you, Mom?" Jen asks.

I pause, considering the question. Am I a different Jess depending on what man I'm with? Maybe once, but not anymore. "I kind of like myself now," I tell Jen honestly. "And I hope one day there'll be a man who likes me this way, too. Just like there'll be a man who likes you. Lots of them."

Have I done my job? Is her esteem properly raised? Can I prevent Jen from growing up to be one of those girls who defines herself strictly through a man?

"You're special exactly the way you are," I say, sounding dangerously like Mr. Rogers. "Do you understand what I'm trying to say?"

"Sure," Jen says, jumping out of the car as we pull into the driveway. "Girl power. We talk about it in school all the time. But I'm still not going out with Drew. He really is a dork."

Dan needs someone to bring along to a big client's party, and I'm drafted. Lucy gives me her okay. She had to zip off to L.A. for a meeting with some network bigwigs the minute Dan got back from Zelda's birthday weekend. Whether Dan would have invited Lucy to the party if she'd been around goes undiscussed.

Dan's my friend. This isn't a date. I know that. Which doesn't explain why I drink three glasses of champagne the minute I walk onto the rooftop garden of the Hudson Hotel. It's a star-filled night, with a full moon, just like Jacques used to order.

"I didn't realize this was going to be such a fancy party," I say to

Dan, looking around at the women in their glittering jewels and couture dresses that are either very, very short or very, very long. As far as I can tell, I'm the only one who went for knee-length. And definitely the only one in Bloomingdale's polished cotton.

"You look fine," Dan tells me. "I love it that you don't need an expensive dress to be the prettiest woman in the room."

He thinks he's being nice, but all I hear is that I don't spend enough on my clothes. And I bet he's wishing that he had his stunning Prada-clad Lucy on his arm.

We stroll around the rooftop, which has been transformed for the evening. The cozy pink-clothed tables for six are bedecked with tiny vases bursting with miniature roses and mirrored trays with rafts of Rigaud candles sending a glow over Manhattan.

"Remind me what we're celebrating tonight," I say to Dan.

"Two big multinational companies becoming one. I designed the new international tax structure for their big merger."

"Looks like a merger," I agree, "but not corporate. More like a wedding. Check out those entertainers wandering around."

"Where?" asks Dan, who's been too busy shaking hands with various business associates to take in the dozens of performers scattered about the room.

"Over there," I say, pointing.

"The guy in the blue tie? He's not an entertainer. That's the vice president of marketing. Nothing entertaining about him," Dan says.

"No," I say, swiveling Dan's head slightly. "The guy next to him. The one who's naked except for a Speedo and spray-painted in gold. What's he? The CFO?"

"Didn't notice him," says Dan, laughing. "Maybe he's one of the summer interns."

Whoever he is, he's joined by three identically Speedoed and spray-painted comrades who begin juggling fire-lit torches, tossing them back and forth, each time higher and higher.

"Risky business," I say. "Hope the deal wasn't that dangerous."

"Nope," he says, but he doesn't elaborate, because across the room, another quartet of performers has caught his eye. Belly dancers. They're spray-painted silver—I'm guessing the merger was in commodities—and wearing teeny, fringed bikini tops and wafty, navel-baring skirts. They sway back and forth in perfect unison, their jeweled belly buttons moving in hypnotizing rhythms. And Dan's entranced.

"Didn't know you were so interested in Middle Eastern dance," I say.

"Yup," he says, monosyllabically, never taking his eyes off the scantily clad quartet.

Dan, the nicest man I know. The least sexist. The nonchauvinist who sees women as friends and colleagues, not objects. Who supports a working wife, equal parenting, and a woman's right to pick up half the check—even Dan can't help ogling available female flesh. And in this case, there's a lot of it. Two of the women have voluptuous bodies. Make that rolls of fat around the middle. But none of the men who are quickly gravitating around them seem to care.

"They're a little chunky," I say to Dan as we join the tide moving toward the dancers.

"You think so?" he asks, obviously not sharing my critical eye.

Apparently it doesn't matter what I think. Most women I know spend way too much time dieting, exercising, slow-burning, fast-walking, purging, pruning, and doing whatever we can to fulfill some ideal image we hold in our heads. Men just want to see a flash of flesh. And they don't care if it's a little flabby. Sometimes I'll notice a girl in a micro-mini walking down the street, and all I see is whether or not she has fat thighs. All the guy sees is that she's wearing a short skirt.

I wander over to the reception table to get our placecard for dinner and notice that I'm going incognito tonight. MR. AND MRS. DANIEL BALDOR, TABLE 4. I've always wondered what it would feel like to be in Lucy's shoes. Actually I have been in Lucy's shoes. Tonight I'll just be in her seat.

I hang out by the half-naked jugglers, wondering who's going to scrub all that gold spray paint off them. Maybe they need volunteers. I don't know who started the myth that women don't enjoy looking at men's bodies. Probably the same guy who started the rumor that size doesn't matter. Sure women are interested in relationships, emotion, blah blah blah, all that stuff. But that doesn't mean we don't appreciate a good pin-up boy when we see him. That flash of flesh works for women, too.

The music changes and the naked Adonises stop juggling. Damn, must be time for dinner. Dan comes over to collect me and casts a good long look at my Gold Gods who are now escorting guests to the dinner tables.

"Those guys are a little chunky, don't you think?" Dan asks, teasing, as he leads me over to our seats.

"All muscle," I explain.

"Hey, I've got some, too," he says offering up his tuxedoed arm. "Feel mine."

I laugh and obligingly rub his firm bicep. Something else the sexes have in common—the need for constant reassurance. Got to throw a man a compliment every so often, too.

"That's one amazing body you've got there, pal," I joke loudly as I turn to take my seat. The man to my left looks up startled, hearing the compliment and assuming it's meant for him.

"Thanks, I didn't think you cared," says a familiar voice. A very familiar voice. He half stands to pull out my chair for me, but Dan's already done it. If the chair goes out any farther, I'll end up on the floor. Which would be par for the course, since the man to my left is Joshua Gordon.

"Josh, hello," I say, extending a freshly manicured hand. I look down to see which nail is chipped. Must be something wrong. I only see Josh Gordon when I'm getting a facial, there's orange paint on my cheeks, or my skirt is snagged on my panty hose.

"You two know each other?" Dan asks, surprised, as he leans across me to shake hands with Josh.

"*You* two know each other?" I ask, equally surprised, as Josh and Dan's handshake turns into congratulatory back-slapping over the merger that they apparently both helped forge.

"This is a helluva deal, and you're a helluva dealmaker," Dan says admiringly to Josh. "Honored to be sitting at your table."

"Not at all. Your restructuring plan for Germany is going to save us millions," Josh replies. "And that Holland idea was a brilliant stroke."

I'm glad the boys are friends but this is about as entertaining as a Matthew Perry movie. Am I going to have to listen to this all night? I play with the placecard that I'm still holding and clamp it down next to the wineglass in front of me. For some reason that catches Josh's eye, and he pauses midsentence.

He looks from the placecard, to me, to Dan, and then back to the placecard that's announced us as Mr. and Mrs.

"Jess, I didn't realize . . ." He pauses. For once he's the one who's flustered. He waves his finger back and forth between me and Dan. "You two . . . you're . . ."

"We're good friends," I say, immediately jumping into the breach. "I'm the ringer. Placecard doesn't know a thing."

I wait for Dan to say that the real Mrs. Baldor is in L.A. on business, but he just lets it pass. Lucy's name never crosses his lips.

"Oh, and let me introduce my friend, Marissa," says Josh, suddenly remembering his manners and putting his arm around the chair of the long-haired, white-blond beauty to his left. She looks us over with a cool gaze and, apparently deciding we're not worth the effort of "hello," gives a barely perceptible nod. Her stick-straight hair hangs almost to her waist. I'm hoping it's not natural and she had to spend at least nine hours at the hairdresser going through that torturous Japanese straightening process.

"Want to dance?" I ask Dan, as the ten-piece orchestra begins playing J. Lo's "Let's Get Loud."

Anything to get away from the table. The way Marissa's glaring at me could cause frost in Bora Bora.

"I don't think I can dance to that kind of music," says Dan.

"Come on, I'll teach you," I say, grabbing his hand. On the dance floor, Dan raises two fists like he's facing Mike Tyson, and moves one foot back and forth.

I grab his hands and shake them. "Loosen up," I laugh. "This isn't a prize fight. You win no matter what you do."

"I've already won. I'm with you, Jess," he says, catching the rhythm now and moving more easily. In fact, he gets so into the music that by the end of the song, he takes off his tuxedo jacket, tosses it on the back of his chair, and rolls up his shirtsleeves. When he rejoins me on the dance floor, the orchestra has switched gears and is now playing that romantic Kelly Clarkson anthem, "A Moment Like This."

Awkwardly Dan puts one arm around my waist, and extends his right hand to take mine.

"Usually you lead with the other hand," I say, drawing on the lessons I learned when I was ten in Miss Hewitt's weekly ballroom dance classes. Back then, we had to wear white gloves and one-piece dresses so the boys couldn't cop a feel of skin by sticking their grimy hands between our skirts and tops. Finally understand the wisdom. Now if I could only convince Jen to wear overalls.

Dan switches position to extend his left hand. "Lucy and I always did it the other way," he admits. "Couples fall into funny patterns, don't they? I guess I'm going to have to learn some new moves."

We find a groove and start swaying harmoniously to the music.

"Never heard this song before, but I kind of like it," says Dan, starting to hum along to the predictable tune.

"It was the hit from that first girl who won *American Idol*," I say.

"What's *American Idol*?"

"You're kidding. It's my favorite TV show. A huge hit."

"Not on CNN," he laughs. "Only station I watch."

I shake my head sadly. "Ah, Dan. This could be the end of a beautiful friendship. You and I clearly have nothing in common."

We dance for a moment or two in silence. Haltingly Dan pulls me closer. "Not the end of a friendship, but maybe the start of something else," he murmurs, barely audibly.

"Right. Maybe we can be ballroom dance champs," I say as we glide comfortably around the floor. "Supposed to be in the next Olympics, I hear. For all of us who never got the hang of pole vaulting."

"Not exactly what I had in mind," Dan says. He stops but doesn't let go of my hand. "Come on, I want to talk to you."

He leads me quickly off the dance floor and guides me to a secluded spot by the rooftop railing that's decorated with twinkling lights and hanging lanterns.

"Everything okay?" I ask.

"Look, Jess, I want to tell you the truth."

Uh-oh. Please lie to me. Nothing good ever came out of a conversation that started with wanting to tell the truth.

"You've been such a great friend," Dan says, looking out over the spectacular view of the city skyline rather than at me.

No good conversation ever came out of "you've been such a good friend," either. But Dan, unaware that he's sent up two red flags already, forges on.

"I've been thinking about this a lot lately. People in my office have been trying to fix me up since . . . well, you know since when." He looks uncomfortable, but he quickly recovers. "I keep saying no because I haven't wanted to go out with anyone. But with you it's different. We're already friends. I can talk to you about anything. And here we are out together and it feels good."

He pauses and turns to look at me. I'm too stunned to speak, but for some reason, I reach out and rub his arm. I think I'm being sympathetic, but Dan sees it as encouragement. He clasps his hand over mine.

"I finally figured out that if I'm going to date, you're the person I should do it with."

His proposition hangs in the air like Glade room freshener. Kind of sweet, but a little too heavy.

"No, I'm not," I say, trying not to let him see just how shaken I am. "I'm not the person you should be with. It's Lucy. You should be with Lucy. Don't try to get back at her this way."

"This has nothing to do with her," says Dan, miffed that I've even brought his wife into the picture. "It's about you and me. I like you, Jess. We understand each other. We laugh. It just makes sense for us to be together."

"It doesn't make any sense at all. For one thing, Lucy's my best friend. I could never do that to her. And besides, you belong with Lucy. You know you do."

"I don't know anything anymore," he says. "No, let me correct that. I know how I feel about you."

"You don't," I say, interrupting before he says something we'll both regret later. "You're just angry with Lucy. You're hurt. You're lonely. I'm not the answer. We shouldn't even talk about it anymore."

I start back to the table, but he grabs my hand. "Okay, I hear what you're saying. I know this would be awkward for you. But put that aside for a minute. Tell me frankly. If it weren't for Lucy, how would you feel about me? How would you feel about us?"

I stand there for a long time, looking at his anxious face. I should cut this off right now. Make it very clear that nothing can ever happen between us. Because nothing ever will. But gazing into his warm gray eyes, I end up admitting more than I intend to.

"I once told Lucy that you were the only husband in Pine Hills I'd want as my own," I say honestly.

"And what did she say?" he asks with a wry smile. "That you could have me?"

"You know her better than you think," I laugh. "But trust me, she loves you. You love her. And you've got to find a way back to each other."

"Hard to imagine that happening," he says as he leans in. He kisses me. It's a sweet kiss that lasts no more than a moment but it lingers on my lips. "I won't embarrass you anymore. Let's go back to the table."

We never make it back to our seats, because halfway around the room, the man in the blue tie who Dan had earlier identified as the vice president of marketing waylays him for some shop talk. I take the opportunity to slip away and head back to collect myself before having to face Dan again. Nobody else is at the table, but I'm glad to be alone. I pick at my arugula and radicchio salad, ignoring all the greens and chomping instead on the toasted pecans and hearty chunks of creamy blue cheese. What the heck. Doesn't matter if my midriff expands. I can always take up belly dancing.

"Abandoned?" asks Josh Gordon, coming over and sitting down in his place next to me.

"Yup. What about you? Where's the lovely Marissa?" I ask, realizing that the seat next to him is also vacant.

"The ice queen?" he asks, accurately gauging the temperature of his date. "She's freshening up. Could take a long time. What do you say we dance?"

Dance with Josh Gordon? I'll probably break my toe. Or worse, his. But I'm certainly getting my share of attention tonight. I guess this knee-length cotton dress isn't so bad after all. I should send Bloomingdale's a thank-you note and an extra ten bucks.

The orchestra segues out of a Celine Dion song and into a new tune. Something I vaguely remember. An old Carly Simon number— "Nobody Does It Better." Who could resist an offer like that? Of course I'll dance with Josh.

Chapter SEVENTEEN

"DON'T PULL OUT THAT ONE—it's not a weed!" Boulder shrieks at me from across the lawn. "Let it live!"

But it's too late. I've already yanked the oversized dandelion out by its roots and I'm holding it triumphantly. Now I stare, trying to figure out what else it could possibly be.

"A zinnia," Boulder says, coming over and taking it from me. He cradles it tenderly, brushing the dirt off the smooth stem.

"Sorry," I say. "Didn't know."

"Poor little plant," he coos to the yellow-petaled orphan, uprooted so abruptly from its bed. "I'll take care of you, baby. Don't worry. I'll even find you a better home."

He clucks his tongue at me, strides five paces across the sunny garden, and kneels on the ground to begin replanting. What, he thinks I can't kill it over there?

I go into the house to get a pitcher of lemonade and some fresh-baked oatmeal raisin cookies and bring them back to Boulder. I sink down on the grass next to him as he lovingly pats the soil around the resurrected plant.

"You're going to be okay, zinnia," he says in a high-pitched baby voice. "I won't let that mean Jessie around you again."

He dusts off his hands and devours a big glass of lemonade in a few gulps. "Mean Jessie with plants and silly Jessie with men," he admonishes me.

"You mean what I told you about Dan at the party?"

"Right. You march back and tell that man you weren't thinking straight last night. New plan. You'll have sex with him, and if it works out okay, he can move right in."

"Boulder, what are you talking about?" I ask, moving some small rocks around the edge of what is now the zinnia bed. "Lucy's my best friend."

He looks at me and raises an eyebrow.

"My best woman friend," I amend. "Girls don't do that to girls. You learn early that you have to be able to count on each other. Simple rules. You don't break a date with a girlfriend for Saturday night just because some guy calls to ask you out at the last minute. Once you get a boyfriend, you still make time for dinner with the girls. And here's the biggie. You don't steal your best friend's husband. Even if they're temporarily split."

"Why not? Where else are you going to meet people?"

"Match-dot-com?" I venture.

"Please, this way's safer. The guy's been preselected. If he's good enough for your best friend, he's probably good enough for you."

"Dan's good enough for anybody. He's great. But that's not the point. He and Lucy have the kids. They're a family. Destroy that and you rot in hell forever. Besides, I know she loves him. She's just been suffering from temporary insanity."

"But Dan said he loved *you*," Boulder says, arms raised passionately, as if he's auditioning for a Danielle Steel movie.

"No, he didn't," I say annoyed. "Don't you ever listen?"

"All I do is listen," says Boulder. "That's what the gay best friend does."

"Okay, well listen again. Dan said he *liked* me. He said we laugh together. He said we were comfortable. Doesn't exactly sound like he's Romeo baying outside my window."

"And if he was?" asks Boulder.

"I'd never do it to Lucy. Friendship. Loyalty. The Girl Scout oath."

"The Girl Scout oath?"

"Do unto others as you would have them do unto you," I say righteously.

"That's the Golden Rule."

"Girl Scout Oath. Golden Rule. Constitutional amendment. What's the difference? I just wouldn't."

"But do you want to? If there were no consequences. No rotting in hell. No bitchy Pine Hills neighbors passing judgment."

I take a moment, thinking about it seriously. Me and Dan. Dan and me. Somebody I already respect. Somebody I already like. Somebody who doesn't speak French.

"Dan's wonderful," I say slowly, letting the words form in my head for the first time. "Who wouldn't want him? He's got all the right stuff. He's smart. He's great-looking. He loves being married. He bikes twenty miles every weekend and he's in great shape."

"So?" asks Boulder, ready to choose my china pattern.

I shrug. "I don't know how to explain it. Maybe it's because he's been my pal all these years. But honestly, he doesn't make my heart go pitter-patter. And I bet I don't make his heart skip a beat, either."

Boulder crosses his arms. "That's a problem? No pitter-patter means no joint checking account?"

"I guess so," I admit. "Even at my age, I'm not ready to give up on real romance. There's gotta be someone out there who's as sexy as Jacques and as nice as Dan."

Boulder sighs and turns back to his plant. "Itsy-bitsy zinny, will we ever find someone perfect for our Jessie?" he asks in that same itsy-bitsy little voice. "Someone she can love and cherish and who'll make the earth move?"

"I'll give you moving earth," I say, laughing, as I dig in and toss a small clod of dirt at him.

He catches it. "You deserve more than the earth moving," he says affectionately. "You deserve an earthquake."

That's my Boulder. Don't want to explain to him that an earthquake isn't usually a good thing. But I wouldn't mind a rumble or two.

* * *

When Lucy asks if I've heard from Dan, I try "yes" and then "no" and then "yes" again. Going for the truth—well, some of it, anyway—I remind her that Dan and I went to a business party together.

"Oh, right, thanks for doing that," she says, looking up from her desk and smiling at me across her office. "At least I know he's not dating."

"Right. Hanging with me instead. I'm safe," I tell her, feeling just the slightest twinge of guilt. And regret. Should I be making decisions for Dan? If he really wants to pursue me, who am I to say he shouldn't? Maybe the pitter-patters would come.

But no. Won't even think it.

Lucy's assistant Tracey comes in with a plastic bag of food from the Au Bon Pain around the corner.

"I thought were lunching at Le Cirque," I say, watching Tracey set out vegetable wraps and iced tea.

"I'm so sorry about this," Lucy says. "Can't leave the office. Waiting for a conference call. My agent Gary Gray swore they'd call me first thing, L.A. time."

"It's still early in L.A.," I say, looking at my watch. One-thirty. That's ten-thirty on the coast. "What time do they normally finish up with their personal trainers?"

"By now," she says impatiently. "Annoys me to be at their beck and call. But Gary says they love love love the show. Kiss kiss. The network president himself wants to talk to me. Len Sunshine."

"Great name. Get his start as a stripper?"

"Close. FM deejay. Then a bit-part actor. Very handsome. Very charming. Could be the only straight man in Hollywood who slept his way to the top."

"Huh? Didn't think there were enough powerful women at the networks to make it worth his while."

"There aren't. But there are plenty of famous actresses. And if enough big female stars adore you, you've got your Saturday night lineup. Everyone loves working with him."

"Can I hang out when the call comes? Put it on speaker. I want to hear a network president sucking up to you."

"Sure. But I warn you. Even with the best of these guys, half of what they say is phony and the other half is fake."

"Kind of like Hollywood boobs," I say, pleased that I can participate in industry banter.

Lucy scrunches her nose. "No, I'm serious. I've had shows turn on a dime. From 'Love ya, baby. You're the best' to '*Hasta luega*. See ya around, kid.' "

"Worried?" I ask.

"Not really," Lucy says, as Tracey announces that The Call has finally come.

Lucy looks meaningfully at me and nods to a chair. "I'll be quiet," I whisper, as she sits down, hikes up her skirt, and perches cross-legged on the desk. Too bad it's not a video conference. But doesn't matter. Lucy knows she's sexy and savvy and she projects that confidence even from three thousand miles away.

"Lucy, baby, doll, it's Gary," says Lucy's agent over the speakerphone. He sounds so hyper that I can practically see him unbending a pile of paper clips while he talks.

"We have Len Sunshine on the line, too," Gary says. "Len, are you there?"

"Right here," says the network president in a deep voice that's still as smooth and syrupy as it must have been in his radio days. "Lucy, I'm gonna get right to the point. Your pilot's great. You did it again. Gonna make a big commitment to you right now. You're on for thirteen weeks."

I love television. Thirteen weeks is a big commitment. I've had warts that lasted longer than that. Although not many relationships.

"That's terrific," says Lucy, glowing and looking prouder than I've seen her since Lily won the science fair. "Appreciate the vote of confidence. Coming from you it means a lot."

"It should. We're behind you on this one hundred percent. Very original. Great graphics. Great choice of music. Thought I'd hate seeing those fucking Olsen twins again, but you did an amazing take on them. Loved everything. But one small little problem. Just a single change we're going to need you to make."

Len pauses to take a loud slurp—coffee? Slim-Fast? Cocaine? No, you don't slurp cocaine. I don't think. Lucy sits stone silent, waiting for the next shoe to drop. Over the speaker, Agent Gary is throwing the shoe. Or more likely, I'm hearing him rocketing a handful of mangled paper clips into his metal wastebasket.

"A single change?" Lucy prods. "You know I'll work with you, Len. Glad to fix anything."

"Great. Good. Right. I want you to fire Hunter Green."

I look over at Lucy, but she refuses to catch my eye and just stares down at the speakerphone.

Gary issues a huge sigh of relief. "Fire Hunter Green? No *problemo*. He's not my client."

But Lucy's not so ready to concede. "What didn't you like about Hunter?" she asks cautiously.

"He's fine. More than fine, he's good. But there are a million guys out there just like him. He's too expensive. We want to bring in someone cheaper. And younger."

"You're wrong," Lucy says bluntly. "There aren't any other guys like Hunter. If the show's good, it's as much because of him as me. He's very special. More like one *in* a million than one *of* a million."

Oh no, Lucy, don't do this. Don't put yourself on the line for Hunter Green. He's not worth it. You've already risked your marriage. Now you're going to risk your career? I want to shake some sense into her, but she's already set her course.

"The guy just costs too much," Len says.

"Then we'll cut costs elsewhere," Lucy says resolutely. "It would be a huge mistake to lose Hunter. You'd lose the whole show. Better if you replace me."

"*No way!*" screams Gary. There's either a tornado in Los Angeles or he's just thrown the entire metal wastepaper basket against the wall. "You're too important," he says, protecting Lucy—and his fifteen percent.

"Gotta agree with that," says Len. "Network doesn't want to lose you."

"Pleased to hear it. I don't want to leave the network, either," says Lucy. "But I've been percolating another project. Let me move on to that one. I've done the hard part on this Hunter show. The format's already set. Hire a producer who costs less than me. The show can run itself as long as you have Hunter hosting. The other project I have in mind could be even bigger."

"Even bigger? How much money will it make?" asks Gary, not bothering to have Lucy explain her idea. The guy has his priorities straight. Who cares about the concept as long as it mints cash.

"New show I'm proposing is a sitcom that could make a fortune," Lucy says confidently. "Len, somewhere on that pile of papers you call a desk is a treatment I sent you last week. Also scripts for the first two episodes. Read them. It's a killer. Call me back."

Only Lucy could fire off directives to a hotshot network president and not get shot down.

"Will do," Len says. "Gotta run. Steven Bochco's on the other line. He's trying to resurrect that singing cop show."

"Loved that show," gushes Gary.

"Hated it," says Len. "Never coming back."

"Good call. I didn't like it that much," Gary amends.

"So listen, how are we leaving it with Hunter?" asks Len, ready to wrap up.

"You're keeping him," Lucy says firmly. "I'll get him to agree to a five percent pay cut. And I'll hand-pick my replacement myself."

"I'm not totally convinced on Hunter, but I'll trust your instincts," says Len. "Got yourself a deal."

Lucy hangs up and I'm speechless. Did Lucy really just give up her job for the man she . . . what? Loves? Didn't the *Feminine Mystique* tell us that's a feminine mistake?

"Don't say a word to me. Not a word," says Lucy, not knowing that I couldn't talk even if E.T. himself asked me to phone home.

Lucy defiantly moves back behind her desk, in full executive mode. "I have one more call to make. Eat your sandwich," she says, punching * 4 into the speakerphone.

Eat my sandwich? As soon as I hear the voice on the other end—and realize it's Hunter—I start to choke.

"Lucy. My Lucy in the Sky with Diamonds," Hunter warbles. "How's my own personal LSD? My addiction. My drug of choice."

John Lennon must be turning over in his grave. If he'd known how Hunter was going to abuse that song, he never would have written it.

"My Lucy, *my* Lucy. The woman who puts diamonds in my eyes and a song in my heart," says Hunter, never one to stop just because he's mixed his metaphors.

"Hunter, a couple of business things," Lucy says, bypassing the schmaltz. "Actually, I have good news and bad news. Which do you want to hear first?"

"The good news," says Hunter. Everybody else I've ever met in my life has always asked to get the bad news out of the way first. Not Hunter. I bet he eats his hot fudge sundae before his peas, too.

"Good news is that Len Sunshine liked the show. Network's picking it up. Thirteen-week commitment."

"Thirteen weeks!" Hunter crows. "That's forever!"

"You're right, it's fabulous. Just a couple of sticking points."

"Is this the bad news?" asks Hunter anxiously.

"Not yet," says Lucy. "Our budget came in a little high. The network demanded some cutbacks. You're not badly affected. Just five percent down."

"And that's *not* the bad news?" Hunter groans.

"I know how much you're making. It's still a great deal," Lucy says.

"I won't do it," Hunter says arrogantly. "Tell the network I won't take it. I won't work for a penny less than I'm worth."

"Yes, you will take it," Lucy says, her tone quiet but firm. "Trust me, Hunter. There are a lot of younger guys who'd take this in a minute for half the salary."

"And they'd only *deserve* half," he says.

"That's true, darling. When the ratings on this go through the roof, you'll hit Len up for a huge raise."

"You bet I will," Hunter says, rallying, and already deciding whether to spend the extra money on the Maserati or the beach house in Malibu. "So what's the bad news?"

"I'm not going to be doing this show with you. Someone else will produce."

Hunter thinks about it, obviously figuring bad news could be a lot worse. But he summons his chivalry.

"You have to produce. I won't do it without you. I'll talk to Len myself," he says emphatically. "I'll use my clout." The clout he doesn't know he's lost.

"It won't matter. I won't do it," Lucy says. Then taking a deep breath she adds, "We can't keep spending time together. It's what I talked to you about last week in L.A. I'm not going to be seeing you anymore."

"You really meant that?" he asks. "But I sent you flowers afterwards. The big Happy Thoughts FTD bouquet. And my note. Didn't you read my note?"

"I did," Lucy says. "And I was very touched when you said that if we stay together I can go with you to Port St. Lucie. For your Lisa Marie Presley interview."

"Lisa Marie's a big 'get,' " Hunter says proudly, now less focused on losing Lucy than on spending an afternoon—or more likely twenty minutes—with Elvis' daughter. "As close to the King as any of us will ever come," he adds reverently.

"I know," Lucy says patiently. "But we can't. Not anymore. It's over."

"Let me understand," he says, finally trying to take in the big picture. "No Port St. Lucie. No more weekends away. No more good times. You weren't joking last week. You're really leaving me?"

"Just going back where I belong," Lucy says, looking up from the phone and staring me straight in the eye. "Or trying to get back there."

"That husband of yours," Hunter says soberly. " I always understood where your heart really was. But I kept hoping."

Lucy doesn't say anything, so Hunter clears his throat.

"I'm really going to miss you," he says quietly. But nothing can get the man down. Not as long as he has show biz. "Real problem is no-body makes me look as good on the air as you do. So who can replace you, who's going to produce?"

"We'll find someone, I promise," Lucy says briskly, eager now to get off the phone and on with her own life.

"Think Steven Spielberg could do it?" Hunter asks self-importantly.

"Too busy redoing his house in the Hamptons," Lucy says, not bothering to explain that in addition to doing home repairs, one of our generation's great movie talents isn't pleading with the network to be Hunter's new producer. "I have an even better idea. I was thinking of Tracey, my assistant. She's learned a lot."

"She'll never be as good as you, but I could see that," says Hunter, mulling over the idea—and probably Tracey's twenty-something attractiveness—for a moment. "Why don't I take her out to dinner to talk it over."

The deal done, Lucy and Hunter say quick good-byes and I go over to give Lucy a big hug.

"You did the right thing," I say. "I had no idea you'd told him last week you were leaving."

"I know," Lucy confirms. "Wasn't as hard as I thought it would be."

"I'm so relieved it's over," I admit. "And you were smart not to stay on as his producer. I just wish you'd taken some credit. Told him that you'd saved his job."

"Didn't need to," Lucy says. "Why hurt him even more? He's not a bad guy."

I ponder that for a second. Hunter is kind of charming. "Think you'll miss him?"

"Probably not. Everything just seems so clear to me now. I can't believe I've been behaving this way. Like some walking midlife crisis."

"Do you think the next decade gets any easier?" I ask hopefully.

"Nope," Lucy grins, flipping back her hair. "Hot flashes. Crepey necks. Upper arms that wave like a flag."

"And too embarrassed to take off your clothes to have an affair," I chime in.

"Which may not be a bad thing."

* * *

When Lucy and I get to the Guggenheim Museum, Zelda is waiting for us in front of Max Ernst's *The Kiss*. She's standing so close that a guard inches over to make sure she's not about to throw paint on it.

"Knew I'd find you here," Lucy says, kissing her mother-in-law warmly on the cheek. "But I'll never figure out why you like this picture so much."

"It's so erotic," Zelda says. "Uninhibited sexuality. After all these years, I still get a tingle just looking at it."

I stare at the colorful surrealistic blobs, hoping for my own tingle. But all I feel is a confused buzz. What does Zelda see that I don't? I can't even tell who's kissing whom. Or who's kissing what. Maybe 3-D glasses would help.

"What always strikes me is the Renaissance composition," says Lucy, putting her fingers up in an L-shape as if framing the painting. "Very Leonardo da Vinci."

"Hints of imagery from the Sistine Chapel," I agree, hoping to sound cultured and not let on that it really reminds me of a finger painting Jen did when she was three.

"Sistine ceiling was Michelangelo," says Zelda, tucking her arm in mine. "But don't feel bad. The other day a student asked me if I'd read Leonardo's new book, *The Da Vinci Code*."

"At least she didn't ask if you'd seen him starring in *Titanic*," says Lucy.

Laughing, we begin to stroll down the museum's spiraling ramps, stopping now and then to admire a painting, but mostly marveling at the architecture. Which is exactly what Frank Lloyd Wright intended. Designed a museum that's more a showcase for itself than for the art. Talk about arrogance. Could have been a big success in television.

"Sorry I missed your birthday party," Lucy tells Zelda as we pass by a Picasso. I turn to get a glimpse of his woman with yellow hair, step back, try to get some perspective, and—whoops—almost fall over the railing. Zelda grabs me but her attention is focused on Lucy.

"I know. It would have been nice to have you. For many reasons," says Zelda.

"Did Dan seem to miss me?" Lucy asks.

"I think he's lost without her," I prompt. But Zelda doesn't bite.

"Not really lost," Zelda says. "I raised my son well. He's a strong, independent man. Great with the kids. Perfect father. Can do everything. Rewired my VCR, helped rewrite my résumé and made charming repartee with all my guests."

"Did he remember to bring you a nice present?" I ask, grasping for something the indomitable Dan might have missed.

"Very nice gift," she says, flourishing her wrist to display a handcrafted silver bracelet. Just the sort of thing Zelda likes.

"Sounds like he doesn't need me at all," Lucy says, obviously hurt.

"Of course he doesn't," says Zelda. "And you don't need him, either. That's the thing about a marriage like yours. You don't *need* to stay in it. Not like my day when the wife was stuck because she couldn't support herself alone and the guy stayed because his wife took care of everything. Now you both have your own, full lives. Nobody's trapped. You both have a whole world of possibilities out there. You and Dan have to choose to stay together. If that's what you want."

"It's what I want," says Lucy earnestly. "I know that now. But I'll admit this has been a really rough patch. I guess I've been pretty impossible these last few months."

Zelda smiles. "I remember my own dad saying that he'd had twenty-five good years of marriage. And that was on his thirtieth anniversary."

"What an awful thing to say," I complain.

"Exactly what I thought back then," says Zelda. "Now I realize my parents were luckier than most. That's a pretty good record."

"Do you think Dan will come back?" Lucy asks anxiously.

"I know he still loves you," says Zelda.

"And I love him," says Lucy.

"Does he make your heart go pitter-patter?" I ask, applying my new Richter Scale for Relationships.

"He does. You wouldn't think so after twenty years," she says, smiling. "But I'd always look at him in the mornings and think how handsome he is. He still makes my heart skip a beat."

"Then you belong together," says Zelda simply.

"What if he thinks I've been too awful? Aren't I supposed to end up throwing myself under a train or something?"

"So you *did* read *Anna Karenina!*" I say, impressed.

"It's not the nineteenth century anymore," says Zelda. "It's not even the twentieth. Men have been having their little flings since Zeus. And women have been forgiving them. So now the tables are turned. Not a good thing when anyone strays, but not so awful that it can't be excused."

"Can you talk to Dan and tell him that?" Lucy asks.

"No. But you'll figure out what to do."

We spend a few more minutes admiring a de Kooning and Zelda's favorite Jim Dine—painting of a heart, so this one I understand—and wind our way down to the restaurant on the Guggenheim's first floor. It's packed with Upper East Side mothers and their children who apparently prefer muffins to Modiglianis. They come to the museum only to eat. And they probably go to the Public Library only to use the bathrooms.

The moment we settle into our seats, Lucy's BlackBerry starts beeping. "E-mails," she reports apologetically. "Must have been no reception upstairs."

She flicks through the messages. "Lily won the backstroke at her swim meet," she says with a smile. "Dean's going to be late at his tennis match. Dave wants to know what time I'll be home and whether he can have the car tonight."

Zelda laughs. "I guess the days of sitting by the phone and wondering where your kids are have vanished," she says.

But instead of extolling the virtues of modern technology versus the time when you had to pray your kids could find a dime and a telephone booth, Lucy lets out a whoop of delight.

"An e-mail from Len Sunshine!" she reports excitedly. She frantically scrolls down to get the entire message. "He loves my new treatment. Says he wants to do the show I proposed. Most creative idea he's heard in months. Well, today anyway."

"That's wonderful," says Zelda, having no idea who Len Sunshine is or what Lucy is talking about, but knowing when a mother-in-law should be supportive.

"So what was the idea?" I ask. But Lucy is wildly typing onto the BlackBerry's tiny keys. Finally she looks up, clearly thrilled. "It's something completely different for me. A sitcom about two women in their forties. One married, one divorced."

"You're doing a show about *us*," I squeal, somewhere between horrified and thrilled. "Who's going to play me?"

"It's not you," Lucy laughs. "Not really me, either. Just about the things every woman our age has to cope with. Like bake sales and Botox. Not to mention sex and cellulite."

"And shopping," I offer, ready to co-produce.

"You got it," says Lucy, grinning. "My pitch to Len was that there really is life between *The Gilmore Girls* and *The Golden Girls*. I'm calling it *The Botox Diaries*."

"If Dahlia Hammerschmidt plays me I'm going to kill myself," I say.

"That's television," Lucy says with a mock sigh. "The show is four minutes old and already everybody has an opinion."

Chapter EIGHTEEN

WORD OF LUCY'S NEW SITCOM makes it into *Variety* and I expect her to rush out to L.A. for casting. Instead, she stays put in Pine Hills.

"Something more important to do first," she says, sitting in her library in full producer mode. She's made a list of twelve possible scenarios. For the next scene between her and Dan.

"First idea to get him back," she says, consulting her yellow legal pad. "I go to his corporate apartment tonight, take off my trench coat, and I have on nothing underneath but fishnets and a garter belt."

"Naked under a raincoat? You sound like a flasher," I say, shaking my head.

"It's a Burberry," Lucy argues.

"Okay, an upscale flasher. Besides, the All-Star Game is on. You could be Striparella come to life and you wouldn't get his attention."

"Point taken," says Lucy, crossing that one off her list. "How about this. A little more subtle. I go to Sitting Pretty in SoHo and have my portrait done. Full-length."

"That's nice," I say with a shrug, "if you think the problem is that Dan's forgotten what you look like."

"Please, darling, don't tell me you've never heard of SP. Everyone's

going. Perfect present for your husband. They specialize in nude photos of middle-aged ladies."

I make a face. "That sounds disgusting."

"Not when they're finished with you. They make you look fabulous. Body makeup artists. Great lighting. And they have Otto, the best
air-brush artist east of Las Vegas. Forget lipo. Otto's much cheaper and
safer. He did wonders with Madonna's thighs."

"I thought that was Astanga yoga. Or Kabbalah."

"Kabbalah. That's an idea I hadn't thought of," says Lucy, jotting it
down on her list. "Maybe I should join a prayer group."

"Save the praying for world peace. Or November sweeps on your
new show."

"Oh, come on, I have to do something," says Lucy, throwing her
pad aside in frustration. "I've tried visualization. You know, imagining
Dan's coming back to me."

"That's called wishful thinking."

"Something's got to work. Last night I left a message on his cell
phone. Played him the entire track of Lovin' Spoonful's 'Darling Be
Home Soon.' He never even called me back."

"I wouldn't call you back, either, if you played me the Lovin'
Spoonful," I say.

"I guess Dan's more of a Bob Dylan kind of guy," she admits. "But
'The Times They Are A-Changin' didn't seem like the right message."

"So tell me how a bike race fits into this whole plan?" I ask.

"That's right," says Lucy, looking at her watch and jumping up.
"It's late. We have to get to Grant's Tomb."

"I thought we were going to praise Dan, not to bury him," I quip.

We rush to Lucy's garage and climb into the car. We're hurtling
down the Henry Hudson Parkway when it suddenly dawns on me that
my legs aren't cramped and I'm not fearing for my life.

"Hey, what's with the Volvo?" I ask. "What happened to your
Porsche?"

"Wrong image. Traded it in," Lucy says, driving at a sedate fifty-
five. "The Volvo is so much more family, don't you think? I thought
this would make a real statement to Dan."

"What statement? That you're insane?" I ask. "You change cars the way other people change underwear."

"Damn, I forgot to put on nice underwear," Lucy says. "Think I'll need it? We could make a La Perla pit stop."

I wish I could answer yes, but I'm not sure what to think anymore. Dan's not responding to Lucy's advances, and he sure seemed ready to move on at the party the other night. I don't kid myself that he was looking at me as his next One and Only. But the fact that he's even thinking about being with someone other than Lucy makes me nervous for her.

The streets around upper Broadway are closed off for the bike race, but Lucy sweet-talks the guard at the security stop into letting her park in the Racers Only area.

"Can understand why he let you in," I say as Lucy minces from the car in her tight pencil skirt and open-backed mules. "Definitely look like you just got off the Tour de France."

"That's what I was going for. The outfit's French. Dior," says Lucy, pulling Persol sunglasses from her pocketbook. Naturally a different pair of sunglasses than she wore when she drove the Porsche.

"This is the first time I've been to one of Dan's races," Lucy says as we head toward the starting line where a group of spectators is starting to gather near the base of the monument. "Pretty spot. All these years living in New York and I've never seen this place."

"Reminds me of the old joke," I say, looking up at the large marble building in the center of the small park. "Who's buried in Grant's Tomb?"

"Grant," Lucy says.

"Nope. Nobody's buried in Grant's Tomb."

"Of course Grant. It's Grant's Tomb."

"Gotcha," I say, laughing as happily as I did in second grade. The last time I told this joke. "He's not *buried*. He's *entombed*. In that big building. Aboveground. Ha-ha. See? Nobody's buried in Grant's Tomb. Get it?"

Lucy sighs. "Yes, Jess. I get it. And I also know the one about not opening the refrigerator door because the salad's dressing. And throwing the alarm clock out the window to see time fly. But knock-knock. We came here to watch the race."

We both turn our attention to the bikers in their carnival-colored spandex who are taking their last gulps of Gatorade and lining up on their Treks and Cannondales. For a weekend hobby, this looks pretty serious.

"Which one is Dan?" I ask,

"The one in the silver helmet," Lucy says confidently. "I bought it for him myself."

"I think it's a popular model," I say, craning my neck to look over the crowd of muscular, well-built racers who are all wearing identical silver helmets and who all, from this distance, are indistinguishable.

The starting gun pops and the racers take off. In no more than a moment, the throng of bikers has disappeared around a corner.

"That was fast. Now what?" I ask.

Lucy shrugs. "No idea. Guess we go have lunch until they're done. Where do you think is good to eat around here?"

I look around at the trees and grass and the Hudson River sparkling a block away. "Hot dog vendor?" I suggest.

Lucy looks at me like I've proposed we pluck a couple of leaves from the tree and forage for acorns.

"Maybe we should skip lunch and go to the finish line," she says, looking around. "Where do you think it could be? I hope we don't have to take a subway."

The woman in front of us turns around. She's wearing a bright yellow T-shirt with a picture of a racing bike and the slogan RICHARD MAKES MY HEART RACE. Now there's a good wife. Or else a stalker.

"New at this, girls?" she asks. "This race is a criterium. Twelve laps. Two miles each. They go in circles. The finish line's right here."

Twenty-four miles of biking? Wish I'd lugged along the Sunday *Times*. Sounds like it's going to be a long afternoon.

But suddenly there's a roar from the crowd and the racers reappear. The bikers are packed together so tightly that if one of them swerves two inches, the whole thing will end up like the chariot race in *Ben-Hur*. And I think the treadmill is dangerous.

"Did you see Dan?" I ask when they've disappeared again in a colorful blur.

"I'm not sure," Lucy says. But always assuming the best she adds, "He must have been the one in the lead."

"Bad tactical move," says Richard's wife or stalker, shaking her head. "Shouldn't be out front this early. Need to save your energy for a sprint at the end."

"Sore loser," Lucy snipes, now confident that Dan is the leader of the pack.

"A very sore loser is what your husband is going to be," snaps Richard's rooter, turning her back on us.

The racers come around and are gone again so fast that Lucy's belated screams of "Go, Dan! Go!" echo in their wake.

"Enough talking. I've got to focus," Lucy says. "Want to be prepared next time they pass." She unties the Hermès scarf from her Hamptons Coach bag—Lucy's idea of going downscale for a weekend bike race—and stands at the ready.

This time we know that the bikers will be back in a blink so we never take our eyes off the curve where they reappear.

"That's Dan!" Lucy screams as soon as she spots him on the outside of the pack, close to the curb where we're standing.

"Dan darling, Dan darling, go, GO!" she shrieks as he approaches at breakneck speed.

Head down, crouched over the handlebars, he of course doesn't look up.

"Dan, GO!" Lucy screams again, waving her scarf practically in his face.

Well, that gets him. Distracted for a split second, he hesitates and goes sprawling off his bike, skidding ten feet across the pavement. Three bikers behind him, unable to stop, crash headlong into each other. A fourth manages to escape the collision, but can't avoid Dan. His Cannondale races straight across Dan's prone body.

"Ohmygod!" Lucy screams. "Don't die!"

I'm pondering whether widowhood is better or worse than divorce—probably better since it's more sympathetic—when Dan stands up and

brushes the tire marks off his chest. Two of the three other wrecked rid-
ers also get up, pulling their now-bent bikes off the course and slamming their helmets in anger. The third one doesn't move. Maybe his wife
will be the widow. Finally the downed rider rouses himself, surveying
his torn and bleeding legs. "How the fuck did this happen?" he bellows.

"She did it," calls out Richard's wife, pointing an accusing finger
at Lucy.

Dan, still dazed, looks up and for the first time sees Lucy. And realizes who brought him down.

"Are you okay?" Lucy asks, rushing to his side.

"Would have been," Dan says, disgustedly kicking the tire on his
mangled bike. "Thought I could take this race. First time I've fallen
this season."

"All my fault," Lucy says, suddenly abashed. "I shouldn't have
come."

Dan slowly pulls off his biking gloves and rubs his scraped knee.
"Surprised to see you," he admits. "You've never been a big fan."

"My mistake. It's a pretty cool sport," Lucy says. "I guess there are
a lot of things I've been missing out on these days."

Two minutes must have passed because the racers who are still on
their steeds come around again and Dan grabs Lucy, pulling her onto
the grass.

"Like standing in the eye of a hurricane," she says, when the bikers
have stormed past again.

Moving far from the road, Dan plucks the water bottle out of its
holder and takes a long swig. "So what are you doing here?" he asks
Lucy at last.

"I came to see you," she says. "I miss you. You won't answer my
calls. We need to talk."

"This isn't the right place."

"It's never the right place," Lucy says, moving closer to him. "So
let me just say my piece right here because it's important. I love you.
I'm sorry. I'm sorry. I love you. We've had so many good years together
and so many good times. We know each other. We love each other. We
can't throw that all away."

Dan lifts up his broken bike and tosses it under a tree. "Love each other, yes. But you're wrong about our knowing each other," he says. "We don't. I don't know who you are anymore."

"Still the same girl you married," Lucy says.

"I wish."

"Here, look. I brought something I think you should see." Lucy opens her bag and pulls out an oversized envelope. It's slighty ragged, has a hint of musty perfume and is fastened shut with a wax seal stamped "LC."

"What's this?" Dan asks, taking it from her and turning it over slowly in his hands.

"The last letter I wrote as Lucy Chapman," she says. "The night before our wedding. Remember? Zelda told us each to write one and put it away. She said marriage isn't always smooth and when the bad times come, we'll need something to remind us that we made a promise for better or worse."

Dan stares down at the envelope. "What does it say?" he asks.

"Honestly, I don't know," says Lucy, "I remember writing it, but not what I said. I couldn't sleep last night and at about four a.m. I padded up to the attic and found these in your grandmother's trunk. They were inside that heart-shaped cookie tin and fastened by a pink ribbon."

Dan gives a little smile. "I remember that cookie tin. The one time you tried to bake for me. And I married you anyway."

"The stomachache only lasted two days," Lucy says.

"But the good times were going to last forever," adds Dan ruefully.

Lucy nods. "If ever we needed this letter, it's now."

Dan slides his finger under the flap of the envelope, fumbles with the seal and breaks it open. He pulls out a thin, pale blue sheet of paper and settles down under a swooping oak tree.

"Why don't you read it to me," he says to Lucy, handing over the page.

She takes the paper and sits down next to him. Both of them have forgotten about me, and I shouldn't be here anyway. I start to head back to the car, but the event must be over because a throng of racers now off their bikes are packing up their gear and blocking my path. I slip to one side of the tree.

"*My Dear Darling Dan,*" Lucy reads. "*If you've opened this letter it must be because you're mad at me. I've done something wrong, even though right now I don't know what it is. No surprise. You keep telling me that part of what you love about me is that I'm a challenge. I keep your life exciting. You say that I may be a handful, but you know you'll never be bored around me.*"

Dan's mouth twitches in a smile. "No, never boring," he says.

"And still a challenge," Lucy adds. "*Right now, on the night before our wedding, I know I want us to spend our lives together. Our whole lives. And if I've done something that in any way jeopardizes that, I hope you can find it in your heart to forgive me. I promise I'll always find it in my heart to forgive you. Love* does *mean having to say you're sorry. And I'm saying that to you now.*"

There's a long silence. Then Dan clears his throat. "Almost sounds like you knew what was going to happen."

"Never," Lucy says ferociously. "I can't explain what I did and I'm not going to try. I can only promise that whatever demon took over my soul for those few months has been banished forever."

"How do you know?" he asks.

"Because it's true what they say. You don't know how important something is until you almost lose it. I'll never be that foolish again."

Dan leans over to take her hand and they sit looking at each other for a long moment. "Where's the letter I wrote?" he asks finally.

"Right here," says Lucy. She holds out a manila envelope with the return address from the office where Dan had worked twenty years ago. "Your turn to read."

With a loud tear, Dan rips open the missive.

"*My Most Beautiful Lucy,*" he says, his voice shaking. "*There can't be anything you've ever done to make me angry. So if you're reading this, it must be my fault. From the moment I met you I've dreamed of our being together and I can hardly believe that's about to happen. My love for you is eternal. If I ever forget that, shake me hard and remind me that even forever is too short a time for us to be together. I hope there's nothing that can ever move you so far away from me that we can't find our way back to each other."*

"Do you mean it?" asks Lucy, sniffling.

"I meant it twenty years ago," says Dan.

"And now?"

Dan takes his time. He looks down at his left hand and twists his gold wedding band, which he's never taken off. Then he reaches for his wife's hand. "Nothing's changed. Nobody could ever make me angrier than you do, but nobody could ever make me happier. I Love Lucy."

"You swore to me you'd never tease me about my name and that TV show," Lucy says, laughing and crying at the same time as she throws her arms around him.

"After twenty years I'm entitled," he says happily, pulling her tight as they tumble over together on the grass.

Good thing he didn't get to race more than three laps. He'd be too sweaty for what seems to be coming next. This could take a while. Guess I'll get a hot dog and take the train home.

Chapter NINETEEN

TAMIKA HAS THE MUMPS.

"The mumps?" I ask, when her foster mother calls with the news, three days before the theater benefit. "Nobody gets the mumps anymore."

"She did," says her foster mother. "Looks like she swallowed a basketball. Or two. Can barely talk."

"Has she been to a doctor?" I ask.

"I'm trying to get someone at the clinic to see her this afternoon."

I should be sympathetic to this poor little girl with her 103 fever, but all I can think of is that her understudy can't possibly sing "The Rain in Spain" the way she does.

A few minutes later, Josh Gordon's assistant Peggy calls me to confirm that Josh needs eleven, rather than ten, seats at the table he's buying for the pretheater benefit.

"If we even have a benefit," I moan. "Our star is sick. The mumps. We're waiting to hear what the clinic says. I'll keep you posted."

"Hang on a second," says Peggy, putting me on hold. While I'm waiting for someone to come back on the line, I expect to hear Lite FM, but instead I'm immediately bombarded with stock updates from Bloomberg Business Reports. Oh, for the Lovin' Spoonful.

A minute later, Josh picks up.

"Nobody gets the mumps anymore," he announces.

Can I teach the man to say hello?

"Hi, Josh. That's exactly what I said. But apparently Tamika has 'em. Two big swollen glands on either side of her face."

"Is that the little girl I saw at the rehearsal, with pigtails and a big voice? She was amazing. A real talent."

"And she's been working so hard. It's just not fair."

"Gotta go," says Josh, abruptly hanging up.

"Well nice talking to you, too," I say into the dial tone. "Appreciate your support."

I hang up the receiver and start strategizing. Maybe the costume designer could camouflage the offending lumps. Turtlenecks. Might be a little strange in the ballroom scene, but can't worry about that now. If Tamika can't sing, how about lip-synching to the cast album? Even Audrey Hepburn didn't belt out the score on her own.

The morning dissolves into endless benefit details. A final proofread of the program notes. A discussion with Amanda about solid white versus red-and-white striped ribbons on the goody bags. A conference call with Pamela and Heather about the dreaded seating chart, which changes as quickly as George Clooney's girlfriends.

I'm in the kitchen trying to decide whether lunch should be a bowl of dry Rice Krispies or Columbo Lite Boston Cream Pie yogurt— 120 calories and worth every one—when the phone rings yet again. I pause a moment before answering. Will I fit into the borrowed Chanel if I eat the cereal *and* the yogurt?

"Tamika's cured," says Josh.

"A two-hour case of mumps? Maybe you should be the next Surgeon General."

"Couldn't make it through the confirmation hearings," Josh laughs. "Besides, I didn't cure Tamika. I just sent my pediatrician over to have a look."

"A doctor in Manhattan who makes house calls? How'd you manage that?"

"Don't ask. I may have to let him win our next round of golf. But he's good. Head of the new Children's Hospital. Turns out Tamika didn't have mumps. He thinks it was a bad allergic reaction and gave her a shot of Benadryl. "

Josh got the head of the hospital to go to 158th Street and St. Nicholas Avenue? Sounds like he had to offer more than golf, but I'm grateful for whatever he did.

"You're wonderful. I don't know what to say other than thank you. This means so much. The show's a big deal for all the kids. But especially for a kid like Tamika."

"No problem," Josh says, clearly embarrassed by my effusive thanks. "Everything else going okay?"

"Yup. By the way, I made that change to your dinner table," I say.

"Peggy tells me we're up to eleven," Josh says. And then after a beat, he adds, "I never asked where you're sitting. If you're not taken, I'd like you to join me and make it an even twelve."

"I never sit," I say stupidly, flummoxed by his offer. "I mean it's not that I stand, it's just that I'll be busy before the show. Helping the kids get into costume, braiding their hair, adjusting the pink gels . . ." I manage to stop blathering before I start reciting dialogue from the show. Though if he asks, I can do it. Since I've heard the kids practicing their lines a thousand and three times, I remember them. Even without my gingko.

"You'll need to have dinner," Josh says.

"Right." I take a deep breath and count to three. Five. "I'd love to join your table. Thanks," I say simply.

We hang up and I notice that I've dribbled Columbo Lite Boston Cream Pie yogurt all over my jeans. Damn. The benefit's Friday. I have three days to learn how to eat.

The next person who has a problem with the seating is Dan, who shows up at dinnertime with a check and an apology.

"I didn't have time to mail this in," he says, handing me an envelope. "Lucy tells me she only bought one ticket. Now we need two."

"That's a change in the seating plan I'm happy to make," I say, taking the check from him. "But you could have just called. I know you're good for the money."

"But you probably think I'm not good for much else," Dan says, stepping inside and closing the door behind him. He throws out his arms to the sides, as if being crucified. "I stand before you as the biggest jerk in Pine Hills. I'm so sorry. I never should have said what I did the other night at the party."

"Doesn't matter," I say, not wanting to go there. "Everything ended up the way it was supposed to. I'm so glad about you and Lucy."

"Me too. You were right about where I belong. It's nice to be home. Together again."

"I bet," I say. Boy, he looks happy. And why not? Back with the woman he loves. Who loves him. And make-up sex is always hotter than August in Dubai. Not that I'll ever get there.

"Sorry you got caught in the middle," Dan says. "Staying such a good friend to each of us couldn't have been easy. But we both needed you."

"My bill's in the mail," I joke. "But you guys really figured it out yourselves."

Dan fidgets and shifts his weight from side to side. "Jess, about the other night again . . ."

"Look, why don't we just pretend it never happened?" I say, walking toward the kitchen and hoping to end the conversation.

"We can't do that. It did happen," Dan says, following me. "And I'm not trying to take it back."

"It's okay, you can take it back," I offer. "Wasn't really you speaking."

"No? Who do you think it was? Sure, I was slightly out of my mind, I'll admit. Angry at Lucy. Hurt. And really confused. But I meant what I said. You're terrific. I like being with you. And I don't want to lose our friendship because I made one stupid mistake."

"You won't. I'm not going anywhere." I look at Dan carefully. Why not. Go for it. "By the way, what was the stupid mistake? Kissing me?"

Dan looks startled for moment, and then he smiles. "Nope. Kissing you was kind of nice. It was kissing my wife's best friend that was stupid."

I grin. "Very smooth."

Dan laughs. "It was a good thing you turned me down anyway. I never would have survived. Too much competition."

"Right. Huge competition for me at the moment. A gay man. An eleven-year-old girl. And my ex-husband, when he's not with his current lover."

"How about a rich Park Avenue businessman who's one of New York's more generous philanthropists."

"What are you talking about?"

"You must know."

"I have no idea. Donald Trump is fighting for me? I wouldn't be interested. Barry Diller? Not that he'd be interested. A Rockefeller? But which one? And how diluted is the money by now?"

Dan laughs again. "I'm not talking quite that rich. But the guy's very nice."

"That lets out George Steinbrenner."

"Come on, Jess, you've gotta know this," Dan says. "It's Josh Gordon."

I burst out laughing, but Dan persists.

"I saw Josh at a business meeting the other day and he kept bringing up your name," Dan says. "Asked about you and me and I told him we were just pals. He was obviously checking because he'd seen us at the party. Very gentlemanly of him."

"He was just trying to make conversation."

"No, he was deciding whether it was okay to make a pass."

"You're so wrong. Josh and I met a couple of times to talk about the benefit. That's about it between us."

"He did mention you were doing a good job."

"Glad he noticed. He's usually more focused on his gorgeous girlfriend and his annoying ex-wife. Anyway, his only interest in me is professional."

"Too bad, I thought you'd be good together," Dan says with a shrug. "Oh well. Maybe not. Win some, lose some."

I start to change my position and say Josh *might* be interested, but I've already done too good a job convincing Dan otherwise. That's the problem with men. They don't know when they're supposed to argue with you. It's really pretty simple. "This dress makes me look fat" demands "No, it doesn't." "I should get a face-lift" requires "Never—you're beautiful just the way you are." And "Josh couldn't be interested in me" calls for some serious disagreeing. If I were talking with Lucy, we could dissect every luscious detail of everything Josh has ever said to me. How he said it, why he said it, when he said it, what he meant, what he could have meant, what he should have meant, what he meant to mean. By then we'd be so exhausted, who'd care what was going to happen.

But Dan just grabs a brownie from my cookie jar and heads to the door. "Don't worry, Jess. If it's not Josh, it'll be someone else. Someone terrific," he says, giving me a warm hug and a sympathetic slap on the back.

"Sure," I say, trying not to sound as disgruntled as I suddenly feel.

Dan offers a quick peck on the cheek and adds, "Thanks for the brownie. Lucy's cooking dinner for me tonight. Don't know what to expect."

"Josh did ask me to sit at his table," I mumble to myself as Dan closes the door behind him. The dinner plan had sounded good for a few minutes. But now it occurs to me that I'll probably be sitting next to the gorgeous Ice Queen, Marissa.

Friday night, two hours before the fund-raiser, Lucy's flitting around the benefit hospitality suite at the St. Regis Hotel. So far, I'm the only member of the committee here. Probably because I'm also the only one without a plush Park Avenue pad to change in—and I couldn't quite imagine wearing my ten-thousand-dollar Chanel loaner on Metro-North. Might have to buy an extra seat for it. And ticket prices just went up.

"Great place," Lucy says, twisting open the small Bulgari body cream in the amenities basket and rubbing it on her wrist. "Love a hotel that gives you a free suite."

"Free with the ballroom and four hundred paid dinners," I say, peering into the mirror to put on another coat of mascara before I get into my dress. "You and Dan want to use the suite later?"

"Don't need it," Lucy says happily. "We're doing just fine back in our own bedroom."

"So absence made the heart grow fonder?"

"Definitely," she says, sighing blissfully. "Dan and I are over the moon. We're back in love. I finally realize he's the man of my dreams. And the second time around is even sweeter. "

I roll my eyes. What is it about being in love that makes people talk in clichés? "I know everyone loves a lover, but I don't know how much syrup I can stand. You're getting sappier than Aunt Jemima."

The suite door opens and Amanda Beasley-Smith and Pamela Jay Barone rush in—decked out in slinky long gowns and enough jewels to make Elizabeth Taylor jealous. Amanda throws a triple air kiss to me and a nod to Lucy, who I quickly introduce. Amanda, eyeing Lucy's beaded Armani, her who-knows-what-they-cost chandelier earrings, and her priceless aplomb takes about seven seconds to recognize Lucy as one of her own.

"You should be on the benefit committee next year," Amanda says.

"Yes, let's have lunch," Lucy says, pulling out the standard Hollywood answer.

A moment later, a tall, lanky man trails in, carrying oversized luggage in each hand. He's dressed in a ten-gallon hat, chaps, and red-and-turquoise Tony Martin cowboy boots. Not appropriate for riding a bull in a rodeo, but might work for throwing some bull in New York.

"This is my favorite hairdresser, Nebraska," Amanda says proudly, dashing over to him. "I corraled him into donating his talents for tonight. For anybody who stops by our suite and wants a touch-up."

"Howdy," I say, welcoming him in.

Nebraska goes into one of the suite's bathrooms to set up a

mini-salon—pulling out gel, moussant, defrizzer, shiner, pomade, spray, and glistening crème.

"I just brought the essentials," he says apologetically. "A little makeshift, but we'll get by."

I look over his collection. "Maybe a touch of shiner for me," I say tentatively. "Tonight's really important. I've been worrying about it for weeks. I mean, not worried about how I look but worried that everything goes smoothly. Donors happy. Kids do well. You know."

"You should *always* worry about how you look," says Nebraska. "But you don't have to think about it when I'm around." He steps behind me with a spray bottle and douses my head with water so quickly that I don't even realize what he's done until I feel drops splattering down my neck. Apparently he didn't notice the twenty minutes of careful straightening and styling I did at home. Or maybe he did.

The rest of the committee—Rebecca Gates, Heather Lehmann, and Allison von Williams sweep into the hospitality suite, each wearing an otherwise-stunning designer gown in the season's most touted color. Biscuit. Doesn't matter what they call it—it's still beige. A color that's not even flattering to a wall.

"Lots of activity downstairs," Rebecca announces excitedly. "The band's warming up and sounds great. People are starting to arrive. And Amanda, you were so right not to go with flowers for centerpieces. We're a serious charity. Those photos of ghettos-around-the-world in the Tiffany frames are much more moving."

"And so cheerful," I add.

Rebecca seems to notice me for the first time. "You better get going," she says archly. "You're dripping wet and not even dressed yet."

"She's not?" asks Allison, stopping to peer closely at my hotel-issued cotton bathrobe. "Isn't that Yves Saint Laurent? I thought it was his new take on the smoking jacket."

I pull the sash on the robe tighter. And, why not? Couture gets stranger every year. But it would take more panache than I have to wear a bathrobe to dinner. Unless dinner was at Hugh Hefner's house.

"I'll have you ready in no time," says Nebraska, pulling the dryer out of his hip holster and brandishing it in the air, in his best Clint-Eastwood-as-hairdresser fashion.

He flicks on the 2400-watt handheld tool—and suddenly everything comes to a stop. The blow dryer is dead. The lights go out. The air conditioner stops whirring.

"Sheeeiiit," Nebraska twangs.

"Must have blown a fuse," says Pamela, looking around the room, as if she might find the fuse box conveniently located next to the minibar.

Suddenly alarms start blaring, and there's a commotion in the hallway—doors slamming, people calling out. A moment later, sirens sound from the street under our window.

Nebraska glances at me in the mirror and then down at the Professional Strength dryer still in his hand. "This critter's more powerful than I thought," he says, with what may be a tinge of pride.

"Don't think your blow dryer did all this," says Lucy, rushing over to the television. When it doesn't turn on, she bangs on it like a broken soda machine, as if she can force the news out of the recalcitrant box.

"Power lines must have fallen," says Heather importantly. "This happens all the time at our house in Barbados during hurricane season."

I look out the window for signs of a hurricane. Or a driving rain. Or even fog. But the sun is shining brilliantly and there's not even a ripple of wind.

Lucy cracks open the door to the hallway where red strobe lights are flashing.

"Probably not a hurricane, but might be a fire," Lucy says. "We'd better get out of here."

"I can't leave," I complain, not budging from my chair. "My hair's sopping wet."

"It'll dry," Amanda says briskly. "Nebraska, do something for her. We have to go."

Nebraska, sharing the sense of urgency, grabs the nearest tube, squeezes some goop onto my hair and quickly crimps various sections of my head. "You're done. You'll be gorgeous," he says, abandoning me and rushing toward the door.

"What did you put on?" I ask, getting up.

"Product," he calls back.

The alarm in the living room of our suite starts clanging and Nebraska looks anxious. "All products are basically the same," he shouts, the screeching noise apparently jolting the truth out of him. But will he admit he ever said that once everything is back to normal?

We charge down the hallway—Lucy, one cowboy, five socialites in strapless gowns, and me with my wet hair glopped with unidentified product and wearing the robe that I never managed to change out of. The elevators aren't working, of course, and in the emergency stairwell, Amanda, Pamela, Rebecca, Heather and Lucy hike up the hems on their body-hugging gowns, whip off their high heels and proceed barefoot down the stairs. The crush of people ahead of us are clambering in controlled panic—no screaming or hysteria, just a steeled determination to get the hell down the stairs.

"What floor are we on?" asks Allison.

"The top. Got them to give us the penthouse," says Amanda, looking for credit. "Seemed like a good idea at the time."

"I can't make it!" wails Allison. "I barely fit in the staircase! My dress is too wide!"

That's a new one, but she's right. Her huge hooped skirt—she could get a job at Colonial Williamsburg—gives her a cute little waspish waist but is so voluminous she could be hiding the entire Confederate army under there. Plus General Lee.

"Get moving, will ya?" barks a man who's trying to push down the staircase. Well-bred Allison spins sideways to let him by and practically knocks over the person in front of her—who shrieks in alarm. Allison grabs at the stiff satin skirt fabric, trying to mangle it into a more manageable form, but no luck. Damn well-made dress.

"Move it!" bellows the man again.

"Screw you!" Allison hollers, losing her cool.

"I don't know why you bought that ridiculous wedding-cake dress in the first place," carps Heather.

Allison looks flustered, but this is a crisis—and she's ready to make the ultimate sacrifice. As easily as the others pulled off their shoes, she pulls off her hoop skirt—revealing a slim silk gown beneath it. These girls are prepared for anything.

"Definitely like the slip much better than the dress," says Heather approvingly.

Allison looks at the hoop skirt, which is now standing all by itself on the landing. "What should I do with it?" she asks.

"Just leave it there," advises Heather. "You can tell the insurance company you lost it."

They start charging down the stairs again, and somehow in the midst of the din, I hear my cell phone ringing and pull it out of my robe pocket.

"Where are you?" asks an anxious voice.

"In the hotel stairwell," I tell Josh into the phone.

"I'm in the ballroom and it's pitch-dark," he says. "You have to get down here."

"I'm trying," I say, as a charging man behind me brushes against my shoulder. "It's kind of scary in here."

Josh hears the tremulous tone in my voice.

"Hey, calm down. We'll be okay. I've already sent somebody out for candles. And we can use flashlights if we have to in the theater. Cheaper than those damn pink gels, anyway."

I try to laugh but at the moment nothing seems funny. "Do you know what happened?" I ask.

"Transformer blew and the power grid went down," Josh says. "Affected a ten-block area. Con Ed's already working on it."

I sigh with relief that it's not a major disaster. "If Con Ed's on the scene, it'll be fixed by next week," I say.

"My money's on Tuesday. But don't worry. I'm just glad you're safe."

I pass the news about the power outage along, and there's a palpable sense of relief in the stairwell. Blown transformer is annoying but not dangerous. We're going to be okay. Twenty minutes later as we turn the stairs to the first floor, the women around me begin smoothing their dresses, putting their fancy shoes back on, and combing their fingers through their shiny hair. Since my dress and shoes are still in the penthouse, all I can do is check my hair. Bad news. Forty flights on a sweltering stairwell, and I'm no threat to the Breck girl.

We make it to the ballroom where all the worried husbands immediately swarm around us, full of comfort and hugs. Amanda's Alden is handsome and doting and obviously hasn't run off with the au pair—though Heather's distracted spouse looks like he might want to. Dan kisses Lucy for a long time—right now even an hour apart is too much—and then breaks to ask how I'm doing.

"Josh was looking for you," Dan says, gesturing toward the throng at the bar. "You should go find him."

Lucy and Dan and the other reunited couples melt into the crowd, and I'm left standing alone in my bathrobe. Not exactly how I imagined I'd look when I was sitting with Josh Gordon tonight.

But apparently I shouldn't have bothered imagining anything, because coming toward me now is a vision in a white sequined dress, white sequined slingbacks and that almost white stick-straight hair that's swinging nearly to her waist.

"Nice outfit," purrs Marissa, stopping in front of me, her white frothy martini glass cocked in her left hand. Her favorite drink or did she order it to match her hair?

"Thanks," I say. "Yves Saint Laurent. Next year's collection."

"Would have guessed Bed, Bath, and Beyond. Last year's collection," Marissa says, shifting her drink-prop to her other hand and posing again. Woman can't take a joke. Woman *is* a joke. How could Josh like her?

"I heard you're sitting with us, even though you're just staff," Marissa says, icicles starting to form around her lips. From the drink? No, they're always there. "Josh is always so nice to people who work for him. Too nice, I tell him."

"Right. Got to get him to stop. Way too much of that nice-to-the-staff thing in this world. But excuse me," I say, backing away. "As staff, I have a lot to do. See you later."

Although when I see her later, it will probably be on Josh's arm. When will I learn not to get my hopes up?

I find the hotel manager who reassures me that electricity or not, dinner will be fine. Steak and salmon entrées are being prepared on the gas grill. "And you were so smart to order sashimi for a first course," he confides, as if I had anticipated tonight's disaster. I call Vincent—who tells me the theater wasn't affected by the power outage. But he's in a frenzy, anyway.

"The lightning could strike again at any moment!" he shrills, flapping his cape in the background.

No use explaining that lightning never strikes twice—because it does. And it wasn't lightning that struck the first time, anyway.

"Should I come over and help out?" I ask instead hopefully, looking for a reason to escape the ballroom. "I can be right there."

"No, no, no," Vincent bellows. "Your job is the dinner. My job is the show. It *will* go on."

But how am I supposed to go on? I hang up, wondering what to do next. My gown, abandoned forty flights up, might as well be on Mars. The dresses for the *My Fair Lady* ballroom scene are just a few blocks away—but no way I'm squeezing into tiny Tamika's clothes. And for once, Lucy doesn't have an emergency backup to pull out of her bag. Okay, I might as well hide out in the ladies' room for the next hour and a half. I'm just on my way there when Josh Gordon grabs my sleeve and spins me around.

"I'm glad you're here," he says, giving me a quick hug. "Didn't see you come in. I was worried."

"Didn't want you to see me," I admit. "I look like an idiot. Sorry about all this. As soon as the elevators are fixed, I'll go back and change. Really sorry."

He steps back but leaves his hands on my shoulders. "Did anybody ever tell you that you apologize too much?" he asks.

"Sorry . . . ," I begin, but stop myself before I apologize for apologizing. "Just don't want to embarrass you in front of your date," I say, trying again. "Marissa's already made it clear I should leave."

"Don't you dare leave," says Josh. "You've made this whole night happen."

But I've already turned and am heading for the ladies' room. Josh follows me and grabs my hand.

"Could you listen to me for just one minute?" he asks. "You've got it all wrong. Marissa isn't my date. She works for me. Attends various business functions with me representing the firm."

"I've heard you're nice to staff," I tell him.

"Too nice." He shakes his head. "Look, Jess, you and I didn't get off to a great start. And it was probably all my fault. So now I'll do the apologizing, okay? I want us to begin again. That's why I asked you to sit with me tonight. As my date."

I look at him, startled. His date? I'm suddenly aware that he's still holding my hand. And it feels nice. A few drops of perspiration are glinting on his chiseled brow. Could it be he's flustered around me for a change?

"Starting again sounds good," I say in a small voice.

"I find myself thinking about you a lot," Josh says slowly. "You're different from anybody I've ever known. Funny. Unassuming. You don't try to be anything you're not. I never know what to expect. It's fun to be around you."

He steps back for a moment. "I have a little something from the Board. To thank you for all you did on the benefit."

He hands me a small velvet pouch, and opening it, I take out the delicate green charm inside, inscribed with a Chinese character.

"What's it say?" I ask, fingering the smooth jade.

"I'm told it means 'Happy Fortune,' " Josh says with a smile. "But I can't guarantee it. For all I know, it means 'Someone on the Board Really Likes You.' Which would be appropriate, too."

I look up at him, wide-eyed, and he smiles. "Actually, it's not from the Board. It's from me. I got it last week when I was in Hong Kong. Put it on your key chain."

"I can do better than that," I say, unhooking the thin gold chain I'm wearing and sliding the charm onto it. I fumble to refasten the necklace, but Josh reaches his arms around me to secure my good luck.

"Looks nice on you," he says. "Sets off your eyes."

"You don't think it's too much with the bathrobe?" I ask, smiling. "I don't want to be overdressed tonight."

"No, it's just the right touch," he says, leaning in and stroking the green medallion lightly with his thumb. "Now I have my good luck."

"And I have mine." I step hesitantly forward to give him a kiss.

"Nice," he says. He wraps his arms around me and pulls me close. We kiss for longer than I would have expected.

Since the lights can't dim to announce dinner, the waiters circulate, graciously inviting people to take their seats. I look anxiously at Josh and then toward the door.

"You're not sneaking out of dinner," Josh says firmly, taking my hand again. "Let's go sit down. Don't worry about the bathrobe. For once everyone will have something to talk about other than the SEC."

Josh is right and it turns out an electrical outage is just what every charity event really needs. The room looks beautiful in the flickering candlelight, and so do all the women. My bathrobe inspires spirited conversation about everyone's most embarrassing moments. Everyone except Marissa, who claims to have never had one. Speeches are kept short, since without working microphones, no one can hear them anyway. And the band, unplugged, unamplified, and unable to do their usual job of making it impossible to hear the person next to you, provides pleasant background music.

We're just finishing up dessert when Lucy comes over to whisper that the hotel now has one service elevator running on an emergency generator. "I told them you're an emergency," she says. "Come on."

I stand up and put my hand on Josh's broad tuxedoed shoulder. "I'll see you over at the theater," I tell him. "I have some things to do backstage, but I'll join you as soon as I can."

"I'll save you a seat," he smiles.

"Who's Mr. Wonderful?" Lucy asks as soon as we've been ushered into the huge, padded service elevator and are blessedly on our way to the penthouse.

"Josh Gordon. And he gave me this," I say, holding out my green charm as if that answers the question.

Apparently it does, because once we're in the room and I've combed my hair, fixed my makeup, and changed into my borrowed gown, Lucy looks skeptically at the sparkly choker that Chanel also sent over for the night.

"I think your Chinese good luck charm works better," she says, noticing that I haven't taken it off yet.

"I like it better, too," I say, airily rejecting what may be my only chance to flaunt a sapphire and ruby bauble.

Lucy looks me over carefully. "You clean up nicely," she says. "Fabulous dress. Your hair looks sexy when it's curly. And your face is glowing."

I scrutinize myself in the mirror. "Must be the new pink lip gloss," I suggest.

Lucy sighs. "Nope, it's your new Mr. Wonderful. Goddammit, we'll never be able to replace men. One good kiss from the right guy still makes you more radiant than a year of dermabrasion."

"And hurts less," I say, grinning.

We go back down in the elevator and walk quickly to the theater where Lucy gives me a big hug. "Let everyone see how gorgeous you are tonight," she says.

"Later," I promise.

Backstage, Vincent has the cast collected in a tiny dressing room for a preshow pep talk. The children have their arms around each other, no longer divided by what school they went to or whether they came from up- or downtown. They're one cast, one big group of friends. And suddenly I realize that however the show goes, it's already been a success.

"You're all *fabulous*," Vincent is telling the cast as I walk in. "You've worked so hard and people have paid thousands of dollars to see you. And trust me, you're all worth every penny. Go out and break a leg."

"He doesn't *really* mean to break it," offers Tamika, now in full voice, recovered from the allergic reaction and wanting to make sure her dance partner doesn't take Vincent's advice literally.

Vincent goes on for a few more minutes, and then the kids put their hands together in the middle of the circle, pulling them up and cheering "Let's Go Team!" as if they're at the World Cup finals. Jen comes over in her ragamuffin costume, a perfect street urchin with smudged cheeks and nose.

"Mom, you look so pretty," she says. "Was your dinner good?"

"Better than you could imagine," I tell her. "And you look pretty cute yourself."

The orchestra strikes up the overture, and the house lights dim as Chauncey calls for the kids to take their places. The curtain slowly rises and Pierce, our Professor Higgins, strolls elegantly across the stage in his morning coat and top hat—borrowed from his father, no doubt—and bumps into flower-vendor Tamika, our Eliza Doolittle, who drops her basket of bouquets, exactly on cue. And in her now perfectly honed Cockney accent, Tamika howls, "Full day's wages, trod in the mud!"

The kids are off and running, and after all the rehearsing and worrying and working, they're just about perfect. I feel goose bumps when Tamika breaks into the first verse of "Wouldn't It Be Loverly," and when she's done and the audience gives her a standing ovation, tears well up in my eyes.

From my position in the wings, I look out across the house and see Dan and Lucy kissing in the second row. Guess they're entitled to miss the show. Cliff and Boulder are right behind them, leading the cheers. Zelda, who makes friends wherever she goes, is engaged in an animated conversation with a gentleman next to her. My well-groomed benefit ladies and their husbands are lined up in a single row, flanking Josh Gordon, who has an empty seat next to him. And it takes me a moment to realize that he's saved the seat for me.

"Go out front," Vincent says to me, his eyes gleaming. "It's fabulous, isn't it? I want you to enjoy it." And he's clearly enjoying it, too. Probably his first success in years.

As the audience is just getting back into their seats from the standing ovation, I hurry out to the front and slip into the seat next to Josh.

"Wonderful show," he whispers, taking my elbow to guide me over. "You should be proud. And happy."

"I am. Both," I whisper back.

He puts his hand on my knee and rubs my beautiful dress. "Look at you," he murmurs into my ear. "So lovely. I liked the way you looked at dinner. But this is pretty darned good, too."

As the musical goes on, I'm torn between focusing on the show and feeling the warmth of Josh's body close to mine. He puts his arm around me, stroking my bare shoulder and then playing softly with my curls.

"Thanks for the second chance," he says. "I have a good feeling about us."

"Me too," I say, stroking the jade charm at my chest.

Just then, the boy playing Liza's father, Mr. Doolittle, steps forward to belt out yet another showstopper. Josh clasps my fingers and rests our intertwined hands on his leg.

"*I'm gettin' married in the morning!*" sings the young boy on stage. "*Ding-Dong the bells are gonna chime!*"

Josh squeezes my hand tightly and half turns to smile at me.

Maybe not in the morning, I think, gazing into his glimmering blue eyes. But anything's possible.

I wonder if Chanel would lend me another dress.